Praise for *The Alaskan Laundry*

"A taut, page-turning narrative, an [...] of characters — all steeped in a wor[...] kelp at low tide, [hear] the creak of [...] rustling of the southeast Alaska rain[...] plunges the reader into the heart and soul of a unique commercial fishing culture and the story of Tara Marconi, as she struggles for respect, love, inner peace, and a place to call her own. A cinematic tour de force, it offers up an empowering message of hope and resilience."

— Nick Jans, author of *A Wolf Called Romeo*

"There are the easy journeys, the ones that take us where we mean to travel, and there are those we shy from, the dark and uncertain treks of the soul. Without flinching, nineteen-year-old Tara ventures from South Philly to the male-dominated 'Rock,' an island off the coast of Alaska. True to her boxer instincts, Tara comes out swinging, unsure what the island will make of her. As layers of her former life wash away, she proves as raw and tender as the landscape, as striking and unforgettable. A promising debut, true to the core — a novel of grit and redemption."

— Deb Vanasse, author of *Cold Spell* and *Out of the Wilderness*

"*The Alaskan Laundry* is a novel of bracing air that gets deep into your lungs. As Tara Marconi reinvents herself in Alaska, we see all facets of the American dream of self-reliance and boundless possibility play out on the stage of the Last Frontier. A strong, singular person grows in these pages. Like a protagonist in a Daniel Woodrell novel, she is stubborn, heroic, and capable of anything."

— Will Chancellor, author of *A Brave Man Seven Storeys Tall*

"A fresh voice in contemporary realism arrives on the scene in this coming-of-age novel. Fierce and flawed, protagonist Tara Marconi leaves the Lower 48 behind to cut her teeth on the Alaskan wilderness, searching for salvation in the notion that 'people come to Alaska to wash themselves clean.' Jones's dynamic love of America's Last Frontier comes through in spare, gripping prose."

— Suzanne Rindell, author of *The Other Typist*

THE ALASKAN LAUNDRY

BRENDAN JONES

A Mariner Original
MARINER BOOKS
Houghton Mifflin Harcourt
Boston   New York
2016

Copyright © 2016 by Brendan Jones

For information about permission to reproduce selections from
this book, write to trade.permissions@hmhco.com or to
Permissions, Houghton Mifflin Harcourt Publishing Company,
3 Park Avenue, 19th Floor, New York, New York 10016.

www.hmhco.com

Library of Congress Cataloging-in-Publication Data
Names: Jones, Brendan, author.
Title: The Alaskan laundry / Brendan Jones.
Description: Boston : Mariner Books, 2016.
Identifiers: LCCN 2015046793 (print) | LCCN 2016008410 (ebook) |
ISBN 9780544325265 (paperback) | ISBN 9780544325272 (ebook)
Subjects: LCSH: Women fishers — Fiction. | Fish trade — Alaska — Fiction. |
Self-realization in women — Fiction. | Alaska — Fiction. |
BISAC: FICTION / Literary. | FICTION / General. | FICTION /
Contemporary Women.
Classification: LCC PS3610.06177 A78 2016 (print) | LCC PS3610.06177 (ebook)
| DDC 813/.6 — dc23
LC record available at http://lccn.loc.gov/2015046793

Book design by Greta D. Sibley
Map by Mapping Specialists, Ltd.

Printed in the United States of America
DOC 10 9 8 7 6 5 4 3 2 1

To my mother
Kathy Gosliner
& her red pen

Whenever a bunch of fellows would get together, someone would start talking about going up north . . . Things were pretty much settled to the south of us. We didn't seem to be ready for steady jobs. It was only natural we'd start talking about the north. We bought out the Russians. We'd built canneries up there. The fellows who hadn't been up was hankering to go. The rest of us was hankering to go back.

— Martha McKeown, *The Trail Led North*

There is a story, always ahead of you. Barely existing. Only gradually do you attach yourself to it and feed it. You discover the carapace that will contain and test your character. You find in this way the path of your life.

— Michael Ondaatje, *The Cat's Table*

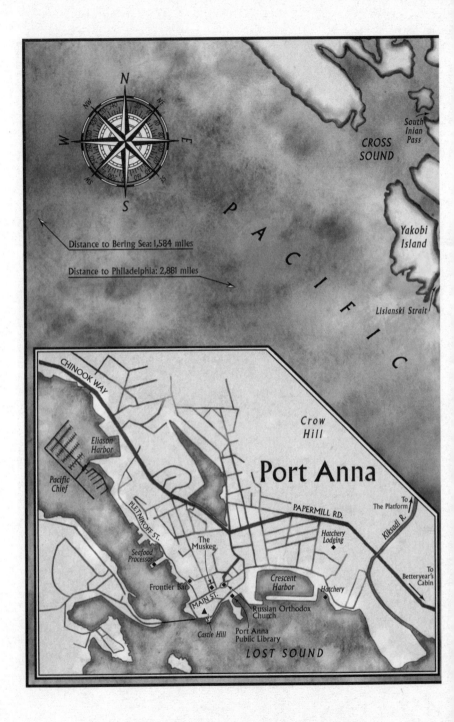

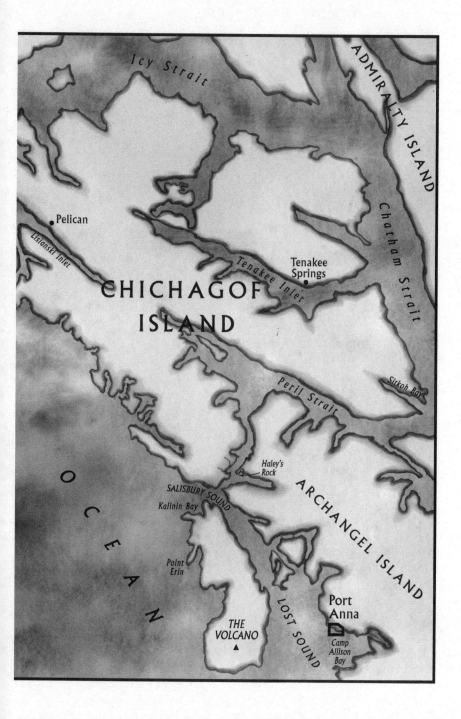

1

THE CAPTAIN'S VOICE ECHOED off the mountainside. "Port Anna. The town of Port Anna, twenty minutes. All passengers exit through the car deck."

She watched off the left rail of the ferry—port, starboard, whatever. Bleached driftwood and tangles of seaweed were strewn across the beach. Above the sand, trees carpeted the mountains up to the dark peaks.

She squinted but couldn't make out much in the thickening fog, just clouds caught in hazy wisps among the treetops. Shouldn't there be factories on the outskirts of town? Suburbs? The air smelled piney, faintly citrus.

She punched her sleeping bag into its sack, tossing salami ends and scraps from her meals during the last four days into the trash. With her thumbnail she chipped duct tape from the cement deck where she had camped. The bottom of the tent was still wet from the first night on the boat, when she had woken to the crack of the rainfly, shiver of the ferry as waves slammed into the hull. Huddled in her sleeping bag, nylon walls contracting and expanding around her like a lung, she had been certain the tape lashing down her tent would give. She'd be trapped in a sail, skittering across the ocean, never to be seen again.

When she finally gathered the courage to step out, as the sky began to lighten, a wave streaked with foam reared up in front of her like some nightmarish opponent, before slapping down, sending salt spray over her cheeks. She spent the next three nights sleeping on a chair beneath the solarium heat lamps, reveling in the warmth.

The ferry heaved toward a break in the trees, threading two islands, crescent sweeps of ash-colored beach on either side, outlines of mountains, faint in the dimming light. Since boarding the ferry she had spoken to no one, feeling like a ghost among the passengers. That's how it had been since she left Philly, as if her vital organs continued to function while her mind went elsewhere, into some alternate universe, the laws of which she could not explain.

She zipped her duffel and returned to her spot. A tall man with a white beard and a weathered face, eyes the color of Pennsylvania bluestone, settled on the rail beside her.

"The Rock home for you?" he asked. H-A-R-D-W-O-R-K was tattooed over scabbed, swollen knuckles. She caught a whiff of oil, and something else, maybe alcohol.

"You mean Archangel Island?"

"The Rock, that's what we call it. A fifty-mile-long, fifteen-mile-wide slab of rock. You're lookin' at the northern tip of it right now, with Port Anna just around the bend."

"I'm from Philly," she announced. Her throat felt sandpapery.

"Yeah, I woulda noticed if you'd been around." He stepped back from the railing, stretching his sinewy arms. "Philadelphia. Capital of America. I got that right?"

She looked to see if he was joking. The wrinkles etched into his cheeks didn't deepen.

He set a palm into the rain, breaking into a jagged smile. "Liquid sunshine. Welcome home, friend. That's what we say to folks from the lower forty-eight when it looks like they might stick around."

"I guess I'll see you," she said, shouldering her duffel.

"For sure. Petree Bangheart." He set out a hand.

"Tara," she said, shaking it.

"Pleasure, Tara."

As she moved toward the car deck she thought how nice it was that someone from around here might think that this could be her home, instead of the brick-and-mortar houses built over the crumbling Wissahickon schist curbs of South Philadelphia. Her mother had always spoken about the magic of living by the sea, her memories of sleeping on a boat open to the stars, cradled by the waves. "Let the hands of Saint Anthony carry you." And now Tara was doing it, signed up to work in a fishing village. This year would be a fist to knock her open, a right cross to shake loose the grime and sadness.

From the protected lower level of the ferry she watched as a broad wooden dock resolved through the mist. Workers tossed ropes, easing the boat to the moorings. Cars were lined up beside a low-slung building in the middle of a parking lot, clouds of exhaust rising from the tailpipes.

She patted her coat, wet with rain. In the pocket was just under two thousand dollars, most of it tip money after a summer scooping water ice at John's, bills still sticky from the cherry and lemon syrup. (She never earned a dime working at the family bakery. A roof and food was pay enough, her father reasoned. Cheap bastard.)

She scanned the coast. She had envisioned Alaska lush and open, wide-skied and dramatic. This world of passageways and forests that seemed to swallow the light felt like some different planet. Where was the spire of the Russian church Acuzio had described? The volcano looming over town? Cabins with smoke curling out of their chimneys?

Inside a ferry attendant unhooked a chain, and passengers filed downstairs to the car deck. The steel ramp leading up from the boat jolted as vehicles drove off. She joined a few pedestrians crossing the parking lot to the terminal, where people were gathered in dulled raingear. One girl, overweight, with small glasses, wearing a pink waterlogged fleece, wet hair plastered to her cheeks, stared vacantly ahead. No one spoke. Her new boss had told her when she had called him from a payphone in Ketchikan that he'd meet her here.

Afraid that he might have forgotten, she started toward the terminal. She thought of a game Connor loved to play, insisting that she choose one word to describe her state of mind. (Her feelings changed with the weather, while his were so annoyingly consistent.) With this army surplus duffel packed with the damp tent and sleeping bag, and her ponytail pulled through her Eagles cap, she'd take "homeless." But homeless with a plan.

As she opened the glass door of the terminal a potbellied man dressed in stained work jeans held up by faded rainbow suspenders elbowed his way out. His brown boots, extending from the frayed cuffs of his pants, appeared clownish. She was about to say that God gave him arms so he could open doors by his own goddamn self when he held out a meaty palm.

"Tara Marconi? Fritz. Welcome to Port Anna."

She shook his coarse hand, then stepped back, taking in his bulk. "How'd you know it was me?"

"Hell," he said, looking her over with small eyes half covered by wrinkled lids. "Not too many curly-haired city gals we get stepping off these boats. Those all your things? Leave town in a rush?"

"Sort of," she muttered.

With his bulk and grizzled face, Fritz resembled one of those Jesuit missionaries she had studied at St. Vincent's, hardened from years spent at some far-flung outpost.

"All set? Truck's right over here." He pointed to a dented gray flatbed with a bumper sticker that read CUT KILL DIG DRILL. Which struck her as strange. Wasn't he running a fish nursery? A stench, some combination of sweat-mildewed boxing wraps and rotting meat, hit her.

"What's that stink?" she asked.

Fritz smiled, showing yellowed teeth. He went around the side of the truck and pointed into the cab. "You stay right there, buster. Toss that bag on the bed, Tara. Let's go take a look-see."

She followed him along the shoulder of the road. He gestured toward a square orange street sign that read END. "Fourteen miles of hard-top on Archangel Island. Seven miles from town one way, seven miles the other. Beyond that, just spruce and hemlock—brown bear territory. Upwards of twenty-five hundred. More bears than people."

A tremor moved through her as they turned onto a gravel road. Trees were on one side, a river on the other. Drops from the branches thudded onto the bright carpet of moss. She looked deeper into the woods, over the plush green mounds along the forest floor. "Do bears actually eat people?" she asked.

Fritz reached for the pouch in his back pocket. "Not if you got your trusty sow stopper."

He took out a gun, big and silver, the kind men with sideburns used in those crime movies her father loved. She stopped walking. "Relax," he said, easing it back into the case. "I'm not holding up gas stations." But all she could think was *GUN*, in the hands of this tired-looking man with blueberry juice staining the tips of his whiskers. Who had a sticker that said KILL on the bumper of his shitty, rusted-out pickup.

"Kid, it's for protection," he said in a soothing voice.

Thorns snagged her jeans as they picked their way along the sandy bank. Scrubby dim beaches with stalks of flattened, sodden grass stretched out on the far side of the stream. Screeching gulls, white as paper, wheeled against the dark sky. The sight of water comforted her, how it curled behind rocks, shadows of stones beneath the rush. One of the stones freed itself from the streambed and darted upriver. A few others followed. With an intake of breath she realized these were fish, thousands of fish, finning in the current.

"There's your smell," Fritz murmured. "Dying salmon."

She watched, stunned, as a gull took a couple of steps in the shallows before jamming its beak into the stomach of a fish carcass. Orange eggs spilled into the current. Tara cupped a hand over her mouth. A grotesque-looking creature, backlit, tore a strip of flesh from a salmon struggling in its talons. It swallowed the meat in gulps, head cocked in her direction. This was an eagle, she realized, not much smaller than the brass statues outside the central post office in Philadelphia.

"Pink salmon. We call 'em humpies," Fritz said. "Males like that"—he pointed to a fish with a hump along its back—"it'll be your job to toss them down the chute. Females we give a whack on the head with a stick of alder, slice open the stomach, and shuck out the eggs."

She put a hand up. "Hold on. Cooz told me this was a *hatchery.* Like we're *hatching* fish, not killing them."

He gazed at her, his melon of a head tilted to one side. Behind him the eagle lofted into a tree.

"How about you hold that thought until tomorrow," Fritz said.

But tomorrow suddenly seemed far away. Right now she was thinking of getting back on that ferry, zipping up in her sleeping bag, and snuggling beneath the heat lamps. Far from this gun-toting man, these zombie fish decaying on the banks, blood-hungry bears, and prehistoric birds.

"So if the females are killed, what about the males?" she asked, ignoring his comment.

"We get a few studs to spray semen over a bucket of eggs. And the rest, like I said, go down the chute. Which dumps"—he ricocheted one hand off the other—"right into my crab pots. Skookum setup. Makes for great stuffing come Thanksgiving."

She bit her lip. The question of whether she'd make it to the holiday hung in the air. This man was challenging her, she decided, some manner of Alaskan hazing. A dull anger lit up beneath her breastbone. The last thing she needed was some fat fuck of a boss ordering her around. If she wanted to, she could be in New York City, by Connor's side, in less than a week. She could reassess. Make a new plan.

When they returned to the parking lot she saw the bright brake lights of one last car receding into the boat. She stood by the flatbed. Her shoes were sandy and damp. Fritz heaved himself into the bench seat.

And then, across the water, behind a number of smaller islands, a thumbnail of sunshine along the rim of the volcano. Just like Mount Etna in the photos her mother had shown her, a dark cone to guide the fishermen of Aci Trezza home each night. Above her, clouds opened to a patch of blue.

"Call those sucker holes," Fritz said. "For the suckers who think it's about to get sunny."

She looked away, leaning into the truck window. Among the squished muffin wrappers and Styrofoam coffee cups, stretched out on the bench, was a hefty white dog with a black and gold streak up his back.

"This here's Keta," Fritz said. The dog peered up at her with clear brown eyes, his whiskers twitching. The smell of mildew and tobacco and wet fur in the truck was almost worse than the dying fish.

Fritz hooked his thumbs into his suspenders. "Listen, Tara," he said, staring ahead through the mud-streaked windshield. "I sure wouldn't think any the less of you if you got right back on that ferry. Save us both a lot of trouble." She waited, listening to his heavy breathing. "Your cousin Acuzio, he was here, what, ten years ago? Long enough to forget what the winters are like, and the sting of hard work."

He was right. Cold sky, the coming winter, the nauseating smells, even this lumbering, weary man—*I don't need this. Not now.* If she didn't go crawling back to Connor—and part of her wanted to, to explain that this was all some awful mistake—she could at least find someplace dry. The Southwest. Santa Fe, even, where Acuzio was working. Get a job scooping ice cream. Find a boxing gym. Train in the afternoons. Just be alone and get her head on straight.

"I should add," Fritz said, rubbing his eyes, "that the last thing I need this fall is someone dragging ass at my operation. We got production goals. It's hop-skip, and I sure don't take well to slackers — especially as we start prepping for next year's run."

The heat beneath her breastbone spread. She thought of her father, at the foot of the stairs, mustard cardigan tucked into his sweatpants, calling her a spoiled brat. How dare he. She had grown up walking each morning to the family bakery, switching on the tiny incandescent bulbs of the Marconi's sign, rolling dough, cleaning display cases, wiping down the aluminum cladding on the storefront. Maybe she hadn't given work at the bakery her all over the past year — but after what had happened . . . *Spoiled brat, my ass.*

The dog perked up as Fritz keyed the engine. The ferry horn blew. Her anger grew hot in her chest. And there, at the far end of the flame's heat, something new. Quieter, reassuring.

An attendant stretched a chain across the pedestrian entrance, as if to say, No, you're not crossing these thirty-five hundred miles back to Philadelphia. Not yet.

She opened the door and got in.

2

AFTER SPENDING most of the muggy Philadelphia summer in Connor's room, scooping water ice during the day, raging about her father at night, she couldn't take it anymore. The "it" being herself, subsisting on Wheat Thins and chive cream cheese, hardly getting out of her torn sweatpants, taping episodes of *The X-Files* to watch over and over, showering only when she and Connor started sleeping together. She had thought the sex would help—and it did, briefly. But after the rush of blood and warmth she only felt emptier. She wanted to disappear, like the dot when she turned off her TV, reduced to a point. To reanimate on some different planet, find some new sun to orbit. Connor tried to help, going out to fetch another box of crackers, a block of cream cheese. If she heard once more that he was there if she needed to talk, she thought she might scream.

One day in early August, while Connor was at his job bricklaying, she woke up barely able to catch her breath. At first she thought she was having a heart attack, or her lungs were shutting down. The walls seemed to close in. She panicked. That same day she tracked down her cousin Acuzio Marconi in Santa Fe.

She remembered his stories about working in what he called the Last Frontier. Catching salmon with his bare hands, running into grizzlies, working at the hatchery, then a fish processor. "Place is huge!" he said. "Instead of America it should be called Alaska and Its Forty-Nine Bitches." Her father at the far end of the table, silencing Acuzio with a glare.

"Are there girls too?" Tara asked, from her chair beside her mother.

"If they're born there. But it's a man's world, shows you what you're made of."

Afterward, as they did dishes in their burnt orange and avocado Formica kitchen, her mother shut off the faucet and took Tara by the shoulders. "This young man, your cousin, he don't know nothing. Alaska, it is like where I come from, where these" — her mother held up her hands and spread long sudsy fingers in front of Tara's face, her nickel-sized medallion dangling over her breasts — "these are how you grow strong. *Si?* It doesn't matter what is here." She patted between her thighs. "*Capisce?*"

When she was in fifth grade Tara did a social studies report on Alaska. She glued eight stars onto purple construction paper, coloring them in with the yellow highlighter her father used to mark late orders at the bakery.

"No, that can't be right," Sister Delaney said when Tara taped a cutout of the state over the rest of the country. Its borders stretched from Canada to Mexico, from Rhode Island to Los Angeles. But it *was* right, Tara insisted. Alaska, she announced proudly to the class, could absorb more than two Texases.

So that horrible day in August, when she was so desperate to leave the city she could hardly breathe, Alaska came to mind. "Cooz," she said, a cloud of wood dust rising as she dropped into Connor's couch. "Help me out here."

"Aren't you going to college or something?"

"I was, to Temple or CCP, but things got fucked. Didn't you work on some island? Can't you find me something? Cleaning houses, it doesn't matter."

"Tara, it ain't no rolling cannolis up there." Over the phone she could hear screaming, kids at a motel pool, perhaps. "I'm telling you, T. It's about as many people on that island as the Italian Market on a

Monday, you feel me? I mean, bears try to chew your brain for fuck-sake."

Bring it, Tara thought. As far as she could get from the clogged gutters of South Philly, the burn barrels, Oldsmobiles sliding past stop signs. As far as she could get from her father — that was where she wanted to be.

A few days later, Acuzio reached her before a shift.

"Hey. I heard what happened. You and your pop talking yet?" he asked. "I heard —"

"Did you find me a job?" she interrupted.

"Dag," he said, his voice going soft. "I'm just so sorry. I mean, I know your pops explained. I was on the road for the wake, and . . ."

Over the past year Tara had perfected her response to this sort of awkward condolence: silence. She was beginning to discover that she could use this to her advantage; just let the quiet echo until you got what you wanted.

Acuzio sighed. "So this guy Fritz, pissy dude with a good heart. He said he could use a hand at the hatchery, starting at the end of September. No overtime. Only other condition is you stick around for the year."

"Done," she said. "You tell him anything about me?"

"Just that you boxed, and could keep up. But I'm tellin' you, he's grumpy as a garden gnome, and you already got two counts against you."

"What," she laughed. "I'm a girl, that's one. And the other?"

She could hear him chuckling on the other end of the line. "That island's gonna turn your head around, little cuz. That's about all I can say about that."

She thought about times in the boxing ring when she had been hit so hard, she thought her head might twist off her spine. "It sounds perfect," she said.

What wasn't perfect was telling Connor two days before she left.

Connor, who had held her hand in third grade to cross Broad Street. Who played Jesus in the Stations of the Cross in fourth grade, and let her color red squiggles across his forehead for the blood of Christ. Connor, who asked her out in ninth grade and who, when she broke up with him after her sixteenth birthday, sent flowers. Connor, who took her in after she fled her father's house, then became her lover. And now she was sitting him down after a long day on the scaffold, his hands spattered with dried mortar, to say she was leaving in two days for Alaska.

His features tightened. The furrow above his nose took on shadow. He wasn't like her father. He didn't rage. In fact, he didn't say much of anything.

She knew it was cruel. But it was time to change her life. And Alaska was the place she'd do it.

3

TARA WAS SILENT as they turned out of the ferry terminal parking lot.

"As I said before, you got two main roads on the island. Think of them like eagle wings. This one here's called Chinook Way. Then you got Papermill Road on the other side. Main Street in town with the Russian Orthodox church — call that the beak of the bird — library down by the water, where there's payphones. Only place you get lost is the woods."

Chinook Way hugged a mountain to one side, and dropped off to the ocean on the other. Islands tufted with trees rose from the water, the surface rustled dark by the wind. There was a newness, a scrubbed quality to the rock faces pushing out from the trees, even the mottled surface of the ocean. Her lungs drank in the clean, moist air. It felt like a place where anything could happen.

They drove into a cloudbank, creamy white outside the windshield, the silence in the cab broken by the steady click of Fritz's blinker. He pulled into a parking lot and stopped the truck at the top of a ramp leading to docks.

"This here's the main harbor. Just to get you situated."

Below was a mishmash of boats of all shapes and sizes, bobbing in their parking spots. "See that big old dark one in the distance there, at the end of the docks? That's a tugboat, where one of my workers tried to hide the other night after getting himself in trouble at the Frontier Bar."

When her eyes found it, black smokestack visible behind the masts and poles, a jolt ran through her. Thick-set, powerful, like the tugs she had watched with her mother on the Delaware River, jockeying barges of garbage upriver. She had to fight the urge to get out of the truck and inspect it more closely.

"You a big drinker?" Fritz asked. She shook her head, unable to take her eyes from the boat.

"Good." He started up again.

Farther on they passed a smaller harbor at the bottom of the hill. Through the dirty glass and fog she made out a quadrangle of dilapidated shingled buildings. Keta raised his head as Fritz coasted to a stop and set the emergency brake.

"What about dogs?" Fritz asked, sliding out. "You a fan?"

She hauled her bag, damp now, from the flatbed. Dogs. She had inherited her mother's dislike of the creatures, and generally crossed to the other side of the street when she saw one approaching. They were dirty, chewed through the plastic coverings of the couch, and kept people up with their barking.

"They're fine," she lied. The dog grunted as he hopped out of her open door. He had a long body and furry chest, a black nose with a smudge of pink at the end.

"You sure that's not a wolf?"

"Wolves don't look you in the eye like that," Fritz said. It was true—the dog wouldn't stop staring. It almost seemed as if he had come out of the truck to get a better look at her. "German shepherd, Aussie, Lab, malamute. Maybe a smidge of arctic wolf? Who knows."

"He's got no tail," Tara observed. The dog's sleek white head jerked up.

"Don't say that too loud," Fritz said in a stage whisper. "He's gets self-conscious."

"Jesus." Tara looked down into the dog's mournful eyes. "Sensitive guy."

"C'mon. I'll show you your new home."

The dog trotted ahead, leading the way across a small bridge. The air reminded her of Oregon Avenue at Christmas, spruce trees trussed up against a chain-link fence strung with oversized lights. Life on this "Rock," as the man on the ferry called it, wouldn't be completely unfamiliar. Her mother's first memory had been sitting atop a barrel of sardines brining by the water, where she had been set to keep the gulls away. This same blood ran in her veins.

They entered a door at one end of a long, single-story building, and went down a dreary hallway. Fritz stopped in front of a door, and the dog leaned against her thigh as he sifted through his key ring. "You grew up in Philadelphia?"

"Yeah. But my mother was from Sicily."

He nodded. "Worked in your folks' bakery? That what Coozy said?"

Not if you ask my father, she thought. "Yeah."

"Well, I am a fan of the baked goods, as you can probably tell." He patted his stomach. "Wife's always trying to get me to cut down, but I tell her I need to put on hibernation weight. Lack of sunlight bother you?"

"I guess we'll find out."

"That's right, soon enough now."

He pushed open the door and extended a hand. There was a single electric burner in the corner, a bed beneath the curtained window, pendant light over a table, and a shower and toilet on the other side of a wood-planked wall.

"You got cockroaches, rats, and all that back in Philly?" Fritz asked from the doorway. He turned the knob on the thermostat.

Was he an idiot? "Sure. It's a city."

"Well, none of that crap here." He pulled a plastic package from his back pocket and tossed it onto the bed. "There's dinner if you like. I'll see you in the A.M., eight sharp down at the hatchery."

6

Brendan Jones

Five-minute walk. Head back out across the bridge, between those old brown buildings to the concrete bunker by the water. Basement. Get some sleep. C'mon, buster. It's our feeding time." And then he was gone. The dog watched her for a couple seconds, blinking his blond eyelashes a few times before Fritz whistled, and he bounded off.

She sat on her bed, looking around, her mind bright with exhaustion. She had made it. From the living room sofa in front of the television, from scraping the bottom of the barrel of lemon water ice, to this bare bones room on an island in Alaska. Right now she needed sleep.

From her duffel she took a framed, washed-out photo of men standing by boats, mending nets, and taped it above her bed. How fragile, even feminine, these dark-skinned cousins of her mother, the men of Aci Trezza, appeared compared to Fritz, with his rainbow suspenders framing his stomach, or the white-bearded man on the ferry with the wrinkles. For all her mother's talk about work, how it kept a person right in the world, Tara was beginning to think work in Italy meant something different than it did in Alaska.

Outside the curtained windows, branches waved in the dark. The baseboard radiators made a ticking sound as they heated. She picked up the package, still warm from Fritz's pocket. Among gimcrack cookware in a kitchen drawer she found a serrated knife and sawed open the plastic. The soft, dark meat tasted of liquid smoke — fish, she realized, picking a filament of bone from her teeth. The springs beneath the thin mattress squeaked as she flopped on the bed.

She tore off another piece, chewing slowly. When she left Wolf Street it had been with not only anger but also relief at not having to trail any longer in her father's dark wake. Not to be shocked out of sleep each morning by the knock of the filter against the rim of the sink as he dumped stale espresso grounds. No more shuffle of his slippers with the collapsed heel on the kitchen linoleum.

Her father's eyes, magnified behind the lenses of his glasses, froze people. It happened with Gypo, her boxing coach, when her father arrived at the gym with sixteen-year-old Tara in tow. Even Urbano's closest friend, Vic, who ran the barbershop up the block from the Italian Market social club, fidgeted under his gaze. And when gifts appeared at their row home — pepper shooters stuffed with provolone and prosciutto, squid marinated in garlic and olive oil, bottles of home-distilled grappa — they were left on the front stoop. No one wanted to risk looking Urbano in the eye.

Connor, on the other hand — how many hours had she spent on the edge of sleep thinking about how they weren't right for each other? Or maybe their timing was off. Her thoughts orbited around him, never coming to rest. It was exhausting.

From her bag she took out a notebook. He hated telephones. Back home, he'd hiss up at her window and they'd meet in the alley, then sit atop air conditioner compressors, kissing, while the rest of the neighborhood slept. Letters. He was old-fashioned like that.

27 September 1997

Dear Connor,

*   I made it! Writing now from this cozy room with log rafters and wooden walls and a kitchenette. You should have seen me boarding that plane in Philly. I kept flipping the ashtray cover in the armrest until someone told me to stop. Then the wheels left the ground, and I could see the city stretched out below, shadow where Passyunk cut through, blip of aircraft warning lights on the radio towers by the Schuylkill River.*

As she wrote, she could see him at a New York City post office, the faintest impression of crow's-feet appearing at the corners of his gray eyes. A lightness in his stride as he walked to the coffee shop. Finding his favorite corner, using the blade of a knife to slice open the envelope.

I slept most of the plane ride, then woke to my ears popping, trying to recall this dream I was having of my mother ahead of me on this pebble beach, pushing through the waves. No matter how loud I shouted she wouldn't turn. Like she just wanted me to follow.

At the Bellingham ferry ticket counter this guy with a tattoo on his neck said, "Don't get eaten alive up there. By mosquitoes, bears, or men." I told him to fuck off. He was surprised and laughed. People seem much less serious here than in Philly. And the sky so much bigger and the trees tall and thick. These wide-open spaces, I've never seen anything like it.

And the ferry! Twice the size of the tugs on the Delaware, a smokestack painted with the Alaskan flag, and everyone on the top deck duct-taping tents to the cement. Chains clattered as the loading hatch banged shut, smoke went up, water churned with the propellers. As the buildings grew small behind us it hit me hard what I was doing. I could hardly breathe, I was so excited.

The first night there was this storm, and that did it for me sleeping in the tent. But on the third day the sun came out, and this land, Connor! Snow-covered mountains and sand beaches and trees stretching as far as the eye can see. The air so clean and salt-scented. We saw otters on their backs, seals with long whiskers barking as we passed. And the mountains, I can't get over them, these glaciers jutting out from jaws of rock like swollen blue tongues. Ropey waterfalls falling from cliffs.

As she wrote she wondered when he would get over his annoyance at her leaving. Sometimes she wished he'd just lose his temper. But that wasn't Connor. When she told him she was going to Alaska, his face grew pinched. In her family people said their piece, then moved on. Although, when she thought about it, her father stewed — until he raged.

She looked back down at the letter. It would be a peace offering, she decided. Not an apology, but something close.

> *The island is strange, though, not what you think of when you imagine Alaska. It's a rainforest, and you can feel it and smell it. When I got here my boss picked me up with his dog, quiet and watchful. Kind of looked like a wolf.*
>
> *Anyway, I know there's more to talk about, but I'm so tired. I'm sorry you feel bad. But I miss you very much.*
>
> *More soon.*
>
> *Youse,*
> *Tara*

As she addressed the envelope she imagined the snicker he'd give at "youse." He never broke into full-throated laughter. They were different that way. Although, thinking about it, she couldn't recall the last time she had really laughed either.

She licked and stamped the letter, then set it on her nightstand. Turned off the light and pulled the covers to her chin.

When she closed her eyes she saw South Philly encased in a plastic bubble, one of those snow globes you shook, flakes sifting between the blocks of brick row homes. Vic cutting hair, Connor's mom at the library scanning barcodes with her red wand. How lucky she was, she thought, to have escaped. Perhaps patience wasn't her strong suit — but what the hell, impatience had gotten her this far. As grim as the island had appeared out of Fritz's dirty windshield, shrouded in fog, she still considered her decision a good one.

A year. Time enough to prove to her father, to Connor, to anyone who doubted her, that she didn't need another person's roof. She would find her own home.

As for her mother, even if the idea of her daughter taking off for Alaska would have frightened her, surely Tara's larger effort to crack open this world of fish and boats, life on the water, would have pleased Serena.

Then her mind darkened and she saw her father in his billing office, smoking his cigars one after the other. His yellow highlighter hovering over orders for more milk, more butter, more flour.

You told me to get out. Now you do the same. Just get out of my head and leave me alone.

4

OPENING HER EYES, she patted the sheets for her watch. A pale strip of light ran down the center of the curtains. "FUUUUCK!" she yelled into the rafters. It was 8:17 A.M.

She threw off the comforter, hauled on her jeans, grabbed her Eagles hat, and ran. At the bottom of the hill she saw a door propped open with a cinderblock. Green tanks surrounded a bunkerlike building. She headed down a set of narrow wooden stairs and saw Fritz talking to a few workers slouched on stools. He crumpled a wax muffin wrapper, shot it into the trashcan, then rapped his knuckles against the glass clock above him.

"I thought bakers woke early."

Breathing hard, she looked over his shoulder. It was 8:36. Not such a big deal.

"Now, I don't know what you thought it would be like up here, but I can tell you one thing. We get to work on time."

"The four hours mixed me up."

"If that was true, you should have been here four hours early."

The other workers shifted. After a moment, he continued — something about the importance of recording data in the logbook: water temperature, antibiotics, and sample growth rates of salmon. "All right, to work, then. Newt, you fill our newest addition here in on what she dozed through."

Fucker, she thought, watching his brown boots disappear up the stairs.

From a shadow in the corner a small man emerged. She made out layers of clothing—a soiled thermal, T-shirt, outline of a wife beater—beneath his overalls. Knobs of bone showed along the back of his neck. With his wispy white-blond hair spinning off his skull, and moon-pale skin, he reminded her of an albino rat—or, more generously, a newborn chick.

She moved to the side as he went for the coffee machine behind her. He filled his stainless-steel mug, shook a cigarette from a pack, and turned. "Late your first day. Classy."

"I'm a classy girl."

He wiped his nose with the back of his wrist. "Follow me."

They went into a concrete room packed with white plastic bins, water cascading between them. He walked like a featherweight boxer—on the balls of his feet, hips thrust forward, shoulders pulled back. Outside in the sunlight she followed him between circular vats of gurgling water, stopping on a knoll, the flat blue-gray ocean stretched out beneath them. Waves lapped on the rocks below. Islands dotted the horizon, and behind them mountains, which appeared cut out from the blue sky, the peaks delicate, like the tips of drip castles she had made on the Jersey Shore as a kid.

A briny, spruce-tinted wind shivered the grass. Newt cupped his hands around a cigarette, squinting as he exhaled. "You do that yoga shit?" he asked, his eyes roaming her body.

"I box," she said, crossing her arms over her chest. "Or I did, back in Philly."

"Girl boxer? Makes sense anyways, where your whole 'I'm gonna kick your ass' act comes from." He clamped the cigarette between his teeth, went up on his toes, and threw a convincing three-punch combination, ducking his head, bobbing and weaving, surprisingly nimble, finishing with a knockout right cross. He pivoted on his back foot, just like Gypo had taught her. Tara brushed hair from her face.

"Back in Kentucky we fought just to get mean," he said.

He leaned in closer. A light down covered the skin where his eye-brows should be. She caught a whiff of fish oil. "Don't let Grandpa get to you. He's so thin-skinned, it's barely enough to stop him from bleeding to death. Ends up taking it out on others."

"Who's Grandpa?"

He eyed her. "How old are you?"

"Eighteen."

"Birthday?"

"March eighteenth."

He flicked his cigarette butt into the rocks. "I'll tell you one thing: old man'll burst a blood vessel if he sees us holding our dicks out here. Word to the wicked, keep your hands out of your pockets, oth-erwise he'll shitcan your ass."

He started back to the building, tossed a scoop of pellets from a plastic bucket over his shoulder, then another behind his back as he passed by the green vats. Tara stopped to watch as a dark cloud gath-ered in the water, followed by flashes like knife blades, sun reflecting off the scales of fish as they rose. Newt shouted back. "Pockets!"

She hurried to catch up, lifting her hands from her jeans. They went down the mossy concrete steps, back into the basement.

"You ever jack off a fish?" he asked.

"What?"

He turned to her. "You got those good boxer's wrists. Might even make you top salmon jacker. Great honor here at the hatchery, some-thing to shoot for, as we like to say."

"I'll make it a goal," she said, again trying not to laugh. She liked this stunted man in his overalls. Maybe, she thought, despite what her mother said, she just didn't match well with quiet men like Connor.

Newt led her to a corner. "So listen to me good here — out of the few thousand salmon eggs in those bins some eight hundred fry will hatch, just like the ones we fed in those tanks. Come May we take the fry out to the open ocean, dump 'em into a holding pen to get them acclimated. That way they're protected from seals and otters and other ocean varmints. At which point they become smolts, maybe four hundred count. Smolts get released, go out and enjoy life, reach adulthood, maybe two hundred make it back to home sweet home. Then we kill 'em, and the process starts over."

"Kill them?"

"They're anadromous—means they die anyway. Fishermen pay us a tax to keep the business going. On top of that, when we got enough fertilized eggs we have a thing where we take extra eggs and send them over to Japan. Eye-koora or whatever the hell them rice-eaters call it. Feel like I'm forgetting something. Oh. Knife. You got one?"

She shook her head. He pulled a small, scratched jackknife from his pocket. "Great Alaskan sin to be caught without. Who's this you got hanging around your neck?"

She touched her collarbone, fingering the gold medallion. "Saint Anthony. It was my grandfather's, from Italy."

"Is that the one they say reached America before Columbus?" he asked, examining it. "Or is that Irish? I don't frickin' know."

"He's the saint of lost people, keeps you safe at sea. My grandfather almost drowned in Italy, but swore Anthony saved him."

"You got heritage, unlike most of us mutts out here. I like it."

He pointed her to a series of stainless-steel racks not unlike the cooling trays at the bakery. "Last year, we checked each egg by hand, with tweezers and a pipette, to see if it was eyed up—you know, alive. Like sorting tick dung out of pepper. This last Christmas Grandpa bought Betsy, our mechanical egg picker." He led her to the far corner, where he patted a red metal contraption that looked like a huge sewing machine, out of place in the room of bins. "All you gotta do is fill the magazine up with eggs. If they're alive, Betsy spits 'em out the one end. Dead, the other. Then they get spread on trays." He flicked a plastic bag hanging from a hook that resembled a hospital IV. "Antibiotics. You'll learn how to switch 'em out. For now, though, why don't we just start you here. With that empty look in your eyes you might fuck up any real work."

"Thanks for the vote of confidence," she shot back.

"You got it, champ," he said, absorbing her sarcasm like a light punch. "Anyone who pisses Grandpa off on their first day at school is all right in my book. Just remember the secret to this state, and you heard it here first. Do what you can, and let the rough end drag. Don't matter what saints you wear around your neck. Here it's just your head, and your hands—and your gut. And now, it's time for you to get dirty."

5

HER JOB was to keep Betsy in action by scooping the pink pellets from the bins, watching as the wheel spun, and then standing by while the laser considered each egg. The work was mind-numbing, not much different from the bakery, and certainly easier than scooping water ice.

That afternoon Fritz stopped her on her way out to dump a bowl of dead eggs. He shouted over the rumble of the pumps. "Work treating you all right?"

She shrugged. "Okay. Where's your dog?"

"Back with the neighbors. I thought I said he wasn't mine."

She could see pits in his teeth, black with tobacco.

"Listen, I volunteer over at the fire department, so you can understand I'm not a huge fan of being late. I tried to make that clear last night."

She looked into the bin of frothing water, imagining landing a right cross on his doughy cheek. Hills of pink eggs filled the bin. She wanted to reach in, squeeze the eggs until they oozed from her fist.

"I'll tell you what, Tara. When I spoke on the phone with Coozy he said you were in tough shape, something about crashing on a friend's couch after a fight with your father. Now, I don't know a thing about what you have going, but as I said in the truck I need a good hand. All these eggs in here become fish in a couple months. Along with that we send roe overseas. And if that doesn't happen, none of us gets paid. Is that clear?"

She lifted her chin and tried to arrange her features in a way that would cut him off—some approximation of how her father stared down men. But she could already feel it backfiring into an insolent, childish expression. "I'm sorry."

He considered, as if judging the sincerity of her words, hitched his pants, and walked off.

Standing in the middle of the room, listening to the rush of water, she decided her time on this Rock would be a boxing match. Keep your hands up, your eyes open.

She'd show them all.

6

IN THE WANING EVENING LIGHT she walked down the hill. Across the channel, mountains made black triangles against the clouds. Not yet four and the sky had already turned ashy.

She went past the basketball and tennis courts, past the small harbor at the bottom of the hill. She caught alternating scents of wet grass, fish, diesel, and seaweed. Despite Connor once telling her that living in Philly was the equivalent of smoking a pack of cigarettes a month, she had never really thought about the smell of the air until she arrived in Port Anna.

She passed the volunteer fire station, middle school, a baseball diamond. She paused to watch men with brown boots pulled up over their calves reading newspapers in the laundromat, sipping from coffee cups while the machines revolved. Everything — the bushes, the trees, even these men waiting for their laundry — seemed to have a sodden quality. As if nothing on the island ever fully dried.

And so quiet. No aircraft rumbling across the sky, leaving contrails. No more bruised purple dome at night. Acuzio had been right. Alaska was no rolling cannolis.

On the other side of a parking lot she found a covered ramp leading down to a broad wooden dock. She went along a central walkway, parked boats rocking on either side of her. Sailboats, fishing boats, yachts, one boat that looked like the landing craft from World War II. Most were rough-looking vessels, long metal poles on either side, webs of wire around the masts. She jumped as water spilled out from the side of a hull. Boats chafed against the rubber balls, making a high-pitched squeak. She ran her fingers along the dull wooden cap on a deck. So different from the slim boats in her mother's picture.

When she reached the end of the main walkway she turned left. A sign bolted to the light post read TRANSIENT DOCK: FOR BOATS WAITING FOR PERMANENT SLIPS, OR VESSELS PASSING THROUGH. ALL MOORAGE MUST BE PAID IN ADVANCE. These were sad, stripped-down skeletons of boats, seemingly lost here at the end of the docks.

At the far end of the walkway she finally arrived at the tug Fritz had pointed out that first day. A high front with a knobby rusted anchor, and an exhaust stack about twice the size of a manhole. The blue-green wheelhouse, built high over the hull, rose and dropped in the surge.

A few dandelions growing from the deck shook in the wind. A curved visor protected the wheelhouse windows. The boat felt to her like one drawn-out sigh, beautiful, lonely and neglected.

Looking either way, seeing no one, she pulled herself up the gangplank, fit her head into a tarnished brass porthole, and peered through the thick glass. Darkness. She stepped back. In the next porthole over, written in block letters, was a For Sale sign.

What sort of person would abandon something so beautiful? How quiet, just the soft squish of the buoy ball against the hull. Waves brushing the planks.

Fritz had mentioned payphones by the library. Eager to share what she had found with Connor, her steps quickened along the docks. She took what seemed to be a shortcut back through town, along a road that curved between buildings clad in corrugated sheet metal. Steam blended into the darkening cloud cover. Thick-woven nets with corks as big as her boss's oversized head were piled in a gravel lot, reminding her of the abandoned piers on the Delaware River, graffiti-stained concrete and broken windows in old factories, weeds growing from truck trailer beds.

A honk snapped her from her thoughts. She looked up in time to see a man at the wheel of a forklift, his wrists swirled with ink. "Look out!" he shouted. She stepped back, out of the way of a procession of men in orange bibs and hairnets following behind the forklift, receding into the billows of steam coming off the building. This must be the fish processor where Acuzio worked, she thought — where boats dropped off their catch.

The road dead-ended and she turned onto Main Street. At the far end was the Russian Orthodox church — its blocky base softened by the oxidized copper dome on top. She followed a street to the water, to a one-story wood-paneled building built on a spit of land. A sign with a carving of an orca leaping out of the water read PORT ANNA PUBLIC LIBRARY. Phone booths were arranged in a circle by the entrance.

She jangled the coins in her pocket. It was just after ten P.M. on the East Coast. Her stomach turned. Maybe Connor would be out in Manhattan, seeing a show, enjoying his new friends. Surprisingly, she missed him. Or, then again, maybe she was just nervous.

Looking at the phone bank, she thought of her father, probably in his favorite corner on the couch, watching a crime show, getting ready to trudge up the stairs to bed. Or perhaps he'd still be at the bakery, in his billing office, working late, leafing through orders for cranberries and candied fruit for panettone — the bread of the rich — in preparation for the Christmas season.

The story of panettone was one her mother loved to tell, of the handsome young noble who flew his falcons by a poor baker's shop and fell in love and married the baker's daughter. He sold his birds to make the luxurious bread to impress the daughter — all in the name of love. "*Colpo di fulmine*, 'the love that is like lightning,'" her mother would say when Tara complained about her father or was irritated with Connor. "It is the men like this, the ones with the big hearts that know in one second—these are the ones for us, *figlia*. But they must wait for us to catch up. It is how it happens with your father—he is so stubborn. We are not easy, *figlia mia*. It is the patient ones who are made for us."

She wondered if her mother had ever seen Urbano drive a fist into the wall. Or use that voice that started way down in his chest. She'd rather rip the phone boxes off their mounts and toss them into the ocean than waste quarters calling Wolf Street. It was Connor she wanted to talk to. Shy, pale, freckled, long-boned Connor, asking in a shaky voice after school one day in ninth grade if she wanted to go ice-skating by the Delaware.

To settle her nerves she walked into the library. People were crowded at the tables reading. An older man in a yellowed engineer's cap glanced up from a magazine. His long fingers clenched the glossy pages. He must be Native, Tara thought. Tlingit. Pronounced *kling-kit*—she recalled from her reading about the island. The man smiled thinly, and she nodded back.

At the phone bank she dropped in quarters and pushed the cold metal buttons. She pressed the receiver to her ear, trying to hear through the rush of wind.

"Hello?"

"C?"

"Yes."

"It's Tara," she said, letting relief bleed through her voice. She wanted to add *I miss you*. And even, *I'm sorry*.

Silence, followed by a shuffling. "Jesus. Where are you?"

"Timbuktu. Where do you think? Alaska."

She listened to his quiet breathing. *To the ship that goes beneath the water, all winds go the wrong way.* This saying of her mother's flashed through her head.

"How's Archangel Island?" he finally asked.

"Fine. I wrote you a letter."

"Did you get mine?"

She pinned the cold plastic of the receiver to her ear. It was because he hated the phone that he sounded so strained.

"No. I haven't checked."

"Check. I sent it to general delivery."

She bristled at the order. A recorded voice came on, demanding seventy-five more cents.

"I sent you something," he repeated. "You should read it, I guess, whenever you have a chance."

With a shoulder she pressed the phone to her and dug in her jeans for quarters. He let out his breath, as if he was pondering something.

"Con? Hang on one sec. I'll call you right —"

And they were cut off.

The change worked through the phone. Instinctively, she looked around for a convenience store or a gas station. Gulls floated in the updraft, heads pivoting. The sound of waves against the rocks. Fuck. The post office might have quarters, she decided. And she could get his letter.

Just up from the church she found it, a single room with a wall of wooden boxes, in the process of closing up. When Tara gave her name, a slight woman handed her an envelope addressed with Connor's large-lettered cursive.

The pages were ripped from a yellow legal pad, and the letters were slanted and jerky instead of his usual neat handwriting. She read as she walked back to the phone bank, where she deposited the change.

19 September 1997

Dear Tara,

If you're reading this now it means you made it to Port Anna. Congratulations. Me I'm sitting here on a beanbag in this high rise in the West Village. Sirens wail over the snores of my hung-over roommate. He still has on eyeliner from last night. It's bizarre here. I mean it beats bricklaying don't get me wrong.

But that's not what I want to write about.

You always encouraged me to say what was on my mind. Maybe it's an ancestral thing. Like my Scots-Irish and Southern blood just doesn't get your first-generation Italian impulse to wear your feelings. How offensive does that sound—but I can't find any better reason for what's happened.

Having a father like I do I understand something about people whose natural tendency is to leave. But who talks these days about staying? What about when things fall apart? I got a taste of how you leave with no warning back in tenth grade. And now you've done it again.

With her index finger she pulled at the metal tongue on the phone, hardly hearing as the quarters spilled into the coin return.

So here's what I want to know. How can I be of service to you now? Because looking back on the past few years I feel like that has been my role. This summer you showed up on my doorstep in the early morning, spent the next three months with me, and ended up in my bed. Saying all sorts of things like maybe you were falling in love. And then poof. Like you're on your own quest for absolution redemption—all that shit they rammed down our throats in school.

It's only memories that stop me from cutting you off now. Times when I felt you softening. Like the night on the life-guard chair. Or Rittenhouse Square. When you slid your head beneath my chin. Whispering in my ear that this, this is where you want to be.

I don't trust you anymore. That's what it is. You hurt people by not having the courage or even taking the time to figure out how you feel. And while you go off and get clean of your sadness or whatever the rest of us are left trying to make heads or tails of it. You're so fierce and impulsive and you expect the world to just heal itself behind you. But that's not how it works.

In the worst moments (like now) I think maybe your father was right. Not in what he said to you — that's horrible, no person should ever have to hear those words — but in what he did thrusting you into the world. Maybe it will shake you free of whatever weight you carry (I wish I knew) that causes you to hurt others so badly.

Connor

Slowly she collected her change and slipped it into her pocket. Back along Main Street she went, not caring when the rain turned the lined sheets in her hands soggy, not paying attention to stares of people on the sidewalk. She stumbled over the wooden bridge, down the hall into her apartment, letting her wet jeans fall to the floor. Steam filled the bathroom as she ran the shower.

What had he wanted to say to her at the end of the phone call? *What weight I carry, Connor? Try losing your mother.*

She stepped under the showerhead, eyes closed, hands by her sides, willing herself to stay still in the scald. *What an awful letter, Connor Macauley. You who pride yourself on being so constant.*

Her hands slipped against the walls, and she curled up into a corner. "To hell with you," she said, jabbing at the shower door with her toe, then kicking at it with her heel. The plastic shattered, slicing into the ball of her foot. Blood mixed with water, rivulets flowing into the drain. Still, she sat there, until the water grew cold. *Maybe I should call him back, wake him and his punk roommate up, and tell him to go fuck himself.* He was just as lost as she was, alone there in New York City. It was a sign of weakness — passing his shyness off as quiet assurance. She saw through it.

She turned off the shower and hobbled to the sink. The toilet paper she used to wrap her foot quickly soaked through. It was a small cut. She wouldn't call him, she decided. Not tonight. Not tomorrow. Maybe not ever. Her life now was on this island. It was a relief to have this truth in front of her. Everything and everyone else could take a flying fuck at the moon.

Superheated, she willed her mind blank until her breathing returned to normal. Calm, despite the throb in her foot. Her thoughts returned to the boat, floating out there at the end of the harbor. How excited she had been to share with Connor what it might be like to live on the water, with a view of the ocean and mountains and islands. It was a clear signal. Separated from the bullshit, the capriciousness of others, that's where she needed to be.

When she thought about the East Coast, she saw it as cities revolving around the sun of New York — Philadelphia like Mercury, Washington like Mars, Boston, Saturn. Here on this island, it was as if her planet had slipped its ellipse and she was floating around some gentler, more mysterious sun. She couldn't see it yet, but she could already feel it, the few times when she stopped fighting and allowed herself to be guided by this new force. It was somewhere in those woods, hidden beneath the ice fields, deep in the river valleys.

7

WHEN SHE CAME INTO THE YARD early Tuesday morning, Newt lay on his back in the grass, smoking a cigarette, a brown boot crossed over a knee.

"Boxer girl! Ten minutes early. Back for more already?"

After barely sleeping, she was in no mood to talk. She hobbled past, tossing a scoop of feed into the tank, then watched as the black cloud of fish converged, showing glimmers of white lips as they fed.

Newt sat up, tossed his cigarette, and took a long sip of coffee from his scratched mug. "You gimped up already?"

"I cut my foot."

"You get a Band-Aid for it?"

A muffled voice called her name. It took her a minute to find the source — Fritz's stubby legs extending from one of the green tanks where he had dug out the gravel. "Go into the warehouse," he ordered. "Fetch me a section of two-by-four — I gotta slip a shim in here. We have a leak."

She trudged across the yard between the sliding barn doors into the warehouse. Her eyes took a moment to adjust. The smell of turpentine and oil and wood reminded her of Connor's workshop, although the place was nowhere near as neat. Strewn across the shelves were wrenches, screws, pipe elbows, fan blades, rubber belts in various sizes. She blew dust off a section of hose and peered through one end, then picked up a wood cutoff.

"The hell are you doing?"

Fritz's round shape blocked light in the doorway.

"Sorry—I was just—"

"Sniffing wood while I'm stuck beneath a two-thousand-pound fish tank?"

He snatched the block from her hands. "You like it in here so much, how about you organize the place. How does that sound?"

"Okay."

He turned on her. "Is that your favorite word? 'Okay'?"

Just go away, you big slug. "No."

"Well, then stop saying it. You're starting to annoy me."

Her fists pulsed as he stalked back into the sunshine. *I'll show you annoyed.*

She spent the rest of the day removing objects from shelves, making a mess she had no idea how to clean up, thinking all the while of how good it would feel to hit Fritz.

"Boxer girl's in the doghouse with Grandpa," Newt said, crossing the floor, holding up a first-aid kit. She took off her boot. He watched as she cleaned the cut.

"Let's get a beer after work. Looks like you could blow off some steam."

She thought for a moment he was asking her out. "At the Frontier Bar?"

"Hell, no. I'm persona non-gratuity there. Surprised Grandpa didn't tell you that story. Anyways, we don't need that warped-table rat-hole. I got an eighteen-pack of Raindogs burning a hole in my backpack. C'mon. You just continue doing whatever you're doing in here"—he let his eyes rove around the clutter of objects—"and I'll introduce you to my favorite drinking spot come quitting time."

When he was gone she wiped down the scarred plywood shelves with a wet rag, then squeezed it out over a bucket. Glancing at the door, she wrapped a rag around each fist and began bobbing and weaving, throwing combinations. She willed her shoulders to relax, the punches coming out more quickly, snapping when she brought them back in. Take the gun out of the holster, put it back. Reach for the cookie, bring it to your mouth.

The first time Gypo put her in the ring, she lost it. She had been fighting a Cambodian girl who had placed in Golden Gloves the year before.

"Just go easy. Breathe," Gypo told her as he held the ropes apart.

But when the bell went off Tara swung wildly. The girl went into a corner, covered her face. Tara thought she was winning until she heard Gypo: "Okay, see if she can take a few." A moment later a hook landed on her temple, then another on the bridge of her nose, sending white flashes across her vision. "You need to settle down, kid," Gypo yelled. But it was no use. She plowed forward, head down, slashing with her arms. The girl stepped back and to the side, and landed an uppercut that hit low, smashing Tara's throat.

"The fuck are you doing?" Tara yelled, lunging at the girl, trying to grab her with the gloves. Gypo separated the two.

"Chick's a brawler," the girl said, spitting out her mouthpiece.

"C'mon," Gypo said, taking Tara by the shoulder and unlacing her gloves. "Hit the showers."

She didn't know why he kept working with her after that. Maybe because of her father, who had dragged her to the gym in the tenth grade when she wouldn't break out of her funk. "You didn't tell me it was no girl, Fava," Gypo said at the time. He put out his hands, pleading. "And c'mon, your only child?"

Urbano just stared back with those serene eyes. Gypo Barsani, a flat-nosed, balding man with thick lips and a purple tint to his rubbery skin, finally shook his head, and it wasn't much later that the smell of sweat and canvas and meat, the snap of jump rope on concrete, the *whomp* of the heavy bag, followed by the tingle of the chain, became the center of her life.

After the fiasco in the ring, Gypo tied a rope between two pillars and had her bob to one side, then the other, move forward a step, pushing off the balls of her feet. "Get the rhythm of it—you know, hear it in your head, like a rap song or whatever crap it is you kids listen to." He gave her a routine: three rounds jumping rope, three rounds shadowboxing in the mirror. Followed by pad work. He'd swing at her and she'd weave out of the way. "Good. Now watch the eyes. That's the secret to it all."

She'd do a few rounds on the speed bag before hitting the showers, which meant going back to Wolf Street because there were no showers for women at the gym.

Just after her seventeenth birthday, Tara went back into the ring with a senior, an experienced featherweight boy who weighed less than she did but had a long reach.

"Just move around," Gypo told them both. "Keep it light."

This time when the bell rang, she focused on his eyes, how they narrowed before he shifted to the left and jabbed. The next time it happened she stepped to the side, put out her own jab, and felt the pressure of his forehead on the end of her glove. From the corner of her eye she saw Gypo nod.

"Thirteen fellas," Gypo said the next day when she came into the gym. "Atlantic City, and a couple over there at the Purple Horizon on Broad Street. That's how many I knocked out with the left hook. You got the jab down. Now it's time we make you dangerous. Go get wrapped up."

That day he demonstrated how to twist from the waist, guard her right cheek, keeping the elbow high as she corkscrewed back around with the left hook. Do it well, he told her, and you could get people three times—once when they were standing, once after their legs gave out, and once more just before they hit the canvas.

Huffing, trying to catch her breath as she stood in the middle of the dimly lit warehouse, she unwrapped her hands, dipped a rag into the bucket, and began to drag it across the shelves, exhausted, just wanting to be left alone.

Mica flecks in the sidewalk sparkled in the lowering sun as Tara and Newt picked their way along the rocks of the harbor breakwater. At the end was a concrete pad with a steel tower built on top, affixed with red triangles and a blinking red light.

He snapped open a beer and handed it to her. The tide was out, and the buttery, low-angled sun lit up the rocks beyond the beach. "Doesn't get better than this, eh?" he said, leaning against a pillar, touching the bottom of his can to the rim of hers. She breathed deep, holding the moist air in her chest. The sea breeze cleared the musty air of the warehouse from her lungs.

"You're lookin' sadder than a midget with a yo-yo. What's picking at you?"

Before she could hold it back a smile broke over her lips. "There it is," Newt chided. "The zombie has a sense of humor after all."

She let the grin stay on her face. "You got me."

"Share a little secret with you," he said, lighting a cigarette, then squinting out into the distance, picking a fleck of tobacco from his lips. "I got this true love named Plume. Little headache from Kentucky with honky-tonk eyes. My eventual future goal is to buy a boat for the two of us. Have her move on up here with me."

When he spoke he jabbed the cigarette at Tara as if she might not believe him, his taut face turning serious. "Let you in on something else. Each one of us here on this island, we got this one little thing holding us back from everything we ever wanted. And it's our job—and it ain't no small thing—to find our channel marker." He pointed at the red light over his head, working on a slow blink. "Something to aim for. But look at me goin' all Baptist minister on you."

Now that she was out of Philly, and away from her father, she couldn't think of what might be holding her back—or pushing her forward, for that matter.

"Me, I had my eye on this one boat, an old tug, tied up way out at the end of the docks," Newt said. "Gal from San Francisco had her. Has her, actually."

"I know that boat," she said. "The one with the smokestack and big rusted anchor."

"That's her. You walked out there?"

"The other day I did. Where's Plume now?" Tara asked.

His brow knit as he pulled on the cigarette. "Eugene, Oregon. Pregnant, turns out."

"Strategy's not working out so hot, then," she said.

He shot her a look. "Maybe it is and maybe it ain't. Important thing is, I'm stayin' clean as a broke-dick dog up here with my eye on that big steak in the sky. Because lemme be the one to tell you—all of us in this state are just getting whipped around on one continuous cycle, washed clean of our sins. You wait it out, be patient, work hard, keep your eye on that channel marker, and by my word there's a payoff." His skin appeared transparent in the last rays of sun. A purple vein zigzagged down his forehead. "If the Newtster aims to get a boat—well then you can set your goddamn watch to that happening."

She shifted on the concrete, drank her beer. Took the knife from her pocket and ran it beneath a fingernail.

"So what about you, Boxer Girl? What's your secret, your channel marker. What sins you got to wash clean?"

"Nothing as interesting as you."

"Oh, I highly doubt that. *Highly* doubt that. Ten cents says you left a man crying back in Philly."

His earnest expression made her want to say more, but she didn't. "How'd you end up here instead of down in Eugene with Plume?"

He took a long sip, and she could see him gathering his thoughts.

"Tell you what. Each man's got his gift, and me, I'm a freak with fish. I swear I can see 'em down there in the reeds, watching the underwater world pass by. I just know how their damp little brains work." He looked over at her as if to see if she was taking him seriously. "I got gills," he said, lifting his ratty thermal, revealing ribs that indeed looked like gills, then sitting back against the rock. "Got my start in eastern Kentucky, a tobacco-turned-cattle farm, grew up fishing and swimming and sometimes ice-skating on a pond me and my cousins dug out of the back forty. At eighteen I go to California to become a Navy SEAL. Best swimmers on earth, right? So I'm making circles around these meatheads, instructors never seen a thing like it, then this damn knee of mine blows out. So I did a little course correction and ended up working part-time here, part-time at the processor with an aim to get on a troller, or maybe the *Adriatic,* the tender down there at the processor. Either that or I stumble onto one of those big-time jobs up on the Bering Sea, go fish for crab."

"Where's that?"

He crushed a can against a rock, pulled open another, took a sip, and wiped his lips with the cuff of his flannel. "Oh, way up north. Dutch Harbor, where all the crazies congregate. Pot at the end of the rainbow, those jobs. But just wait until spring rolls around and herring starts. Opportunity abounds. You just gotta be quicker, work harder than the next guy. Maybe it'll rub off on you and you'll quit looking like a fat boy sitting alone in the school cafeteria."

It was probably an accurate assessment, she thought, watching the tip of his cigarette glow in the twilight. She resisted the urge to tell the story of her father's outburst by the stairs, pounding his fist into the horsehair plaster, and then what he had said.

Newt tossed his cigarette into the water, picked up his backpack, and stood, ducking his head beneath the triangular steel braces. "Anyways, good to know you're just about as fucked up as the rest of us. C'mon. You got some work ahead of you tomorrow."

8

THE FOLLOWING DAY she attacked the warehouse. Her hair in a ponytail threaded through the back of her Eagles hat, she tested circulation fans on an extension cord, coiled sections of hose, aired out mildewy tarps and refolded them. Grouped PVC pipes into neat piles, forty-fives and nineties, couplings, four- and eight-foot sections, labeled drawers for copper nails, wing nuts, gaskets.

By lunch her back ached from the steady, repetitive bend and rise, and her morning surge of energy was gone. Rain hammered away on the corrugated metal roof. This shitty work, being banished to the shed, was all because she hadn't fetched Fritz his precious shim fast enough. She hadn't spent four days on a ferry to deal with this chaos.

"Damn, you work slower than molasses going uphill in January." Her head snapped around. It was Newt, peering at her in the dim light. "You dreaming up some time machine in here?" And then he was gone.

To trim her misery she tried to focus on good memories. Driving in Connor's beat-up Mazda truck to Runnymede, New Jersey, a picnic on the hard dirt of a pitcher's mound. Wrapped in blankets on the lifeguard chair at Cape May. That night in Rittenhouse Square when he held her, and she felt, for the first time, her heart grow shy in her chest.

And, further back, her mother sweeping the house, pushing dust from the foyer onto the sidewalk, watering her ceramic pot of basil on the kitchen windowsill. Removing the sofa protectors for guests and zipping the plastic back on when they left. The aroma of marrow bones, gravy bubbling, at 1005 Wolf Street for the Sunday meal. The gold medallion around her neck jostling over the ironing board as Serena pressed a white blouse for Tara's first day of school, putting knife-pleats into her wool jumper, folding bobby socks while Little Vic cut off one of her braids at the dining room table. How furious her mother had been.

In these memories her mother was always in motion: leaning out the second-story window of the bedroom at Christmas with a broom in one hand, using the handle to arrange strings of colored lights into the branches of the maple. *Uno, due, tre!* — Tara's job to push the plug into the socket. Urbano on the stoop, unlit cigar shaking between his lips as he clapped. The lights shedding an amber halo on the pavement below. Early winter morning walks to the bakery, sidewalks coated in frost, Tara shocked from half-sleep as her mother flipped on the fluorescent lights in the kitchen. The ticking sound as the oil in the deep fryer heated, Serena fetching a tray of precut cannoli dough from the walk-in freezer.

She recalled one morning a couple months after her sixth birthday when she and her mother watched on the grainy black-and-white television in the bakery kitchen as flames destroyed sixty-five row homes. Her mother wept as she filled the pastry tube. "What kind of country is it where a city bombs its children and no one does nothing?"

The side door slammed. Tara jumped, fearing Fritz's grumpy wrath.

"The hell kind of show you got running in here?" Newt snatched a section of pegboard from her hands, split it, and tossed the pieces into a burn pile. "Thing's about as warped as a dog's hind leg. C'mon, we got some work ahead of us. I like having you around too much to see Grandpa fire your slow ass."

He plugged in a table saw near the door, took the pencil from his hat, measured and marked, then handed her a pair of safety glasses. "Now just feed it nice and gentle, flat, slow and low like a turtle, otherwise it'll catch back on you. Grandpa loves him a good organizational storage box. There you go, keep it flat. You done this before?" He took up the ripped section, then showed her how to hold the strips of plywood tight against the fence, just as Connor had once done.

"Blade's sharp as a rat turd on both ends, so watch yourself," Newt said. He swiped the chop saw, handed her pieces to hold while he drilled. "Glue it and screw it, and you'll have something to show for the day. Hey," he said, trying to catch her eye. "Hey, Molasses. You okay? You hanging in there?"

She fit a screw into the drill. "I'm good. Thanks."

9

BUT SHE WASN'T.

As the days contracted further, the sun barely clearing the mountains to the south, the island seemed to fold in on itself, caught in a bubble of October twilight. Her bones ached despite layering undershirts, thermals, and sweatshirts to keep out the damp. At the end of the day she wanted nothing more than to crawl back into bed and float, semiconscious, waiting for the sun to return. When the clouds finally did part, the sun was halfhearted, low-angled, slicing at the buildings, sparking raindrops that dangled from spruce tips.

At odd moments a wave of sadness enveloped her, and she could hardly move. She remembered her mother's casket being lowered into the ground in the plot overlooking the Schuylkill. Standing on the green felt, wanting desperately to sink into the earth with her.

She often thought about Connor, sometimes blaming him for the wedge of his letter, at other times for sleeping with her when she was so open, so needy. But most often now there was just the steady beat of missing him, wanting to feel his warm breath on her neck.

In the evenings after work she went to the docks and walked among the boats, listening to the now-familiar squeak of the buoy balls. Sailboats, fishing vessels, and skiffs crowded the stalls, bouncing in the swell. Men on the docks who before had given her quick, sidelong glances as she approached now acknowledged her with short nods.

Newt had tried to explain to her the differences between the fishing boats — trollers with their folded poles, seiners with the elevated wheelhouses and broad decks, and longliners with the aluminum chute extending off the stern. But they all just looked like tough, tired horses in their stables.

She liked catching snippets of conversation among the fishermen, who stood with their brown-booted feet propped up on the side of a boat, smoking cigarettes and speaking in low tones. A foreign language of drags and tides and fathoms. Or who dipped stiff-bristled brushes into buckets and scrubbed down the deck, or sent wheels of orange sparks into the water from grinders. The docks, limbs extending into the water off the central work float, were alive.

As she walked she thought about how quickly the house on Wolf Street changed after her mother died. No longer the lingering smell of garlic and meat, the basil plant in the window, the electricity in the air when her mother laughed. Homesick? What home was there to be sick for?

When the ache set in, she reminded herself that she was here, on this island, safe. Then the tugboat came to mind, dark-windowed, floating there at the end of the docks. Waiting.

10

SHE ARRIVED AT the hatchery at 7:50 to set up the egg treatments, check the temperature of the water in the incubator trays, fill the magazine on Betsy. With care, she hung antibiotics, piercing plastic bags with a twist of the nozzle, taking note of the survival rate in the sliding trays, recording it in the speckled journal.

Fritz had done an inspection of the warehouse, where she had labeled each compartment, grouped widths of wood together, and scrubbed the planked floor with degreaser. "You sure took your sweet time with it," he grumbled, looking around. "And I guess now you're the only one here who knows where anything is."

He was such a grim bastard. Newt flashed her a don't-you-dare-open-your-mouth look. And she didn't.

She fed the fry, swept the cement floor of the workroom. *Be the first with a broom in your hand, the last with a beer* — this was written on the blackboard above Fritz's desk. She had made a vow to follow the dictum.

At night she went back to her efficiency apartment, closed her eyes, and tried to think of one thing she had done since first arriving on the island that was successful. Three weeks, and she had organized a warehouse. Even sleep, the most elemental task, came with difficulty.

As she lay awake she pictured her father back home, moving up the stairs, chalky heels sticking out from his slippers. Had he just headed back to his office and smoked a cigar after he kicked her out, as if nothing had happened?

How many times had she heard the story? (The Marconis had a way of repeating family lore, the details shifting but the thread staying the same.) The doctors had told Urbano's parents, Grandpa Joe and Tara's *nonna,* that they wouldn't be able to have children because of the high lead levels in Grandpa Joe's blood. He had spent much of his teenage years working for a shoemaker on Snyder Avenue, soling nails clamped between his teeth. Tara's *nonna* miscarried four times. When she gave birth to a son, Grandpa Joe took to the streets howling, calling the neighborhood over to examine his child's large head and thick black hair.

Instead of a traditional Italian name, Grandpa Joe wanted to call his son Hercules, the last mortal son of Zeus who sprayed Hera's breast milk across the heavens to create the Milky Way. Her *nonna* would have none of it, and settled instead on Urbano, figuring — correctly — that he would be a man of the city.

As a teenager Urbano boxed. To hear Grandpa Joe tell it, his son was never much of a fighter until he got hit. And then — forget about it. "Your papa, he coulda gone pro with that temper of his. Just need to get him riled before a fight. He got those stone eyes, scared the shite out of those Irish boys." Tara had seen the photos at the social club of Urbano's arm raised high, blood running from one eye. People respected him, even when, as a teenager, he chose to linger in the kitchen in his sweatpants, studying cake recipes with the women instead of playing stickball on Manton Street.

After high school Urbano joined the Army. Korea was over, and he served two years in peacetime. In Philly he returned to the bakery, grew the business, but quit socializing. He stopped boxing, didn't flirt with the girls at the public swimming pool, stayed in his billing office during the Italian Market festival. He took on the nickname Fava for his oversized head, and was still single at the age of thirty-five, interested only in his bakery and relaxing with a cigar at the Italian Market social club with his buddy Big Vic.

With his wife nagging him for *nipoti,* Grandpa Joe decided to play matchmaker. Soon he had a stack of Polaroids, a few cameos, and one oil painting spread over the parlor table.

After much consideration he selected a wide-hipped, long-limbed, curly-haired woman from the old country, the notch at the base of her neck filled with a scoop of shadow. This was Serena Isola, a distant cousin to Big Vic. From a fishing village on the eastern coast of Sicily, fourteen years younger than Fava.

Grandpa Joe mailed Serena's father a letter about the wonders of South Philadelphia, and his virtuous son — a quiet, intelligent man who didn't cheat or gamble, and owned a bakery known throughout the city for its cannoli. As a good faith gesture he included a picture of Urbano standing beneath the lit-up Marconi's Bakery sign, dressed in a three-piece worsted suit with a gold watch chain. A ticket for passage from Naples to New York City followed, along with a diamond-studded bracelet and a thousand dollars in cash. Serena's family sent word back that by Christmas 1972, their daughter would be in the New World.

Even as preparations were being made, Urbano insisted with shakes of his shaggy, graying head that he wasn't interested. But when Serena arrived, wearing the glittery bracelet on her thin wrist, medallion of Saint Anthony nestled into that notch at the base of her neck, it became clear to anyone who knew him that Urbano was smitten. "He's a slow cooker, my boy," Grandpa Joe always said. "Not a loud sonofabitch like his old man. But we broke him. We got him now."

For a wedding gift Grandpa Joe ordered the concrete dug up outside his son's row home, and planted a red sugar maple sapling. The very same one Serena would decorate each Christmas. Waiting patiently for Tara to plug in the lights.

11

WHEN SHE TOLD Fritz that one of the tanks was low, he sighed and heaved his bulk from behind the desk. "Newt handy?"

"He's off at the processor."

He spat a stream of tobacco into the grass and handed her a fish net. "C'mon then. Use the handle to chase away the fry so I can see what the hell's going on."

Outside, she followed his instructions, herding the swarm of fish to one side. He scoffed, spit again. "Another goddamn leak. Where's Newt?" he repeated.

"Processor."

He stomped off without saying where he was going. Tara busied herself organizing the workbench, hanging up individual tools and arranging the wrenches in descending order. Thinking about how disappointed Fritz had looked when he realized Newt was gone. Like he might as well have been left with no one.

Hearing a high-pitched honk, she went outside, watched as Fritz bucked a construction lift into the yard. He slid out of the seat, ran truck straps beneath the leaking tank, climbed back in, then throttled the engine and lifted the tank.

"Your hands cold?" he shouted. Confused, she shook her head.

"Well, then get them out of your damn pockets. Hold that tank steady."

She cursed silently. She wanted to be a good worker, but he made it so difficult. He fiddled with the joysticks, jockeying the tank to where he liked while she tried to keep it in one place. Waiting for him to point out something else she was doing wrong. He scooted out of the seat and stopped a minute to look into the clouds.

"Might be working against the rain — snow, even, if the temperature drops hard enough. You look cold — you all right? Wanna go back and take a warm shower?"

Her knuckles itched. With his orangutan body he'd be slow and cumbersome. She'd stay out of range. She could take him.

"I'll be fine."

But he was already under the tank, inspecting the leak. "I'd ask if you ever worked fiberglass before, but I'm pretty sure I know the answer."

"We iced cakes with it at the bakery."

He ignored her. "Just do your best to keep the thing still while I work with the sander."

"Okay," she said back, in a lilting tone to let him know she was purposely annoying him. When he came up he gave her a knotted glance, as if to say he didn't have time for her games, switched on the sander, and began moving the pad over the worn-away section.

Thirty minutes passed, an hour. Even in the dimming afternoon light, through clouds of sanded glass, she could see his pissed-off expression when the tank wobbled. He reminded her of her father, not only in his bulk, but also in how he seethed.

"Earth to Philly! Would you hold the damn thing still? I can't build up any pressure."

She tightened her grip. It was either that or let go and start beating the fat fuck. She looked around the yard. At her wits' end, she shouted over the whine of the sander. "You know, there's a better way to do this."

He shut off the tool. "What did you just say?"

She didn't care. Let him fire her. "I said, there's a better way to do this. Like, if we find something to set the take on."

He slipped the facemask from his mouth. With the curved red

marks on his cheeks he looked like an astonished, obese clown. Shreds of tobacco coated his tongue. *Go on*, she thought. *Say something insulting.*

"And how, my little genius, are we going to set it down with me still able to sand under it?"

Desperate, she searched the yard. Cinderblocks poked out from the weeds. She pointed. "What about those?"

After a moment he said, "Well, hell. Go."

She heaved four out of the wet grass and positioned them on end where they would catch the tank when it was lowered. He returned to the wheel of the lift. Her mind played the scene forward, the heavy fiberglass coming down over the blocks. "What about tying a rope to the straps so I can pull the tank when you lower it, make it easier to position?" she suggested.

"What, did you fall on your head or something?" he said. "Go on then."

She ran across the yard, her face flushed. After organizing the warehouse she knew exactly where to look. Back outside, Fritz watched as she knotted the length of rope to the truck strap. He slid out of the seat, undoing the lump.

"Now pay attention." He folded the rope on itself. "Pretend this here's a rabbit. Rabbit goes up out of the hole, over the log, around the tree, back over the log, gets scared and heads back down. Got it?" He sent the end through the hole, around, then in again. "Simple. You try."

Her fingers shook. "The rabbit comes out, and then he . . ."

"Goes over the log."

"Over the log, and around the tree."

"Back over the log . . ."

"Back over the log into the hole."

She held up the result, a ropey pile of nothing. He shook his head, retied the line, and eased the tank down. She adjusted the cinderblocks until the base of the tank hit squarely.

"Good!" he shouted, turning off the lift. He poured resin into a bowl, squeezed in hardener, then dipped long strips of mesh into the syrupy liquid. It smelled bitter as he smoothed the layers with a plastic spackle knife. "Here, use this one," he said, handing her his respirator. "Didn't think you'd be helping out, otherwise I woulda grabbed a spare. My eggs are so scrambled, it doesn't matter anymore."

Flakes melted on her forehead as she took the sander and began smoothing the fiberglass. Fritz stood up, hands on his hips, watching her.

"We just might make a worker out of you yet, Marconi."

12

THAT NIGHT, standing in front of the long mirror in her apartment, Tara traced the imprints on her cheeks left by the respirator. Shadows over her jaw from a summer of crackers and cream cheese were filling in. Dirt from the warehouse was trapped in the pores of her nose. When she ran her fingers through her hair, they caught on snags of matted curls. Grime rimmed her nails.

Still watching herself in the glass, she pulled off her tank-top, splashed water on her face, then leaned forward on her hands. Her ribs appeared darker, thicker. A shadow split the muscles of her stomach. After the day spent fixing the tank, she felt stronger, in a different way from boxing. As if the strength from punching the heavy bag were vitamin C and what she was doing here at the hatchery were the thing itself, an orange.

After her shower she slipped into sweatpants and climbed beneath the covers, the springs of the bed sagging. The temperature had dropped, and flakes drifted through the cone of light outside her window. Closing her eyes, she slipped a hand beneath the waistband. She came steeply, almost the moment she touched herself, imagining Connor over her, sweaty, that concentrated, intense expression on his face. She lay there, waiting for sleep to come, trying to ignore the feeling of the room closing in.

It wasn't happening. She dressed quickly, buttoning her coat to the neck. Hands shoved deep into her pockets, she walked toward the tug. Her rubber boots squeaked in the snow, which made a latticework in front of the mountains. Standing in front of the boat, she watched as flakes buffeted the wheelhouse windows, silver tracers melting into the black water. Her lungs hurt with the cold. The For Sale sign dangled from a corner in the porthole, rimmed with orange rust. If it had been outside, she would have ripped it off.

Back at the apartment, she flipped on the pendant light and took out a lined pad. As she sat with it on one knee, tapping the end of a pen against her front teeth, she thought of the time she had been frustrated with Connor for turning down a role in the spring play at St. Vincent's. He kept insisting he wanted to remain behind the scenes, build sets in his workshop. They got into an argument on the sidewalk in front of the house. She told him he never took chances, that he lacked the courage to just go for it.

When she opened the door, her mother was already wearing her winter coat, and Tara knew she had been listening.

"Come, *figlia*. We go to decorate the bakery."

"Ma, I'm tired. I just wanna sleep."

"Come," she said, taking Tara's hand.

That evening, as they kneeled in clouds of cotton in the display window, snapping together train tracks, her mother said, "Do you not see? He is so patient. *Lui ti corteggia*. And you don't care at all."

"He's not courting me, Ma."

Serena jabbed at her own eye. "I see what I see. And I also tell you something else. Ones like this boy, when they see who they love" — she flicked her fingers to mimic an explosion — "ka-boom they go, like a balloon with too much air. They have been saving all their lives. And then — *basta*."

"Ma, it's not like that."

Her mother shook a section of train track at Tara. "You wait and see. I tell you now."

27 October 1997

Dear Connor,

It's 2:17 in the morning. I can't sleep. The snow turns everything white. I'm just back from walking to the harbor.

I wish we could talk in person. It would be so much easier.

I know we're on our separate paths, and that's probably for the best. I'm still angry at your letter. But I'm also sorry. I hate the idea of you alone in that city. I hope you also understand how fucked up in the head I was. Like I'm starting to see how little I really know.

She stood up, pulled her shoulders back, and took a sip of water. The floorboard radiators ticked. In the window she could see the table and herself reflected above the letter. She took a step closer and saw, beyond her reflection, snow balanced on the branches of the spruce trees. After a moment she could feel the cold through the window.

Okay. I'm going to put down this pen and fold this into an envelope and send it before I catch myself. I miss you.

Tara

13

IN THE CHILDREN'S SECTION at the library she found a book called *The Young Seafarer's Book of Knots*. Illustrations and step-by-step instructions for tying the bowline, laid out in sequence.

At the fishing supply store by the processor she bought a spool of thin braided twine called gangion. Back in her apartment she turned on the dome light over the table, nipped off a section from the spool, and opened the book.

Even putting the twine up against the drawings, it was difficult to figure out on which side to set the loop. She tried it this way, then that, pulling on both ends. Her result was bumpy and awkward compared to the elegant illustration.

She flung the gangion at the photograph on the wall. Fritz had tied his bowline on the tank in just a few seconds.

On Monday morning she found Newt smoking a cigarette. "Grandpa got you practicing knots?"

She held out the string. "You know how to do a bowline?"

He tossed his butt into a five-gallon bucket filled with sand, holding the door open, and started inside. "Keep at it. It'll come."

That evening she pounded a tack into her shower wall with the heel of her boot. She stood beneath the showerhead, her curls flattened against her cheeks, line tied to the tack, making loops. A knot came together, one she thought might be right, but when she tried the same exact thing again the twine snarled in a bunch.

She threw a jab at the wall, misjudged the distance, and grazed her knuckles. "Fucker!" she shouted, then looked guiltily at her duct-taped door. Her knuckles bled into the water. Frustrated, she tried again, the line twisting and looping over itself, snagging before coming undone. "*Cazzo*," she hissed. "You piece of shit."

She looked down at the mess in her fingers, turning her hand in the stream to wash off the blood. "Settle down, Tara. Just settle the fuck down." The water had turned tepid and her skin puckered. *I'm not getting out of this shower,* she told herself, taking up the line once more. Make the rabbit hole, bring the rabbit out, jog him around the log, then back down. She began to shiver as the water grew cold. She held the knot up, blinking away droplets. Ah. That looked right.

She dried, then took her result over to the book on the table. Right it was. She flipped a page and made a bowline with a bight, fashioning a loop, pushing the doubled-over line through the opening. Slowly, the parts cinched, one loop tightening over the other until the knot was made fast. Not so bad.

The next afternoon after work, when she reached into the shower to throw the handle, her arm got sprayed with cold water. Except this time she had an idea.

She returned to the store and bought miniature blocking, which she screwed into the stall, setting up a pulley system. She looped a clove hitch over the handle, the two ends oriented in opposite directions, then ran the line through the pulleys, took the end over the side of the shower door. When she pulled on it, the sound of water startled her, along with the realization that she had mastered some small piece of the universe.

For the moment, she felt a little less lost.

14

ON THE MONDAY before Thanksgiving, Tara found Fritz behind his desk. He glanced up as she reached for the logbook, adjusted his reading glasses, which made him look like an overgrown Santa's helper, and squinted at her.

"You got big Thanksgiving plans?" he asked.

"Me?"

"Yeah, you," he grunted. "By the way, that patch on the tank's holding."

"Oh yeah?"

He nodded. "Join us. Fran, my wife, enjoys meeting new folks." He didn't look up, as if that settled that. "Now get on out of here — go take a walk in the mountains or something. Explore. Don't be such a sad sack."

Planks burped brown water as she walked up Crow Hill. Stepping into the tree cover, she smelled a rich mix of wet moss, spruce, and salt in the air. Wooden flights of stairs crisscrossed between the trees. *Hill my ass,* she thought, breathing heavily.

As she went, she fooled with a spruce twig, folding it over on itself, practicing the bowline, liking how her fingers were gaining memory of the movements. How stupid of her, she thought, never to ask her mother what she knew about fishing, paying out line, making these knots.

She angled off the trail, ignoring the tears thorns made in her jeans. A creature chattered above her, charging back and forth along a tree limb. Through a break in the needles she saw the blanket of the ocean, the cone of the volcano rising from the gray, and headed toward it, bending back branches to see better.

Looking over the water, she remembered a night in eleventh grade when she heard a raspy sobbing coming from her parents' bedroom down the hall. When she peered around the doorjamb she saw her father holding her mother to his shoulder. They had their backs to her, black outlines of bodies in front of the blue light of the muted television.

"Each day," her mother said, "it is like she goes farther from me. Like there is something, you know, that — *scares* her. In *Sicilia* I talk to my cousins. We figure out how to make it better. But here in this city . . ." She lifted her hands, dropping them with a slap against her bare thighs. "*Amore*, I am no good at it."

As she stood listening, Tara realized her mother was talking about her.

Alone in the woods, wanting to chase this memory away, she went up on her toes, shuffled her feet, and shook out her shoulders. She threw a couple jabs at the tree trunk. "Double jab left right hook," she heard Gypo snap. "Jab uppercut followed by the right. Combination, then get out of there."

It began to rain, drops filtering through the branches. Winded, she let down her fists. She started back, this time gathering speed on the stairs, hopping high so her momentum wouldn't cause her to slip on the dark wet wood. *Just a little faster,* she thought, pushing off her toes, trying not to fall. *Just a little faster and I'll be good again.*

15

FRITZ GAVE THEM the Wednesday before Thanksgiving off. (He needed time to prepare his crab dishes.) Feeling lost without work, Tara headed to the bookstore, where she found a card with a woodcut print on it that showed a couple huddled together against the side of a mountain. Her palms began to sweat.

Maybe her letter had fallen out of the mail plane, helicopering down over one of those glaciers she had seen from the ferry. She could picture it, soggy, lost in the swirls of dirty ice.

Behind the bookstore she found a coffee shop called the Muskeg. The room had a grotto feel to it, reminding her of Little Vic's basement beneath the barbershop, with the windows looking out onto the sidewalk. She ordered coffee and a slice of salmonberry pie, and set the card in front of her.

November 26, 1997

Dear Connor,

Sitting here in this café. It's dark, just a few windows looking onto the sidewalk. Kind of like your garage.

I thought of you when I saw this print. They say you shouldn't hike alone up here. More on that in a moment. But it also made me think of our trip to the shore, the blankets we wrapped up in.

She set her pen down and looked around. *Now you're getting sappy and nostalgic.* Then she found herself meeting the eyes of the older, long-fingered man she saw at the library the night she called Connor. He wore the same workman's cap, same peaceful expression. *C'mon, Tara. Take a minute and figure out what you're trying to say here. Don't get distracted.*

> *Connor, I'm sorry. I miss you. But I'm going to wait to hear from you before any more letters.*
> *I apologize for being a little shit. For what happened over the summer, for sleeping with you then leaving like that. For tenth grade, going quiet. There are reasons I wish I could tell you. Soon.*
>
> *Tara*

As she reread the letter she heard a sound and looked up to see the man from the library in front of her.

"Do you mind?" he asked, lowering into a chair with his coffee cup and a few cubes of sugar. He had a drawn, ageless face, and sloped shoulders—he could have been anywhere between fifty and seventy. "Excuse the intrusion. You appear to be hard at work."

"It's fine."

"Betteryear," he said, reaching across the table. She shook his hand. Improbable distances separated the joints of his fingers. She caught the scent of old grass, and something else, cucumbers maybe.

"Tara Marconi."

He touched the bill of his patched engineer's cap. "Did you just arrive in town, Tara?"

What was that Newt had said about men in Alaska? *The odds are good, but the goods are odd.* "I did," she said. She was about to add "just before I saw you at the library," but caught herself.

"Well, as I said, I don't mean to distract you. I just thought I'd introduce myself." He pulled on leather biking gloves and stood. "I'm often in here, reading the papers. Ah—and if you don't have plans for Thanksgiving, we do a big meal at the Alaska Native Brotherhood Hall. Come if you like."

"Okay."

"Happy day."

"You too."

She looked back down at her letter.

PS. If you see my father tell me how he is. I'm assuming he's figured out where I am by now, if he even cares. If I call I know he's just going to hang up.

Oh. And if I had to pick one word now — empty. Not in a bad way.

After mailing the letter she returned to her studio and set to baking. Chilling the butter until it was hard to the touch. Folding pads of it into the flour. Halving, seeding, roasting the squash three pieces at a time in her undersized oven. She rolled out the dough, kneaded a shred between her fingers to test the consistency. Dripping in ice water, salt. In her head she heard the tune of a Sicilian folk song she couldn't name. One her mother hummed when she was baking. Her father would recognize it. She remembered him sometimes humming along, even singing the Italian lyrics in a soft, wavering voice.

She watched her hands as she built the crust, working slowly around the rim of the pie pan, pressing down with her thumbs with just the right amount of force, careful not to thin the dough, which needed more butter. She stopped, her hands gripping the pie. Tensing her stomach, trying not to move, for fear of starting to cry, and not being able to stop.

16

FRITZ AND HIS WIFE, FRAN, lived in a cabin built on piers over the water just down from the library. The kitchen was already bustling when Tara arrived, people opening ovens, pouring cream and splashes of orange juice into sweet potatoes, crumbling seaweed and shreds of king crab into stuffing. Fran smelled of patchouli, and wore a hooded Baja shirt and fleece pants with burn holes in the fabric. After hugging Tara, she set the pie on the counter. "This looks delicious — Fritz mentioned something about you working in a bakery. Wine? Beer?"

"Beer is great."

Tara froze when she saw the back of a woman working over the stove. It was the set of her shoulders, her head bent over a pot. Just like her mother.

The woman set down a potato masher, reached for a carton of milk, gave a generous pour. Fran handed Tara a beer.

"You gotta hold the darn thing tight if you want this to work," the woman said, turning. She was reedy, with a smoker's body and straight, graying hair — nothing like her mother. Tara held tight as she wrenched off the cap. "Laney," she said, clinking Tara's bottle with a glass of white wine.

"Tara."

She had polished skin and wide-set eyes traced with black liner. Beneath her apron was a red shawl. Laney sliced a lemon, squeezed, then motioned to Tara for another one.

"You work with that lunatic Newt?"

Tara took a slow sip of beer. "I don't think he's a lunatic."

"He didn't tell you the story?"

"What story?"

Laney walked the line of being obnoxious. And yet her straight-forward manner made Tara feel at home.

"The story of him hiding on my tug and getting dragged off by the police."

Her heart thumped. So this was the woman who was walking away from the tug.

Fritz yelled her name from another room. "The lion tamer calls," Laney said, giving a coy smile.

He was in the den off the kitchen, watching football with a can of beer balanced on his stomach, his fur-lined slippers perched on an ottoman. "Have a seat."

The room was wood-paneled, its walls hung with a black and red Tlingit quilt and ink prints of rockfish. "Cowgirls," she mumbled, dropping into the couch. The Dallas Cowboys were playing Tennessee.

He closed one eye and looked at her, as if measuring what she meant. The exchange with Laney had made her bold—or maybe it was the day off, and writing the last letter to Connor. She also felt she had earned this respite from the hatchery, the right to sit down with a beer and watch her least favorite team in the world lose. She fooled with the ends of a quilt on the sofa, folding half hitches between her fingers. "I watched the Eagles beat the Cowboys. December tenth, 1995. It was like, seven degrees out."

He massaged the bridge of his nose. "Bunch of grown men in tight pants that should be working, if you ask me," he said.

Dick. Couldn't he say anything nice about anything?

But the memory of the football game with her father warmed her. Watching as the Eagles kicked a field goal in the final seconds, how Veterans Stadium had erupted with sound, and Urbano had pumped his fist in the air. The smell of espresso grounds and cigar smoke, and that earsplitting noise.

Some thirty-five hundred miles away, her father was watching this same game at the social club with Vic and the crew. Maybe Little Vic, too — he was over eighteen. Or perhaps Urbano was at Wolf Street, tapping his cigar against the saucer and shaking his head as a Cowboys runner slashed for a gain.

She looked around the room. Draped over the porch railing was rope — or line, as Newt had said. She fetched it, then stood over Fritz.

"Hold out your wrist," she ordered.

He leaned forward, his stomach bunching over his thighs. "What's this? Some Italian magic trick?"

"Just do it."

In quick twists she tied a bowline, looping the rope along the crease of his skin, then pulling it tight.

"Not bad," he said. "You know how to put a bend at the end?"

But she was already doing it. After that she made a clove hitch, a trucker's hitch, a mooring hitch, a double-half hitch, until his smile was gone, and he just looked down at his wrist as the knots pulled together.

"Well, call me an asshole," he said, chugging his beer and standing. "Is that what you were up to all those hours organizing that warehouse?"

"Go to hell."

She meant it, and her heart beat, waiting for his response. He just beamed up at her, lifting his empty can. "Another?"

When he returned from the kitchen with two beers, he said, "You talk to Laney in there about that tug you seem to have taken a shine to?"

"What makes you think that?"

"You kidding? I saw you googly-eyed the other day. Miracle that it's still floating."

She thought of the boat rocking in the waves, then suddenly saw it slipping beneath the surface — a horrible image.

"That's coming back," she muttered at the screen.

The referee picked up his yellow flag, flipped on his mic, and called "holding." Fritz smiled. "You know your football."

Fran called them to the table. Glasses clinked. Chipped clay bowls of stuffing and sweet potatoes and cranberry sauce with ginger and orange, as well as various dishes incorporating Fritz's Dungeness crabs collected from the bottom of the chute at the hatchery, made their way around. There was no turkey, just venison Fritz had shot a couple weeks back on Crow Hill. Laney ladled a scoop of thick, dark gravy over Tara's meat. "So you've got that city look in your eyes. East Coast? Boston?"

"Philly."

"The city that bombs itself, right?"

Frozen for a moment by the memory of her mother sobbing at the bakery, Tara stayed silent. By the time she recovered, Laney was speaking with her neighbor. Fran leaned toward her, patchouli scent mixing with crab and gravy, and started in on the story of how the Russians made Port Anna the capital of their fur-trading enterprise, bringing down Aleuts to hunt otter. Then how the Tlingits had stood up to the Russians, destroying their village. She felt a tap on her shoulder.

"Can I interrupt the history lesson?" Laney said. "I could use company."

Tara excused herself and followed the woman out the sliding door. It was windy on the deck. Clouds skirted across the sky. Laney repinned her hair with a chopstick, then cupped her hands and flicked up a flame.

"You're on edge, I can tell," she said to Tara, exhaling smoke into the wind. "I get it, all these men around. Like you can't find your groove."

"I'm doing all right."

They both turned to a rumble and tracked the path of a plane as it descended over the smaller islands. "Fritz told me you were asking after my boat. If you're interested, come out for a glass of wine some evening. For a go-getter like yourself, I'd halve the price. Say an even thirty K."

Before she could respond, the door opened and a crowd joined them. Tara and Laney watched as a dog on the beach knocked over a toddler who cried until she found a shell and forgot about it.

Back inside, Tara dropped down in front of the television. The game was in the fourth quarter, and Dallas was losing. Laney balanced a plate of pumpkin pie on her knobby knees.

"Lord above, this is amazing," she said, holding up her fork. "Your mom teach you?"

Tara shook her head, watching the screen. There was a *thunk* in the kitchen followed by a tinkle of glasses. Fritz came in with three whiskeys.

"Drink up, ladies," he said. "Tara, that pie in there is off the charts. Coozy sure couldn't do anything like that. I never asked — where is that kid these days?"

"Last I talked to him he was out in Santa Fe, working on an organ for a church or something. Yeah, baby," she said as the Oilers kneeled on the ball.

Laney held out her glass. "May our daughters have rich fathers, beautiful mothers, and dry homes."

"That's supposed to be 'sons,'" Fritz said as they clinked and drank.

"Yeah, well. Us girls over here changed it to 'daughters,' didn't we?" Laney winked at Tara, and they drank.

17

EACH AFTERNOON she walked to the post office, only to see the white light from the workroom in the back of her mailbox. She had written on Wednesday the twenty-sixth. Connor should have sent a letter back by now.

Finally, on the second Friday of December, an envelope arrived, postmarked from New York City. Resisting the temptation to tear it open in the post office, she hurried down to the Muskeg. Her heart quickened as she used her knife to slit open the envelope.

4 December 1997

Dear Tara,

Thank you for the last two letters. I apologize for not responding earlier. I do appreciate you writing instead of calling. It gives me time to sort my thoughts. It was hard and nice to hear that you miss me. But thank you for taking time out of that snowy night to write.

Empty doesn't strike me as such a bad way to be.

It's good also that you've discovered a small well-lit place for a cup of coffee where you can read and write letters. Down here I have Caffe Reggio, by Washington Square, home of the first cappuccino. I feel a bit like an animal in my high-rise cage so it's good to get out and walk around.

What else? I found an off-Broadway theater to intern in. I'm taking these theory classes where we study the affects of colonialism. It sheds interesting light on South Philly.

That's all.

It's good that you're finding your true north.

Godspeed in your journey,

Connor

She flung the sheets on the table in front of her. It was bullshit. This wasn't Connor, who looked at her with such careful concern that awful summer. Who waited for her to walk home after school. There was nothing personal in the letter. It was detached. She read it again, then decided it was worse — pompous. Like he was at this fancy college, and all of a sudden he was beyond cool, while she was shucking baby salmon from their mothers' bellies in Alaska. She was pouring out her soul, writing about the hardest thing she had ever experienced, and he came back with this cold piece of shit.

She crumpled the letter and threw it into the wastebasket. *Fuck you, Connor Macauley. I'll show you separate paths.*

18

A WEEK BEFORE December twenty-third, she and Newt perched on the drizzle-wet concrete pad of the channel marker, the red light blinking silently above, a soggy eighteen-pack of beer torn open between them.

For a while they talked about Plume, the excruciating details of her letter describing the birth of her baby boy. Two days later, she reported, the father was arrested on assault charges.

Newt snapped open a fresh can. He had been drinking two beers to her one. "I'm tired of making shit money being a cleaning lady at the hatchery. I'm a goddamn fisherman," he said, shaking his head. "Needing to get my fisherwoman up here beside me."

Earlier that day they had finished a deep clean of the killing shack, dipping wooden brushes into buckets of bleach and water, scrubbing dried blood from the nubby walls.

"What about the processor?" she asked.

"It pays good when you get overtime — but a spot on the *Adriatic*, the tender. That's when you start pulling away from the rest of these mules."

"It'll pan out," she told him.

He took a swig, looked to the side, and burped, giving her a glance. "That what they teach you in Catholic school? It'll pan out? Like it panned out for Jesus?" He sighed, running fingers through his hair.

She didn't consider herself religious, and was surprised when this offhand comment offended her. "You should just shave it," she told him.

"I should, shouldn't I?" he said, picking loose strands from his fingers. "Like feathers hangin' on for dear life."

They drank in silence.

"I met that woman who owns the tugboat," Tara said.

"Laney?"

"Yeah. She told me there's a story. Grandpa ignored me when I asked about it."

"There most certainly is a story."

"Tell."

He crushed his can against a rock, reached for another. "That boat's got its hooks into you, doesn't it? You know what B-O-A-T stands for? Break out another thousand."

"Tell me the story."

"You tell me first. What's got you so gaga over it?"

She shrugged. "Maybe it's a ridiculous idea. I don't know. Maybe it's like falling in love. It just . . . is."

Newt watched her carefully. She didn't feel like talking about this. "Your turn. Tell me the story."

He grinned. "So I finish up with the navy down in San Diego, then hitchhiked north."

"I got that."

"Up in Seattle I found out Plume was pregnant."

"Living with the guy who just got put away."

"That one. So I spent a couple weeks on the streets, stole a tray of croissants from a bakery, threw them up, ate a hamburger from a trashcan, that sorta of thing. Slept with the hobos by the tracks — I mean bad, rough shit. Caught a break on a ride north on a tender out of Seattle, and picked up a job at the processor just in time for herring. First day at work, fish coming in at all ends — you can't imagine.

Air chunky with salt, no spit left for a swallow. And all the while I'm workin' hard, thinking about Plume in Washington, how to give her and her baby a good home."

"And you thought of the tug."

He gave her a stern expression, took a long swig of beer.

"Sorry. Go on."

"So I go over to the Frontier on my break, and it was like stepping into a cattle car, full of hairy, cigarette-smoking, fish-smelling, beer-swilling motherfuckers. Boys doing bumps right off the bar. And that she-man of a tender pouring tequila quick as old boys could shoot 'em back."

"Nice."

"And I see on the chalkboard someone's put a World War II tug-boat up for sale."

"*Pacific Chief.*"

"That's the one, out there on the transient. I ask a fisherman about it, and he tells me it's two thousand square feet of living space, couple wood stoves, one you can cook on. Married couple had it until the bride fucked some seiner while the husband was off playing grab-ass, chaining himself to the Forest Service building. Keep in mind here, this is my third day in town. Follow?"

"Got it."

"So that same night I go down to the harbor to have a look at the tug sitting at the end of the docks like a queen on her throne. Those brass portholes, horseshoe stern, even that sea mist color they painted her. Loved it, just like you do. So anyways, the next night I get the number off the chalkboard and go to the library and call. I tell the gal Laney I'm making bank at the processor and maybe I could rent to own or some shit. She says meet me in twenty at the Front, she'll be in a red cape or whatever she calls that fancy blanket of hers."

He tossed his can to the side, then fished around for the last one.

"Nasty March storm that night, wind going forty out of the southeast like a dog blown sideways. I wedged my way through the herd to the head, and there in the urinal was a hundred-dollar bill, right beneath the scent cake, left by some highliner. Idea being, as I later found out, your boat's not catching fish, you need that bill good, don't matter it's been pissed and spit on more than a Nashville whore. And the guy who put it there couldn't care less because his boat is catchin'."

"Did you take it?"

"Like a babe out of the fire! Snatched that bill right up, ran it under the faucet, stuffed it into my jeans. I got the Plume fund to worry about, after all. I don't give a hairy shit. Plus I needed a good luck omen to get me that tug.

"So I get back out to the bar, and there's the pretty lady herself, wrapped up like a Christmas gift, waiting beneath this big ol' scratched bell with a knocker the size of a bull nut. Lady like that needs a drink a-sap, I figured. I took hold of the crab line on that bell and pulled, hard as I could. CLANG CLANG CLANG. And you shoulda seen it, T. Suddenly me, little old Newt, was the hot shit. It was like I grew a foot and got some hair and straightened out my teeth and had my own boat. Big guys — king crabbers, loggers — slapping me on the back, the whole place happier than a stump full of ants. All I was missing was Plume in Laney's place, but I knew the way things were going that would soon change."

She took a sip from her warm beer.

"I started whooping it up, ringing the shit out of that bell. CLANG CLANG CLANG! Didn't matter that Laney was yelling at me, only made me ring harder. Then there's the bartender looking at me colder than a mother-in-law's love. I turn to Laney, to ask like a good Kentucky gentleman what she's having. She yells into my ear that I probably owe the bar a thousand bucks." Newt shook his head. "And it dawns on my thick skull that you ring the bell, you're buying drinks. For the whole damn place. I tell the tender I hardly got half that to my name. I was scared I'd be the death of her, her face got so red. Then out came her baseball bat."

He looked out as a boat eased past the breakwater. "Tara, it was not my proudest moment, but I ran like a black man from a Klan meeting. Past the processor, into that wind, rain like carpet tacks in my eyes. For god knows why I went to the end of those docks, straight to that tug of yours, hid right behind the windlass on the bow. When I peeked out I seen what musta been the whole damn police force at the top of the ramp, all the blue lights goin' at once. This one cop yelling through the bullhorn"—he cupped his hands around his lips—"'NEWTON SCARPE. YOU RUNG THE DAMN BELL. TIME TO PAY UP, SON.' End up standing the next day in front of the judge, who says, and I kid you not, 'Boy, get the hell outta my courtroom, and don't let me ever set eyes on you again.' So now I'm banned at the Front. And it's just as well, because all that money I'd be spending on pull-tabs and beers really needs to be going to the fund."

He laughed and looked at her. "As I said, we all pay for our sins here, one way or the other. No rest for the wicked. Story of this god-damn state."

19

LIFE ON THE ISLAND seemed to grind to a halt as they dropped into the heart of winter, darkness shrouding town. People spoke in hushed tones. The middle of the day was, at best, twilit.

As work played out to a steady rhythm, she thought less of Philly. Winter had cast a spell, encapsulated her. The gloaming on the island matched her mood, allowing her mind to hibernate while her body never stopped moving.

Bizarrely, there were more solstice gatherings in Port Anna than Christmas parties. Fritz and Fran invited her to their beach for a bonfire. Newt would be there, and Laney, along with others from Thanksgiving, Fritz said.

Instead she walked down the hill, across town to the docks. The portholes on the tugboat glowed with light. On the back deck was a stump of wood with an ax sticking out. A shadow moved across the wall. She thought of Laney inside, painting on black eyeliner before going out for the big evening. Tara had planned on knocking, perhaps having a glass of wine with the woman, but, as she stood there, decided against it.

It began to rain as she went back toward town. A cold, freezing rain that made the backs of her hands ache. Rising up on her toes, she threw a couple jabs, followed by a right.

It pained her to think of her father struggling up the basement stairs with the dank-smelling boxes of Christmas decorations, his thick fingers sorting through the paper-thin glass ornaments on December twenty-third, the first anniversary of his wife's death.

That night she had been preparing for her final Golden Gloves fight. After training with Gypo she walked over to Connor's and fell asleep on the couch in his woodshop. They had just started spending time together again, and she had been stopping by his house after her workouts.

She woke to the noise of sirens, and Connor standing by the door. "Something's going on," he said, looking down the block.

There would be hell to pay — over an hour late for the lighting of the Marconi maple tree. Even her father, she was sure, would break his usual silence and comment on her lateness.

She grabbed her gym bag and coat and pushed past Connor, running up Manton toward home. People moved to the side, making a path on Eighth Street, where red lights swabbed the brick facades. At the far end, on the corner of Eighth and Federal, a dark-haired woman was sprawled on the asphalt. She wore the same purple flowered dress her mother had put on that morning. Her father stood above the kneeling EMTs in his mustard cardigan, the cuffs bloody. An Oldsmobile idled just beyond the stop sign.

Urbano watched her as she approached, his green eyes wide and empty. Each word uttered so slowly, as if he was speaking in some foreign language. "She was out looking for you."

Over the past year these words had played on an endless loop, always in his deep, resonant voice. If it weren't for you, my wife would still be alive. That was what he meant. Although now, as she circled the library, listening to the rhythmic sound of the ocean brushing the boulders, she heard just sadness.

At the payphones she sifted through the change in her palm. The conversation would be short — she wouldn't need more than a few quarters. Her stomach lurched when he picked up.

"*Figlia?*" he said in a low voice.

"P-Pop," she stumbled. "How'd you know it was me?"

He spoke with gathering force. "Who else calls at this hour?"

She waited. Growling, he said, "I spoke with your cousin Acuzio." The start of his temper, that wintry slow-brew of rage. "Your mother and I, we gave you a good life. And this is how you treat us? It's disrespectful. Disgraceful. Alaska." He made a spitting sound. "You are like an old woman with a lamp, looking for trouble. You have no idea what —"

Gently, she dropped the phone back in its cradle.

Down on the beach Fritz and Fran had already started burning stacked wooden palettes. In a daze she walked in the direction of the flames. More people had arrived, and were singing songs celebrating the sun's return, each one matched to the tune of a traditional Christmas carol.

> Deck the halls with streams of sunlight . . . It's solstice time, so
>   long to the night . . .

Huddled over lyrics, hoods making shadows over the paper, the islanders resembled monks, save for the shouts and dancing. Fritz stomped around the fire, rain pasting his thinning hair to his skull.

"Tara!" he shouted when he saw her. He held up a potent-smelling purple liquid. "*Glogg!* Island tradition. Have some."

Sparks from the flames swirled into the darkness. She finished her cup and Fritz ladled out another. Snowflakes caught in the wool of his sweater, in his beard, which had thickened over the winter. A conga line formed, hands waving in the air. She felt palms on her waist, closed her eyes.

"Hey, girl — I saw you out on the docks tonight." She turned. It was Laney. "When are you gonna you grow a pair and knock on my door?"

Before she could respond, the woman was off, dancing by the fire with Newt, who skipped in his Xtratuf boots, his yellow teeth shiny in the firelight. When he saw Tara he grabbed her by the wrist and twirled her, letting out a rebel yell that hurt her ears.

Later, after a few more cups of wine, masts and troll poles zig-zagged in her vision as she stumbled up the beach to the sidewalk. She lost her balance and crashed into the bushes, struggled to her knees, her breath coming out in puffs. The snow had turned back to rain. Drops knocked against her coat. She let herself fall again, wheezing softly. When she opened her eyes she thought she saw her mother there beside her, just inches away, a heart-shaped face framed by dark curls, as if reflected in the thin glass of an ornament.

"Mama," she groaned. "Mama, make it stop."

She squeezed her eyes shut, then turned and looked again. A shiver went through her. She didn't want her mother to see her like this, caked in snow, drunk, about to vomit. Lost on some island in Alaska. She turned on her back, looked up at the sky, and whispered into the dark, "I just miss you so much."

20

AFTER NEW YEAR'S she began to grow more efficient at moving from task to task — washing incubation trays, scrubbing concrete floors with bleach, picking sticks and leaves from the fish ladder. Newt had switched over to working at the processor, where the money was better and he had a shot at getting a job on the tender. Occasionally she considered responding to Connor's letter, but at the end of each day she just wanted sleep.

"Don't get too comfy in your routine," Fritz warned. "Things around here are gonna change pretty quick soon as they let out the wolves."

The wolves, Newt explained, as they met up on a Friday for beers on the breakwater, were the low-riding seine boats that began, toward the end of February, steaming into town from points north and south.

At the beginning of March she took one of her walks out to the harbor to see the tug. Newt was right — the place had been transformed. Seiners were tied up on the transient float, rafted together three and four deep. When she reached the *Chief* she saw grass growing from the seams of the hull. Mussels and seaweed coated the planks beneath the waterline. Tara chewed the insides of her cheeks.

Laney's head appeared around the side of an Adirondack chair, red wool shawl wrapped around her shoulders, glass of white wine lifted. "You better scurry on up here before you get snatched by one of those hungry herring boys."

Tara gripped the knots on the rope railing and pulled herself up the gangplank.

"Help yourself to the grigio in the galley there," Laney said. "There's a glass above the sink."

Slowly, as if drifting back into some favorite dream, she stepped into the house. She stood for a moment in the warmth, letting her eyes adjust, breathing in the diesel and cedar scent. Wood crackled in the cast-iron and porcelain cookstove. On top, a teapot billowed steam. Copper pans hung from the beams, their lids nearby, arranged in descending order of size. Firewood stacked on the other side of the bookshelf along the wall — all of it just as she had imagined.

She found a glass in a varnished oak cabinet, then joined Laney, who wore her same dark eyeliner, wavy hair piled with a chopstick. They clinked glasses and looked out past the breakwater toward the volcano. A sea lion exhaled, surfacing to watch them. The wine was fruity and strong, and immediately made her lightheaded. Waves washed against the wood hull. Tara resisted the urge to pick at weeds beneath her chair.

"So what's the verdict?" Laney asked.

"On what?"

"The boat, silly."

Tara paused, thinking of the rusted anchor chain, thick as a fist. Or how the wheelhouse curved, the steel visor protecting the oak sash windows.

"I didn't really get a chance to look around. But that cookstove in the kitchen's pretty cool."

"Don't let someone hear you say 'kitchen' on the docks. Galley is what we call it. You ever get Newt to tell you the story?"

"He told me."

"Dude hid right up there, behind the windlass," she said, pointing to the bow. "Just about a year ago to the day."

Laney rose and grew serious, pacing on deck. She wore heels. What a strange woman.

"So the Rock being what it is, I'm sure you've heard Doug and I are filing for divorce. I should tell you that when we hauled the boat out, we sank a hundred thousand into planking beneath the waterline. There's a couple out of San Francisco, cello musicians with the philharmonic, who're talking about towing her to the Bay Area, starting a music school or some yuppie crap. I'm flying back there tomorrow."

Tara bit her tongue. Laney seemed about as yuppie as they came, though lined with a go-to-hell Alaska attitude.

"Here's the thing. She hasn't moved since we hauled her out, and that was six years ago. If she doesn't go a hundred yards under her own power, that harbormaster tows her out to state tidelands and hires an excavator to tear her apart." The ends of her shawl fluttered in the wind. "Still interested?"

Tara spoke slowly. "My mother grew up in a fishing village in Italy, and she loved boats. So yeah. It just makes sense to me. But I don't have thirty thousand dollars."

Laney dismissed this with a wave of the hand. "If it's in your blood you'll find a way. Listen, I need to get packing. But quickly, I'll show you the living quarters."

They took their wine inside. Laney pointed out the Monarch cookstove, which worked great with lint from the dryer as fire starter. Then the head, with its toilet sized for a kindergartner. Three quarter berths, small rooms with double bunk beds, were situated around the salon. "All heated by wood," Laney said proudly, nodding toward the ax outside. "Chopped by yours truly."

As Laney climbed a wooden ladder Tara imagined the woman in her heels, splitting wood. She had always considered her mother tough, but had trouble thinking of her living through a divorce, swinging an ax, retaining her elegance at the end of the docks like Laney.

At the top of the ladder the room opened around a bed. Books, mugs with dried tea bags at the bottom, envelopes torn open, were scattered on a slab of plywood to one side. Tara recognized the pine ceiling from looking through the rusted portholes. A hammock swung gently on the other side of the exhaust stack, which was connected to a smaller wood stove.

"And here — the *pièce de résistance.*" Laney opened the door onto the wheelhouse, a half-circle of sash windows high over the water. The boat's shiny wooden wheel was almost as tall as she was. Worn leather straps allowed the far windows on either side to slide up and down.

"The catbird seat up here," Laney said. "Whaddya think?"

It was magnificent, sitting on the water so far above the other boats. "I love it," Tara said.

Laney smiled. "Yeah. I knew you would."

21

"IDES OF MARCH," Fritz murmured, spitting chew juice into a mug, filling in the crossword folded out on his stomach. "Ain't that funny. Wonder if they did that on purpose."

Channel 16 on the VHF chattered in the background. Fritz was waiting for the Alaska Department of Fish and Game to put the seine fleet on two-hour notice. Tara made entries into the logbook, measuring the average size of the fry, the water temperature of the tanks. Fritz had forbidden anyone else to make reports, with her cursive so neat and precise.

"So I was out picking my pots the other day," he said, "and who should come on over in his skiff to pay a visit but your pal Betteryear."

"Who?"

"Tall old Native dude."

She hadn't seen the man since that time in the coffee shop. Months ago. She had been avoiding the library, steering clear of the payphones.

"Oh yeah?"

Fritz leaned back in his chair and spit a stream of tobacco. "Yeah."

She finished transferring information from her notebook to the log and stretched her arms above her head, making a squeaking sound that caused Fritz to grin. She set neoprene waders out on the workbench to patch them. Fritz adjusted the waist of his oilskin pants.

"You ever hear the story about that old guy?"

She focused on her work, squeezing silicone onto the tip of a Popsicle stick, thinking about her money saved — just over twelve hundred dollars. "I haven't."

"July, maybe ten years ago. Guess he was steelhead fishing up north. It got hot in the sun, so he stripped down to his long underwear, no shirt, when all of a sudden a bear comes charging out of the brush. He had his thirty-aught on the gravel bar beside him, Winchester seventy, holds five zingers. Took him four to knock down that bruin, which skidded to a stop ten feet from where he stood." Fritz spat. "And then, not two seconds later, from farther upstream comes a smaller one sprinting like all bananas through the shallows. Old man had one shot left, so he took his time, hit the bear dead in the brainpan. Ended up under the thing as it bled out. Finished putting on his pants, stropped his knife, and spent the next two days skinning and boning."

"No shit."

He nodded slowly, tapping the end of his pen against the newspaper. "You know all that stuff Fran said at Thanksgiving, about the Tlingits getting a raw deal — don't get Betteryear started. Man's got a temper."

She thought about him in the coffee shop. "He seems pretty chilled out."

"Trust me, he's not."

After a couple more minutes of listening to the VHF, Fritz heaved himself to standing, adjusted his suspender straps, and took his coat from the hook. "Gonna go change out bait on the traps."

"Roger."

Alone, she sat on the stool, listening to the thrum of water from the tote room and the back-and-forth on the radio. The smell of silicone was making her woozy.

Her thoughts returned to standing with Laney in the wheelhouse of the tug. It made no sense, the idea of working so hard for a boat.

She could find something less expensive, a double-wide trailer by the water. Then again, falling asleep in that hammock, having that piece of history, making it her home . . .

Sighing, she went into the yard to begin feeding the fish.

The next morning when she arrived at work, Fritz shooed her. "Take the flatbed—just drive out Papermill Road toward the church until you see parked cars. Here, use these." He handed her a pair of binoculars.

"Where am I going?"

"To the opener. Go! Just get out there before you miss the wolves."

She drove past Maksoutoff Bay, up the hill, past the Lincoln Log church and Salmonberry Cove, and back down to the water. And there they were, the seiners, forty or so tacking back and forth in the ocean. With the binoculars she made out names: *Storm Chaser, Perseverance, Leading Lady, Defiant.* Pointed snouts, gunwales just above the waterline, sodium halide mast lights as bright as near planets. Skippers in wraparound sunglasses leaned out of wheelhouse windows, smoking cigars, steel coffee mugs in hand. Crews dressed in bright orange and green raingear stood poised on decks. A horde of floatplanes buzzed overhead, on the lookout for balls of herring, Fritz had told her, the pilots reporting back on scrambled channels to the seiners.

People had set up picnics on patches of grass and on the roofs of houses across the road, sharing jars of smoked salmon and pickled herring. A VHF radio from a car broadcasted the district commissioner counting down from ten.

"Nine, eight, seven . . ."

"Let the dogs out!" someone yelled.

"Five, four, three, two . . . Open season!"

A roar echoed off the mountainsides as clouds of black smoke rose over the water. Rooster tails spewed from jet-powered skiffs dragging folds of black net from the boat decks, making a wall of mesh. Herring flashed like coins as the mesh drew tight, fish pocking the surface. She watched a deckhand punch the web, working to free a caught log, cursing loud enough for her to hear. Just off the rocks two boats barreled toward each other, neither conceding position, the larger one veering off at the last second. There was the screech of steel ripping, followed by a flurry of expletives over the handheld radio. The larger boat began to sink. Two other seiners gathered up their nets, positioned themselves on either side, squeezing the sinking boat between them, keeping it afloat. Like coaches at a football game, an arm on either shoulder, they nursed the injured vessel off the field, back toward the harbor.

Thirty minutes later the fishery closed. She took the rest of the afternoon to hike up Crow Hill.

The forest had turned chartreuse with spring, shoots of new growth spearing the soil. A few bears had been reported around town, groggy after hibernation, digging through garbage, one snatching a Labrador from its chain. Not wanting to take chances, she sang Prince's "Kiss," trilling the falsetto. A bottle of bear spray jostled at her hip, its plastic safety removed.

A couple thousand feet above the sea she reached the lookout and watched as the fleet made its slow return to town. Newt was down there somewhere, working in that steam-shrouded processor. He'd probably go through the night.

As she walked back down, she couldn't escape the feeling that she was just beginning to scratch the surface of life on the Rock. *Give it to me. I'm ready.*

22

IN MAY, two months after the herring opening, Fritz called Newt back from the processor. Pink salmon had started to appear in the slough at the hatchery.

"Here we go again," Newt said, snapping on his bibs and duct-taping a hole on his Xtratufs. "Giddyup."

A few times she tried to drum up the courage to call her father back. To apologize, perhaps, for hanging up on him. Or to say that she was fine, and they'd speak sometime in the future. But she didn't want to. If anyone needed to apologize, it was him. In the meantime, she had work to do.

Her job was to corral the dark schools of fish up against the aluminum weir and scoop as many as she could. The spawning males, some a couple feet long, had overdeveloped snouts and jaws. Their teeth snagged on the waders she had patched so carefully, ripping new holes, letting cold water seep into her long underwear. Her legs were soaked.

"This fucking sucks," Tara yelled up to Newt. "I'm wet as shit."

"C'mon up here then. We'll switch."

Outside the killing shack, Newt showed her how to seize the male fish by the meat of their tails and fling them into the chute, while females were dropped on a stainless-steel tray. "You're not tapping them awake, you're knockin 'em dead," he said, gripping a female just behind the head and setting the skull on the cinderblock. "Downright mean to be hesitant." He raised an alder stick wrapped in heavy-gauge copper. *BANG*. The tray shook, the salmon quivered, the yellow eye dimmed as the body went slack. "There you have it. Dead as an iced catfish."

It was miserable work. She preferred being inside the killing shack, using a finger-razor to slice open the females' stomachs, dumping their skeins of orange eggs into a five-gallon bucket, sealing the bucket by pounding on the lid with a rubber mallet.

Throughout the day they switched off. Fritz had hired a couple students from the college who reminded Tara of how she had been her first weeks — trudging around, unsnapping their bibs at the end of the day while Newt and Tara loaded buckets onto the flatbed. Lazy.

Things grew more exciting whenever Fritz came down to the slough, a doughnut or coffee in his hand, and yelled, "It's baby-making time!" Newt showed Tara how to select seven virile males with prominent humps and long jaws. One by one she rubbed the spot just above the anus, releasing a stream of milky white liquid over the eggs of twenty-seven females. Newt patted her on the back.

"Keep it up, you'll be chief salmon jacker in no time. Just a little lower, give it a good pinch." She pushed him out of the way. But he was right: she did have the touch. She shook the bucket until the eggs were covered in a film of milt, then tossed the writhing male salmon into the chute. "Spawn and die," Newt chanted, two fingers held above his head like a rock star. "Spawn and motherfuckin' die!"

As summer wore on she refined her moves, knocking fish a centimeter behind the eye, flinging spent males over her shoulder, one after the other, into the chute. Fritz watched from the doorway of the shack. "If I don't look out, some fisherman's gonna steal you away and make a worker out of you."

He gave them Sundays off. At the Muskeg, mandolins, banjos, guitars, and fiddles emerged from beat-up cases pasted with stickers. A bright-eyed older woman pulled out an accordion, and soon they were all playing, the fiddle so mournful, it made the roots of her hair hurt. She realized she was counting again, trying to recall when Connor had sent her that short letter. Just before Christmas. A card would be good, she decided. Brief and informal. In the bookstore she selected one with an old cabin rotting into the woods.

June 17, 1998

Hey, Connor,

I just wanted to drop a note to let you know I'm still alive up here. Putting away money with that tug I told you about in mind. It has a messed-up engine or something. The woman who owns it is an odd duck. Maybe I'll just end up with a little fishing boat.

She considered what she had written, unsure why she was going on like this.

Are you back in Philly for the summer, maybe up on the scaffold again? I'm working at the hatchery, killing fish. The work's not so bad once you get into a groove.

I hope you're enjoying your separate path.

She hesitated over the signing, then scribbled, *Yours, Tara.* She put the card in the postbox and walked back to her apartment in the rain.

23

SHE GOT HIS LETTER on the Friday before July Fourth. She set it in front of her at the Muskeg, after getting a slice of pie and a coffee, but she couldn't bring herself to open it. Then she placed it on her bedside table, waking in the middle of the night to rest it in her palm, trying to glean its contents. The envelope felt warm to the touch.

Saturday, Coast Guard helicopters thundered over Main Street. Newt snagged Mary Janes tossed from the backs of fire trucks, and made faces at the Civil Air Patrol kids waving from the boat trailer.

"I'll be right back," she told him. "Don't move."

She weaved through the crowd, then walked up the concrete steps to Castle Hill, the spot where Alaska had been transferred from Russia to the United States. She sat on a stone wall overlooking the water. A rope tinged against a flagpole. Her hands trembled as she slit open the envelope. If anyone had the right to be angry, she thought, it was her. He shouldn't be able to put her on edge like this.

She looked over the roofs of town, then down at the letter. From across the water she heard the steady beat of rotors as the helicopters returned to the base.

27 June 1998

Dear T,

Thanks for the card. Pretty and sad this moss-covered cabin being swallowed back into the woods.

*It's good to know you're alive out there. I was beginning to
doubt it. The boat sounds lovely. Failing means you're playing right? Good for you keeping on. There's an old schooner on
the Delaware. They're looking for volunteers to work on her. I
was thinking about doing it this summer if I can find the time.
Sounds like you have a similar project ahead of you if you get
that tug. Yeah I'm putting some hours with the crew bricking.
Helping my mom out where I can.*

*On another note I've also been taking improv classes. Trying
to loosen up. The idea is to put yourself in someone else's world.
And to never say no. I'm bad Tara. I mean really bad. Like my
brain just doesn't react so quickly.*

*It's good (I think) that we're living our own lives now.
Although I will say in all honesty when I try and spin my life
forward I bang my head against you. You are experiencing
something powerful on that Rock of yours that has nothing to
do with me. And I have my own world. My father (surprisingly) is all of a sudden trying to broaden his role in my life.
Impromptu visits to New York. My mother can't stand to be in
the same room with him — you know all this.*

*But you you're falling in love with a place — and perhaps a
boat — instead of a person. Either way Alaska seems to soften
you. I think this is a good thing.*

That's all for now.

C

She folded the letter, then went down the hill to find Newt.
He wanted to go out to the docks to watch the fireworks. As they
walked, Connor's words turned over in her head. He had responded
so quickly. It took her off-guard.

His father was a weird dude who dressed in French cuffs and
pressed shirts and kept a neatly trimmed beard. He worked with

banks in France, or something like that. When she thought about it, she realized Connor never really talked about the man. Then again, she hadn't been great at asking questions.

They reached the end of the docks. When she strode up the gangplank of the tugboat, looming in front of them, Newt stayed behind, uncharacteristically bashful. "Does Laney know you're here? She's not my biggest fan."

She knocked on the padlocked door, then cupped her hand to the glass. Chairs were arranged around the galley table, plates stacked in the dish rack. "She won't mind," Tara said. Her words, spoken into the glass, echoed.

"Hey, check this out."

She turned to see the top of Newt's balding head disappear down the hatch into the engine room.

Below, his penlight flashed over an unplugged chest freezer, chunks of rigid insulation, a workbench cluttered with mason jars filled with rusting screws. "Laney said to stop by, but I don't think she meant for us to sneak on," Tara said.

"Scared money don't win, T."

"Look who's all gung-ho now."

She followed as he ducked beneath a bulkhead. The beam reflected off the engine block. Newt ran his palm over the cast-iron, gasping. "Geezum crow—thing's the size of a goddamn school bus! You could take a bath in these cylinders. Look here," he said, running his fingernail along a crack. "Probably hasn't run since Moses split the seas."

"Six years," Tara said, tracing her hands along a copper pipe leading to a cylinder. "That's what Laney said."

"Hell of a lot of elbow grease into this old girl to get her running."

They climbed into the living space. Her eyes followed the white beam as it worked over the cookstove. A fine coating of dust covered the burner plates, the pots hanging overhead.

"Jesus Lordum Christ, yes!" Newt said as he opened the porcelain-plated oven, tapped the thermometer with a nail. He rapped his knuckles on the insulated exhaust stack. "Molasses, you better start thinking about picking up work at the processor. Get you enough money to buy this bitch."

"Don't call her that," she said softly, walking forward into the salon. Buttery yellow cedar and orange splits of hemlock were stacked beside a built-in settee, up to the brass portholes. Now that they weren't in a rush, she took time to examine the portholes from the inside, running a finger along the green oxidation coating the screw threads, rapping a knuckle on the glass. Tall narrow doors with cracked porcelain enameled numbers led to the berths. She opened one, looking inside to a neat bunk. "It's just so fucking cool."

"Yeah, cool until it's fish habitat."

"Laney fixed it up before the divorce."

"A million ways to sink a boat, girlfriend. If you can't run her a hundred yards, then the harbormaster will put on a demonstration."

They climbed the ladder topside. Laney's bed was made, her things on the plywood table gone. In the wheelhouse she could feel Newt's sly mind at work as he gripped a spoke of the oak wheel. "The rudder on this bitch must be big as a barn door."

"Don't call her that," Tara snapped. "Jesus, have some respect."

"Look at you, all defensive."

She reached up and twisted a knob on the ceiling; they both started as a bladeless windshield wiper scraped glass.

"Variable speed," Newt marveled. "Damn, those old-timers didn't mess around."

They jumped as a boom echoed over the water. White and blue reflected on the back walls. Newt pulled a leather strap and a window dropped into a recess. Acrid air blew in as fireworks lit up the cloud cover.

"You saw those lights and you thought the police were coming for you again, didn't you?" Tara said, slapping him across the shoulder blades, laughing.

He ignored her. "Well, looks like you got your channel marker. Took you almost a year to learn how the island punches. Now it's time to punch back."

24

THE NEXT DAY she went by the harbor office at the top of the docks. Beneath the glass countertop was a collection of photos showing derelict boats seized by the harbor, left to crumble on the beach.

"Can I help you?"

The harbormaster, taller than Tara, adjusted a mouthpiece away from her lips. Over her collarbone she had a washed-out banner of a tattoo that said *No Matter How Far I Go, Always at Home*.

"I just wanted to know what was happening with the tug out on the transient."

The woman shook her head. "What is it with that old tug and you pie-in-the-sky girls? Can't seem to get it into your heads this is a working harbor. For fishing boats. Not houseboats."

"Do you know when Laney's coming back?" Tara asked.

"Who can say, the way that girl jet-sets. All I know is I'm sick of looking at that tug."

The phone rang. The woman leaned in toward Tara. She flipped down the mouthpiece to answer. "I'm tempted to do everyone a favor and just sink that old slab. Good morning. Port Anna harbormaster."

25

IN THE BOOKSTORE Tara bought another card, this one a woodcut of a muskox, a mountain goat, an elk, a bear, a puffin, and two seals crowded around a blanket, tossing a person in a fur-hooded parka into the air.

July 28, 1998

Dear C,

She gnawed the top of the pen cap. She wanted to tell him about the pea-sized salmon eggs, the threads of silver slipping into the black plastic disks. Also of the mink she saw clawing into the broken fridge where Fritz smoked the sockeye he dip-netted from the falls across the channel. The astringent smell of WD-40 each morning as she descended into the basement. The voltage that shot up her arm as she wrapped her fingers around a salmon tail. Holding females steady with one hand the way Newt showed her, bringing down the club of alder, the crunch as the skull collapsed.

She sighed.

Thanks for your letter, for telling me your news. Good for you branching out like that. I can't imagine you doing improv. Gutsy.

Life on the Rock is good. The salmon have arrived at the hatchery so we're hard at it. The summer days are loooong—it's light until almost eleven. It rains ALL THE GODDAMN TIME. At first it bothered me, but now I'm getting used to it, growing some shell to deal with the wet.

There are rhythms on the island that don't exist in Philly. All to do with fish, the winds, where the sun sets in the sky, and the smell in the air. When I first got here (thinking back on it now) I felt like I was holding my breath. Panicking. Just wanting to be back in Philly. By your side, planning an adventure

She stopped writing. Why did her words feel so clunky, so stilted? And why this sudden intimacy?

With her pen she scratched out everything following "Philly."

Just wanting to be back in Philly. Now it seems like I'm beginning to understand the island, its knots (I've gotten good at tying them!), the people. And the tug. I can't stop thinking about that boat.

As for the other stuff, Connor, I'm not sure what to say. Some part of me gets excited when you say you keep hitting up against me when you think down the line.

Please keep telling me your news. And I'll do the same.

She reread the letter, then thought back to the other one he sent, so short, dismissive. She paused, about to sign *Youse*, then just wrote *T*, and mailed it from the post office.

26

AT THE BEGINNING OF AUGUST, the run of pink salmon slowed. In the meantime, Newt pestered her about getting a job at the processor.

"I got the Plume fund, and now it's time for you to start a *Pacific Chief* fund. It doesn't take an Einstein to see you're sticking around. Get Laney on the horn. See what tune she's singing."

"I'll figure it out."

"You're wound up tighter than Dick's hat band is what you are. Listen to your buddy Newt."

So she did. But when she reached Laney, an urban curtness seemed to have replaced the woman's friendliness. "I'll need twenty-five thousand cash and the boat's yours. That's my bottom. I was asking sixty-five. As I said, I like the idea of it going to a young go-getter like yourself. But I can't go lower, so please don't try and bargain. I've got those folks talking about towing her south, and they seem serious."

Tara cursed beneath her breath. It was stupid to even be thinking like this — she had about a tenth of that stored beneath the sink. There must be some license required to drive a boat like that. She couldn't weld, knew nothing about engines . . .

Laney's voice softened. "Listen, Tara. I liked you from the get-go. I think we would have been good friends. If there's a way of making it work, let's do it. Scrounge up the money, give me a call."

From the library she walked to the harbor, climbed up onto the deck of the tug, and looked around. She picked a tuft of grass growing between the planks, pinched it between her fingers. That strange gravity she had felt before, pulling her toward the island — this boat was its source. She could see her mother here, stepping into that galley, setting a basil plant in a porthole. And she could see herself in that Adirondack chair, staring across the water toward the volcano.

She flipped up her hood against the rain and walked from the harbor to the post office.

In her box she found a manila envelope doubled over and taped. Inside were flannel pajamas wrapped in plastic, along with a letter written on yellow legal paper.

August 6, 1998

Dear Tara,

I hope these PJs keep you warm for your second Alaskan winter (which should be starting right about now by my calculation). I was going to wrap them and tell you to hold off for Christmas. But I know you better than that.

You asked in your last letter about me. Picture a long-boned freckled guy in a black jumpsuit with a headset on and a clipboard, running around backstage at a small theater off Broad Street. Costume racks, dressing rooms, even a woodshop for set design. I'm the stage manager. My job is to keep the rabble in order.

We just ran through the dry tech. Show looks pretty tight. I agreed to be an understudy for a minor role (you'd be proud — unlike that stupid Guys *and* Dolls *play in high school, I said yes) but generally I just make sure everyone gets to where they're supposed to be. I quit improv. It was a lost cause although I'm doing my best to take its larger lessons to heart.*

For sophomore year I'll have my own place on the Lower

East Side with a couple other acting buddies. I'll continue studying postcolonialism. My father offered me a room in Lyon winter semester. It's tempting. But I want to stay close to the theater.

Thank you for being in touch. I hope the PJs keep you warm.

Connor

She folded the pages, then stepped out onto the sidewalk, the door sucking shut behind her. A snow-slurry was caught in the needles of the potted spruce tree; drips from it splotched the envelope. The pajamas were printed with a pattern of blue anchors.

At the Bunkhouse, warehouse lodging by the processor, where Newt lived, she knocked on his door. "Yo yo."

"Can you set me up an interview at the processor? I'm ready to make some money."

He gave a lopsided grin, took a flask from beneath his cot, and toasted her. "Looks like baby's ready to play baseball. It's about time."

27

A TALL, BEARDED MAN with a lazy eye introduced himself as Trunk. He took her into an office attached to the processor's main floor and held a clipboard up to his face.

"Marconi. What's that, Polish?"

She tried to smile, then realized he was serious and stopped. "Italian."

"You know the difference between words and numbers, Marconi?"

"Yes."

"Can you multiply and divide by ten?"

"Yeah."

He brought the clipboard closer to his face. "Can you work for extended hours in the extreme cold?"

A memory of being a kid, shut in the bakery freezer, flashed through her. "Yes."

"You'll be required to distinguish shades of color to identify abnormalities or defects in the fish." He looked up at her. "Your eyes both good?"

Better than yours, she thought. So many of the men on the Rock seemed to have been spit out the end of a meat grinder.

"They work fine."

He read haltingly. "Employees are regularly exposed to toxic or caustic chemicals, and risk electrical shock and vibration. The noise can be unusually loud. You'll be required to stand for long periods at a time, walk, use your hands to finger, handle, feel, and reach into fish." Again he looked up. "All that good?"

"Okay."

He set the clipboard aside. "Pay starts at seven sixty-five an hour. That's two bucks over minimum wage. Anything over eight hours a day is time and a half. Same for anything over forty hours a week. Good?"

"Fine."

"You know what a king salmon looks like?"

She paused, thinking. "Not really."

"How's it different from a coho?"

She thought. "Bigger?"

He shook his head. "You'll learn. King salmon opener starts August fifteenth. That work?"

"That's a Saturday?"

He paused from standing and cocked his head at her. "Oh, excuse me, your honor. Does someone not work on Saturdays?"

Her heart thumped. "I'll be here."

She left the processor and went back to her apartment to check beneath the sink where she had been storing her money. Two thousand six hundred and seven dollars. She half jogged to the bank, where she opened an account, feeling like she did before a Golden Gloves match.

Let it be cloudy. She could keep up with the work. Blue skies were for suckers anyway.

August tenth, the following Monday morning, when Fritz came down the stairs, she asked if she could have a word. He sat behind the desk, adjusted his suspenders to give his belly room, then snapped his fingers against a puck of dip.

She took a breath, then started in. "I know it's not the end of September, but —"

"You know that day your cousin told me you were interested in coming up here?" he interrupted. "I says to my wife, I say, 'Fran, if this girl even makes it off that ferry, she won't last longer than a week on the island.' You believe that?"

He pried open the container. The room filled with the rich, sweet scent of tobacco as he fashioned a plug with his fingers.

"I believe that," she said slowly.

"And look at us now. Almost a year later, you tying bowlines with your eyes closed. Whacking fish dead, tossing 'em one after the other into my crab pots." He stood and topped off his coffee mug. "How 'bout you gimme one more day in that warehouse, making it nice and neat. That work?"

She nodded. "That works."

"I'm rooting for you, Tara. Like I said before, buying an old wood boat's about the dumbest thing you can do. But I've seen kids like you before. Once you got the itch, there's no turning back."

On impulse she hugged him. He patted her gently on the back.

"Thanks for your hard work. Don't be a stranger at Thanksgiving."

28

TRUNK TWISTED TO LOOK AT THE CLOCK. "You're early," he muttered. "A good twenty goddamn minutes early."

He assigned her to a locker, then set a rubber apron, hairnet, and a pair of orange gloves in her hands. "You here to make money or just the bare minimum? I don't care either way, I'd just like to know, 'cause I got a couple different tracks for folks. Your buddy Newt, for example, he wants to—"

"I'm saving to buy a boat."

"Oh yeah? Which boat's that?"

"An old tug down in the harbor."

His eyes grew wide. "The *Pacific Chief*?"

"Yeah."

"You shoulda said you were crazy before I hired you."

He introduced her to Bailey, a guy from Boston with the wedge-shaped head of a pit bull who wore a ragged Red Sox hat and had *Southie* with a four-leaf clover tattooed between his thumb and index finger.

"Show her the ropes," Trunk said, retreating to his office.

"C'mon," Bailey said. As she followed she recalled the tattoos on his wrist—he was the one who had almost run her over with the forklift back when she first arrived.

"Where's Newt?" she asked.

"Re-Re? Not sure. So this is the frozen side, this big wheel here you use to sort fish and make boxes. That machine over there is the glazer — it coats fish in a film of sugar water." It looked to her like a huge pasta maker. He took note of her expression. "Just don't touch it, about all you need to know."

They walked to the other side of the building, silver scales on the concrete floor reflecting back the overhead fluorescents. A line of workers, most of them Asian, in aprons and hairnets, slid schools of fish along the stainless-steel trays, knives and spoons flashing as they pulled out guts. "This is the fresh side, where the fish come once they're offloaded."

"You know if Newt's working today?" she asked.

He turned to her. "I already said I don't fuckin' know."

"You just said you didn't know where he was."

"Jesus Christ — you a lawyer or something?"

They crossed back onto the frozen side, where he pushed through plastic flaps. The temperature dropped. Shelves were stacked with rectangular boxes, frozen white fish piled in wire cages. Bailey's breath came in puffs.

"Get orders there in the wall-box, set up a pallet, fill it up with whatever — black cod, king, coho, halibut. Bang it out quick." She crossed her arms, already shivering. He focused on her chest. "Trunk likes to put you in here early. See how you do with the cold. We call it the brig."

Newt better have a good excuse, she thought as she followed Bailey back out. Convincing her to take this job, then disappearing, leaving her to deal with this prick, who led her now into the flash freezer. A network of copper pipes along the low ceiling. Whole salmon were laid out on trays. He picked one up. "Check for gouges and nicks, any damage. Fish gotta be mint before they go in the box. You see something, slip one of these red rubber bands on the tail and they get number-twoed. Clear?"

He looked off to the side. He could stare at her chest no problem, but not into her eyes.

"Crystal."

"So you're Re-Re's buddy?"

"Who?"

"Re-Re. Little man. The one you keep annoying me about."

"Yeah."

"Heard he got a job on the water, on the *Adriatic*."

It was a good excuse. A very good excuse.

"Where you sleeping?" Bailey asked.

"I just moved into the Bunkhouse. I thought you said you didn't know where he was?"

He shook his head. "Fuckin' incredible. Bang it out," he repeated, and walked away.

That night she lay awake beneath the scratchy wool covers, hearing the snores of men through the walls, breathing in the chlorine smell of the floors. Her mother's photo of Aci Trezza was set up on the windowsill. The payphone down the hall rang. And rang. And rang.

There was no way it was him, and she grew annoyed at herself for even thinking it might be. Their lives weren't converging (and who ever said she wanted them to?). It wasn't like there was a market for postcolonialism, or whatever he was studying, on the Rock. Or for bricklaying, for that matter. She couldn't see him living on a tugboat. His dry letters were proof. He was becoming a New Yorker. Their time apart revealed how fundamentally different they were from each other. Better to know now.

The phone stopped ringing. She turned on her side, shut her eyes, and tried to sleep.

29

JUST AS BAILEY PREDICTED, Trunk stuck her in cold storage, sorting through boxes and stacking pallets for shipments to be loaded into refrigerated tractor-trailers. Her clothes weren't warm enough. After work she went to the Pink Cheetah, the local secondhand shop, and picked up a red wool halibut coat and a torn watchman's cap.

Her second day at the processor, August sixteenth, boats began to drop off fish. Trunk switched her to the docks. They lifted bags from the holds of trollers, dumped salmon onto the steel sorting table, where workers checked the bellies to make sure the fish were properly cleaned, and separated king from the coho, chum, and occasional sockeye.

"Kings got black lips, dots on the tail. And smell 'em. They smell strong, not like the others," Bailey muttered at her.

After just half an hour she had let three cohos, a sockeye, and two chums past. Bailey came out. "You're useless. Back into the brig you go."

Blood tingled in her cheeks as she pulled box after box from the shelf and stacked them on a pallet. After an hour the tips of her curls, poking out from her cap, were frozen. When she bent to check a label and match it to an order form, a stab of pain shot down her neck and bloomed over her back. To get the blood flowing she hopped on the balls of her feet, imagining rope slapping the concrete beneath them. She windmilled her arms, then shadowboxed, pretending she was Rocky going up against the cow carcass.

The compressors hummed. Powder-white halibut, piled in metal cages in the corner of the freezer, looked impassively back at her.

She was eight or nine — young enough to be screaming and wreaking havoc in the kitchen, dodging around the mixing bowls — when her father had locked her in the freezer.

It started with her mother trying to roll dough as Tara careened around the bakery floor. Serena finally slammed a rolling pin against the edge of the table. "*Cazzo!*" she yelled. Urbano flew down the back stairs, seized Tara by the wrist, and dragged her into the walk-in freezer, crowded with silver bowls of dough covered in plastic wrap. Whimpering in the darkness, among the bricks of butter, not sure what she had done, she just stood there, and grew sure her mother didn't know where she was, and her father had forgotten about her. It was terrifying. After what seemed like hours, the door opened, light and warmth as she clutched Serena's thighs.

And then, years later, in eleventh grade — which she thought of as the year when she first understood that leaning over the tub of water ice at John's was a way to get guys to pay attention to her — she found herself crying into Little Vic's chest as they stood in the back freezer, cylinders of water ice stacked around them. She told him about that night in Avalon, about the club, cocaine, the guy with his braided necklace.

"Holy shit," Little Vic said. "Your pops would kill the kid."

"Which is why you don't tell anyone. You hear me?"

"Your mom told you not to say?"

Tara thought back to it. "Yeah. She did."

"All right," Little Vic said. "I won't."

30

AFTER HER THIRD DAY OF WORK at the processor, the lower left side of her back hurt so bad, she couldn't fall asleep. The droopy springs at the Bunkhouse didn't help. She woke in the middle of the night with a pain extending along her hamstring to her heel. She wasn't meant for this work. Maybe Acuzio had been right all those years ago, and her mother wrong. This was a man's world.

Salmon came in heavy. She struggled in the freezer to keep up, shadowboxing every fifteen minutes. At lunch Trunk told her to take an hour instead of the usual thirty minutes. "You look like shit," he remarked.

She walked from the processor to the Muskeg. In her booth she gripped the mug in both hands, glorying in the heat moving up her wrists. When the seat shifted she jumped.

"Geezum. Didn't mean to scare you." It was Fran, Fritz's wife. She wrapped a tea string around a spooned bag, squeezed drops over a mug, set it on the table. "You look like a ghost," the woman said.

"I'm fine."

Fran's paper-blue eyes focused on Tara. "I was thinking—Fritz said you moved to the Funkhouse?"

When Tara smiled it felt like her skin was cracking. "I think they soak the halls in chlorine each afternoon. It makes me nauseous."

Fran's neck folded as she considered this, tapping a finger on her lip.

"There's this couple near our place on the water, musicians. They've got a cabin kind of like ours, built over the rocks, which they're selling. This summer they adopted a dog—I call him Buddha, because he's totally Zen, like he just skipped being human in the wheel of things and went straight to enlightenment." Fran smiled. "If you wanted to stay there and look after him, it might work out for everyone, long as they don't sell the place. He's a sweet older guy, shepherd-malamute mix. It's a cute little—"

Tara grabbed her arm and pulled the woman toward her. "Keta. I met him. Yes. Please. When?"

Fran set down her mug, smiling sadly across the table. "They've put you through the ringer. Come over this eve."

"They might not let me off until late."

"Don't worry about showering after work. I'm used to it."

Just after ten Tara limped into the mudroom of the cabin with Fran, dropped her duffel on the clay tiles, and removed her boots. The house was compact and neatly arranged. The wine-red cabinets in the kitchen had rounded edges; the floorboards were tight-grained and honey-stained. (These were things she knew Connor would notice. He'd like it here.)

"Nice, right?" Fran said, holding a wool wrap around her shoulders with one hand as she flipped lights. "The owners, they're into old wooden boats, and this is about as close as you can get without actually living on one. Built by a shipwright, so everything's snug."

"Is that the couple talking to Laney about the *Chief*?" Tara asked.

Fran looked back at her. "They'd have to be even crazier than I thought they were to go through with that," she said.

As she slipped off her boots, Tara examined a photo of the couple—smooth-skinned, playing cellos in the rainforest. Beautiful people: her blond and tanned, a mane of hair spilling from his felt hat.

"Fritz said they're selling this place?" Tara asked.

"That's right. They travel around the state each summer teaching and giving cello performances. Nice people. Just not entirely, well, realistic."

She heard a sound from the other room and turned to see the white-muzzled dog tap-tapping toward her.

"You remember me?" Tara said. "From all that time back? You kept my legs warm in the truck."

The dog's ears, rimmed in black, pointed forward. He seemed to be appraising her with his brown eyes. He leaned his weight against her shins, craning his head up as Tara tugged her fingers through his fur.

"Some wino fisherman abandoned him on the docks," Fran said. "This couple took him on, then one of them got a gig playing Carnegie Hall or something. Poor kid."

His shoulders softened as she pet him. "Looks like you'll get along just fine," Fran said. "Here. I'll show you about his pills."

Around midnight, after a walk along the beach, Tara set food in front of Keta. The dog peered back at her. "Go get it!" Tara said. He didn't move. "Eat!" Nothing. "Fuck it. Don't eat," she said, going toward the bathroom. "See if I care."

When she returned from brushing her teeth Keta was still sitting there, watching her over his shoulder. Drool from his cheeks pooled on the tile. She was tired, and had no patience for this. Breathing in deeply, she gave the dog a final, enthusiastic "Okay!"

He loped over to the bowl and began crunching kibble between his teeth.

"Weirdo."

He shot her a quick, seemingly hurt glance and returned to his food.

After dinner he joined her in the living room, where she filled the wood stove with crumpled newspaper, a package of fire-starter bricks, and a few branches of yellow cedar from the kindling box. When she dropped in a match. smoke kicked back into the room. The dog wheezed, shook his head, sneezed.

"What? You want to try? I never said I knew what the hell I was doing."

She opened the door, adjusted the knobs until the fire evened out and began to feed into the chimney. The spiced, peppery scent of yellow cedar filled the room. When she shut the door, the flames shot up. So much better than the Bunkhouse, she thought, taking a pillow from the couch and stretching out by the stove, wanting to accumulate as much warmth in her sore body as she could before returning to the brig the following day. The muscles in her leg relaxed, and the heat loosened the knots in her lower back.

Keta crawled across the rug toward her, poking with his pink nose, nestling his snout beneath her jawbone. "Oh, I see. Now you're ready to snuggle." She adjusted, trying to read her book, something about a man homesteading and running a trapline in Alaska's interior. Keta's chest rose and fell, his breath moist on her neck. The potbelly wood stove let off waves of heat.

"Christ almighty, that's disgusting," Tara said when the dog released an airy fart. She waved the pages of the book in front of her nose, shoving his hips with a socked foot. "You're a nasty, gassy, pill-popping creature, aren't you? No wonder they left you behind."

Ears flattened against his skull, the dog skulked to the other side of the room. With a huff he leapt onto the couch and curled up, watching her. When he blinked the two dark orbs of his eyes disappeared. "Jesus," she said. "Hey. I'm sorry. I shouldn't have said that."

She dropped to her stomach, crawled across the room, and patted the rug in front of her. "C'mon. Please."

Hesitantly, he put his two paws onto the rug, then his hips, white tail nub shaking as he settled in front of her. She pulled his frame closer, resting her cheek against his shoulders, listening to the steady beat of his heart. With her hand she cupped one of his paws, rubbed the rough pads with the tips of her fingers.

"I'm sorry," she said. "I'm so sorry."

31

THE NEXT MORNING, when she woke up at five thirty by the wood stove, Keta had his chin on her stomach. When she rose, he yawned, watching her. She knelt in front of him and dragged out his eye boogers, like her mother had done for her when she was a child. "You must clean away dreams," Serena liked to say.

After letting him out to pee, she sank his pills into a spoon of peanut butter, told him to sit, and tried to get him to eat. When he refused she grew frustrated, held his mouth open, and shoved the pills to the back of his tongue. He coughed, shaking his head, trying to clear his throat.

"I'm sorry, buddy. I gotta go."

He stood in the mudroom, watching. After closing the door she stopped, opened it again. He was still there, unmoved.

"Go lie down! I'll be back soon."

She made it to the processor by six thirty, took her bibs and hair-net from her locker, buttoned up her jacket, and pushed through the plastic flaps into the frozen world of the brig. When she bent to slide out the first box, pain oozed down the back of her neck, unfurled over her shoulders. It felt like punishment, except this time for bigger things. For leaving Connor. Her father. Philadelphia. "Jesus Christ," she muttered to herself. "This is fucking unreal."

When she stood up straight a bolt shot down her left leg, worse than the day before. Her cheeks were numb, and she couldn't feel her toes. She wasn't even fifteen minutes into the morning. She thought of Keta back at the house, still sitting in the hall, wondering if she was ever coming back. Her joints ached. Her arms didn't want to bend at the elbow.

A lift pushed through the flaps. She hobbled out of the way as Bailey worked the forks under the pallet. "Staying warm?" he yelled, then honked twice and gunned the vehicle. Fucker.

Maybe people who made it in Alaska were just built of tougher stuff. Some Nordic ancestry better suited to the cold and wet and scream of machinery. Philly hadn't prepared her for this. Although Gypo told her she had grit. She had fought Golden Gloves. She just needed to calm down and put aside the cold. Pretend she was covered with Keta's thick fur.

At break her ears, despite being covered in fleece, throbbed. Her feet felt like concrete blocks. She filled a Styrofoam cup with steaming coffee and stood by the humming machine to absorb what scant warmth she could.

It was hopeless. She had never taken a knee in the ring, but another six hours in that freezer wasn't physically possible. She just wanted to be back by the fire with the dog.

"Someone looks worse for the wear."

She turned. Newt stood in the doorway, arms crossed.

"You asshole!" She set down her cup, staggered across the room, and hugged him. "Where have you been?"

"Easy, easy," he said, laughing. He smelled of diesel, sweat, and fish. His eyes appeared flat, lacking their usual spark. "Weeklong circuit on the tender. Captain Jackie rode me like a goddamn mutton-buster."

"I don't think I can last the day in that freezer," she blurted.

"That's funny, because I don't think I can last much longer on that tender. Feeling beat as a five-pound bag of smashed assholes, I am. But we'll grind it out 'cause we're made of the tough stuff. How's the Bunkhouse?"

"I'm housesitting. Looking after a dog."

His face knotted. "I got some bad news for you. Don't get all worked up when I say it."

"I have some bad news for you too. I'm on my way to Trunk to tell him I'm quitting."

"T, we passed the tug on the way back into town. She's being towed south."

She stopped. "What do you mean, she's being towed south? The boat's in the harbor."

Newt shook his head. "Word on the street is there's gonna be a music school on her, or some similar insult to that boat's original purpose."

Her voice shook as it rose. "Newt, that's why I took this job. That's why I'm stacking fucking boxes in Antarctica. You lined this up, then you're not even here? And now this?"

He poured brown liquid from a flask into her coffee. "Calm down, okay? Have a drink. What is it with that tug? There's other boats."

She took a gulp, letting the scald of the coffee and alcohol spread through her throat. "I'm not going to calm down. This whole island's fucked. No one does a goddamn thing they say they're going to do. I can't stand it."

He took her arm. "Tara, I've got a plan. Trust me."

She shook him off, pulling her bib over her head, knocking her hat to the concrete floor. "*Fangoul* to that freezer, and screw you, too, for leading me down this path."

She walked out of the processor, then over to the Bunkhouse, down the hall to the payphone.

"Sorry," Laney told her. "As I said, I would have preferred the tug to stay on the island. But it's best for the boat, best for everyone."

"Bullshit," Tara said, shifting the phone to her other ear, feeling the pressure of her anger building in her chest. She shut her eyes. "You knew I wanted that boat."

"Yeah, I did, but you didn't have the money, okay? We've all got our own shit—it's not just about you, girlfriend. I'm going through something called a divorce, which, I can tell you, is no walk in Central Park."

Tara sidestepped her words, although they rang true. She needed to get her head out of her ass. Still. "You said these new owners were starting a music school or some horseshit?"

"And what were you going to do? Transport armed troops again?" Laney shot back.

"At least get the engine running. And by the way, your friends who are buying the boat suck. I'm taking care of the dog they left behind."

"I need to go, Tara."

She slammed the phone down, kicking at the baseboard. Spoiled San Francisco brat, that's what she was. High-heeled bitch with her white wine and red shawl and chopsticked hair.

Back at the processor she put on her bibs and hairnet and gloves and elbowed her way between the flaps into the brig. She glanced up at Trunk, who was standing in just shirtsleeves, looking back at her.

"What?" she asked, grabbing at the first form and scanning the shelves for boxes to pull. "You got a problem too?"

He shook his head innocently, his eye bouncing around. "No problem. Just that Newt said he got the glazer working and needed a hand making boxes. But hell, someone needs to cool off by the looks of it. Maybe it's best you stay here."

She was freezing, thought her head might split with cold if she remained another minute in the freezer. Still, she worked on stacking the pallet, finding the next box on the list.

"Tara," Trunk said, watching her. "Hey."

"I'll wrap this up and come out. Okay? I got it."

He watched as she finished the stack, arranging the end of each box flush with the other. Then she followed him through the flaps, feeling close to fainting. *It has to be genetic,* she thought as he switched on a conveyor belt, *how he just doesn't notice the cold.* Across the room Newt flashed a thumbs-up, dragged over a rack from the freezer, and began slipping fish into the glazer. Frozen black cod dropped one after the other onto a revolving wheel.

"Okay. Deep breath. Good?" Trunk asked.

She stared back at him, willing herself steady.

"Remember back in our interview when I asked you about counting? Here's where it comes in handy. Your job is to measure up each fish coming down the belt, finish boxes between forty-nine point five and fifty point five pounds. Scale is already tared out at one point five, which means we've accounted for the weight of the cardboard. Watch."

Trunk quickly put together three boxes, trading out fish only a few times. As he worked she began a reassessment of his stupidity. People out here who wouldn't understand a Philly parking sign somehow had a way of just *doing things* well.

"Got it?" he asked. "If these are seven-ups, about how many fish do you need?"

Fifty pounds. "Seven."

"That's right. Make a box."

She did. Then another, slapping fish onto the scale, slinging them into the box, and tying a loose knot in the plastic bag. The fish kept coming, an endless flow of frozen gray bodies emerging from Newt's glazer. Trunk walked back to his office.

After a few boxes she ran into a hitch. The red numbers on the scale flashed 44.2 pounds. Each fish she put in the box was either over or under. She grasped at tails. The wheel brimmed over with fish, and one clattered onto the cement. Newt hit a red button, stopping the belt. Trunk came out of his office. "The fuck's going on?" he yelled.

"Jammed nozzle on the glazer," Newt said, holding up a wrench. "I'm on it."

Trunk's lazy eye bounced around the room, landing on Tara. "Well, c'mon. We got fish coming up our ass."

"Trick is to find your magic number," Newt whispered from behind her. He shuffled through the fish, put together a box, wrapped the plastic, fit the cardboard flaps together. "Seven. Always shoot for a seven-pounder instead of just starting wherever. Make sense?"

He returned to the glazer and restarted the conveyor belt. As she began packing she wondered if there would ever be a time on this island when she was good at something, just one damn thing. Or at least content, with nothing on her mind. She thought of being on the end of the breakwater with Newt, beneath the blinking red channel marker. She needed to apologize for snapping at him. And to Laney.

Her hands accelerated as she sized up the ashy bodies. What else was there but to keep going? Fish after fish, box after box, and go home at the end of the day to fall asleep with the dog by the fire. Feed the sweet love his pill, and do this all over again. Hopefully a bit better the next time.

32

HER BODY, which had rebelled so fiercely, began to accommodate itself to the rhythm of the work, the endless stream of fish along the conveyor belt. Her orange-gloved hands stretching out to take that one, sure this one would work. 49.7. Perfect. Her hands sweated, grew clammy in the rubber gloves. An hour until break. A doughnut. Slap of the red button and they were going again.

It was as if she had broken through the forest into a clearing she hadn't known existed. She could breathe easier, spend twelve, even fourteen hours a day on her feet. Just so long as she didn't have to go back into that freezer. With the tug sold, all she had was Newt, and these fish, one after the other. Like she was buying time but getting paid for it.

Her second week at the processor she clocked eighty-three hours, boxing fish and scooping guts on the fresh side when the tender arrived with its filled green totes. Calluses at the base of her fingers thickened and turned a dirty orange. Muscle rose like a plate of armor over her collarbone. When a Ukrainian kid pinched her ass, she whirled around and hooked him across the face. Stunned, the boy stared back at her, bleeding from a gash beneath his eye. "You've gone wilder than a fifth ace," Newt said in the break room.

Nights, she showered, put on Connor's flannel pajamas, walked Keta along the spit's narrow beach, and fell asleep in a nest of pillows in front of the wood stove, the dog breathing warm beneath her. Despite the long days (which were quickly growing shorter, she noticed), her mind felt numb. She kept wanting to respond to Connor's letter, to thank him for the gift (she had kept the tag on, imagining his fingers as he examined the purple numbers), but her brain couldn't put together the words. At the end of the day she felt exquisitely exhausted, no space to reflect.

The first week of September, Fran informed her that the San Francisco couple's house had sold. Before Tara returned to the Bunkhouse, she gave Keta his pills, cleaned his eyes of sleep. The dog ran his pink tongue over his black gums. "I'll come by Fran's to take you on walks. Promise."

As she walked down the hall of the Bunkhouse, the awful antiseptic smell burning her nostrils, she found herself crying, already missing the animal. She put on her pajamas and listened to the hum from the plant, certain that he had already forgotten about her.

33

TWO WEEKS INTO SEPTEMBER — a month after Tara had started at the processor — Trunk called her into his office.

"I got a proposition. I give you a raise to eight dollars, you take a couple days off."

She stared across the desk, confused. Trunk waited for her response, his lazy eye appearing to bounce in his head.

"You're gonna burn yourself out, friend. I've seen it happen. There's a whole island out there. Have some fun for godsakes before your time on this green earth is through."

When she knocked on Fritz's front door, he opened up with a heavy sigh, wiping his lips.

"Aren't you supposed to be slaving away in the fish dungeon? Or — let me guess — you want your old job back?"

Behind Fritz, Keta stepped into the hall. When he saw Tara he jabbed his head between her legs, letting out a high-pitched whine.

"This is why I'm here," Tara said, kneeling to rub the dog's cheeks. He gave her a tongue flick.

"Wow, he's stingy with his licks," Fritz said.

"I was thinking of heading up Crow to the lookout. Thought maybe I could take him along."

"Take him period as far as I'm concerned," Fritz said. He slapped the dog's hindquarters. "If it were up to me, I'd use him for crab bait. Wouldn't I, buster?"

Tara hugged the dog, who dropped his chin on her shoulder, panting in her ear.

"He's just an old grump with no one left to yell at," she said.

As they walked through town, Keta strained against the leash, sniffing fence posts, his nubbin of a tail wagging. At the trail she let him off, and he bounded along the planks, veered into the muskeg, paws sinking into the green carpet. Loping between the trees, he really did look like a wolf, she thought, save for his floppy white ears.

The earth was soft under her boots, which had turned glassy with moisture. Streamside, she cupped a hand and drank. Keta clambered down and lowered himself into a pool, before clawing back up, shaking, spraying water, and sitting down beside her, chest heaving. His pink nose tested the air.

They continued climbing, following the wooden steps crisscrossing the side of the mountain. She thought about the herring opening, that feeling of being ready for the next step. And here she was six months later, heading into the winter with a job at the processor, and no plans to return to Philly.

Up ahead of her the dog stopped. She walked to where he stood, pausing when he gave a low, guttural *woof*. She caught a brief scent of something musky, rotten. The woods had grown quiet. The black and white hairs over Keta's shoulders quivered. She heard a branch snap. At first Tara thought it was a large man with a backpack, about fifty feet up the trail. Then she saw a flash of teeth. Keta's lips rose, a low rumble coming from his throat.

"Holy fucking shit," Tara whispered. A heat spread over her cheeks, followed by an awful hollowness in her body, the recognition that she was at the mercy of a creature who knew no reason.

She took a step back. The bear rose on its hind legs and sniffed the air. Wind ruffled its golden chest fur. Keta growled louder. Tara tried to take another step back, but her legs wouldn't move from where she was standing. Time stopped. Then Keta let out a true bark, squaring his body in front of Tara. The bear snorted in response, snapped its jaws, and fell, its forelegs grabbing the air before they hit ground. Then it charged, its body elongating as it narrowed the distance. Keta threw out his front paws, lowering his chest and barking furiously as the bear came toward them. Tara gritted her teeth and stiffened.

The bear skidded to a stop less than ten feet away. The animal seemed to absorb the light of the woods, its small eyes peering at them. An oily, rancid scent washed over her. Ears flat against his skull, trembling, Keta continued his slow growl, his head almost on the ground, haunches high in the air. Thirty seconds? A minute passed? Finally the bear let out a huff and moved off through a break in the bushes.

Tara held still, waiting until the crunch of breaking branches eased into silence. The dog turned, jaws open. He gave her a quick look, then stared in the direction the bear had gone. When she touched his head he still didn't move. Through his fur she could feel the rush of his heart.

"You . . ." was all she could say. Words held no meaning.

They started down the mountain. Tara took the steps one at a time, the dog staying just ahead of her. Then she was running, palming tree trunks to stay upright.

At the Muskeg she tied Keta outside, slipped into a booth, and watched the line of people at the register. She felt a weight in the seat beside her, and squeezed her hands into fists. There was the smell of cooked greens, and grease. Betteryear.

"Tara?" he said. "Are you okay?"

"I was just charged by a bear."

"This is not a good word to say aloud."

"Bear, bear, bear," she said angrily, her voice rising. She held her face in her hands. The stopper at the base of her throat, just above her breastbone, cinched as she started to cry.

"Come," he said after a moment. "Let me walk you home."

The three of them went along the water. Keta stayed by her side, close enough to brush against her leg.

"This is a trauma," Betteryear said. "Perhaps I could help teach you some things to make you feel safer in the woods, and avoid this happening again. Have coffee with me tomorrow morning."

She couldn't think, and just petted the dog, holding him close to her thigh. "Okay."

Dogs weren't allowed at the Bunkhouse, but she didn't care. Keta settled on the laminate floor in a pile of her clothes, crossing his legs and resting his head to one side. She dragged the mattress and the wool cover to the ground and pulled the dog to her, burying her face in his fur. When she whispered thank you, he breathed a long sigh. It was probably just a reflex, she thought. But he might have meant "Yes. Always."

34

THE NEXT MORNING the temperature dropped. It rained lightly. On the way to the coffee shop, at a ramshackle house by the police station, a couple tables were set up beneath a tent. Among the clothes and board games and saucepans she found a dog-eared book on diesel boat engines. When a man with a great waterfall of a white beard came by, she pointed at a rusty rifle hiding among the dish racks and pots. "That thing work?" she asked.

He lifted the gun. "Barrel's crooked as a duck's ass. Good for bear, though. Winchester Seventy, thirty-aught-six."

She considered telling him she had been charged the day before. "What about a license to shoot?" she asked.

He laughed. "You're not in the lower forty-eight no more, sweetheart. You can walk down Main Street with this baby strapped to your back. Hundred bucks and she's yours."

She glared at him. "I've been here a year."

He held up the oil-stained engine instruction booklet. "Alaska girl, I'll even throw this in. Seventy-five bucks and you got a deal."

At the Muskeg she leaned the rifle against the wall by the children's blocks. As she waited for Betteryear, she thumbed through the diesel-splotched manual, tapping her foot to fiddle music, reading about the importance of building air for a direct-reversible to allow for as many starts and stops as possible. No spark plugs. With the tip of her finger she traced the arrows showing the path of air, how it traveled from the tanks into the steel, then copper pipes to create compression in the cylinders. Which started combustion, which turned the crankshaft, which turned the propeller to make the boat go.

Basic, yet unimaginable. She ran an oily palm through her hair, then began to fool with the rifle. Soon she had figured out the spring-loaded release for the bolt, how to empty the magazine, pull the trigger, and reset it. She was sipping from her coffee mug, pleased with this small victory when Betteryear settled in a chair across from her.

"Ah, Tara," he said, nodding at the rifle. "What have you done?"

"I know. It's bent. I just got it at a garage sale."

He looked back at her with something in his face, disappointment perhaps. For a moment his expression reminded her of Connor. Not quite condescending, but close.

"Before hunting you should learn to gather."

"Gather?"

He stared her down. In the city this meant fight. Not so on the island. "Yes. Plants. Mushrooms. Berries. I've got baskets in my truck. We could go right now, if you like. It won't be dark for another few hours."

She thought about it. Tomorrow she was scheduled back at the processor. But her body felt so worn down. She flipped the pages of the manual with her thumb. Now that the tug was gone, what did it really matter? Then again, going into the woods with a man she didn't know—a man Fritz said had a temper.

"The two of us will be fine," Betteryear said, in a gentle voice. "Promise."

"Okay," she said, shouldering the rifle, starting for the door.

Flakes melted into the asphalt as they walked along the street. The cluck of chickens, a crumple of a tarp in the breeze, the smell of brown sugar and liquid smoke from fish brining on decks. Betteryear seemed to glide, his basket swinging an arc from one hand.

The faint disk of the sun hovered just above the mountains across the channel. The descent into darkness didn't worry her as it had last year — she knew what was coming. This year she watched how everything seemed to draw in closer: objects, people. As if intent on sharing heat.

They turned onto a gravel road, which dead-ended into an unfamiliar trailhead. Kiksadi River chattered between the trees. She missed having the dog by her side.

"You are nervous," he said. "Please, relax."

He took a couple steps off the trail, then lifted a dome-shaped mushroom from the moss. Its cap looked like a burnt loaf of bread.

"It's not only bears that can kill you in these woods. *Galerina marginata*. Poisonous. But luckily," he said, swooping his fingers over the earth, reaping a handful of butterscotch stems, "galerinas are rare. This here is *Craterellus tubaeformis*, also called yellowfoot, or winter chanterelle. Look at the ridges on the underside. Ridges, not gills, like the poisonous variety. The winter chanterelle is your best friend."

She held the chanterelles to her nose, smelling the damp earth. She walked by his side toward the river. The chatter of the water made her anxious again, how it drowned out nearby sound.

He picked a creamy white mushroom from the base of a tree, flipped it, and ran a finger over points along the underside. "Sweet tooth. Also called hedgehog." He smiled as if they were both in on some great secret.

"Edible?" she asked. He dipped his head, shutting his eyes. "Oh, yes. And oftentimes close by . . ." He crouched and peered beneath a tree, gave a satisfied smile. "Reach beneath the hemlock here. I think there might be a surprise."

She dropped to her knees, ignoring the wetness, and extended her arm into the root cave.

"Farther," he said. "Lie down on your stomach."

The order annoyed her, but she obeyed, reaching in until her shoulder pushed against the trunk, patting the dry dirt. She didn't like this, having her right arm pinned. Her fingers touched soil, twigs, then a rubbery coldness. "Yes?" he said. The root gave with a soft tear. She brought the mushroom into the light, brushed dirt from the thick stem, and ran her fingers over the spikes along the bottom.

"Hedgehog?"

"That's right," Betteryear said, taking the mushroom from her, nestling it into the basket. It was, by far, the largest of the bunch.

"How'd you know it was there?"

He shrugged. "I had a feeling."

They picked until the basket could hold no more. "Now that you know how to gather, you must learn how to cook. And then one day we'll hunt with your rifle, and shoot a deer. Yes?"

The rifle had been for bear. But she wondered if she could do it, pull the trigger on a deer. She had heard stories of people hunting in upstate Pennsylvania. It would be an adventure. "I'd like that."

She asked Betteryear to drop her at the docks. Before returning to the Bunkhouse she walked out to the transient, just to make sure the tug hadn't miraculously reappeared. It hadn't. Nothing but the sound of rigging against the masts, and the high-pitched screams of the buoy balls chafing against the bull rail.

35

WORK AT THE PROCESSOR slowed down. Chum salmon were finished. Now that she wasn't clocking overtime, she felt antsy.

At the end of September, Newt took her aside in the break room and announced his plan to save money. "The woods, T. We'll live in the woods. The price is right. Free."

"No way," she said, looking out over the floor. "I'm not living like some bum."

"Stop thinking like a city girl," he said.

She bristled. "Who around here has been charged by a bear?"

"Bears won't pay us no mind."

"Who's 'us,' anyway?"

"Bailey. Maybe that crazy redheaded Frenchy, too."

He meant Thomas, the lanky, fine-boned new arrival on the processor floor, who had a shock of red hair and freckles, and smoked cigarettes in the break room while squatting against the wall. He had been studying politics at a university in Paris, he told them, when he decided to travel. He ran out of cash in Alaska, found the job at the processor.

"Newt, you're not making sense. It's about to be winter."

"What makes sense is you getting out of that shitty Bunkhouse and saving to buy a boat. And me getting Plume north. You've been through a winter here. It ain't no worse than Kentucky — just a matter of holding your breath." He started back to his station, tacking sea cucumbers up on the plywood. "Think about it, T. It's a good one. And I think you know it."

36

SHE KNEW HER FATHER WAS STEWING, furious, but couldn't bring herself to call. On top of that she still hadn't responded to Connor's letter. It was tempting on the island to just shut off contact with the rest of the world, shove it away into a corner until she was ready to re-engage.

She had seen a card in the post office, an aerial view of Archangel Island with the volcano in the background. From above, the town appeared like a thumbnail along the coast, with ice fields and glaciers visible in the alpine. She bought it, then drew an X by the processor.

October 2, 1998

Dear Connor,

Here you can see Port Anna, and all the beauty that surrounds her. The mark is where I stay. Thank you for my early Christmas present. I sleep in them every night. They make me very happy.

More soon,
Tara

37

THE SUN TRACED A SHALLOW ARC over the mountains as Tara, Newt, and Thomas walked along the gravel road by the Kiksadi River.

"Just to look," Newt reassured her. "But I'm telling you — it's perfect." Thomas walked ahead, bending his tall frame over to inspect mushrooms in the long shadows cast by the trees. Tara recognized them as galerinas — poisonous. "Although that kid, I don't know. Comes off as dumber than two sacks of hair. You seen him sort fish? He's got two speeds, slow down and stop."

The trail ended at the river. A hopscotch of boulders made a crossing. On the other side a game trail. Tara stayed silent as they walked, stripping hemlock needles from a branch, crushing them between her fingers and breathing in the piney alcohol aroma. After days of rain and a few snow showers, cold sun filtered through the trees, casting shadows over the river, swollen with snowmelt and opaque with glacial deposits. It would be nice to be lulled to sleep by the sound of running water, she thought. But the idea of living with no shower nearby, no stove? It still seemed far-fetched.

After a couple miles Newt called out, "Hey, Frenchy! Hang a right up this hill here."

They scrambled up the side, Thomas grabbing on to tree roots. At the top, spruce and hemlock circled a slight depression in the forest floor. Wood smoldered in the center, a glow of embers in the ash.

Bailey emerged from a tent at the edge of a clearing wearing a sweat-shirt with the sleeves lopped off. He eyed Tara, then Newt. "I thought we said man-town out here. That girl's a pain-in-the-ass bitch."

Before she could announce that she had zero intention of living in the woods, the skin on Newt's cheeks drew tight. He settled his weight on his back foot.

"Whatever," the big man muttered. "You fucks make your own goddamn site way over there. *Way* over there. And you said you'd bring a chainsaw, Re-Re. I don't see that around." He lumbered off toward his tent.

The three of them stood, listening to the babble of the river. "Why does he call you Re-Re?" Thomas asked.

But Newt was looking into the trees, his eyes moving from one to the next, and she knew he was planning something neither she nor Thomas could envision.

38

FOLLOWING THE TRIP INTO THE WOODS, Newt wouldn't veer from the idea that they should build a platform. "Give it a couple months, T. Try it out. Trust me. I'll make it watertight."

"We're not cavemen, for godsakes."

"You need some vision, girl."

Trunk gave them Columbus Day off. The Sunday before, they headed back to the clearing, this time with two-stroke oil, a mixing jug, and a thirty-inch used chainsaw Newt bought off an old-time logger.

Tara made a deal, mostly to get Newt to stop pestering her. If he could build a satisfactory home, then she would come back with her things. She already had her rifle, slung over one shoulder, a sleeping bag, and her half-used roll of duct tape. Thomas carried the chainsaw, the orange cowling over the engine a shade darker than his hair.

"That thing have bullets in it?" Newt asked her.

"Yes." She had purchased 180-grain 30-aught cartridges from the hunting store.

"You ever pull the trigger?"

"Nope."

"What about you, Pierre? You know how to use that chainsaw?"

Thomas held the tool in the air. "I will figure it out."

Newt shook his head. "Jesus Christ."

At the top of the hill Tara set the rifle against a tree trunk. Bailey was nowhere in sight.

"Go on then," Newt said to Thomas. "Let's see you try to fire it up."

Thomas stooped over the saw, held the bar, flipped up the hood on his merino wool sweater, and pulled the cord. The engine turned over, coughed, and died. "Gimme that," Newt snapped. He pulled out the choke, yanked the cord, and the machine wheezed to life. "Don't teach ya that in gay Paree, do they?"

Thomas looked on, mesmerized, as the small man made a neat slice into the tree, then moved around to the other side. "Timburrrrr!" he crooned, branches snapping as the trunk crashed down. He shoved a wooden pole with a rusted hook on one end at Tara, showed her how to use the tool to roll the hemlock onto the rocks. He bolted the Alaskan mill to the chainsaw.

"Time to plank this bad girl up," Newt shouted.

"I can try?" Thomas asked, as he watched Newt push the saw through the tree.

Newt let off the throttle. He turned to Tara. "That medallion protect you from chainsaw massacres?"

Thomas leaned in, pressing on the trigger. Curled yellow shavings caught in his sweater. He was handsome, Tara thought, watching a leather lanyard with a bone amulet bounce against his chest. When the chain got stuck at a knot, Thomas yanked at the saw, the toothy grin still on his face. Newt shook his head, undoing the bar with a couple twists of a brass key.

"You're not the smartest peanut in the turd, are you?"

"What?" Thomas said.

"Watch out. C'mon. *Vamonos*, or whatever."

After the planks were cut, Newt used scraps of cedar and the chainsaw to fashion four stakes. "Batter boards," he explained, pounding them into the earth. "Mark out our perimeter. Look big enough?"

Tara shrugged. "Good with me."

With a handsaw he made a notch in the top of each stake, then ran gangion through to make an outline. Despite his yelling and ribbing he was a patient teacher, demonstrating how to use sixteen-penny nails to fasten joists, posts, and the ripped boards. Clacks echoed through the forest. She noticed it took her about half as many hammer swings as Thomas to pound in a nail.

"It's the boxing that makes you good with that thing," Newt told her, flashing a grin. "All that training was good for more than getting hit in the head. Help you build a home."

It was fun to see her friend excited like this. Newt gave Thomas the handsaw and told him to cut alder saplings from the riverside, demonstrating how to lash them together through the tarp grommets. Newt scampered up a hemlock and draped the alders in a collage of canvas and tarps. Tara marveled at her slight friend. He couldn't spell worth a damn, but had some freaky engineer's sense about how the physical world went together. He howled from high in the branches. "Tell me one of you brought duct tape!"

She tossed up her roll. He held it in the air. "If you haven't learned yet, Frenchy, this is why Americans win wars while you guys keep getting rammed in the ass by the Nazis. It has a light side and a dark side and it holds the fucking universe together."

When he finally came down, the trio retreated to a mossy hill. Newt wiped his forehead and looked back at the platform. Breathing hard, he set a hand on each of their shoulders.

"Well, dip my balls in sweet cream and squat me in a kitchen full of kittens. If we don't have a cozy little home of our own making."

39

THE NEXT MORNING she woke with the light, rose from her sleeping bag, and stretched. The air felt cool and clean, the sky white through the branches. Everything so quiet. Thomas was half out of his sleeping bag, stretched over the rough-hewn planks, head curled into one arm. As she lay there, listening to his soft snores, the chatter of the river moving over the rocks, she thought of her father. What day was it? Monday, October twelfth. Urbano Marconi would be in his billing office, trying to reach suppliers, cursing Christopher Columbus if they were closed. Tracking special orders to see what ingredients the bakery would need in the coming weeks.

She unzipped the sleeping bag, the denim of her jeans cold and damp on her thighs. The fire was down to embers. She pulled her hair back, arranged wood from Newt's pile, and blew on the coals as she had seen people do on television. Her father's heart would break, or perhaps harden even more, if he could see her in the woods like this, saving to buy a tugboat, starting a fire.

The sticks were slick with dew, but she was able to coax up a flame and get water boiling. "Look at you, scaring up fire at first light," Newt said. His cheek still bore the print of his flannel cuff. "Fuck. I need coffee."

He stared into the woods, the forest floor dappled with sunlight. "Interested in a run to town?"

They walked along the river. At the bookstore she found a card of a fishing boat framed by tree branches beneath the stars. The boat mast wrapped in Christmas lights, alone in a dark bay. While Newt went off for coffee, she wrote.

October 12, 1998

Dear Pop,

    I just want you to know that I'm safe. The winters here are dark, day after day of rain, but it's not cold. I'm sorry for hanging up on you.

    Work has slowed down a bit so I'm making more friends. I don't know when I'll be back

She started to write *home,* then stopped. Thinking of her small room, with its rabbit-eared television on the dresser and knobby bedposts, then of the platform out in the woods with its freshly sawed plank scent. She dotted a period after *back.*

Your daughter,
Tara

That night in the clearing Newt's flask went one way and Thomas's pinky-sized joint the other. He had spread wool blankets over the platform, arranging their sleeping bags in neat lines, then pulling logs to the fire to sit on. Sticks of hemlock and alder hissed as they dried in the heat. She brought out her duffel and the rest of her things. Newt leaned back, evidently pleased with his success.

"Damn, Frenchy, that's some good Alaskan bud," he said, inhaling deep and holding it. "Makes my face feel like grape jelly," he squeaked.

She thought of Keta back in town, imagining him curled up in the warmth by her side. It felt more like her first time camping than being a bum on the sidewalk.

Although he had moved his tent a good fifty yards from their new platform, the fire and weed drew Bailey, who banked chain-sawed branches against a rock, sat on a five-gallon bucket, and stared into the flames. She was thinking of heading to her sleeping bag when Thomas reached for her hair. "So this is your mother or your father who is so beautiful?" he asked. She batted his hand away, glaring. Bailey snapped out of his trance.

"Hey, Re-Re. Check out Pepé Le Pew over here. He's kicking game."

Thomas rose and fetched a bottle of wine from his backpack on the platform. He removed his shoe and whacked the heel against the bottom of the bottle.

"The hell you doing?" Bailey said.

"Watch. It is a trick for the cork."

"You gonna get her drunk, then make your move?"

A log popped, letting off steam. Thomas grumbled at the wine bottle. She thought of her rifle, wrapped in a garbage bag beneath the platform, box of bullets in a Ziploc.

Newt, hands held out to the flames, spoke in a flat voice. "I wouldn't underestimate Tara getting the best of either of you boys. And if she doesn't, well, there's my skinny ass to deal with. I'm small, but I'm one mean motherfucker."

The paleness of Newt's head in the firelight, the coldness in his eyes and his voice, cut even Bailey short. Thomas quit with the shoe.

She loved her friend so deeply right then.

40

AFTER HALLOWEEN, work at the processor dropped to five or six hours a day. She arrived in the dark, nine in the morning, and packed spot prawns from Hoonah Sound, black cod, the few winter kings that came through. Newt did his best to keep things light.

"You just wait, T. You and me, we're gonna run this town. I'll be fishing my face off with Plume running gear, and you'll find another boat to fall in love with. It's gonna be peaches, just you wait and see."

She was growing accustomed to life on the platform, and even found herself enjoying how the sound of rain dripping from the alder leaves grew louder the farther she got from the river. Hedgehog mushrooms popping out beneath hemlock stumps after a downpour. The slow flap of eagles, the commotion they made as they settled into the branches. Not that she wouldn't have enjoyed a night on her bed with a tub of cream cheese, a box of Wheat Thins, and the ears on her television adjusted just right to watch *The X-Files*.

But that might come. One day. Right now she didn't want to think about it. Instead she took pleasure in having all her belongings so close to her on the platform, arranged in the duffel. Nesting her jeans at the bottom of her sleeping bag so they were loose and warm come morning. Stoking the fire for coffee. Doing what she needed to do.

41

A COUPLE DAYS INTO NOVEMBER a group clad in Gore-Tex pants, faded leathers, surplus sweaters with European flags sewed onto the sleeve, materialized in the clearing. Pierced and tattooed, they called themselves the Alaskan Travelers. Newt joked about charging them rent.

"They'd probably pay with clamshells or some shit," he said.

Thomas made friends with a German woman, in her thirties or perhaps early forties, named Frauke. She had short bleached-blond hair and a spotted pit bull named Nanny. From across the clearing Tara could hear the sharp commands.

"*Komm,* Nanny! *Sitz! Braver Hund.*"

The barbell in Frauke's nose gave her a doleful look, made sinister by a missing front tooth. She wore a washed leather jacket and army-green pants with pink trim and an assortment of flaps and buttons and pockets and safety pins and zippers. Staying indoors, she told them all, damaged your aura. Tied to her belt was a leather pouch that held chits of paper, an inspirational quote on each. Every now and then she'd take one out and stare at it, her lips mouthing the words, before crumpling it up and eating it.

"She is pure," Thomas said, a step ahead as the three of them made their way back toward the clearing. "She has no wall to her reality, you know? She tastes each second in this life."

"Yeah, she tastes it because she doesn't work," Newt said.

Disgusted with the growing crowd, Bailey sequestered himself on the far end of the hill. But he also made friends with a gray-muzzled Lab "looked after" by a pixie-faced, waifish girl from Oregon. The dog followed Bailey as he cut wood, sat by a cast-iron cauldron to boil water.

One evening, when they were all sitting by the fire, Newt setting a grate over the coals to cook black cod tips soaked in soy sauce, Frauke tapped Tara on the shoulder.

"I tell you your fortune. Yes?"

Elbow on one knee, smoking a cigarette in her tank-top and cargo pants, Frauke resembled a soldier. The tip of her tongue worried the empty socket in her gums.

"Sure."

She tossed her cigarette into the fire, untied the leather string, took out a note from the pouch, shiny with age, and studied it. Newt arranged the fish with a fork.

"It is difficult for me to say. But basically it is that unless you try something higher, then you will always stay lower. Yes?"

Tara thought. "Like, don't waste your time on bullshit."

"Ah! Exact."

Thomas, looking up from one of his Foxfire books, said, "Nanny does not waste time on the bullshit."

Frauke sighed. "In Germany it is a rule that your dog is polite."

Keta would behave himself out here, Tara thought, as she watched Newt turn the fish. She resolved to stop by Fritz's to walk the old guy.

"Want some?" Newt asked, looking at the pit bull, who had been staring at the sizzling links of fish.

"I do not eat the gluten," Frauke answered.

"I wasn't talking to you, honey," Newt said. "I was addressing *das Hund* over here."

"Nanny? Ach, she is fasting."

"The dog?" Newt asked incredulously.

"Yes. For two days. Liquid only. No fish, no solid."

"Jesus, Frau-cakes," Newt said. "You can't make a dog fast."

Frauke's slight grin disappeared. She stood, walked toward the canvas flaps in front of her tent. "Nanny. *Komm*," she ordered. Nanny continued to salivate by the fire, panting, watching the pan.

"Nanny! *Komm!*" Frauke ordered.

"Eh-oh," Thomas said, reaching out to give Nanny a pet as she loped over. "Off you go."

"*Braver Hund*," Frauke said. "No beg, *mein Schatz*."

Newt looked over at Tara and shrugged. "Woman seems to have forgotten where the dog is in the food chain. Let's hope the woods don't remind her."

That night the full moon cast a flinty glow over the tents. There was the zip of a sleeping bag, a whisper followed by a laugh. Newt had retreated to the platform.

Restless, unable to sleep, Tara sat by Thomas, watching the coals pulse red in the breeze. Since the one evening when he tried to open the bottle, he had been keeping his distance.

Nanny poked her nose through the canvas. Thomas tsked, trying to coax the dog. Slowly her body emerged. She sat on the other side of the fire pit, panting.

A few minutes later the pixie girl's Lab with the graying snout trotted up to the fire, a deer bone in his jaws. Without warning Nanny lunged. The old Lab yelped as the pit clamped down on her neck. Seconds later, he lay quivering in the mud.

Screams followed — Frauke in German, Thomas in French. A few of the travelers spilled out of tents to watch. Nanny gnawed serenely on the bone, growling when anyone approached. The pixie-girl and Bailey emerged from a tent, skin gray in the moonlight, Bailey pulling on his boxers and the girl in her underwear, shouting, throwing herself on the bloody Lab. Newt yelled in a groggy voice from the platform, "Everyone just shut the fuck up. Some of us gotta work in the morning."

Chilled, Tara made her way to the platform and zipped herself into the sleeping bag, looking back as people milled by the fire. Frauke and Bailey dragged the dog carcass out of the clearing. The girl sobbed, head in her hands.

"Another scene like this and I'm back at the Bunkhouse," Tara told Newt. But he was already asleep.

42

A COUPLE WEEKS before Tara's second Thanksgiving, Betteryear invited her to gather the last mushrooms of the season. They would hunt for deer once the snow arrived, he promised.

After foraging they drove in silence past construction vehicles along the shoulders of Kiksadi River Road. The basket, filled with winter chanterelles, hedgehogs, and a few ragged-looking shaggy manes, bounced on her lap. A truck came toward them, and Betteryear lifted two fingers. She watched through the windshield for a response but saw none.

Betteryear shook his head. "All this is sacred land, a Tlingit graveyard. And now they're buildings houses. It's obscene."

When she didn't say anything he smiled over at her, his gloomy mood shifting. "Would you like to know how to prepare the mushrooms?"

"Sure."

Instead of a right he took a left on Papermill Road. She realized he was bringing her to his home. It was okay, she decided. She was growing tired of eating fish from the processor boiled in shrimp ramen, which she and Newt bought in boxes. Occasionally Newt's cans of refried beans and cream of mushroom.

A sheen of twilight reflected off Maksoutoff Bay. They climbed a hill. Just past the Church of God he parked the truck in a gravel pullout with a set of mailboxes. She followed him down a winding path to a cabin built just beyond the beach line. Roof shingles were bleached bone-white by the salt air. Stones and shells made a tinkling sound as the waves receded.

"Go explore," he told her. "I'll be inside."

She slipped off her boots, folded the cuffs of her pants, and waded into the water, cupping her arches to avoid being stabbed by shards of shell. Waves lapped against her shins. She recalled a dream of trying to catch up to her mother on a curved beach just like this one. Seaweed draped over her mother's shoulders, ocean gathering at her ankles as the tide receded.

A candle flickered in the uneven window panes of the cabin. Gray smoke rose from the chimney. This is what she had imagined all those years ago when she heard her cousin speak at Sunday dinner, when she read her report in fifth grade.

A worn stone step led into the cabin. Inside was a boxy room, with a single bed, made neatly with a quilt folded at the bottom, and a blanket chest at the foot. In the far corner a flitch counter and chipped porcelain sink sat beside a wood stove. An assortment of cast-iron pans gleamed in the candlelight. A fat orange cat jumped from one of the wooden chairs around a rough-hewn wooden table and rubbed against Betteryear's pant leg as he kneeled on a braided rug and built kindling in the wood stove.

"Is this a trucker's hitch?" she asked, examining a knot on a clothesline.

"It is." The air turned smoky as newspaper caught, and the cedar kindling crackled. Two bear skulls flanked him on the wall.

"Did you kill those?"

"You're so curious," Betteryear said. "Has it always been like that?"

"I don't know," Tara said, picking at the hard chinking between the logs. "In Catholic school the sisters always told us curiosity was a bad thing."

Betteryear fanned the fire with his cap. He had more hair than she expected, black flecked with gray. He took down a metal colander from among the woven baskets hanging from nails in the rafters, and tipped in the mushrooms.

A gust blew branches against the leaded glass, and a brown curtain billowed over an open casement window. Raindrops hit the panes, then ran into the crosspieces.

"You should be careful, wading in the water like that," Betteryear said as he separated mushrooms onto a muslin cloth.

"Why?"

"*Kushtaka.* The land otter spirits, shape-shifters. They come up from the sea, take human form, usually a dead relative, and tempt you into the water." The fire snapped, and a tremor ran through her as she thought of her dream. The cat yawned. Betteryear took a bulging pillowcase from a nail on the wall, shook out a mound of Labrador tea leaves. "Then you drown," he added. "Did you know, speaking of names, what yours means?" She shook her head. "The other day in the library I looked it up. In Polynesian mythology it is a beautiful sea goddess. Your mother must have known this."

"Maybe," she said in a soft voice.

"Tell me about her," he said.

She watched as he took a teapot from the wood stove and poured boiling water over the leaves. He handed her a mug, and she sat down at the table. Tired, feeling drugged from the heat and exhaustion, she said, "My mother was killed. December twenty-third, two years ago this Christmas."

"Did you hold secrets from her?" he asked.

"What? No."

The cat snored by the fire.

Betteryear crossed the room, lit a scarred propane camp stove over the sink, turned, and rested a hand on her shoulder.

Through the wool of her sweater she could feel the uncomfortable warmth of his palm.

"Listen," he said, before she could pull away. "No sadness to-night. Just good food. Yes?" He patted her head. "Come. You wash mushrooms. I'll start dinner." He set the filled colander and a wood-handled brush in front of her.

There was a fishy smell, followed by a clatter as he dumped a bowl of shells into a pan. "Limpets in seal oil," he explained. "Are those mushrooms ready?" he asked.

"Sorry."

When the nubs of meat from the limpets dropped out of their cone-shaped shells he added the cleaned chanterelles, hedgehogs, and chopped shaggy mane — also called a lawyer's wig, he informed her. In a separate cast-iron pan he heated olive oil and garlic, pushed chopped eelgrass off a wooden cutting board, the rich bright scent filling the cabin. He handed her salmonberry relish and pickled bull kelp in ce-ramic jars, naming each food, directing her to put them on the table.

"Here," he said, pulling up a rocking chair with a bear pelt over the back. "This is for you. Would you mind setting our table?"

Flames from the wood stove reflected off the scarred spruce ta-bletop. She laid out burlap placemats and muslin cloth napkins and silverware on top, then watched as he lowered a filet of white king salmon on a bed of sour dock, a tart rhubarb-like green that grew, he said, in the tidal grasses. He covered the fish with dulse, a seaweed the color of dried blood, wrapped the package in green skunk cab-bage leaves, and slipped it into the wood stove.

While the fish steamed he lined up gumboots — chitons found on ocean-lashed rocks — flesh-side up, over a grate over coals. At the table, he demonstrated how to remove the eight shields of armor along their back sides, then scooped out the orange gonads with a finger before setting them on a shred of dried seaweed. She hesitated for a moment, then took the food. The meat tasted sweet, like lob-ster, with a burnt salty scent.

"*Ka-ta-rina ru-sti-cana*," she chanted, the Latin name he had taught her for gumboots.

"That's right," he said. "What a spectacular memory you have."

Billows of steam released as he unwrapped the singed skunk cabbage. He was right: the good food reassured her, set her at ease. They ate the mushrooms and limpets and fish with their hands, blowing on the flakes of salmon to cool them. Bleary-eyed from the food, Tara stretched out by the fire, alongside the cat, who blinked its good eye at her. Betteryear slipped on glasses, lenses smudged so badly they barely reflected the flames. He pulled a book from the shelf.

"Do you know," he said, arranging a tallow candle on the table beside him, "that there exists, in Tlingit mythology, a curly-haired woman named Lenaxxidaq? During the new moon, at low tide, she gathers mussels, then leaves them for the poor."

She found it hard to picture a Native woman with hair like hers. "Really?"

He peered over his glasses. "Each household she visits, she brings happiness and prosperity."

She shifted away from the heat of the stove. "Whoever wrote that definitely didn't have me in mind."

"Perhaps not," he said, shutting the book. "But it is a sign that you were meant to be here, in this cabin, at this very moment."

He set a lamp on the floor and lowered himself in front of her. The cat rose, arching its back, and walked over to the bed in the corner, glancing at Tara before hopping up on the quilt. She turned on her side, put an arm out, and rested her head on it, watching him. Lamplight threw his eyes and mouth into shadow. "You look so sad, Tara."

The panes rattled against the wind. When she allowed her eyes to close flames danced on the backs of her lids. For a moment she felt light, free, removed from her own body. Her awareness thinned, and soon she was asleep.

43

THE FRIDAY before the holiday it snowed. Flakes white as the underbellies of salmon sifted down. A high-pressure system with a northwesterly followed on Sunday, bringing blue sky and a biting cold. Ravens hopped on the crust of snow, black-purple feathers varnished by the sunlight. Squirrels flitted along the tree branches, chattering away.

When Betteryear said there wasn't enough snow to hunt, she asked if he wanted to go to the Muskeg to hear bluegrass instead. He grew tense in public, she noticed, lost his grace, walking through doors first, rarely looking anyone in the eye. But she felt good beside him, protected by the breadth of his knowledge. She liked how slowly his eyelids worked, his long fingers as they tugged a salmonberry from its stem. How he rode his French bicycle everywhere, coasting the last twenty yards before stopping, just one foot on the pedal. How he pronounced words with clipped vowels. His patched workman's cap, like Big Vic and some of the old Italian men wore back at the social club.

They sat for a bit in the Muskeg, drinking coffee and listening to music. He flipped the corner of his paper down and announced he wanted to take care of a couple chores back at the cabin.

"Would you like company?"

"Of course."

Outside he blinked in the sun as they loaded into his pickup.

"You have plans for turkey day?" she asked.

"Probably the big potluck at the Alaska Native Brotherhood, along with the rest of the island."

She flipped up the collar of her coat, her breath coming out in ragged clouds. Fritz and Fran had no way of getting in touch with her. She wasn't even sure she wanted to return to their house, although she'd get to see Keta.

Betteryear started the truck. When she tried to shut the door it wouldn't close. He said something over the engine. When she slammed the door harder Betteryear hollered. "Look!"

She jumped. "Jesus, settle the fuck down," she said.

"I don't enjoy repeating myself."

She saw that the corner of the saddle blanket covering the bench seat was caught. She pulled it up. "Just don't shout at me."

He rested a hand on her leg. "I'm sorry, Tara. I—I don't know."

Her good mood was broken. "Take me to the woods, please."

They drove in silence. When they reached the trailhead she sat in the truck for a couple minutes, listening to the engine. Betteryear did not speak.

Finally, she got out, shut the door softly behind her, and started into the woods. A couple minutes later she heard the rumble of his engine as he pulled away.

44

ON THANKSGIVING, Thomas, Newt, and Tara heaped salmon dip, whale meat, roasted seal half-covered in tin foil, smoked ham, and butter-soaked stuffing onto doubled-up paper plates. The heavy clouds had returned, bringing the metallic scent of a more serious snow.

When she scanned the room she saw Betteryear, sitting alone. She waved. He gave a half-nod, wiped his lips. "Seal tastes just about as rubbery as it looks," Newt said, making his way down the table of food. He sniffed a chunk of whale. He was leaving on the tender the following day to do cukes, and had announced his intention of stuffing himself before the trip. "We gonna sit with your buddy?"

Across the room she saw Betteryear start to stand.

"Hold my plate," Tara said, breaking out of line. "I'll be right back."

When she reached him she wished him a happy Thanksgiving. He blinked. "A happy Thanksgiving would have been if white people had gone back to England after we fed them. It disgusts me. All of it. This whole island."

Lifting his tray, he began to walk toward the kitchen.

"What's going on?" she asked, following him.

"They're starting construction along the road through our graveyard."

"I'm sorry," she said.

"It's not you, Tara," he said, worrying his thin lips. "I need to leave this place."

She watched his back, then returned to where Newt and Thomas were sitting. "Here. I got you filled up," Newt said, tearing a bun apart.

Thomas, unscrewing the lid of the salt shaker to dust his food, examined Tara. "Does your Indian friend take you hunting?" he asked.

"Yeah," she said, studying him across the table. "Before the end of the season. He's waiting for a good snow."

"*Merde*," Thomas said, sawing into turkey. "You are so lucky. But don't you think it is strange that the Indian people celebrate this day. You know? He eats here with all the white people, and it is his land."

"Fuck you, Frenchy," Newt said, buttering his bun. "Don't ruin my meal with your bad thoughts. I need the sustenance. I swear, T, this chick Jackie on the *Adriatic* is gonna be the death of me. She hardly gives us time to eat. Thinks she's leading Pharaoh's own army out there."

"Like you said, we're made of the tough stuff, right?"

"Unlike my sturdy French turd over here, playing Davy Crockett with his *Frau* in the woods."

Thomas smiled back. "You are crazy, my friend. *Loco*."

After the meal Newt and Thomas said they were heading back to the clearing before the snow started. Tara wanted to check her postbox. Which was absurd, she knew, because she was the one who owed Connor a letter after that flimsy postcard. A longer letter, one she had been putting off writing.

Just before splitting up, Newt narrowed his eyes at her. "T, you know I'd fight tigers in the dark for you, right?"

"I know it."

"So don't get mad when I ask. You got your head on straight with that old guy?"

"Betteryear?"

"Yeah."

She considered. Even if he could be a pain in the ass, she liked spending time with him. And knowing she had a roof to sleep under, a warm fire to sit by, made a difference. Even if things did get strange.

"I know what I'm doing."

"T, you've got a lot of good qualities. But knowing what you're doing ain't one of them."

45

HALFWAY INTO THE FOLLOWING WEEK Trunk called her into his office.

"Good Thanksgiving?"

"Fine," she said. "Yours?"

"Great. My ex had the kids. Close the door," he ordered. She pulled a chair up to his desk. "I got good news and bad news."

"Lay it on me."

"Last night your buddy lost an eye."

Her head snapped up. "Newt?"

He nodded.

"What do you mean, he lost an eye?"

"He cut a line under tension. It came back at him and ruptured his eyeball. They bandaged it up, dropped him in Juneau. He'll be back on the Rock in a couple days."

"Oh my god," she said, feeling the onset of tears. She knew fishing was dangerous. But this? Just last Thursday they had shared that meal. Could he still work? Save for the Plume fund? "That bitch on the *Adriatic*," Tara murmured.

"She's been called a lot worse, trust me. And that leads me to the good news. Bailey's off to graze in greener pastures, he got a job on a herring crew. Which puts you next in line for the tender spot. Interested?"

"What about Newt?"

He stood up, and so did she. "Go pick him up from the airport, if you like. No doubt he could use the help. In the meantime, get yourself a crew license. Won't be for a long stretch, just two days to finish up the cuke season. If Jackie doesn't hate you maybe she'll give you a shot at salmon next spring. You ship out December sixth, a week from today. And hey." He looked hard at her. "You're a good hand. Don't let anyone tell you different."

Her chest warmed. "Thanks."

"I'm serious. Keep that in mind, no matter what that viper says."

46

NEWT MADE A JOKE OF IT at the airport, holding his arms out in front of him like Frankenstein as he emerged from the gate. Gauze covered the right side of his face. A sly, embarrassed grin worked over his lips.

"Greetings from a gimp," he said.

She hugged him, feeling the long, taut muscles of his back. "Damn, Newt. I'm so sorry."

"Ach, it's part of the business. Our numbers all come up sooner or later."

"Do you have bags?" she asked.

"Just broken ol' me."

On the ride back over the bridge she stole glances at his eye patch. Little Vic had broken a leg once on his Huffy bike. Connor had told her stories of tools falling from scaffolding and knocking workers unconscious. But nothing like this.

"Truth was, I hardly felt it," Newt said. "Darn thing snapped back so fast. I was down in the hold cutting loose a brailer bag of cukes and bang! 'Cept now I get these goddamn headaches that are like to blow the cap of my brain off." He grimaced. "And I gotta figure out a way to make money." Immediately she felt bad for accepting work on the tender. "Fuck it," he said. "I'm not going back into those woods just yet. I don't give a flying shit about that bitch of a bartender. Let's go to the Front."

But when they walked into the Frontier, Cassie brought out her bat. "Dude just lost an eye on a boat, give him a beer," a fishermen at the bar pleaded.

"I don't care if he lost his left testicle to a ling cod. I'll call the police. Like the judge said, you stay the hell outta my bar."

Tara expected Newt to fire back, but he just turned around, head hung. They picked up a suitcase of Rainiers and headed out to the clearing, which appeared abandoned, save for quiet voices coming from behind Frauke's canvas. Tara made a fire, and they sat drinking.

"Who knows," Newt said. "Maybe that bitch'll hate Bailey more than me."

Tara crushed a can beneath the heel of her boot. "Trunk asked me to go," she said. Newt looked up. "He said Bailey got a spot on a seiner."

"No shit." He picked up a hatchet and balanced a piece of cedar on the stump. "Well, at least we're keeping it in the family, right? Maybe that old she-devil will be sweet seein' as how you've got a vagina."

"I'm sorry," Tara said. "Should I have said no?"

"Quit that. If I was you I'd run through my knots. Fuck if I can't hardly chop wood," he said, throwing aside the hatchet and sprawling by the fire. "Can't quit this headache either. Damn noggin's about to crack open."

"You want tea?" she asked, setting the kettle on the grate.

"Hell no. This Vitamin R does me right. Truth be told, I'd rather be back in that Juneau hospital with a broken back and colon cancer than do another tour with that wack-job. Oh — almost forgot to say it. You hear word on the tug?"

"I haven't heard anything."

"We saw it being towed back north. Laney was out there drinking wine with a couple that looked like they walked straight outta the Patagonia catalogue. For my money they're back tied up on the transient at this very moment."

"Wait," she said, her heart pounding. "The *Chief*'s back? You're sure."

"Hard to mix up that vessel with anything else."

The water started to boil. She fetched a mug from the platform. When she came back Newt was already snoring, beer in one hand about to tip. She set the can aside, draped a blanket over his legs, added wood to the fire, and watched as the flames caught, hoping it was true.

47

DECEMBER SIXTH—a cloudless, wind-scoured Sunday, the temperature hovering just above freezing. With the collar of her halibut coat up, she marched out to the docks. No one answered her knock on the *Chief.* She left a note for Laney: *Please find me.*

When she arrived at the processor to meet the *Adriatic,* Trunk came out of his office.

"Someone on the phone for you," he said.

She assumed it was Laney, calling to say the boat was still for sale. *Please,* she thought. *Please let it be.*

"Hello?"

"*Figlia?*"

Her legs went gummy. She heard the click of his espresso saucer as he ashed his cigar. "You are occupied?"

"No," she said. "It's fine. Is everything okay?"

"Yes, yes, everything is fine. Connor told me this is where you work. And—I received your letter in the mail."

He cleared his throat. There was a tentativeness in his voice she hadn't heard before.

"The man I spoke with said you were about to go on a boat. Is this true?"

She felt Trunk's eyes against her back. *Go away,* she thought.

"It is. For a couple days."

"Like your mother's father in Sicily."

Even when she had been alive Urbano rarely spoke about her mother's past. And since her death he hadn't talked about her at all.

Trunk waved a hand in front of her face. "Tara. It's go-time."

Fuck the tender, she thought.

"There is something I need to talk to you about, *figlia*."

"What?"

"It is something serious. Do your work, then call me when you return."

And he hung up.

"That your old man?" Trunk asked as she set down the receiver. She ignored him, pushed past, and went onto the dock to allow her mind to turn over. It made no sense that he had searched her down at the processor, figured out when she would be arriving. And what could he want to talk to her about?

She dropped her duffel on the dock and waited. Beneath her was the *Adriatic,* a cement-decked boat with a castle on the stern. Did it have to do with her hanging up on him? He was angry. Maybe he wanted to formalize their split. Put it in writing. Make the disowning permanent.

A compact, muscular woman walked over, reaching back to re-knot a blue handkerchief over her blond bob.

"You lost?" she asked. The wind made it difficult to hear.

"No, just waiting to get on the boat."

The woman looked toward the processor. "Trunk said they were sending a dude."

So this was Jackie. "Guess not. He's in his office if you wanna ask him."

Gulls screeched, fighting over fish waste. Jackie paused. "You green?" she asked.

"Green?"

"Yeah, green. As in a greenhorn. *Cheechako.* I just had someone lose an eye doing something very dumb, so I'm not in the mood to have beginners on my boat."

"That was my friend. We worked in the cannery together."

"This isn't a *cannery,* it's a seafood processor. So I'll take that as a 'Yes, Jackie, I'm green.' Where did you grow up?"

It was the woman's tone that made Tara cant her left shoulder forward, drift her weight onto the ball of her right foot, and prepare to drop this obnoxious woman who had driven Newt so hard. Loose strands of hair blew around the woman's eyes. Tara reshouldered her duffel, pulled her hat low. This was about the last thing she needed.

When she started to walk away the woman gripped her shoulder. "Keep your fucking hands off me," Tara spit.

"Okay, okay. God, you're strung tight. Better than being some hippie. Go on, throw that bag and bibs on deck."

Without waiting for an answer, Jackie slid down the steel ladder onto the boat. Tara watched from above.

"C'mon!" Jackie shouted. "Now or never. We're pulling out."

After hesitating, she tossed her duffel, followed by her bibs, which landed with a slap on the concrete deck.

Inside the galley Jackie poured herself a cup of coffee, then handed one to Tara. "I gotta say, I liked the look in your eyes out there. You got fire in your belly."

Her anger evaporated as she looked around. There was a small wooden dish rack beside the stainless-steel sink, a gas stove with a griddle scoured clean, and a Hoosier cabinet filled with jars of smoked and pickled salmon and string beans. Striped linen kitchen cloths hung above the sink. After so much walking around in the harbor, dreaming about life on the tug, here she was, finally on a boat.

The hull shuddered as the engines fired. "Cut her loose, my bride!" a voice yelled. They both went out on deck. Jackie introduced Tara to Teague, her husband, who had a white goatee and wore ripped fleece pants. "You know how to remove line from a cleat?" he asked.

"Yeah."

Husband and wife watched as Tara dragged the braided rope through the water, coiling it like a snail's shell as she had seen others do. Her heart rate only slowed when Jackie flipped a thumbs-up.

Black exhaust rose from the stacks as they steamed down the channel beneath a clear sky. She stood by the gunwales, looking back toward town, like the deckhands she had watched so many times leaving the processor.

The forests and mountains that had appeared so threatening when she first arrived now insulated her, and the seven miles of road on either side of town that before had felt so constricting now were just long enough — she couldn't imagine ever being stuck in a traffic jam on the expressway, in the shadow of a tractor-trailer, again. As for her father, she knew he was waiting for her call. So it went. She'd call, when she was good and ready.

As they approached the outer harbor she saw the *Pacific Chief* tied up at the corner. The boat looked lonely, its anchor hanging down like an elephant tear. And there, on deck in her Adirondack chair, Laney, red shawl blowing in the wind.

"Hey!" Tara yelled across the water, waving with both hands. "What happened?"

"We got as far as Petersburg!" Laney shouted back.

She cupped her hands around her lips. "Is it still for sale?"

"Twenty-five!" Laney returned.

I don't care if the galley leaks, she thought. *That's my boat.*

48

LIFE ON THE TENDER WAS INTIMATE, self-contained. Seldom, except when she was in her small bunk, was she alone. There were always eyes on her, making sure she worked, and worked quickly. Teague wasn't bad, just flirtatious in a jokey, harmless manner, even as he told Tara about his wife, how she had grown up in the bush, homeschooled until third grade, walking seven miles to town and back.

"Her and her brother could either take a dog or a gun with them for bear," he said, shaking his head. "She was eighteen when she learned a toilet flushed. Imagine that."

Teague anchored in a bay near where the divers worked, red flags raised high, yellow hose coiling around the boat as they walked the ocean floor for sea cucumbers. He got on the VHF to advertise the price per pound, encouraging folks to unload with the *Adriatic*. As the first boat motored toward them, Tara watched Jackie, her rosy windblown face, blue handkerchief holding back her blond hair. The woman had bony, birdlike shoulders, and wore a wool sweater with frayed cuffs and a darned collar. There was an invincible quality to her, Tara decided, an air of the Viking out to plunder.

"Ready? Boat coming in, starboard side. Tie her off," the woman said as they went out on deck. She spoke in a tone that wasn't mean, but it didn't leave room for nice, either. Oblivious to her beauty, which would have turned heads in the Italian Market.

"You got a fender you can throw down?" the diver called up. He still had his hood on.

"A what?" Tara asked. He looked at her like she was stupid.

"A fender! A buoy ball."

Jackie came from behind and tossed one overboard. "C'mere. Now watch. If we do salmon it'll be more of the same. We open the hold, hook up brailer bags to the lift, twirl a finger in the air to signal Teague, and up she comes. *Si?*"

After lowering herself into the hold, Jackie gave a whistle. The hydraulics moaned as the bag swung above the deck, oozing pink slime from the sea cucumbers, nubby creatures that resembled giant caterpillars. Jackie handed the line attached to the bottom of the bag — the "tag line," she called it — to Tara, and she did her best to hold the sack steady as Teague read off numbers from a glow-in-the-dark LED scale. "Good," the woman said. "About twenty more like that."

As night came on it began to rain. The tips of her curls sticking out from her hood dripped water down her neck. Teague switched on the deck lights, flooding the deck in white. They kept at it until almost six A.M., waiting for the last boat to clean cukes and unload, and still no hint of sun. When Tara began to unbutton her raingear Jackie shook her head. "Not yet, *señorita*. Need you to check levels on each of the totes, send hoses into the ones that are fullest, make sure they've got seawater to keep them fresh. Yes?"

Her hands and face were covered in cucumber slime. She just wanted to crawl into her bunk, not bother with showering. "No problem," Tara said.

"Listen, girlfriend. You stick with me, you'll be tying knots quicker and pulling line harder than men twice your size. Yeah?" She clapped a hand on Tara's shoulder, giving a squeeze. "Doesn't get much easier than this. Trust me."

"Thank you for giving me the shot." But the woman was already on her way to the wheelhouse, removing her gear.

That night, brushing her teeth in the head, she thought about Jackie, growing up in her homestead with her brother, deciding between the dog and the gun. She wondered whether it might be possible to become like her one day, working so furiously, barking orders. With her toothbrush extending from one side of her mouth, she hardened her face, like she had seen her father do. Men respected Jackie, it seemed, were even afraid of her at times, handing over their permit card without any argument over weights. She'd love to see the small woman give her father hell. He wouldn't know how to handle her.

She spit in the miniature porcelain sink, washed it down. Tending bar, slinging coffee, or gaffing fish, women in Alaska carried themselves differently from women down south. As if each one of them had passed through a ring of fire before coming out the other side, flame-tested and hardened. The slag of the past burned off, cooling in the salt air, charting their own course.

49

WHEN THE *Adriatic* returned to port she went straight to the *Chief* to get the story on the tug. A plank had popped on the way south, Laney told her. They diverted to Petersburg, where the boat was hauled out on a railroad winch. The ordeal convinced the cellists that the boat, in the end, wasn't suitable for a music camp.

"Fairweather San Franciscans," Laney said. "I'd include myself in that group," she added.

They were sitting at the galley table, drinking wine. "So you still interested in the boat?"

"I am."

"And you know you need to get the engine running, otherwise the harbormaster sinks her."

"I understand. I'm reading up on it."

At the bank she deposited a pile of cash. This gave her twelve thousand, including payment from the tender. Then she went to the coffee shop and selected a card of a totem pole in the woods.

December 21, 1998

Dear Connor,

Just as she began to write, a shadow fell over the page. Betteryear stood above her, a mug of tea in one hand. Without asking, he slid into the bench beside her.

"You know," he said, slipping on his glasses, pointing at the card. "This is a Tlingit funeral pole. Here" — he tapped with a long finger — "in back of the carved raven is a hole for the ashes."

She was in no mood for this.

"There's something wrong, Tara. I can see it in your face."

She sighed. "I just want to get this off."

"Are you writing to your father?" he asked.

"No. A friend."

"From where?"

"Home," she said.

"Home?"

"From Philly."

"What does 'home' mean to you, Tara?"

She did not want to have some philosophic conversation. She wanted him to go away.

"I'll leave you alone, Tara. I'm so sorry for interrupting your thoughts."

When he finally left, she scrawled on the front, just beneath the totem pole.

I'm lonely. I love you. I'm sorry. I wish you could come here. It would be so much easier if we could touch. I need to tell you something. To just write it.

She stared at her handwriting. It looked like graffiti, barely legible. After a minute she ripped up the card, dumped it out with her coffee, and started the long walk back to the clearing.

50

ON THE TWENTY-THIRD, she pulled herself out of her sleeping bag. Newt bought beers and told her to meet him at the channel marker. On impulse she swung by Fritz and Fran's to see if Keta was there. At first the dog seemed to ignore her, hardly looking up as she pet him. Then she knelt and whispered in his ear.

"Hi, sweet you," she said. "I'm so glad you didn't leave with those people. I thought you might have forgotten about me."

When he didn't move she turned his head toward her, pressed her forehead against his skull, and stared into the dog's unblinking eyes. *Funny, I was thinking the same thing*, the dog seemed to say back. She switched tacks. "Hey, monkey. I'm sorry. I've been busy. Okay? But I'm here now. I promise I won't abandon you. My resolution for the year."

After a few seconds he freed his head, gave her a quick look, then trotted out in front. When they got to the breakwater, he wouldn't go out on the rocks until she was there beside him, her fingers trailing along his back.

"Dog likes you," Newt said as Keta picked his way among the boulders. "See how he keeps making sure you're okay?"

When they were arranged in their usual spots, Tara leaned against a steel post, calmed by the rhythmic flashing of the light, Newt handed her a beer. Keta sat on his haunches, the sun reflecting gold off his white fur. Clouds swam like fish across the sky.

"Any word from Plume?" Tara asked.

He looked up at her, veins blue beneath his pale skin. "Not a word."

A whale exhaled toward the end of the landing strip at the airport. Keta watched the white funnel of mist come apart in the breeze.

"You know, my old man called me at the processor, just before I went out with Jackie."

"That right?"

"He said there was something he wanted to talk about."

They drank, watching the clouds for a couple minutes. "What's he like, your dad?" Newt asked.

She stroked Keta's silky head. "You know, today was the day she died."

Newt said nothing. She felt her stomach heave, then took a breath.

"Right before I left, like six months after my mother was killed, I'm coming back up the stairs late at night, sandwich in one hand. And there he is, favorite mustard cardigan tucked into his sweatpants. I'm standing there holding my cheese sandwich. He asks me something, like if I was planning to start giving him a hand at the bakery anytime soon. I must have looked down for a second, because then I hear this crack, and he's got his fist through the plaster, hollering that it was my fault my mother died, that I never lifted a finger around the house, that all I did anyway was watch TV and eat his food. Spoiled good-for-nothing brat, that's what he called me." She swallowed. "I told him he could go fuck himself, ran out of the house in my pajamas, then spent three months at Connor's. That's when I called Acuzio, who got me the job with Fritz."

Keta whined softly. She was petting him too hard. The breeze blowing through the hemlocks along the coast made a brushing sound.

"Well, all I can tell you is —"

"I know, Newt. Do what you can, and let the rough end drag."

"Well, that too," he said. "But I was gonna say he sounds like a prick. Maybe he's calling with his tail between his legs."

Tara shook her head. "Urbano Marconi doesn't do tail between his legs."

"Well, then here's another one. We're put on this green earth to learn to love honestly and cleanly. Simple as that."

"So?"

"So we're all tumbling around in the Alaskan laundry out here. If you do it right you get all that dirt washed out, then turn around and start making peace with the other shit. Maybe even make a few friends along the way." He winked at her.

"I'm trying," she said.

"I know you are," he said seriously. He stood and slap-boxed on the rocks with Keta, who bared his teeth and growled. "It's pretty damn obvious."

51

AT THE BEGINNING OF JANUARY the Alaskan Travelers filed out
of the woods in a ragged procession, responding to whatever mag-
netism drew them hither and yon. With their sleep rolls and scav-
enged bones and unused cans of bear spray lashed to their backs,
fishing rods broken down, blanks rubber-banded together. A mam-
moth tooth hung around a neck with dental floss, a new tattoo of
the state on the underside of a wrist. Then it was just Newt, Thomas,
Tara, and Frauke.

It snowed. One afternoon, walking in the half-light back home
from work, she found Betteryear mounting his bicycle in front of the
Muskeg. They chatted for a few minutes.

"You said you wanted to learn to hunt — now is the time. Yes?"

Even if he made her uncomfortable, this was something she felt
she needed to do. The season closed at the end of the month.

"Yes. I'd like that."

They drove in his pickup to the shooting range at the end of the
road. He showed her how to brace the stock of the rifle in the notch
of her shoulder, breathe in, exhale, squeeze the trigger at the bottom
of the breath. The gun lurched, the sound echoing against the mountainside. Betteryear looked down-range at the target with binoculars.

"You're up and to the left," he said. "Which means you're squeezing the trigger too hard, pulling it."

"The barrel's bent," she said.

Betteryear squinted. The snow made everything bright. He walked the length of the range, at least a football field, and set up a can. "Let me see," he said when he came back. He lined up on the stand, closed one eye, and pulled the trigger. The can hopped, making a tinny noise as it fell to the gravel.

"Not bent that much," he said.

"Wow. Kickass," she said, genuinely impressed. She had been shooting from twenty-five.

They spent another couple hours at the range. By the end she was hitting the can at fifty yards as often as she missed it. But Betteryear still wasn't pleased.

"You're distracted," he finally said, picking brass shells from the gravel. "I don't hunt with people who do not have a clear head. It's supposed to snow again in a couple days. We'll go then."

That night she crossed the river in the rain and started up the trail, cursing the old man and her whole situation. She had been dreading zipping into her damp sleeping bag, how clothes piled at her feet constricted her legs as she slept. The incessant chatter of the river grated on her ears.

When she climbed the hill she saw Frauke moping around the edge of the clearing, the woman's skull visible in the rain beneath her wet blond strands.

"What's wrong with her?" Tara asked Newt.

"Brown bear ate her dog," he said, settling beside the fire.

"What?"

"The two of them were out Red Lake Road, came upon a sleepy sow. Ripped the dog open like a sardine can, apparently. Frauky-kins covered herself with the bike frame to save her own skin."

Tara looked across the clearing. The woman was picking notes from her pouch, mouthing the words, then putting them in her mouth and chewing. Newt lifted his eye patch and swiped a finger.

"Don't scratch at that," Tara said.

"You call your old man?" he asked.

"Nope."

He nodded slowly, then rose and headed to the platform. "Don't be so stubborn. Or, be stubborn when it comes to the tug. Not with these things."

As she went to sleep that night she got that lightheaded, thin sensation of dread that came right before she did something difficult. Although not as bad, and not as deep as she had felt it before.

Her friend was right. It had been a month. Tomorrow she'd make the call.

52

THE NEXT MORNING she woke in the dark, dressed without making a fire, then picked her way along the trail. She walked quickly beneath the lights of Papermill Road. Huddled against the cold, the ocean a black sheet in the dark, she dialed Wolf Street from the library payphones.

"Hi," she said, confused when a woman answered. "Is Urbano there?"

"I think he is sleeping," the woman said in accented English.

It was almost nine in Port Anna, which would mean one in the afternoon in Philly.

"Who is this?" Tara asked.

"It is Eva. Tara?"

"That's right."

"Oh. Yes. Please wait." Static. Bizarre that Eva, with her grim lips and that flowered apron with the red fringe, who had been mopping tiles at the bakery when Tara left, was now answering the house phone.

Her father came on, huffing. "*Figlia*. I have been waiting to hear from you. You're back on land."

"Yes. I am."

Silence. "How are you?" he finally asked.

She flipped her hood over her head to better hear him. "Fine. How are you?"

He gave a small laugh. "I'm sixty-two now, and my belly grows.

Your mother and I shouldn't have waited so long to have you. Did you celebrate Christmas?"

She had expected him to be angry she hadn't called sooner. And Christmas — it was always her mother's job to bring up cardboard boxes of ornaments from the basement, wrap gifts decorated with twine and twigs from the maple tree outside, and, of course, do the lights. It surprised her he would bring this up.

She couldn't take it anymore. "Pop, was there something you wanted to talk to me about?"

His voice grew even. "*Figlia,* I must ask you something." He took a breath. She swallowed, a shiver moving up her spine. "Since you left town, I've talked to people. To Vic. He said something happened to you."

And she knew.

It was as if winter accelerated through her body: leaves dropping, pond icing over. Such shame.

She took a breath. *If you're going to say it,* she thought, *say it.*

"Is what Little Vic told his father true?" he asked.

She never thought she'd have to do this. Bile rose in her throat. "I don't know what you're talking about."

An edge moved into his voice. "Don't lie to me, Tara."

She exhaled to a slow count in her head, trying to remember that feeling of not being angry. "I've got to go, Pop."

"Tara, you tell me what happened. As your father I have a right to —"

"I really need to go, Pop. I have stuff to do."

"Do not leave me, Tara."

And she hung up.

It was almost dark by the time she climbed the hill to the clearing. Thomas was busy pumping the knob on a red gas canister, trying to start a camp stove. Newt's voice floated out from somewhere between the trees. "Need to prime it first, goof."

As she approached the platform, she smelled gas.

"What's up?" Thomas asked, taking a lighter from his ripped Carhartts and drawing up flame. Frauke kneeled beside him, watching the stove vacantly.

"Did you leak in the bowl, dumbass?" Newt shouted, stepping into the clearing. "If you didn't prime the goddamn —"

It was as if someone had switched on a floodlight. Frauke tumbled off the platform, slapping at her cargo pants. Thomas seized the pot of *glogg* he had been preparing and tossed it over the flames, which just roared higher. Fire clawed up the near wall, tarps melting in great yawns.

"You are one true fucking idiot," Newt shouted, running toward them. Tara dragged her duffel from the platform, then tried to grab her sleeping bag, but it was already melting, the heat seeming to shrink the interior fabric. They used five-gallon buckets to douse the planks with water from the river until the wood was charred and steaming, the wool blankets ashed, their home destroyed.

She started to walk away. "Hey!" Newt shouted, breathing heavily. "Where you going?"

"I don't know," she sighed. She waved a hand over her head. "Away."

She could hear his voice at her back, but the river drowned him out.

As she walked out of the woods, and up the hill toward Betteryear's cabin, her father's question played over and over in her head. *Is what Little Vic told his father true?*

In the end, she decided, the only person who really needed to know the truth was Connor.

It was time to write the letter.

53

Dear Connor,

   I had a phone conversation with my father that didn't end well. I don't know what people in the neighborhood are saying. But it's time you know something. I'm sorry it took me so long to do this.

   Do you remember my 16th birthday when you had tickets for us to go see a play? "The Lovers" I think it was called. I ended up asking if we could do it some other time, some weak excuse. That night, March 18th, Friday, my birthday, I went out with these girls I met at the roller rink up in the northeast.

   First off, as you know, I never really had girlfriends at St. Vincent's. (My mom kind of played that role, I spent so much time at the bakery.) So when this one older chick asked if I wanted to go out, I was all nervous. She could drive, and said she'd come by my house to take me out. I had on this miniskirt and remember looking in the mirror, thinking it was cool. Adult. Putting on purple eyeliner like I had seen the girls wear. Of course when I came down the stairs Ma said no chance in hell, and sent me right back. So I found a skirt I could fold up and shorten when I got out of the house, and put the eyeliner and lipstick in my purse. Did my hair, then heard a honk.

   I remember Ma holding the storm door open as I climbed in that Pontiac blocking traffic on Wolf. Already I could hear *her in the morning. "Che cazzo fare with these cozze" — "the fuck are you doing with these ugly girls?" The back of that car smelled of car freshener. Zooming along Delaware Avenue out of the gravity of South Philly felt amazing. (Maybe it's how you felt after writing that letter to me. Like you were escaping some weight.) We drove under the El into Kensington, a neighborhood my father always said was forbidden. We pulled up to this building with a bass so heavy it made the windows of the car rattle. I remember half of me hoped the bouncer wouldn't let us in. But when we reached the front of the line, he just waved us through.*

Inside it was the exact opposite of all those corny St. Vincent's dances, you know where the nuns came around with a ruler and told us to leave room for the Holy Spirit? Of course I tried to act all grown up, nodding my head to the music. When I opened my eyes this guy in a rugby shirt was asking me if I wanted a drink. I said no. "Take a bump from the stump," he shouts, and shows me this mound of white on the back of his hand. I looked around for Christina. "Go on," he says. What the hell, I thought, leaning over, sniffing. Immediately the world grew sharper, like my fingers were electrified. The guy said he wanted to go for a ride. I found my friend, making out with some dude in the corner, and told her I'd be right back.

You remember our senior year the time we drove to the shore, to Runnemede and took a blanket onto the pitcher's mound of that diamond? And I said I didn't want to take the Ben Franklin Bridge over the Delaware? Well, this is why — it reminds me of being in his BMW convertible. At first it was cool, watching the buildings grow small in the mirror. I had this soapy drip in my throat, my nose burned, the world seemed to be coming on so fast. He wore some sort of braided necklace and tapped the top of the gearshift to music I couldn't hear. His

*wrists made him look like he was on the wrestling team — I tell
you this to try and explain. I remember him resting a hand on
my thigh, and then I put my palm out and let it dip and rise
with the wind. I remember thinking of you back on Manton
Street, reading a play on the couch, or working on some stage
set. "I'm taking you to Avalon," the guy yelled. "My parents have
a house there." And that's when I started to freak out. I say I
have a curfew and we should turn around, and he tells me to
relax. And then my mind splits into like ten different interior
screens, and I'm looking at them all at once. I can't figure out
which to focus on. My body numb, like I'm slowly spilling out
of myself. There in front of my eyes I see everyone I love — my
mother, my father, Big Vic, my Nonna, Grandpa Joe. And you.*

*When we park the lifeboats pulled up on the sand are famil-
iar. He takes my hand. Wind shifts the grass sideways. Rush
of the waves, and the crash. It was a beach I had visited with
my mother — we had come here and she had told me about
Sicily, and how one day I would visit the island. "These people
will welcome you as family," she told me. And this — it sounds
awful, in light of what I am about to write — made me think of
you, wishing you were on that beach with me so I could tell you
about this time with my mother and her stories.*

*We had just about reached the waves when he starts kissing
me like he can't wait another second. He puts my hand on him.
When I push back he tackles me, pinning my shoulders. Clamps
a hand over my mouth. I scratch at his necklace and he shoves
me down. I mean, strong. And then I'm looking up at the purple
sky, the jerk and grind in the sand. Awful.*

*Why didn't I tell anyone? Here's why. The next morning,
when I went into the bathroom I see a splotch on my neck. It
hurt to walk. My mother called for me to come downstairs. I
knew they were both waiting in the parlor, my father in his*

corner on the couch. She would yell at me for staying out after curfew, and for hanging out with these girls. And he would just watch.

I found a penny. I had heard at school rubbing it on your skin would make a hickey go away. Just as I started the door opened. And there was Ma. She got this cloudy look on her face, then came back a few minutes later with spoons chilled in the freezer, ice, and peppermint oil. She shook drops over the splotch and kneaded them in with her fingers. There was a plasticky smell left in my nostrils, and the peppermint oil took care of that too. With her fingers she smoothed on makeup. I could swear as she worked her hands had this language of their own. She caught my eyes in the mirror. Put your words in order, Tara. These things happen to women. I know about it. We all know about it. This is what I thought she was telling me.

When she took her fingers from my neck, the spot had disappeared. We went downstairs. What a nice birthday it had been with my new friends, I told my father. We got lost in Jersey. But no, I will not be seeing those girls again. And because she was not angry, he wasn't either.

And that is what happened. What led to my father taking me to Gypo to learn to box — I think he was at a loss how to deal with a 16-year-old who stopped talking. And perhaps it led to this island where I am now.

I don't know what writing this will change. I'm not even sure I'll send it. I just know these words have been building inside me. And it's time you know.

Yours,
T

54

ON HER SECOND NIGHT AT HIS CABIN, as Betteryear predicted, it snowed, the beach and trees blanketed white.

"Would you like to hunt today?" he said over tea and berries. "You can bring your rifle."

She had told him about the burning platform, and stomping out of the woods like she did. It was a childish reaction, and she regretted it now. But she was done living in that clearing.

"Yes," she decided.

At the trailhead she adjusted the rifle on her shoulder. The letter had been sitting on a wooden soap crate that Betteryear had set up by her cot. Stamped and addressed, its white envelope giving off some faint nuclear glow. Now she had it in her duffel, in Betteryear's pickup.

Her boots squeaked in the snow as she followed behind him. This was nice, enjoying the brief hours of daylight, behind this man, so quiet and intent on the trail. She liked the worn leather strap of the gun, the shift of the stock against her hip. After sitting for so long the day before, tearing that letter out of her, the movement felt good.

After an hour all they had seen were star-shaped mink prints. As she watched Betteryear's easy gait ahead of her, she worried her scrambled head was keeping the blacktail away. She willed herself to forget about the platform burning, the letter in the bag, even Betteryear's sharpness when the saddle blanket caught in the door. *Let it all go,* she told herself.

When he stopped in front of her, dropping to his knees, she almost ran into him. He drew a finger to his lips as she crouched by his side. "Look," he said, running the tip of his finger along the outline of a hoof in the snow. "See how it zigzags, how he drags his hooves." She examined the slot followed by a scrape, felt his warmth through her wool pants. "Doe move in a straight line, and their hooves are U-shaped, and don't have this split-toed look to them. This is a buck, what we're hunting for. Clean edges on the track. Fresh."

He rose and walked, slower now, heel-toeing. "If you see something," he whispered, "you tell me. I don't want you shooting that gun."

They gained elevation. Betteryear removed his glove and spread a palm in a bowl of melted snow. "Feel. This is where he bedded down. A couple minutes ago. He moved when he heard us." She did, detecting a vague heat.

Snow began to fall again, making a whisking sound as it sifted through the hemlock needles and fronds of yellow cedar. Their rubber boots squeaked. He shifted the rifle off his shoulder and cradled it in one arm. A movement caught the corner of her eye and she froze, looking off to the side. Just tree trunks, branches, snow. She was about to turn away when a peculiar geometry stopped her. The triangle of a leg, the line of a back, and the white fur of a neck — the shapes resolved into a deer, standing with its back to her, about fifty yards away. It hoofed the forest floor, dropped its head, and nosed away snow.

She hissed, then clicked her tongue. Betteryear turned, glaring. With her chin she motioned to the right. He twisted, raised his rifle to his shoulder, and leaned against a tree trunk. With a thumb he pushed forward the safety, a glint of red just behind the bolt. She shifted her body for a better view of the deer. A twig snapped. The cat lifted its head, ears aimed toward them. And it ran.

When the explosion came Tara yelped, clutching her ears. Betteryear pulled back the bolt, and the shell fell into the snow, sizzling before going quiet. The smell of cordite and scorched brass filled the air.

"You scared him," he said matter-of-factly. "Come. Let's see."

The deer lay on its side, purple tongue lolled out between grass-stained teeth. Blood leaked from the chest into the snow. A few feet beyond the body was what appeared to be a small animal convulsing.

"*Gunalchéesh*," he said. "Thank you, deer, for giving your life to us, so that we may continue to live."

She crouched beside him. "*Gunalchéesh*."

He took the ears in his fists, lifting the head. Ears that had responded to *her*, to a sound *she* had made just moments before. He held out a bone-handled knife. "Slice the neck."

"What? Isn't she dead?"

"It's a buck. And yes, the heart is in the snow over there."

She swallowed, looking over at the shape, which twitched a couple times, then went still. She had just watched a heart stop. A life gone. A halo of red-tinged slush grew around the muscle, and she felt a sadness for this creature that had looked across the woods at her. At that moment her anger at her father seemed so small.

She dropped to her knees and began to saw.

"You must apply pressure," Betteryear instructed. "When males rut their necks grow thick."

She pressed harder. Downy fluff drifted across the snow. A jet of blood splattered her wool coat, tapered to a drizzle, and began to bead on the waxy fur. "That was an artery," he told her. "Keep going. The windpipe and esophagus come next."

She gripped the deer by the back of the neck and sliced until the ribbed tube of the trachea split. Betteryear took cloth bags from his backpack and dragged the deer over to a mound of moss.

"Stand behind here and help."

She held the ankles as he swiped off the scent glands on the hind legs, then made an incision along the stomach, turning his knife and dragging the gut hook, revealing the gray bulge of intestines. A musty, coffee-ground scent filled the air. The stomach slid out with a squelch, followed by ropey intestines. He went in again with the knife, making a circle, carving out the diaphragm.

The stench of fish that first day had been awful, a brown sea rot. But this was something else entirely. And the purple-green glop of it — this could very well be her stomach on the forest floor, her guts spilled into the snow, the stench of her empty cavity filling the air.

"Come. Give me your hands," he told her. She lowered to her knees. "Both of them."

She crouched closer, up to her elbows inside the deer as he guided her palms into the warmth of the chest, the cuffs of her coat brushing ribs. She focused on the tree trunks in front of her.

"There," he said as her hand moved over what felt like a mound of hardened Jell-O. "Close your fingers. Pull."

She coaxed out the liver, wine-red and floppy in her hand.

"And now the heart, which I've already done for you."

It was warm, a fist that fit into her palm. The snow around it had melted, and the bullet had shredded the ventricles. Jellied blood, the purple of grapes, clotted the valves. A muscle like this, just slightly larger, had quickened the other night when she hung up on her father. Had hammered in Avalon as that boy had done what he did. And would hammer again when she put the letter in the mail.

Betteryear took the heart from her, peeled back a membrane, and sliced with his knife where the flesh came to a rounded point. He held the flat of his blade out to her.

"Eat," he said.

"You're kidding."

"Trust me. Your body is repulsed by what you're seeing. But once you eat, your stomach will grow calm again."

Closing her eyes, she chewed, the rich taste spreading to the sides of her tongue. When she swallowed she gagged, then swallowed harder, determined.

"Good, Tara. Remember this," he said. "Our first blacktail. The next one will be yours to shoot."

He went back in, pulling out the lungs and the rest of the multicolored innards. He cracked the pelvic bone, removed the milk-white tangle of scrotum and penis. The blood in the snow reminded her of cherry water ice at John's. Pebble-shaped droppings leaked out of the anus. He sliced around each hoof, and pulled the hide off with a rasping sound. From either side of the spine he carved the backstrap, two stoles of meat, then nicked out webbing between the ribs, dropping the shreds into a plastic bag.

"We'll soak that and make jerky."

They flipped the deer. With the tip of his knife he took the tenderloins from the backside. She held the legs wide as he arced the knife around muscle, carving away hindquarters, loosening the plate of a shoulder, which slid easily off the rib cage, then dropped them into the cloth bags she held open.

"Have you ever tasted tongue?" he asked. She shook her head. "Hold this. Pull."

She felt the grit of taste buds against her fingers as she gripped the tongue. He maneuvered the blade of the knife between the chipped moss-colored teeth, prying the jaw open until it snapped. He dug at the root, tugging out the puce-colored muscle.

"Good boiled. Tender."

Her stomach had settled. They spent the next twenty minutes slicing out burger meat from the neck and hindquarters, then loaded the cotton bags, soaked through and distended, into his backpack.

"Must be a good seventy pounds of meat," he said, giving little hops to gauge the weight of the pack. He opened the chamber of the rifle, pushed in a round, threw the bolt, and flipped on the safety. "Are you comfortable pulling the trigger if we run into a bear?"

She brought her rifle to her shoulder, spotted through the scope, training the crosshairs on a tree trunk.

"Yes."

. . .

That evening, on the beach in front of the cabin, Betteryear clamped plywood to the sawhorses. He set the meat on the board and began carving from the forelegs and hindquarters, tossing scraps in a bowl for the table-mounted meat grinder. He showed her how to shave off globules of fat, pat the cuts dry, and separate them into piles. He ran an extension cord from his generator and plugged in a vacuum sealer, and they packaged the steaks, the warble of the sealer followed by a soft zip as the plastic heated. The burger grinder made a rhythmic squeaking sound as she turned the crank.

When she went inside with the bowls of packaged meat, she saw that he had washed her blood-splotched coat and hung it above the stove to dry. The orange cat splayed its body across the rug by the fire, turning at the hiss of droplets from the cuffs against the cast-iron, blinking its leaky eye. Betteryear dangled a cut of heart over the creature, who took the meat down in gulps.

He cooked the liver and heart with golden chanterelles on the single burner, boiled the tongue, setting it with a bowl on a muslin cloth in front of her. Carefully, she peeled off white skin, revealing the muscle beneath. Betteryear fried the backstrap in a buttered pan, poured huckleberry wine into a canning jar, and raised it toward her. "I give thanks for your good eyes," he said.

The words lit her up from the inside. Flushed with the compliment, she cut the meat carefully, using the same hunting knife she had used to sever the buck's neck, held a cube of heart on her fork, squeezing it between her teeth, letting the juice run over her gums. The backstrap was more like tuna than any sort of beef she had tasted.

"Oh my god," she murmured.

"Yes," he said. His eyes, a lazy black, were glazed with firelight. The muscles of his face, so taut over the course of the day, relaxed. He dabbed the sides of his lips with the cloth napkin, flipped the tines of his fork, and pointed toward her. "This is food from where you live, Tara. Do you know that?"

She looked across the table at him and found herself resting her hand on his. "Thank you."

He took her hand. Quickly she stood and began clearing the table. Then she remembered the letter in the duffel.

Tomorrow, she told herself. Tomorrow she'd send it.

55

AFTER DROPPING THE LETTER into the mailbox, the metal door echoing with finality, Tara used Betteryear's pickup to gather what remained of her things on the blackened and half-collapsed platform. There was the smell of gasoline and wine and wet ash as she packed jeans, a sweater, waterlogged and sooty, into a garbage bag. It started to rain, clouds crowding into the valley. She heard a sound and turned as Thomas stepped out of Frauke's tent in a T-shirt and boxers.

"Eh-oh," he said, waving, appearing sheepish as he turned to the platform.

"Hey. You seen Newt?" she said.

Thomas shrugged, sniffing and looking up into trees. "He is working. On a boat called the *Spank* or something."

"Cool."

In the long twilight she walked the harbor to the tug. She considered sneaking aboard through the engine room, making a fire, sure Laney wouldn't mind. But when she peeked in the porthole she saw buckets and tools crowding the floor. The place was a mess.

Back out at Betteryear's she dried her long underwear and gloves on the clothesline over the stove. The wind picked up from the southwest. Gray clouds shrouded the volcano. Betteryear hummed as he prepared a sweet-smelling soup with blue crabs and seaweed and limpets, king salmon wrapped in eelgrass and nori. Sitting by the wood stove, with a cup of hot tea in her hands, she felt a lightness in her shoulders. Warm, full, hypnotized by the promise of sleep, and good food to eat. She thought of the tug, alone out there on the corner, and felt as if she was failing the boat in some fundamental way.

In the predawn hours, she woke on the cot to what she thought was the silence after the rain. Moonlight filtered through the windows. Outside she could hear pebbles tumbling in the waves.

She smelled a grassy scent, then looked over to see Betteryear's smooth, unlined face gray in the moonlight. He was crouching by her cot.

"What the fuck?" she said, sitting up on her elbows, pulling the squares of the quilt over her chest.

"Sorry, sorry, I — I was just checking."

"Checking what?"

He shook his head and stood. She could see the whites of his eyes. Stiff-legged, he crossed the room to his corner. "Sorry," he said again. "Just checking to make sure you are safe."

56

Dear Tara,

My god. Where to begin.

First off let me just say—I am so sorry.

Then unequivocally: thank you. Thank you for caring enough about me (is this a selfish thing to say?) to travel back to this. As I read I began to cry. With relief? Sorrow? It's so hard to say. I think some part of me had been waiting to hear these words.

I wish you felt you could have told me. Part of me is angry that you didn't but maybe that's for me to get over. We were so young.

I only hope now that this rock of yours will have helped you get clean of this pain.

So much more to say. So much more I'd like to ask.

Soon,
Connor

57

IN MARCH WORK ACCELERATED as shoals of herring spawned along the coasts of Archangel Island. She moved quickly, energized by the sun and warmth, stretching her arms high to ease her back, rolling her head as she walked along Pletnikoff Street. She felt lighter. Secrets are funny, she thought. The great weight they hold. And then — the thaw.

She moved her things from Betteryear's to the Bunkhouse, paying with cash. By now she understood well the formula at the processor: work longer and harder than the person, usually male, beside you, and you'll be fine. Trunk had put her in charge of the frozen side, except for the glazer, which Newt tended better than anyone, even with his bad eye. When trays of boxed herring came out of the flash freezer, cemented by their own sperm to the stainless steel, she jammed the flat tip of the bar beneath the cardboard and rocked the boxes loose with a thrust of her hips. If they didn't shake free she'd push the box off the tray and the opaque, heavy ice would shatter over the concrete.

The herring came in so fast that Trunk called the district manager and asked him to hold off on a second opening to allow the workers time to catch up. He enforced mandatory overtime and spent his days gloved, wrapping boxes in plastic, shouting to be heard above the jam of the glazer and rumble of the conveyor belt.

She had gotten a small taste of life on the water and knew now she preferred to be catching instead of processing. She still hadn't heard word if she was getting another shot on the *Adriatic,* but doubted it. At least overtime paid, and her tug account grew.

On the last day of herring she paused for a moment in the bathroom at the Muskeg. She stood closer to the mirror, turning her head to one side. Her hair had grown coarser, the furrow over her nose deeper. A ruddiness to her skin that hadn't been there before. She splayed her palms in front of her chest, calluses dark with work. *Bring it,* she thought. *Bring on all of it.*

58

AT THE HARBOR Betteryear zipped her into a one-piece float-coat to keep her warm and buoyant, then weaved the skiff between larger boats clustered just outside the breakwater. She skimmed a finger over the waves, considering this trip with him, after what had happened the other night, a last kindness.

The *Chief* appeared dark and shut up. Maybe Laney would take a down payment. Or even allow her to start fixing the engine, using what little she had learned from the manual. She could drain the diesel from the lines, make sure there were no obstructions. Change out the filters. Anything to stop depending on others for shelter.

Up on the docks people gathered, a few holding wreaths.

"Blessing of the fleet," Betteryear explained over the grumble of the outboard. "A ceremony to keep boats safe for the fishing season. Eleven thousand years my people have subsisted on the ocean," he continued. "We could rake herring off the Sound. Now the Japanese businessmen show up with suitcases of cash and these boats rape until there is nothing left."

The harshness in his voice surprised her. She thought of the opalescent, shimmering herring frozen in the trays, unsure if he blamed her as well.

They cruised beneath the bridge, trading off sips of nettle tea from his thermos. He shifted to one side of the bench and asked if she wanted to sit. She did, and he handed her the tiller, showing her how to twist the throttle. The hull bucked forward. Betteryear seized the gunwales with both hands.

"Easy, easy!" His long fingers, surprisingly warm, wrapped around her hand. "Small movements."

On the open water it was too loud to speak. They ran the length of town, past the ferry terminal, where the road ended. He pointed out landmarks — a rockslide, the head of a stream — to steer toward. It was a thrill, opening the throttle, feeling the thud of waves beneath the hull. He pointed her toward the back of the bay, then told her to slow. He reached over the port side to lift hemlock branches frosted with herring eggs from the water, broke off a twig, and handed it to her. "Here. Try this."

She ran the needles between her teeth, sucking off the grain-sized eggs. Bitter and salty at once, they exploded between her teeth.

Betteryear arranged the branches in a waxed box, then took over the engine, throttling up until they reached a collage of islands on the eastern edge of Lost Sound. The open water and rush of the wind cleared her head. When he brought the boat into a slot in the boulders of an island and helped her out, she felt good again, just happy to be in this wild place, among these slick rocks strewn with fronds of seaweed, the cinder cone of the volcano rising across the water.

"There is a saying among the Tlingit that my grandmother repeated," Betteryear said as he handed her a plastic bag. He crouched above a tide pool. Waves lashed the faces of stone. "'When the tide is out, the table is set.' You see now what she means." With a knife blade he scraped tangled black fronds from the rock face, then stretched a sheet to the sky. "This is *Porphyra*. Like a woman's stocking. Nori."

They fell into the quiet of work. From around the corner she could see back toward town. How small it looked, just a dash of buildings beneath the mountainous, tree-covered expanse. A pearl of light in the lowering sun.

An oily sickening odor filled her nostrils, a smell different from the salty, anaerobic brine of low tide in town. "That's deep seaweed," Betteryear said, standing. "Come. Let's move away from it."

They walked into a cove, where he bent to one knee and sifted sand between his fingers. "The old tribes here, my ancestors, crushed these shells to have a place to pull up their canoes so as not to damage the bottoms."

Tara watched him. "My mother talked about the scraping sound the boats made at the end of the day in the town where she grew up."

"It must have been difficult for her to go from the old way of doing things to living in a city," Betteryear said. "Leaving her home like that. I can't imagine."

Tara picked up a seashell and ran the blade of her nail along the ridges. "I never saw her home in Italy, but I like to imagine her there. It's like she had two homes."

Betteryear considered. "That's a beautiful thought, Tara."

He unbuttoned his shirt and waded out into the mud flats. His skin was taut over his muscles, his arms long and sinewy. Grass swayed back and forth with the current. He timed the waves, reached into the water, and came up with a handful of dripping plants. "Eelgrass roots," he announced. "We can make seaweed wraps with these."

As they walked farther along the coast, Betteryear stopped by a tide pool. He identified sculpins, purple shore crabs, pink and green anemones. "Patience," he said as she tried to wiggle a cone-shaped limpet off a rock. When it wouldn't come she worked her nail beneath the rim, and the creature came loose. She dropped the speckled shell into a separate bag. He gave a small nod, then walked ahead, ghosting over the rocks.

She noticed all of it, the white and pink flowers on Siberian miner's lettuce, the soft green frills of yarrow. He reached toward a bed of moss, selecting a stalk. "And this is bedstraw, or cleavers. Feel," he said, handing it to her. "Run the stem between your fingers. When you swallow it, it hooks into your throat." He pushed it against her wool jacket. "It also clings to fabric. You see? But still so tasty." He nipped off licorice fern — the weevil-shaped roots he dug up, splitting the fruit and handing her a piece. "And this is good for sweetening tea."

She chewed. "Tastes like a black Twizzler."

"No," he corrected. "A black Twizzler tastes like licorice fern."

She felt drunk on words as he continued to tell her about the difference between wild cucumber, or twisted stalk, and false hellebore, which had darker, more fibrous leaves. He grew excited when he came across a particular wild mustard plant.

"The Latin name of this one I enjoy, *Cochlearia officinalis.* Notice the basal rosette, how the leaves clasp the flower stem. It looks like an ear, doesn't it? *Cochlear.*" He handed her a sprig. "Spicy on the tongue." Slowly, she put the plant in her mouth, grinding the fibers between her molars. It did taste spicy, faintly like mustard.

"It's so nice to be able to pass down this knowledge. And you are such a fine listener. Just like the crushed shells for the canoe, like the guano from the birds coming off the ocean that fertilizes this island — too soon we forget the stories that instruct us. Take for example yarrow," he said, holding up the stem of the soft-frilled plant. "*Achillea millefolium,* named for the great warrior of your Western tradition, Achilles. In love with his own glory. He was a student of the healing arts, and used yarrow to tend to the wounds of his soldiers. But he was no better than Katlian, the Tlingit who slayed Russians by the thousands. But who learns about Katlian? No one, this is who."

Moisture turned the calves of their boots shiny as they walked through tidal grasses, the bags of limpets and greens and seaweed knocking against her knees. When they reached the skiff he held out his hand, his palm cold and damp from the water. She settled on the bench as he shoved the bow off the beach and leapt in, paddling out to depth, dropping the outboard, pulling the starter, and pointing them back toward town. His running lights were out, he explained, and he wanted to be back home before dark.

The sky had clouded over. She caught his eye and he smiled. She was eager to get back to land.

59

IT RAINED FOR THE NEXT COUPLE DAYS. A cold, serious rain that bled into April. She racked up hours, slept at the Bunkhouse. Newt was out of town. Packing fish and sleeping, this was her life.

Toward the middle of the month, Trunk called Tara into his office.

"You passed," he told her.

"Passed what?"

He squinted, trying to make sense of something on his clipboard. "You'll be starting in May on the *Adriatic*. Work through September. Should make a nice bit of cash long as you don't fuck it up." He handed her the board. "Fill out your 1999 crew license, take it on upstairs, and the girl will set you up. Jackie and Teague are driving the boat up from Petersburg, should be here the seventh. You can get in some hours on the frozen side until they arrive."

With the twenty-two hundred in cash in her locker, plus the thirteen thousand in her bank account, she was at just over fifteen thousand. Her meals would be covered on the tender, and she would have nowhere to spend money. If she completed the summer with Jackie, if nothing went wrong, she could have the tug come fall. Wake early, get the engine to run. Spend quiet evenings cooking by the wood stove, plucking leaves from the basil plant.

She loaded up on the forklift and was driving it out of cold storage when she saw, by the open gate, Thomas waving at her. When she came over he hugged her long and hard.

"What's up?" she said, pulling away.

Frauke stood by the roll-up door with her old-school external frame backpack.

"We go to California," he said.

She could feel the burn of Trunk's good eye through the glass. Frauke barked something in German.

"Well, good luck," she said.

"And you too. You will have no regrets, you will see."

At the end of the day she returned to her locker. The door was half open, the lock gone. In the bottom, where the $2,200 had been, she found a note on the same paper Frauke used for her sayings. *If you don't have dreams, you have nightmares.*

"Motherfucker!" she screamed.

She went across town to the police station, a cinderblock building by the fire station. The dispatcher, a pretty, heavy-lidded woman, told her that the police could apply to the magistrate for an arrest warrant, which would be on the books if either Frauke or Thomas came back.

"Forget it," Tara said. It wasn't worth fighting. She'd just have to work harder.

60

WHEN TARA SAW JACKIE on the docks she was tanned, her hair straw blond.

"Good winter off, girlfriend?" Jackie asked.

"Made it through, with a few bumps. You and Teague?"

"Bunch of us went down to Mexico. Surfing, *palapas,* back to the basics. Heard you got robbed?"

"Yeah, well. They'll get theirs."

Jackie started down the ladder. "I heard something about how you and Newt were out living with those crazies in the woods? It have anything to do with those folks?"

"I'm done out there," Tara said quickly. "Just ready to work."

"Good. It'll be straightforward, go up the circuit, pick up our load, c'mon back and drop it off. May to September. You have time to run down to the post office before we head out. Tell them to forward your mail to the processor. Welcome aboard."

When Tara returned to the boat, Jackie introduced her to Miles, the engineer, a quiet, thick-bodied senior in Port Anna High School who wore faded Carhartt overalls. "Miles is the town wrestling star," Jackie announced. "A whiz with the engine, with a nasty sweet tooth."

They loaded up, threw the lines, and pushed north along the channel past the tug. After a brief look, she went down to begin moving into her bunk for the summer.

61

AS THEY RAN she found that she enjoyed spending time in the wheelhouse with Teague. She liked his drawl and his stories, particularly when they involved landmarks along their path — how this boat ran aground in this bay here, how the Tlingits once maintained a fish camp there.

On the second day of the trip she watched their progress on the computer screen as Teague made the gradual turn from Chatham Strait into Peril Strait. Tree-covered mountains rose, jagged, along the coastline. Teague said that all the land to her left was protected wilderness.

"Thank god," she said.

"Bullshit. It was God who gave us these resources. Now here we are sitting on our hands instead of fulfilling our duty of cutting those trees down."

She recalled Fritz's CUT KILL DIG DRILL bumper sticker. The men up here were funny. They seemed to pride themselves not only on surviving Alaska, but on conquering it. She thought of Connor backstage with his headset, a clipboard in one hand, making a note. He'd be good at working, she decided. But he didn't have the swash-buckling nature of the men here. The built-in power of dudes like Miles.

They anchored in a drizzle at the back of a bay. "On the beach over there is where a picnicking family discovered a local hunter cached by a brown bear," Teague told her. "Kids found him folded in half like a doll. Stuffed at the base of a tree, a little after-hibernation snack."

She peered into the woods, and thought of telling him about the time she had been charged up on Crow Hill, how Keta had stood in front, protecting her, when Teague picked up the VHF to make an announcement that the *Adriatic* was buying.

Like distant stars, the mast lights appeared on the horizon. Teague made a list of trollers ready to unload.

"You met Irish yet?" he asked. She shook her head. "He'll be our first. Cranky old-timer. Eighty-three, and he still works alone. Can't wait to be at the front of the line."

Tara went down the stairs and pulled on her bibs and gloves in time to drop fenders off the side. As the troller eased in, she looped line over the cleat. Irish paced the deck, chewing his blistered lips. He had a shock of white hair, a weathered face, and thick-lensed glasses. Behind her she heard the snap of Jackie's elastic wristers, and watched as her skipper hopped down onto the smaller boat and lifted the hold cover. She cursed.

"C'mon, Irish. Coho should face the same direction, otherwise their scales come off. Jesus, what a fucking mess."

The man lifted a hand in the air but didn't speak.

"What are you waiting for?" Jackie snapped at Tara. "Fish aren't getting any deader."

She lowered herself into the hold. Silver scales floated like confetti. She dug the blood-slimed straps of the brailer bag out from the pile of fish, hooked the straps to the steel eye. Jackie gave a twirl of her finger. "Up!" The hydraulics groaned, the elastic spreaders made a bang as they sprang loose from the side hooks, and the bag rose.

"Gimme that tag," Jackie said to Tara, stepping back onto the *Adriatic*.

"What?"

"The tag! The tag line!" Jackie reached over and grabbed the rope tied off to the bottom of the bag, threw her weight away from the

Northern Star, heaving the brailer bag over a tote. With a gaff hook in one hand she went back into the hold, came up with a fish, and set it on the V-groove of Irish's tray. She opened the belly flaps, frowned, reached for the Vicky knife duct-taped to her suspender.

"This is some sloppy horseshit, Irish," she said, scraping with the knife and flinging purple goop to the side. "Blood in the central artery and in the armpits. Swim bladder remnants. And this?" she held up a fan of ruby-red gill rakers. "Are you shitting me, Irish? You didn't even clean out the head!"

The old man continued to look out toward some invisible spot in the distance as Jackie used the honed edge of a spoon to squeeze out the remaining threads of blood from the sides of the fish.

"I'll tell you what, Irish. I wouldn't be caught dead handling a fish like this. And I *goddamn well* don't have time to do your work alongside mine. You've gone through your ice, your fish are belly-burned, and they've lost their scales. These are all gonna get number-twoed, you're not gonna be able to afford your gas. Am I making sense to you, old man?"

Tara stood there, feeling embarrassed for the skipper, who took a pack of cigarettes from his wool vest and shook one loose. If Jackie had yelled at Urbano like this, it would have been a much different story.

"I'll ask again: Am I gettin' through, Irish? I'm not fucking getting through, am I? Waste of my fucking time. We'll buy your shitty fish, but they're all number-twoed, good for cat food. If you don't like it, sell 'em elsewhere."

The rest of the day was more of the same—Jackie bitching out skippers, sniping at Tara, giving a quick nod of the head when the catch was acceptable. It was dark when Tara hosed down the deck, water running pink through the scuppers. She used the hand-powered pallet jack to rearrange totes to make more room for the next day's fish. Links on the chain clacked as Teague pulled the hook and the engines fired.

"Go grab a few while we run up the line," Jackie told her. Zipped into her sleeping bag, staring up at the ceiling inches from her nose, her muscles felt long and tired.

She understood now why Newt had grown so frantic before a trip on the *Adriatic*. Jackie functioned in a perpetual state of frustration. At the same time it made Tara proud to see this small woman take on the world.

62

THE NEXT MORNING, after finishing her chores around the boat, Tara poured a mug of coffee and joined Teague in the wheelhouse. They worked their way up Lisianski Strait, spruce and hemlock thick along the water's edge, cliff sides slick with rainwater. To the north she could see the front end of a glacier between the tree-covered mountains. Teague told her how fishermen had drowned in a storm here a few years back after alerting the Coast Guard that the boat was going down in Lisianski Inlet instead of Lisianski Strait.

"Trust me. One day, when you get a boat of your own, you'll find yourself in the shit. Something will go wrong, something you couldn't have imagined, and you'll have to make the right decision."

"Hope not," she said.

"Hope doesn't have a damn thing to do with it. That's just the game we play out here."

They approached a silty green line separating glacier water from the blue ocean. "Watch this pod," Teague told her, pointing out the window at the porpoises playing in the wake of the boat. When they reached the lighter water the critters broke off, turning around back toward the deep blue. "Buckos don't like all the sediment," Teague said. "Least that's what I think. No one really has a clue."

A buoy rang mournfully in the swell. With the binoculars Tara watched sea lions piled at its base, their wire-thick whiskers twitching as they jockeyed for position. Teague mulled over the tide table, stroking his goatee, trying to decide whether to shoot South Inian

Pass, a tidal bottleneck about half a mile wide and three miles long connecting Cross Sound with Icy Strait. "Hold on to that greasy hat of yours — this is a nasty-ass bite of water."

The scow's twin screws churned against the ebb. They passed whirlpools and oily boils of water. He pointed to odd shapes on the depth-finder screen.

"Sunken boats," he said. "They all want to go home, to the ocean floor. From dust to dust, and all that."

She looked toward the distant mountains, snowcapped and craggy, thinking about the *Chief,* with its broad shoulders and horse-shoe stern, slipping beneath the ocean. It wasn't possible. Teague broke the silence to identify the Fairweather Range, chipped teeth of mountains outlined against the horizon, the summit of Mount Fair-weather more than fourteen thousand feet from the water's surface. Maybe one day, she thought, she'd power the tug through this pass. Already she could hear the bang of the engine, six cylinders pound-ing in line, charging against the moon's gravity.

They anchored off the ash-colored beaches of Homeshore and went on Channel Sixteen. Trollers appeared, poles lifting in jerks as they came closer, great birds folding their wings. "You think you can get these folks unloaded?" Teague said. "Jackie's down in the engine room with Miles."

She snapped on her bibs, pulled her hair back in a high pony-tail, slipped on her hat and safety glasses, then went on deck to catch trollers' lines and pull them snug over the cleats. Teague worked the levers while Tara hopped down and grabbed the hook out of the air.

"Lower!"

Down it came. She pushed the straps past the catch, twirled a fin-ger to the sky, then up went the bag, its bungees snapping free from the stainless hooks. Teague watched, steel coffee mug in one hand, as she followed the bag, leaping back to the tender.

"You stay out from under that load, hear?" he yelled down. She released the fish into the tote and began sorting. When the skipper came out from the wheelhouse, his permit card in hand, Teague joked. "You gonna have my deckhand do all your work, or what?"

The skipper snorted and dropped back down to his boat. "Hook attached to a lead took off the tip of my deckhand's thumb. I guess we gotta head on back to town."

"Damn. You still got the thumb?"

"Soakin' in milk there in the hold."

"Milk?" Teague shouted.

"Yeah, milk."

"That's teeth, buddy. You soak broken teeth in milk. A thumb is flesh. Wrap it in a steak."

"Fuck that. I ain't wasting a steak on that lazy sonofabitch."

"Just slice off a piece then, duct tape the thumb into it."

"Well, it's coming off his rib eye. Dumb shit. Yeah, I'm talking to you in there!" he yelled into an open sash window. "He's gonna have to catch a rockfish if he's hungry. His goddamn fault for losin' the thumb in the first place. Cost me a whole goddamn trip, now I'm supposed to give up a steak."

They unloaded the last of the trollers, pulled anchor, bucked the tide across Icy Strait to Hoonah to take on ice, then ran with it down Chatham Strait. Through Sergius Narrows at slack tide, then back to Port Anna to unload at the processor, untying early the following morning to do it all over again.

63

FRITZ HAD BEEN RIGHT. Unlike most Alaskans, she hadn't been raised with work — an understanding of how engines ran, how houses fit together, how food arrived on the table. Knead, cut, roll, brush, punch, crumble, soften — this was what her parents had taught her. So different from the gearwork of life, the origin of things: squeezing milk from a cow on an Illinois dairy farm, flaking hay from the bed of a pickup on a Wyoming ranch. Learning how to rip flitches in an Oregon woodshop.

In her first month on the *Adriatic* she had watched Miles, after taking one look at a bolt, reach for the proper socket head, metric instead of inches. Her muscles lacked this knowledge, how many twists were needed to remove that bolt. She didn't know to smear nickel on the threads before tightening it back up. And each time she thought she had mastered a skill — tying a bowline, learning how to feather an orbital sander, working the pallet jack — she was confronted with yet another mystery of the mechanical world that laid bare her ignorance.

On the other hand, she could make cannoli. She recalled the time her father taught her. "Your mother is correct," he began by saying. "Cold hands make the best pastry. Except with cannoli. To do that, your hands must be warm. Here. Towel off."

He turned the thermostat on the fryer to 350 degrees, then carefully laid squares of dough into the oil, keeping them plunged with the flat of the tongs until they turned pecan brown. "Always wait until the last minute to fill, otherwise the shells will lose their crunch."

She learned the correct amount of pressure to squeeze the custard of mascarpone, chocolate chips, and a few drops of amaretto into the cooled shells. When she overfilled he remained patient, waiting by her side until each cannoli was lined up neatly on the wax paper, then followed behind, watching as she slipped the metal tray into the display case.

It made no difference if it was frying shells or working through this bag of fish to make sure no chums were mixed in with kings. Attention to detail and speed, these were the main ingredients. Maneuver the totes with the pallet jack and signal Teague so that when the tote came down its feet fit into the one beneath it. Do it well, do it quickly, and already be thinking about the next job.

It made her cringe to remember her first weeks on Archangel Island, daydreaming in the warehouse while Fritz lay under the tank, waiting for his shim. Worse were those memories of being sprawled on the couch as Connor worked, or dragging her feet through her chores at the bakery.

Miles didn't speak much, except when either diesel engines or wrestling became the topic. She enjoyed sitting with him on the stern deck, protected from the wind by the house, two of them leaning back in plastic lawn chairs, boots propped up on the gunwales, watching the wash from the props. He introduced her to the thin, uneven Backwoods cigars, which they smoked while Jackie's pressure cooker clattered in the galley. When she told him about the tug, he walked her through the basics of a direct-reversible engine, how there was no transmission or clutch, and the cylinders reversed order when the boat had to move backwards.

"Pure power," he said, stabbing the air with his cigar. "Fuckin' bomber."

He surprised her by listening carefully when she talked, and she found herself telling stories, how her *nonna* died with ground veal beneath her engagement ring, which she never took off, even when making meatballs. How her father was an only child because of the lead in his father's blood. She showed him a few basic boxing combinations, and laughed when he attacked her with a double-leg takedown, dropping her on deck.

"The hell's up with you two," Jackie hollered, sticking her head out the galley window. "Don't you burn down my boat."

"She sneaks up on me in the engine room," Miles said as they took their seats, and he relit his cigar. "A ghost. But she likes you. Your buddy Newt, man. She rode him hard. I blame it on her, what happened."

"How so?" She leaned in closer to hear him, getting a whiff of his diesel and sweat scent.

"It was a short weekend trip, doing cucumbers. He was already going twice the speed of any normal drag-ass deckhand, which is why so many of the divers unloaded with us—he'd get them unloaded so quick. Still, she kept pushing, you know, in that way she does, like she's pissed off at the world. Constantly busting his balls, giving him shit about his teeth, going bald, how weird he looked, whatever." He ashed over the gunwale. "That night some new guy in the fleet had overloaded his brailer bag in the forward hold, and it got stuck when Teague tried to pull it out. Newt shoulda called for the hook, lifted the bag to take tension off. But he knew Jackie was watching, so he just slashed with his Vicky. I heard this god-awful scream, and he came up, blood pouring down his cheek."

It rang true—despite his testy nature, Newt was the sort who kept on pushing until he fell apart. "Thank god I know engines better than she does," Miles said. "Anyways, this is my last season with her, even if the money is good."

They both glanced up at a noise. But it was only the jars in the pressure cooker, glass shaking in the hard boil.

"Just keep your eye out," Miles said. "That's about all I gotta say about that."

64

ON JULY FOURTH, in the middle of the king opener, they anchored off Salisbury Sound, in Kalinin Bay. The tender had been inching its way back up the line, keeping pace with the trollers working off Point Erin. Teague set a pot and brought up a couple red king crabs before pulling the hook the following morning. Jackie defrosted spot prawns and boiled up the crab for dinner. Teague melted down a brick of butter and spread newspaper over the galley table.

"Now, this," he said, digging out meat from a crab leg, "is how we do it in Alaska."

Tara rose, went into the galley, and brought over a plate of cannolis from the refrigerator. When Miles took a bite he rolled his eyes back in his head and pretended to go into shock.

"Now, where in the Sam Hill did you learn to make these tasty little hot dogs?" Teague asked.

"Bakery."

Miles laughed. She was feeling nervy, and glared up-table at Teague.

"You playin' around?" he asked.

"No—I was raised in a bakery in Philly."

"Your mom's a baker?"

She just nodded. "Well, I don't care what anyone says about you, Tara Marconi. You all right in my book."

· · ·

The next morning Jackie found Tara in the galley as she cleaned the fry-pot she had used for the shells. She stood for a moment, watching as Tara scrubbed.

"I've been meaning to tell you. You're not a natural fisherman."

Stunned, she stared back at her skipper. "Excuse me?"

"But it's okay," Jackie said, taking a granola bar from a cabinet, peeling back the wrapper, and tearing off a bite. "You try harder than any sonofabitch I've ever seen. Oh—another thing. Your father's been calling the processor. Trunk said to put an end to it. He's not your secretary."

"When did you hear this?" Tara asked, shutting off the water.

"Don't go getting all worked up. Spoke with Trunk the other day."

Her heart rushed. She wondered if he was hurt, if he had fallen on the stairs. "Well—I need to call him."

"And that's why I'm telling you. Tomorrow we put in at Hoonah to pick up ice and mail. You can do it then."

No good would come of it. He'd pick up, she'd refuse again to answer his question, and one of them would get angry.

She wished he would just leave her alone.

65

AS THEY CROSSED ICY STRAIT to the small town, Jackie sent Tara into the hold to break up the last of the ice, which had frozen into a block. Each time Tara stabbed at it with the edge of the shovel, the berg threw back shards into her eyes. Finally, she stomped it with the heel of her boot, breaking it in half, before working down each chunk.

"Now, this is what I call a job well done," Teague said, when she came into the wheelhouse to pour a glass of water. "Not a damn tree left."

At first she thought he was talking about her. Then she looked out the window. The hillsides were clear-cut. "Native corporations," Teague said. "They know how to get shit done."

Teague's goofiness, originally charming, had turned strange. If her father had seen him giving her these eyes, there would be a problem.

"You wanna go throw lines?" he said.

After making fast she found a phone outside the liquor store at the top of the ramp. A single Plexiglas booth. She stood in a line of fishermen, repeating to herself that she wouldn't hang up on him, not matter what. Out of the corner of her eye she saw the folded arms of a man behind her. In a tan work coat with oil-splotched shearling lining. Purple tattoos on his knuckles.

"Your turn, honey."

She was about to tell him to fuck himself, then recognized his sad blue eyes and thick white hair.

"Did I stutter?" he said, pointing toward the phones. "We ain't got all day. Go on and make your call."

His eyes appeared glazed, the wrinkles in his face deeper, the tone of his voice tighter. Petree, the man from the ferry. She held her tongue, stepped forward, and shoved quarters into the slot. The receiver smelled of fish oil and still held the warmth from the previous hand. She flattened her ear to the phone. Her heart knocked as she dialed. Her father picked up on the second ring. His voice sounded thin.

"Yes?"

"It's me, Pop."

She waited for his anger, bracing herself. *Figlia,* he breathed. "Where are you?"

"In a small town. North of Port Anna."

"Where?"

"Hoonah."

"What are you doing?"

"Fishing, Pop."

"On a fishing boat?"

"I'm on a tender. Other boats unload their catch to us, then we bring it back to the processor, where it gets frozen and packaged."

His voice grew raspy. "They said they couldn't tell me where you are. Vic said he'd get a map, and put it on the wall in the parlor here."

She looked for a folding door on the booth, but it was broken off at the hinges. The idea of him tracking her on a map was hard to believe.

The man behind clicked his tongue. "Hey, daddy's little girl, you gonna be all day explaining how to fish?" Another male voice said, "Maybe when she's done she can give me a private lesson." Chorus of laughter.

"Hold on —" She cupped a hand around her mouth and turned. "One second, okay?"

"Tara," he pleaded. "I need to know when you're coming home."

There was the old tone, the insistence. "I don't know, Pop."

"C'mon!" the man from the ferry bellowed. "You got a line behind you, honey. Call your dad later."

"Are there other people with you?" he asked.

"No — it's fine —"

"I'm having a hard time hearing, *figlia*."

Eva came on. "Tara? It's me. Is everything okay?"

"It's fine, yes." She turned again. "If you just shut the fuck up I'll be off. Okay?" She spoke back into the mouthpiece. "I wanted to say I'm sorry for hanging up on him. I thought he was going to be angry."

"He just wants to talk to you. Maybe there's another time to call back."

"Okay. But tell him to stop calling the processor, please."

Eva took a breath. "Yes. I will tell him, Tara. Call from someplace where he can hear you. He just wants to know you are safe."

Carefully, she set the receiver into its cradle, then stared forward, trying to push her insides back down. He had sounded so anxious, so desperate to know where she was, what she was doing. Even — was she imagining this? — apologetic.

"Hey," the man behind her said. "It's been two seconds, honey. You wanna get out of the way so the rest of us can call?"

Like a string of lights the muscles lit up. Her left hand drew into a fist as her wrist moved through the air, her knuckles hooking into Petree's skin, digging under his cheekbone. His bloodshot eyes wide, he made a gasping sound. Instinctively she pushed, moving out of range, but not before one of his arms seized the nape of her jacket and jerked her toward him. She was close enough to smell the damp diesel on his coat, the stink of half-digested hops and ginger on his breath. "You little fucking cunt bitch, I'll rip your fucking throat —"

She felt a hand on her hip. And there was Jackie, popped up between them.

"Petree, Petree, Petree." His Adam's apple twitched, his eyes still fastened on her. "What did I tell you about fighting girls? You're not careful, you're gonna get yourself a reputation."

"She unloaded on me!" he said, pointing at his cheek, flushed red. He looked back at Tara. "I know you, anyways, you little shit. Where I seen you before?"

"Let's go," Jackie said, guiding Tara by the waist. Petree spat at them. Tara turned. "You don't remember, do you? You said we'd meet again, and sure enough."

Jackie slapped Tara on the butt. "Hoo-ah girl! I knew it from that first day we met. Never seen someone throw a punch like that."

"I told him. He wouldn't give me two seconds of peace."

Jackie dug into her coat, waved an envelope in the air. "Maybe a letter from your boyfriend will calm you down. Don't worry, I won't tell Miles. Get some rest while we run south. You deserve it after that performance."

She took the envelope. Connor's handwriting.

When they reached the boat she went straight to her berth and closed the door, trying to even out her breath as she unfolded the pages.

June 24, 1999

Dear Tara,

    I'm not sure where this letter will find you. By now maybe you're above the Arctic Circle hunting whales. Or fishing for crab out in the Bering Sea. I guess it's been a bit, and I wanted to know how you're doing. And also to tell you about what goes on here . . . wait for it . . . in the thrilling metropolis of Kansas City! (I'm already starting to sound like a New Yorker.)

    I actually love it here. I'm interning at this small theater company for the summer. And you'll never guess what play we're doing. "The Lovers" by Brian Friel. It's actually two one-

act plays called "Winners" and "Losers," but we're doing just the first half (casting it as an island — my idea after thinking of Port Anna).

And guess what? I'm Joe Brennan. The director said he liked my height and sincerity and understated nature. So there you have it. Back on stage I go.

That's been my life. Living in this little room up above the theater with a mattress and a lamp on top of a box. While you — who knows.

Before jumping in the Mazda and hitting the road for Kansas I went back to Manton Street. The downtown skyline has expanded. People move in from NYC by the truckload — this couple with a greyhound dog the size of a small mule bought a place a few doors down from your pop. Vic and Sal and all the old Italian dudes don't know what's going on. People are calling it the "Mexican Market" instead of the Italian Market. Oh and City Council is considering outlawing burn barrels. Crazy. Nicodemo Scarfo got out of jail, so now everyone's on edge waiting to see if he'll get revenge for his son being shot up at Dante and Luigi's. You remember that? Halloween 1989 guy came in with a mask and hit Nikki Jr. nine times but didn't kill him. (I can't help but think your pop knows more about such things.)

I'm not really sure why I'm writing you like this. Just want you to know that the city you left still exists. And that I'm out here in Kansas City. Thinking of you.

Love,
Connor

The volume of blood in her veins seemed to have doubled — either from the fight or the letter, she couldn't be sure. She folded the paper, pinched her fingers, and ran them over the crease. Then unfolded it, read how he had signed, relieved to see it still said the same thing.

She felt emptied out from the fight, but the letter had lifted her spirits. Or maybe it was speaking to her father on the phone, hearing this new gentleness in his voice.

Topside in the galley, Miles and Teague were chomping away on the rest of the cannolis. "Motherfucking Petree Bangheart," Teague said when she walked in. "That guy's a myth. And you go and hit him. Un-fucking-believable."

She set bread on the cutting board and began smearing peanut butter and jelly. Miles gawked at her. "You're a fucking badass."

"I was on the phone with my father," she said, slapping the halves together. "He wouldn't shut up. What was I supposed to do?"

The two men exchanged glances. "Miles, you be sure to give me a signal if I ever don't shut the fuck up," Teague said.

"Yeah, me too." The two of them broke into laughter.

Sick of the boys, she returned to her berth and sat on the bottom bunk eating her sandwich. For the third time she read the letter. This time she thought of her father slamming the storm door, kicking the television off its stand after Nikki Scarfo got shot up.

She lay back, set the pages on her stomach. Maybe he was signing all his letters these days with *love*. If only she could see his face. Then she'd know.

66

THE *Adriatic* repeated the two-week circuit, unloading totes in Port Anna, taking on fresh ice, then turning around and heading out again, north by the cape, waves shattering against the rocks. At Lisianski Inlet they cut up along Yakobi Island, turning southeast to tie up in Pelican, a boardwalk village built into the side of a mountain.

"You're looking a bit worse for the wear," Teague told her. "Someone needs to go see Joleen."

Joleen was the owner of Gem's, Teague said, the bar known for sponsoring "Teeny Weeny" contests, where fishermen wore white boxers while Joleen sprayed them down with cold water. "She wanders around in her bathrobe hugging people. About the nicest woman you could hope for. No grumpy fishermen you need to flatten."

Tara was just glad to be off the boat again. At one end of the boardwalk was an abandoned cold storage, held up by barnacle-encrusted pylons. Inside she breathed in the mildewy air, running her palms over the rough-hewn spruce beams, trying to compose a response to Connor in her head.

He was right, she was leading a good life in Port Anna. She had been given a second chance on the tug and intended to make it happen this time. Before returning to Philly she wanted a roof and a bed of her own. And yet, after reading his letter, and hearing her father on the phone, Philly seemed closer. Urbano telling Vic to get a map made her want to cry.

She imagined the flames rising out of the burn barrels at the market, cabbage-scented cardboard boxes broken down and shoved inside to keep the vendors warm. Fires in the refinery fields flickering in the south. Radio towers blinking over the Schuylkill River. Or maybe all of this had changed in the past couple of years. Or — more frighteningly — maybe she had changed, and none of this would move her in the way it once had.

She left the cold storage and continued along the boardwalk, trying to shake the growing feeling that walking here, along these planks, shimmering with rain, in some half-abandoned boardwalk town, she was wasting time. She passed a house built into the hill, heard country music, and pulled open the heavy wooden door. She could use a taste of the raucousness Newt had described at the Frontier, something to take her out of herself. But inside, it was just a few men hunched around the horseshoe-shaped bar, smoking and drinking from Mason jars.

She ordered a shot of whiskey and settled onto a stool to read an outdated Juneau newspaper, ignoring the sidelong glances. At her back the door opened.

"Gotta keep the locals happy, right?" a man said, walking behind the bar and plopping a cleaned salmon into the sink. "Fish tax paid. Where's my lovely Joleen? I need a hug."

You've got to be kidding, she thought. It was Petree, in his shearling-lined coat, tearing open a ginger chew, looking like some out-of-work Marlboro man. She so wished she had worn her Eagles hat, to pull low over her eyes. As he took a stool beside her she saw the tattoos along his knuckles, and along the broadside of his wrist, one of the Big Dipper, stars connected by barbed wire, the North Star, in the shape of a fishing hook.

"Well, I'll be goddamned, if it ain't the fightin' kangaroo her own self." He slapped Tara on the back, then rested a finger on his bruised cheek. "Boys, anyone wondering where I picked up this shiner, here's the left-handed source."

She looked around the bar, thinking this would end in another fight, one she would certainly lose. Instead he motioned to the bartender, who poured two beers and two tequilas. He pushed a shot glass toward her, raised his own in her direction, ignoring the lemon slices and saltshaker. "Swear you woulda taken my head off if I hadn't been quick. No hard feelings?" After a pause she threw back her glass. The alcohol bit into her cheeks.

"'Nother round over here!" he said, slapping his palm on the bar. "You like working for that ball-buster of a skipper?"

She shrugged. He focused on the bottom of his empty glass. He drank twice as fast as Newt on the breakwater. "So what do the parents think of their pretty little daughter all the way out here in Alaska?"

She pushed away her beer and stood.

"What, did I hit a nerve?" He turned to the guy beside him. "You hear me say something?"

She put a twenty-dollar bill down on the bar. Petree stammered. "Hey! I said it's on me. Don't go. I swear I remember you back from somewhere."

"The ferry," she said. "We spoke on the ferry, when I first got here."

She allowed the wooden door to slip shut between them. It was ten P.M. and still light. Cliffs rose on the other side of Lisianski Strait. Even without a night at the bar, she felt better, she decided.

The tops of her hands shined orange in the boardwalk lights as she walked toward the boat. Milled nail heads, like the ones they had used to build the platform, shimmered. Back on the *Adriatic* she fried bacon, shredded hamburger and dropped it into the grease. The meat burned the roof of her mouth. She spit it on the floor, then found herself holding on to the Hoosier cabinet, laughing until her stomach hurt. At what she wasn't sure. Maybe Connor in Kansas City, acting. Or how happy his letter had made her.

That night, full and warm, and a little drunk, she fell right asleep.

67

IN EARLY AUGUST, after almost two months on the boat, the *Adriatic* made tight in Tenakee Inlet, a thirty-five-mile gouge into the east coast of Chichagof Island, just off Chatham Strait.

"About sixty year-round residents," Teague told her. "Everyone washes in a poured concrete bathhouse built over natural hot springs. Crazy, right? Used to be called Robber's Roost 'cause it's where Soapy Smith's gang settled after Soapy was killed in the Juneau Wharf shootout . . ." She nodded as he spoke, peanut butter and jelly sandwich in one hand, hot cocoa in another, eager for him to shut up so she could return to her bunk and catch up on sleep. Finally he did. She was dressed in her flannel pajamas, zipped inside her sleeping bag when there was a knock on the door.

"Planning on becoming a grease monkey?" Jackie said, poking her head in, nodding at the book, *Diesel Boat Engines Made Easy*. "I'm going for a soak. Wanna come?"

She heard the snap of cards from the galley as Miles shuffled for a game of cribbage with Teague, the whoosh of the teakettle being filled, the clack of it lowered onto the stove.

"Thanks. I think I'm gonna hang here."

The door swung fully open. "No thinking allowed on this boat. C'mon. Hop to. Oh, and naked bathing only. Town ordinance."

It was just after ten — the sun had set behind the crotch of the inlet, and a flinty light covered the water. They walked at a leisurely pace, past the phone booth at the top of the ramp, the playground by the harbor, crossing a wooden bridge to the single gravel road that ran from one end of Tenakee Springs to the other. Jackie's flip-flops slapped against her heels, flinging up stones. She wore Teague's black fleece pants with the rip up the backside, which spread as she stooped to inspect clusters of blooms along the edges of the road.

"State flower of Alaska, the forget-me-not," she said, pinching a small flower. She pulled up a larger, violet-petaled stalk and tucked it behind Tara's ear. "Nootka lupine, for my hard-driving deckhand."

The woman, usually so grim and focused, seemed serene, happy, even. "Wouldn't mind retiring here," she said, nodding at a black pipe jammed into a stream. "There's your drinking water. And that" — she looked toward an outhouse built at the end of a pier — "your shit-ter. See how they do it? Two flushes a day, each at high tide. Way life should be."

That salty, spruce-tip, tinny ice field smell of Port Anna (at least when the fish weren't running) — Tenakee Springs was braised in it. Purple light from a television shifted over the windows of a house, mimicking for a moment the color of the sky. The fragrant woods appeared to push the buildings along the coast into the sea. A maze of wooden stairs led up the hill, connecting A-frame cabins, perched among clumps of salmonberry bushes. A generator grumbled. From somewhere came the slap of a nail gun, followed by the pounding of a compressor.

Jackie switched on her headlamp. A gust of rain sent sawtooth alder leaves scurrying through the white light. They quickened their pace, crossed another stream, flowing from the uphill side of town through a culvert to the sea. Then Snyder Mercantile, a ramshackle building with peeling asphalt shingles, its false front lit up by flood lamps. SINCE 1899, the sign read.

"And here we are," Jackie said. A peeling slab of plywood showed bath hours in black paint: WOMEN'S 2–6 P.M. AND 10 P.M.–6 A.M., MEN'S 6 A.M.–2 P.M., 6–10 P.M. Jackie smiled and pushed open the door. A few older men were toweling off. "Boys," she said, setting down her basket on the bench. Someone grunted. Tara kept her eyes on her boots.

"We'll just get out of your hair here," one of the men said in a sarcastic tone. Jackie was already pulling off her thick woolen sweater and stepping out of fleece pants. The men gathered pouches of soap and shaving cream and left, the door knocking shut behind them.

The changing room was sheathed in tongue-and-groove panels. Knots bled through the steam-faded paint. The rusted oil furnace in the center rattled, a gasp of cold air pushing down through the exhaust.

Tara tugged her sweat-stained tank-top over her head, the draft from the furnace pricking her skin. The purple flower fell from her ear. When she reached down to pick it up the world took a heave. Boat brain, that was what Teague called this. She squeezed her eyes shut. When she opened them she glimpsed Jackie's nipples, the color of dirty pennies. Her body was square-shaped and knobby, as if her arms and legs had been hastily attached to her trunk. She crossed the room, the dimples at the base of her back shifting.

"Shall we?"

Tara forced herself to walk, one foot in front of the other, focusing on the planks pocked with small divots. Jackie held the door open. "Floor looks like a golf ball, doesn't it? From the caulks of logger's boots. Old boys coming in here after weeks out in the bush. Now we get to do the same, right? After you."

A single bulb hung from the ceiling, illuminated the steam. Moonlight gave the corrugated fiberglass on the atrium roof sheeting a toxic glow. Rain sounded like pebbles.

"Town rule," Jackie said, tossing Tara a bar of soap. "Suds up before you get in."

Jackie lathered her skin, using a cut-off Clorox container to rinse. Tara did the same, then braced herself on the edge of the bath, lowered her body into the water, and shut her eyes.

"Nice, right?" Jackie said.

Stone pressed into her back, massaging her muscles. Slowly, her stomach evened out. She allowed her body to go limp, her head slipping under. When she came back up, her eyes still closed, she heard Jackie's slow breathing.

Enough with these letters, she thought. Christmas, she'd go back to Philly. Connor could pick her up from the airport in his Mazda, and she could look at him, watch his expression, and just know.

But first — the *Chief.* She was making about a thousand dollars a week. If she could survive through September she'd have about twenty-one, then have the remaining four by Christmas. Or maybe Laney would accept a down payment. She'd get the boat, run it a hundred yards, and fly back to Philly. Surprise them all. That was the plan.

She felt a foot on her knee and opened her eyes. Jackie sat across the pool, small shoulders just visible above the water's surface, arms spread along the ledge of the bath. Her head appeared helmeted, hair dark and wet against her skull, cheeks shiny with moisture. When Jackie's heel slipped between her legs Tara gripped the ankle, pushed it away. "What are you doing?" she asked.

Jackie stood, resting her hands on Tara's shoulders. "Kiss me, sweetie." She pushed a knee between Tara's thighs. Her muscles wouldn't fire. Jackie twisted a fist into her hair, bent her head, and ran her tongue over Tara's lips. Tara turned and vomited over the concrete curb.

"What the fuck!" Jackie yelled, springing back.

Swallowing down the bile, Tara hauled herself out of the bath, taking the stairs by twos. Shivering, she pulled on her pants, thrust her feet into the rubber boots, stumbling as she pushed open the bathhouse door, and emerged into the evening light.

"Hey, T! Hold on! Hey, I'm talking to you."

Jackie was in the doorway, naked, dripping, small breasts sagging like poached eggs. She crossed the gravel, wincing as stones jabbed into her feet. "Jesus, would you calm down for a second?" Jackie reached out. Instinctively Tara jabbed, hitting the woman just beneath the right eye. She made an *oof* sound, and stumbled back, falling onto the gravel.

"I told you — keep your hands off me."

Tara pulled up the hood of her sweatshirt and ran. Past the tarped four-wheeler, the teapot house, the clumps of Nootka lupine and for-get-me-nots. A voice from a house asked if she was okay. She kept going, hearing only the rhythmic crunch of stone beneath her boots. She crossed the bridge, passed the playground, and stopped by the phone booth at the top of the ramp.

On deck she could see Miles, back to the wind, face illuminated by orange flame as he relit his cigar. Above his head, a trouble light glowed yellow in its wire cage. Taking a breath, she walked down the ramp, onto the *Adriatic,* went past him to her bunk, and began packing her things.

68

SHE SLEPT ON THE FLOOR of the library, an open-air shack filled with moldy paperbacks and VHS movies. In the morning Snyder's Mercantile opened. The cashier, a lavender-scented girl, faded denim apron over her swollen stomach, let her inside and said she'd brew coffee. It was an unusually hot day, the sun alone in the sky.

The girl plugged in a plastic fan, which made a grindy, knocking sound as it tried to turn. Tara stood by the counter as coffee percolated, the smell of grinds waking her.

"You know anyone headed to P.A.?" she asked the girl.

"This fella comin' in right now."

A reedy older man in a clean pair of Carhartts stomped up to the counter and set down an eighteen-pack of Rainier beer alongside a few boxes of white wine.

"Hey," she said, not surprised to see Petree. The man chuckled, shaking his head.

"Now I remember you, from that day on the ferry. You seemed like a little gerbil back then. And now look at you, in your work pants and Tufs. Fish blood behind your ears."

Tara moved to one side. He had shaved his white beard, and smelled like Vic's barbershop, hair tonic and talc.

"You clean up well," the girl behind the counter said.

"Yeah, well, I got a date with my new boat. Figured I'd dress for the occasion."

The fan continued to knock. The idea of spending twelve hours on a boat with this man was worse than spending the rest of her life in this outpost.

"Hey," he said, turning to Tara again. "Don't I recall you saying something about an old tug? I know all about them engines. If I could preside on you to help me keep a Jimmy six seventy-one good and primed on the way south, we'd both win out. You know anything about that?"

She recalled the engine—favored by fishing boats—from the book she had bought at the garage sale. "You don't have a reservoir?"

His eyebrows shot up. "That's right. We'll be running off containers."

Tara gestured with her chin at the beers. "And you'll be drunk on those the whole way down, I'm guessing."

Petree fondled his change. "How 'bout this. I'll lay off the Vitamin R until we hit Lost Sound. It's either that or you're gonna end up delivering a baby."

Tara looked at the girl, who was doing some sort of complicated breathing.

"All right. As long as I don't have to dress up to meet some stupid boat."

"Aw, don't be saying that too loud," he said, looking hurt. "She'll understand."

They walked through town to the harbor, where Petree untied the *Invictus*, a drab-looking squat double-ender troller, the wheelhouse hardly big enough for two people.

"Need to get the fuel pump fixed, probably a new tank welded up. Few other things. But she'll fish," he said, resting a hand on one of the cedar poles. "Little thirty-eight-footer. She'll get in the shallows while the big boys are out there dragging the forty-edge."

He set the boat due east, and they coasted out of the harbor. In the open water he showed her how to switch one jug of diesel for another, making sure the hose nested deep inside the can. Tenakee Inlet grew small behind them. It felt as if she were coming up from the underworld.

69

AFTER TWO MONTHS OF CIRCUITS on the *Adriatic,* she could sense where they were by the wind. The wind off Glacier Bay, near Homeshore, that brought with it the tinny smell of blue ice. The unfettered wind off the cape, how it wrapped around her. Chatham Strait's flinty williwaw wind, funneled between Archangel Island and the mainland. And the softer, spruce-brined wind of Peril Strait, which they turned into now, ZZ Top blaring on the deck speakers. The scent of sap and needles as they ran along the coast.

"You doing all right back there?" Petree yelled. He held out a box of white wine.

"Deal was no alcohol," she shouted back.

He raised a finger. "We said no Vitamin *R,* Kangaroo. Don't worry, wine just makes me chatty. It's the beer that makes me mean."

His skin, shaved and glistening before, now appeared torn, crêpey, like dough with not enough water. White whiskers sprouted from his cheekbones.

"What's with calling me Kangaroo?" she asked.

"You know, like them fighting kangaroos in Australia. Don't expect them to box."

She smiled at this. "You ever been on the *Pacific Chief*?"

"That old tug? Owned by that good-lookin' couple? Gal with the red shawl? Had sex with the feller up in the wheelhouse? Heard she zipped herself in a Tyvek suit and scrubbed every inch of that bilge. Came out the other side black as a leech."

He was a treasure trove. "That's a new one."

"Yeah, with the hippie trust-fund husband."

"I'm saving to buy her."

"Then I'd say you're plumb crazy. She's got a cracked engine block. That witch of a harbormaster's on the edge of sinking the darn thing, and I can't say I think it's a bad decision."

There was a break in the trees. They were passing Sitkoh Bay, to the north. She saw something at the far end, and took up binoculars from the binnacle board. It was the *Adriatic,* with boats unloading on either side. Teague worked the hydraulics from the bridge. And there was Jackie, hopping up to grab a tag line, dragging a bag of salmon over the tote. Miles hosed down a Traico, her job.

"Dumb bitch," she whispered.

She wanted to see if the woman's eye had swelled up, and adjusted the wheel on the binoculars, bringing her into sharper focus. But she couldn't tell.

"Seemed like the two of you were pretty tight in Hoonah. Something go sour on that boat?" he asked.

She lowered the glasses. "You could say that."

They arrived at the Narrows as the sun set, just after seven. Petree took a rolled chart from netting strung between the ceiling beams, pushed aside out-of-date tide tables, a used paper towel cylinder, bills, amber pill bottles, electrical tape, and unfurled the map in the galley, pinning the edges with four Rainier cans. He tapped the chart with a finger.

"They dredged just about twenty-four feet here; that's where we'll cut, between the two islands. Over there you got a rock and a submerged ledge. Head out on the bow and look for whirlpools, logs, dead sea lions, anything that might sink us."

The passage couldn't have been wider than a few lengths of the boat. Tangles of bull kelp were draped over the rocks, wrapped around bleached spindles of driftwood. Whorls of it spun off the bow. The tide pushed hard on their stern as they cut through boils of current, rushing past the islands. A row of cormorants on the rocks, shapes vague in the evening light, shuffled around as they passed. How much closer she was to the water on this small troller.

"Live to see another day," Petree said when she returned to the house. He rolled up the map, eyed the four beer cans on the table.

"We had a deal," Tara warned.

They tied up to a mooring buoy by Haley's Rock, on the southern side of the mouth of Fish Bay, a couple hundred yards offshore. The sky held its tint of soft blue as trees along the beach darkened. It was a warm evening — no wind, the water bathtub calm. Off to one side she heard the flat splash of a fish jumping. The bay stretched out in front of her, dark and silent.

"Lookee there." He pointed to a pumpkin-colored half-moon rising behind the trees. "Ring around the moon means cold, that's what the Sourdoughs say. Maybe it'll start feeling like Alaska again, instead of this swamp swelter."

"Hey, you know anyone looking for help on one of these trollers?"

He held a spotlight like a gun and shined it into the trees. The tide had spit driftwood onto the gravel flat. Drops of popcorn seaweed glittered. Green eyes blinked from the tree line. "Ever shoot a deer?" he asked.

She thought of Betteryear, alone in his cabin on the beach. His cat with the leaky eye. "No. But I saw one shot."

He nodded. "Thought maybe I could send you in for some dinner. Season opens in August. Guess Bambi gets to see another moon. That's fine, because we got Bullwinkle waiting inside. What'd you ask? No — you'd have to do like the rest of the world, walk the docks. Either that or put your name up on the chalkboard down at the Frontier. Sounds like you're checking off the bases, working at the hatchery, on the tender. Troller next in line."

He surprised her by cooking moose quesadillas, hot to the touch but cheesy and dripping with fat. Afterward she heated water on the

Brendan Jones

stove, then went out to do the dishes. A few stars shined beyond the halo of the moon, which had paled as it rose over the trees. With the pot she ladled seawater. Poured it into a tub until the temperature was right, and began to scrub.

The current pulled at the boat, swinging it around toward the beach. A wind started in from the north, cutting through her sweatshirt. Moose fat gummed up the sponge, but she didn't mind.

Back in Philly she knew her father would be pulling out the sports section of the *Philadelphia Inquirer,* reading it with his espresso. The Eagles would be having their first game in about a month. She adjusted her hat, splotched with oil and dried fish blood, and thought of being huddled by his side on that cold day at Veterans Stadium.

After switching off the deck light, she took a last look at Sergius Narrows. The channel marker blinked red, on and off, keeping the boats safe through the night.

70

MORNING SURF DASHED WHITE against the rocks at the back of Salisbury Sound. Petree had been right about the weather; the sun shined, but it was colder, and windy. And there, through a break in the islands, was the ferry terminal.

Petree kept his tattooed hand loose on the helm. "Imagine that. Two years ago you and me was up on the top deck, chatting it up."

All of it—Fritz, his gun, muffin, the dying salmon—seemed from another life. Before she could tie a bowline, or bleed a fish. How close she had been to getting back on that ferry.

Boats heaved to in front of the processor. Skippers stood on deck smoking cigarettes, watching the docks, waiting to unload, monitoring the VHF to check their place in line. Petree took over, elbowing the *Invictus* up to the crowded work float at Eliason Harbor. White sparks fell into the ocean as welders worked on back decks. She tossed her bibs and duffel onto the planks.

"You end up buying that old tug, you let me know," he said. "I don't mind playing around with those direct-reversibles. Might be fun, a change from these tetchy Jimmys."

"Right on."

She wanted to go directly to the tug, but stopped off at the processor along the way.

A young woman behind the fake-wood paneled counter said that Jackie had called ahead. For a moment Tara became nervous, wondering if she was about to be arrested for disorderly conduct or assault. Instead the woman handed her an envelope. Inside were bills.

"Five thousand three hundred and two dollars and eighty cents," the woman said. "Jackie said to record your time as ending today, which is weird, because they still haven't tied up."

"Is Newton Scarpe in town?" Tara asked, slipping the envelope into her halibut jacket, ignoring the girl's confused expression.

"Little guy with the eye patch? I think he's out trolling on the *Spanker*."

This was good news. The *Spanker* was a highliner, run by the owner of a float house in Camp Allison Bay, the skipper one of those rare people in town that folks called "fishy"—he had a nose for where salmon schooled.

"Some guy also left this for you."

The girl handed her another envelope with *Tara Marconi* scrawled on the front. Inside she found a note from Fran.

August 2, 1999

Greetings, Tara,

Just a quick missive to let you know we are having to let Keta go. Would you be interested in taking him? Otherwise we will need to give him to the pound. Love and good blessings.

Your friend, Fran

She checked the calendar behind the counter. August sixth.

From the office she ran along Main Street, past the church, toward the water. When she knocked, Fran answered. Before she could say anything the dog shoved his snout between Tara's thighs, whining softly. "It's all right, it's all right," Tara said into his ear. "I'm not going anywhere." Fran looked down at Tara, as if questioning whether this was true.

"I'll take him."

"You sure? He needs his medicine, which isn't cheap, although I've got almost a full bottle here."

The dog pressed harder against her. "I'm sure."

"Well then, he's yours. Let me grab his food and leash."

When Fran left, the dog gave a quick lick of the cheek, followed by a little dance, hopping on his back feet and panting.

"We'll be good," she told him. "I don't know how, but we'll be good."

When Fran returned, Tara started to ask if she could stay the night. But the woman gave a quick wave and shut the door.

"So much for hippie love," Tara said, looking at the dog. Without waiting, Keta bounded across the gravel parking lot. She followed, leashing him, but he strained in the direction of the docks. He didn't stop pulling until they stood in front of the *Chief.* Laney appeared at the galley door.

"Goddamn. You found a wolf."

"Can we stay?" Tara blurted out.

Laney smiled, then performed a quick curtsy, her feet clad in worn rabbit slippers. "It would be my pleasure. C'mon aboard."

That night the three of them sat in front of the fire, cedar popping in the wood stove. Laney sipped her wine while Tara told her about the *Adriatic.*

"You did the right thing," Laney said.

"You mean getting off that boat?"

"I mean hitting her in the face."

Tara drank half her glass. "I want this boat."

"Why?" Laney asked, her tone challenging. "I mean, don't get me wrong, I want you to have it. But why?"

She thought but couldn't say. It was as if she was just floating, and the hooks of her logic were rolled up, out of the water. "It's not like I'm boat shopping," Tara said slowly. "I don't know. I can't stop thinking about her."

"You're stubborn," Laney said. "And angry. I could tell from that first Thanksgiving. You think getting the boat will solve your problems. Trust me, I tried that."

The woman watched her. The ears on her bunny slippers flapped as she crossed her legs. "You get me twenty-five thousand dollars, and we're good. Okay?"

Tara swallowed. "Yes."

That night before sleep she took the dog for a walk along the docks. Pumps gurgled, dumping warm water from the bilges. Lines creaked against the bull rails.

At the bulletin board on the work float she put up a sign. *Deckhand for Hire: Hard-working, can cook. Two years' experience.* She paused, looking down at Keta.

"How will they reach me, monkey?"

Leave note on board, or for Tara Marconi at the library, she wrote.

Not tired, she walked down the street to the Frontier Bar, took Petree's advice, and wrote the same on the chalkboard.

They slept that night in one of the quarter berths off the salon, Keta snoring softly beside her. It was nice to feel the sway, slightly out of sync with the rise and fall of the dog's chest. She tracked in her mind the different parts of the engine beneath her, the connecting rods joining the cylinder heads to the crankshaft. How when you spun open a valve, air released from the tanks to the cylinders, starting combustion. One day, she swore to herself, she would hear that sound. The engine would fire, and the boat would move beneath her.

The next morning she took Keta on a walk to the Frontier Bar and library. No responses to either of her advertisements. She returned to the tug.

"Give me something to do," she told Laney. "Anything. Just keep me busy."

The woman bent and pushed aside the stern hatch of the *Chief.* "I know you've been reading about the Fairbanks-Morse. Why don't you go visit with it for a while. And, if you want to keep moving, organize the cargo hold."

In the engine room, with the caged bulbs shedding light on the cylinders, each one the size of a garbage can, she took off a plate, then peered into the casing. A brass piece of machinery attached to the crankshaft, which was the diameter of a small tree. Try as she might, she couldn't imagine it spinning.

She set to work filling carts with empty bottles of degreaser, sections of hose, a broken Zodiac foot inflater, and various other useless items, which she left in the harbor dumpster. At the end of the day, as Tara was spraying down the deck, Laney came up from the cargo hold, then put a glass of white wine in her hand.

"Damn," Laney said. "You don't let the grass grow, do you?"

She bent down and pulled a weed from a deck seam. "Not if I can help it."

71

HER THIRD DAY ON LAND she walked up to the post office. Keta seemed chipper, peeing on every patch of moss. Her heart sank when she saw the empty box. For some reason she had been sure she'd find a letter from Connor there.

If Newt were here they'd split a pack of Rainiers, head out to the breakwater, and make easy sense of the world. She considered asking Trunk for her old job back, but couldn't let go of how satisfying it had been to be out there with Petree on the *Invictus*.

She needed to make at least four thousand dollars in the next three months. On top of that, it felt wrong to be walking around like this while the rest of the fishing fleet was on the water. And yet there was nothing left to do except wait.

At the bookstore she bought a pad and settled into her booth at the Muskeg.

12 August 1999

Dear Connor,

I think this is the first time I've ever mailed a letter to Kansas. Hopefully it will catch you before you return to NYC.

I can't believe you got the lead in a play! And of course I remember Nikki Scarfo. He was down at the social club a few times. My father flipped out when they shot him.

She took a sip of coffee and reread. Her words sounded detached, unconcerned. Happy.

> *I got a dog. A big wolfish guy named Keta, a malamute-shepherd mix. He calms me. Although I'm agitated now, because I don't have work, even if I'm learning about the tug's engine. I think I told you — I need to move it a hundred yards, that's the deal (or it will be if I save enough money to buy it). I've been doing my best to get a head start reading up on the mechanics.*
>
> *Thanks for your letter. I miss you too. I'm thinking about coming back for Christmas.*
>
> *Love, T*

Before she could scratch out this last thought, she folded the letter, slipped it into the envelope, and mailed it. It was how she felt right then.

72

SHE WALKED ALONG THE BEACH WITH KETA, watching as he sniffed the tide pools, inspected the rocks. They checked the library for messages again. The woman at the front desk handed her a slip of paper.

"The guy sounded a little crazy on the phone. He said you could reach him at this email address. Kingbruce at Alaskanet dot com."

She hadn't ever been on email, so she went to the library computer and followed instructions to open an account. Growing warm with anticipation, she sent a message.

> This is Tara, you left a message at Port Anna Public Library. I'm looking for deckhand work.

A few seconds later the flag on her mailbox went up.

> Hi Tara. Opening on a crab boat. Bering Sea. Can you cook? How many years on the water.

She answered:

> Hi King Bruce. Yes, I can cook—I'm Italian. I have 2 years on the water.

This was a lie—two lies, even, and she knew it. But she had also been around long enough to understand this was how things got done.

> Yeah let me know if you need me. Thanks, Tara.

She stared at the computer screen, willing the flag in her inbox to flip. When it did, her hands shook as she clicked open his message.

Could use another hand. pasing thru PA October 3 maybe earlier.
check HO and meet us when we tye up. 3% share King Bruce f/v AK
Reiver. Okay?

She looked out the library window. The Bering Sea! Up by Russia, on the big boats. Making the big money. Her heart grew loud in her ears as she hen-pecked the keys.

YES

Giddy, she hit the send button.

She closed out her session and stood, looking around the room. And there, sitting in an armchair by the magazine rack, was Betteryear.

"Tara," he said, reaching for her hands, half standing. "It is so good to see you."

She smelled his scent of grease and cooked greens, saw how his lips shook. He appeared older, but squeezed her hands firmly.

"I'd like to spend time with you," he said. "Are you free tomorrow? There's a special place I'd like to go, perfect for relaxing, especially after your hard work on the tender. Yes?"

"I can't tomorrow," she said. "I have things to do."

"I see. Well, we can have dinner on Sunday. Does that sound good?"

She didn't want to spend time with him. Then again, he had been so generous with his knowledge, his food. "Is it okay if I bring my dog?"

"Yes. Seven P.M. We'll make beach asparagus."

When she left she swung by the Frontier one last time to check the blackboard. Beneath her post someone had written in neat capital letters: 6 P.M. TOMORROW LEDA'S REVENGE.

That night, walking out the docks toward the *Chief,* Keta stopped in the middle of the walkway. He pointed his nose into the black sky and began to yip. She looked around, wondering what had set this off. His yips blended into a long howl. The sound made her shiver, the wildness and bravery of it. Her chest overflowed, and then she was leaning back, howling into the night. The two of them bayed together, until a fisherman came out of his wheelhouse and asked if they would please keep it down, he was trying to sleep.

73

SHORTLY BEFORE SIX P.M. the following day she tied Keta at the top of the ramp and went off to search for *Leda's Revenge*. As she walked a rasping sound set off a dim memory. It made her think of Connor in his shop, but something else as well — her father, in khaki pants, on his hands and knees, refinishing the floors of their house on Wolf Street. An early memory — she must have been three or four. Her mother watching from the kitchen table, smoking a cigarette. Strange, now that she thought about it, that her father had never been allowed to smoke cigars in the house.

The rasp came from a newly painted troller, with the outline of a raven perched on the "G" of LEDA'S REVENGE, stenciled in black over the flybridge.

"Tara?" A man stepped forward and offered his hand, rough and swollen. "Zachary," he said. His beard, flecked with thicker gray whiskers, was darker where a dust mask had covered it. Dust coated his eyelashes. "Can't figure out for the life of me what makes more sense," he said, looking over the deck. "The orbital sander or the jack plane. Guess the fish don't care either way. C'mon aboard. What boat did you work for?"

"The *Adriatic*," she said, stepping over the gunwales.

"Ever trolled?"

She shook her head.

"When people in town advertise themselves as having experience, that generally means trolling."

She knew this. It hadn't stopped her from putting up her note. Black grime outlined his nails.

"How long are you looking to work?"

"I've got a job crabbing in October."

"On what boat?"

"The *Alaskan Reiver.*"

He gave a tight smile. "Usually guys with years of experience get those spots. I assume it's for the two-week king crab opener?"

"That's right. The skipper said it was an emergency."

He pulled at his beard. "So we're coming up on the middle of August now, which gives us about a month and a half. Usually work alone, but I could use a hand. My main priority is safety. We go out, fish tough, have a good time, come back a bit richer, and in one piece. That make sense to you?"

"That works."

"Here's my proposition then. You be up front with me, I'll be up front with you. I can say off the bat that I don't like that you haven't fished before. And I also don't like that you put you had experience when you don't. So you take the marine safety class they're offering this Friday, pass it with flying colors, and we'll fish the salmon opener Monday, August sixteenth. If it works out we'll do coho in September, maybe chum depending on the run. I'll start you off with a ten percent deck share, and we'll take it from there. Then you go north to the Bering in October and crab. Deal?"

She didn't like him calling her out like that. On the other hand, this scheme meant she could pocket a few thousand trolling, and then the crab boat would put her over the top in October. From the way people spoke about crabbing, way over the top.

"Deal."

"Only thing I'll ask is that you buy yourself a survival suit after your course. Here." He handed her a wad of bills. "Consider it an advance. In the interest of safety."

"One quick question."

"Shoot."

"Can I bring a dog?"

Zachary looked into the air. It was something Fritz used to do—peer into space, part serious consideration, part you've got to be fucking kidding me.

"Does he get seasick?"

Tara watched him. "I'm not sure."

He smiled. "Good. Bring the dog."

74

TARA ARRIVED EARLY to the weekend marine safety class, held on Sawmill Creek Road, in a purple board-and-batten structure across from a trailer park. She set down her new survival suit on the table. A clean-cut, handsome curly-haired man poured her a cup of coffee.

"What boat are you on?" he asked.

"*Leda's Revenge.*"

"Zachary Sachs. You're in good hands there."

Older men with pasty, weather-beaten faces, double-fronted Carhartts, and caps slick with oil residue took their seats around the classroom. The instructor split them into smaller groups. The men removed immersion suits from their orange rubber sacks and practiced slipping plastic bags over their feet before stepping into the neoprene heels. "Sixty seconds or less," the instructor said. When he set off the clock, she shoved her fists into the mittens, zipped up, Velcroed the flap over the lips. Encapsulated in the suit, Tara felt like a school mascot.

They learned how to set off flares, board a life raft, test an EPIRB, call in a mayday on the VHF, providing coordinates, boat name, and details of the problem.

"Details like, we're fucking sinking, git your lazy coffee-drinking Coastie asses out here," one of the trollers joked.

Outside the building, they gathered around a welded stainless-steel structure, open on both sides, built to simulate an engine room.

"Okay. I want you to imagine that this is not only your livelihood, but also your home. With all your possessions, your dreams, your hopes, all of it sinking from beneath you. Now I need a volunteer." The instructor's eyes roamed over the crowd, settling on Tara. "Feeling lucky?"

It was like stepping into the boxing ring, she thought as she climbed over the side, spreading her feet, finding her balance on the diamond sheet-metal floor.

"Bring it," she said.

He handed up a plywood box. "These are your tools. If you fail to stop the leak, you drown, along with the rest of your crew. Ready?"

"Ready."

He smiled, then turned the lever on a plastic ball valve. A leak sprang from the floor, soaking her jeans. She jumped back, shooting him a look.

"You said you were ready."

"The box, box," someone chanted.

She dumped the contents onto the deck, thinking of Newt, how he would know exactly which tool to grab. She seized a tire scrap and wrapped it around a wedge of two-by-four, hammering it into the gash. A geyser erupted from a pipe. She took the vise grip with a chain and ratcheted a boot over the rip. Water squirted against her leg, coming from the stuffing box, where the crankshaft exited. The only tool left was a wrench. She used it to torque down the bolts.

Breathing heavily, she looked around. Drips from the roof hit the bill of her cap.

"Congratulations," the instructor said, smiling as her classmates began to clap. "You live."

75

SUNDAY, August fifteenth, the night before the king salmon opener, she took an unlocked bike out to Salmonberry Cove.

In Betteryear's cabin she stood at the burner, shuffling beach asparagus and cubes of chicken-of-the-woods with a hand-carved spatula. Out the window she caught a glimpse of Keta, roaming the beach, investigating tide pools. Betteryear didn't want him inside, scaring the cat.

There was the *whomp* of the handle as Betteryear shut the door on the wood stove, followed by a click as he slid the catch home. It wasn't that she didn't want to be there; she still enjoyed the seclusion of the cove, the sound of pebbles receding with the waves. But there was so much afoot. She was excited to fish with Zachary, and to make good on her promise to Laney.

"You still have your rifle under the cot, don't forget," he said, coming into the kitchen. "It's hunting season. We should get you a deer of your own."

She concentrated on the orange chunks of mushroom, the twig-like stalks of beach asparagus turning bright green in the cast-iron pan. "One day. But my plan now is to make money and get the tug. I'll crab up north on that job I told you about, then go back to Philly to see folks."

He stood in front of her, interlacing his long soapy fingers.

"And after that?" he asked.

She looked around for plates. "I'm trying to be patient."

"Move in here," he blurted. "To the cabin."

When she didn't answer he moved closer. "Tara, listen to me. I've known you since you first came here. Trust me when I say this boat makes no sense."

The cat, curled on the quilt at the end of her cot, yawned. She looked out the window for the dog.

"All I'm asking is that you think about it. I could build an addition. *We* could build an addition. I'd teach you to use hand tools. And we could make dinners. I wouldn't charge rent. Just help with gathering, canning, keeping things clean and swept."

She extinguished the burner, set the pan on a potholder, and took two plates from the shelf. His whining was beginning to grate on her.

He took the plates from her hands and gripped her shoulders. "Tara, let me help you. Please." His lips were shiny with saliva. She saw they were trembling. "Please, Tara. I know what I'm doing. Trust me. *This* can be your home."

The words jarred her. She imagined herself twenty years into the future, hair streaked with gray, bent over the stove cooking mushrooms. Keta buried at the tree line, Betteryear soon to follow.

She drew away, grabbed her coat from the hook, and pushed open the door into the rain. Betteryear followed. "Where are you going?" She took her bike from where it was leaning against the tree. Keta watched Betteryear. "What about dinner?"

She pushed down the pedal, rising high in the saddle.

"I need to get ready for fishing."

"You don't understand!" he shouted at her back. "You have *nowhere to go!*"

She pedaled up the trail, bouncing over roots. Keta followed at a trot. Betteryear shouted something else, his voice melting into the sound of the rain. Her lungs burned as she climbed.

Keta kept pace as she coasted past the church, looking up every couple of seconds at her, panting. On the curved stretch to Maksout- off Bay, she began to sob in gasps. Past the trailer court, turning onto Kiksadi River Road. Keta lagged behind, and she stopped to wait.

The new asphalt shined beneath the recently installed street lamps. Grave plots blurred between the trees. Her thighs hurt. When Keta caught up, his tongue lolled out to one side. She biked slowly, tears and rain running down her face. She wanted to sit by the river, in the darkness, and just think with her dog.

When she dismounted at the trail, Keta began to whine. She qui- eted her breathing. The dog kept glancing up at her, making small yips.

To her right a shape rose from between the trees. A dull, vegetal smell, decaying earth, proteins breaking down, drifted through the air. The dog's lips went up, and he stepped forward, growling. *Kush- taka,* she thought. Land otter spirit. Death-bringer. Her punishment for running away like she did. For not listening to Betteryear. For not seeing beyond her own grief. She repositioned her bike in front of her body, backing toward the road. The shape kept pace, ignoring the dog.

"What do you want!" she screamed. It stopped. Her breath came in hitches.

Bailey stepped into the light. "I thought you were done with the woods, girlfriend." When he took another step toward her Tara raised her fists. "What, you think you're going to box me now?"

Out of the dark Keta lunged at him. Tara screamed as Bailey brought down a beer bottle on the dog's shoulders. She hit him on the side of the head, his skull hurting her fist. Keta yelped, then con- tinued to bark as Bailey sauntered back into the woods, laughing.

Shaking, Tara crouched and felt the dog's bones, wincing when he whimpered in her ear.

"You're all right, love. We're good."

She walked, dog by her side, to the harbor. On *Leda's Revenge* she found a can of beef soup for Keta, and pet his soft head as he ate the brown chunks in gulps. When she curled up on the bunk he sat on his haunches and faced the door.

76

EARLY THE NEXT MORNING, on a blowy Monday, Tara woke to the sound of Zachary unloading groceries.

"Ready to catch some fish?" he said.

A hearty, upbeat nature was exactly what she didn't want to deal with now.

"Got some good reports at Fulton Island, and some at Dos Santos Bay, near the southern tip of Archangel. Salmon are like the rest of nature, I guess," he said, arranging milk, butter, and eggs in the icebox. "Hard to predict." He held up a package of bacon. "Don't tell my wife."

The dog stepped onto the docks, stretching, keeping a wary eye on Zachary.

"Whoa! You didn't say you were bringing a wolf on board."

"He's chilled out. Doesn't bark."

"You look like you could use another five hours of sleep."

"I'm fine."

She ignored his raised eyebrows as she brought more groceries into the galley. He climbed the ladder to the flybridge, then hoisted up the roof so the chute from the processor could drop into the hold. Their ice appointment was for five A.M. He gave her the job of inflating the buoy balls until they made a hard knocking sound against her knuckle.

THE ALASKAN LAUNDRY   255

"Cut her loose there, partner," he shouted down. She undid the
bow, stern, then the midship line, and stepped aboard.

"Forgetting something?"

"Shit," she said. The dog watched her, standing on the end of the
dock. With a pulse of the engine Zachary pushed them back.

"You might as well undo our shore power while we're at it."

"Shit," she repeated. The boat swiveled, tilting the blue dock post
where the yellow cord was attached. She hopped back onto the dock,
threw the breaker, and swung the cord over the bow.

"C'mon, love. Hop hop!"

With a surprising nimbleness Keta leapt over the gunwales onto
the deck, giving Tara a quick lick when she leaned down to kiss his
cheek. Again Zachary backed out, then swung the boat around the
breakwater of Crescent Harbor and cruised beneath the bridge. Cars
passed above, the sound of tires over the joints echoing off the water.
Tara leaned against the hold, watching the sun rise behind town, jeal-
ous of Keta snoring away on the galley bench. Seasons were made or
broken by salmon openers, she knew. She needed to get on with it.

When they approached the pilings of the processor, Zachary
threw the engine into reverse and a backwash kicked out from the
stern. She waited with a line in one hand, then leaned against a pil-
ing, caked with barnacles and scallops and a few starfish, to make
them fast.

"The tide's pulling us," Zachary said as she seized the rope and
began to tie a clove hitch. "Just come right on back to the boat." Unsure, she looked back at him.

"Here. Always go from bow to stern when you tie off to pilings.
And leave some slack so the hull doesn't rub."

A voice came from above. "Holy shit, is that Tara Marconi you
got on board?"

It was Trunk, peering down, earphones around his neck. "You
stealin' my employees, Sachs?"

"What can I say?" Zachary shouted back. "She was ready for some real work." He turned to Tara. "Tie her off at the bow, then come and help me with this hatch cover."

Trunk lowered the hooped cylinder of the ice chute. "Tell me when!" Zachary dropped into the hold, caught the chute, and shouted up.

"All right!"

There was a rumble, and then the familiar bang of Trunk hammering on the chute with his wrench, followed by the scurry of ice chips. Zachary filled the stern hold, then the two sides.

"One minute!" Zachary hollered. Trunk hit a lever and the ice slowed. Zachary pushed the chute over the side of the boat.

"Y'all stay safe out there," Trunk shouted down. "And you take care of yourself, my lady."

She leaned over the gunwales. She liked how he said this, as if she were some aristocrat. "I will."

The hatch cover slid home with a whomp. The sun broke through the clouds, lighting the volcano a rusty red as he motored out past the breakwater. "You get seasick?" Zachary asked.

"I didn't on the tender."

"That old scow doesn't bob up and down like this one. If you need to throw up, just go right over the side. You wanna lie down?"

"I'm good, just hungry."

"Make lunch."

She smeared peanut butter and jelly onto a tortilla while he checked the tide tables. The RAM of the autopilot made barking noises as it shifted, the system keeping the boat oriented west-south-west, just off the volcano.

"You bring food for the dog?"

Keta's ears perked up. He looked between them.

"Nope."

Zachary shook his head, turning the knob on the VHF, adjusting the volume. "Well, I hope he eats fish."

Southeast Alaska waters, Cape Decision to Cape Edgecumbe, small craft advisory. A weak trough will dissipate over the panhandle Monday. A high-pressure ridge will build across the panhandle and eastern gulf Monday night. A weather front will move northeast into the central gulf by Saturday morning, with southeast gales up to forty knots diminishing to fifteen knots late. Seas sixteen feet.

Zachary grimaced. He opened the tide book again, and looked toward the volcano. A green-tinted line of clouds moved east off the ocean. The teapot on the Dickinson clattered against its railing. She handed him a sandwich, which he ate in large bites, holding a paper towel to catch loose jam.

"You ever take wheel watches on the *Adriatic*?" She shook her head. "Just keep an eye on the radar, and ahead of you for dead-heads—floating logs. If you see one, go in the other direction. Red channel markers on your right, green on the left. I'll be right back. The other day the bilge was pumping oil. I want to make sure we're okay."

She stood in front of the wheel, keeping one hand on the dial. It was like a video game, making sure the image of the boat remained between the red and green points on the screen, and out of the light blue shallows. Glancing up at the radar every now and then, watching the blobs of islands and boats shape and reshape every few seconds. There was an intermittent whine, and she stayed quiet, trying to hear what it might be, until she realized it was the dog.

"You need food, don't you?"

When Zachary returned, Keta was eating the second half of his beef stew. Zachary lit a cigar, the wheelhouse filling with its odor. "That's good beef. Coming out of your crew share."

"I'm new at this taking-care-of-another-creature thing," she said, moving over so he could take the wheel. "Sorry."

He smiled to show it had been a joke.

"So why didn't you finish out the season with Teague and Jackie?"

One thing she had come to appreciate about Alaskans: when it was clear you didn't want to talk about something, people laid off. So she felt confident he'd let it drop when she said, "It just didn't work out."

Except he didn't.

"It gets squirrely on the water, especially in these small boats," he told her. "I like to have a sense of who I'm working with, where they've been. That's why I put you on that safety course. So if there's anything I should know, tell me before we put gear in the water."

She stared out the window. They were rounding the far side of the volcano. Ravines, still filled with snow, swirled off the rim. "We had a misunderstanding, and I left."

"And you hit her."

That was another thing about Port Anna. No secrets. "Yeah, I hit her, okay? If you had some guy getting up in your face, what are you going to do? Smile back at him?"

He drew on his cigar, exhaled out the window. "Depends on what the guy was in my face about. I also heard you were in a scrape up in Hoonah."

"What the fuck?" she said. She felt a wetness on the back of her palm, Keta nudging her hand with his nose. "If you don't want me on the boat, drop us on the next island. We'll figure it out."

He pulled back on the throttle. For a moment she wondered if he was actually doing it. Then she saw they were coming into a cove. Small waves looped over themselves, breaking onto a narrow strip of beach.

On the flybridge he hit the kill switch on the generator. The silence echoed off the rocks. Back inside he said, "Listen. Like I said back at the docks, honesty is boat policy. I need to know who I'm working with."

"Should I get dinner started?" she asked.

He waited.

Fuck, Tara thought. This was a mistake. It was always a mistake to go anywhere with a guy you didn't know. Things never ended well.

"Tara," Zachary said. "Just be up front with me. That's all I'm asking."

She exhaled. "Okay. In Hoonah I was on the phone with my father, trying to talk to him, and this guy kept harassing me. It was my fault. I hit him. And with Jackie it was worse. Things got really weird in Tenakee. And she deserved it."

He picked at his beard, thinking. Finally, he gave a small nod. "Okay. Let's get dinner started."

Cooking calmed her. She sliced potatoes and onions into browning bacon while Zachary picked up the radio station, blues of some sort, and set to repairing his glasses, one arm held to the frame with a shred of electric tape. Gray wafts of smoke rose in the still air as he soldered. He put down the glasses, fed a handful of chips into his mouth. Flakes caught in his beard. "This bruiser over here keeps a good eye on you. Watches your every move."

She kissed Keta on his bony snout. "So how'd you end up in Port Anna?" she asked. This was the standard Alaska opening gambit, she had come to learn. She wanted to break the awkwardness. Thankfully, he went along.

"Well, I was going to a yeshiva in Kew Gardens Hills, in Queens, New York City, and I met a beautiful woman outside a synagogue. We married, everything was fine, then her parents were stabbed in a mugging. And she decided that, if we were going to raise children, we would bring them up in a place where they would feel safe. I had read about this half-baked idea in the 1920s of Roosevelt's to send ten thousand Jews a year to Southeast. So I thought, why not check it out? We hitched up to Bellingham, caught the ferry, bought a boat, and I started fishing. Thelma found a job as a dispatcher at the police station, while I learned the charts, the pinnacles." He held his glasses away from his face, then slipped them back on, eyes large behind the lenses. He wiped his fingers with a wet cloth. "And that's my story."

"I've got a friend, Newt—"

"Guy on the *Spanker*? One eye? Works like a demon?"

"That's him."

"Yeah. I like that kid."

"He has this idea that the state's on one continuous wash cycle. The Alaskan laundry, that's what he calls it. Everyone coming north to get clean of their past."

Zachary looked toward the islands. "I've seen some folks get pretty dirty in the process. Take Newt, for example."

She set out plates and silverware. He had a point.

"So how'd you get hooked up with King Bruce?"

"The crab guy? You know him?"

"I know *of* him. He's down an eye as well."

"You're kidding."

"I am not. Comes with the territory, I guess. You feel ready to work those volcanic reefs up there in the Bering Sea? That's a whole different game."

After dealing with Fritz, living in the woods, navigating her way through Jackie, Petree, and Betteryear, she felt like she could deal with anything.

"What happened to his eye?"

"As I heard it, he was stepping into a crab pot to change out a bait jar. The boat took a wave, the door shut, and the pot went overboard with him inside. He was on his way to the bottom until he kicked open the door, swam up, and whacked his head against the hull. Knocked himself out cold. His boat circled back, and some deckhand trying to save him hooked him in the eye with a pike pole. When he woke up he was half blind."

"Man."

"Coming clean exacts its price."

"I guess."

She scooped food onto the blue enamel plates. What would her price be? Had she already paid? The other night with Bailey? With Betteryear? The platform burning in the woods?

"One thing I can tell you," he said, "it's no country for a *nebbish*."

"What's a *nebbish*?"

His reached out to scratch Keta's chin. The dog seemed to smile, showing his long teeth. "Everything, as far as I can tell, that you are most definitely not."

77

THE ALARM BLEATED. She peeked off the side of her bunk: 3:44 A.M.

"Time to go fishing!" Zachary barked, rolling out of his bunk. "C'mon, doggie. Up and at 'em. Tara, wanna lower the poles?"

When she returned he had pulled the anchor and was motoring into the ocean. Keta stood by the hold, blinking as the sun broke the horizon. Even after almost two years in Alaska, it still struck her as bizarre, the sun up at such an hour. Zachary held up a bottle of corn huskers lotion. "Keeps the hands from getting too rough. Also, tape each of your fingers. When we get deep enough I'll throw in the gear. Make sure Wolfie stays away from the troll pit. I don't want him getting a bug in the eye."

She called Keta into the galley, where he made himself comfortable in the corner that offered the best view of the wheelhouse. It worried her that she had no idea what Zachary was saying—gear, troll pit, bugs. Keeping one eye on their depth, she wrapped her fingers. Zachary came back in. "Now, this is what we're searching for," he said, pointing at the pixelated fish finder. "Needlefish. Gear up. We're wading in bait."

"I haven't brushed my teeth or peed."

"Fish on!" he drawled, watching a large rubber band connected to the line stretch and contract. "C'mon! We got action. I'll show you how."

She watched carefully as he brought in the line, unhooking each leader, arranging the flasher—a reflective, rectangular piece of plastic — neatly in front of him. When a fish came up he clubbed it, gaffed it through the gill plates, heaved it into the landing bin, freeing the hook by pulling the leader tight.

"This is a bug," he said, holding up the fluorescent rubber lure. "What the fish bite."

He worked one gear below frantic — club, spike, land, take out spoon, next leader. When he missed a fish, save for a short hiss of frustration, he just kept on going, confident another fish would come through soon enough.

"Give it a shot," he said as he set out his Styrofoam float. "Start with the main."

She turned the crimped copper knob and the wire started coming in. Clips hurtled toward her. When she tried to slow the line down she turned the knob in the wrong direction and a clip accelerated into the blocking, making a knocking sound.

"Fuck," she said, backing off.

He came over, worked out the tangle. "Patience," he said, wedging a spoon on the end of the cleaning knife into the clip to make sure it snapped shut. "Try again. Slow this time."

She did, setting the leader on the clothesline strung at the back of the house, then realized there was a fish on it. She pulled in the line hand over fist, leaned over the side, raised the gaff, then brought it down toward the head. She missed, hitting the boat.

"Again," Zachary said. "Concentrate."

This time she brought the fish high out of the water until it spun in the light, prismatic. Focusing on its smooth head, she sank the steel point of the gaff hook through the gills, then lifted it into the landing bin.

"There it is!" Zachary shouted. "Success."

She watched as the salmon's charcoal lips opened and closed. Its body thick and torpedo-shaped, its back rainbow with a bronze sheen.

"Jesus, they're beautiful," Tara said.

Rollers lifted and dropped the boat as they continued to work through their lines, Zachary moving through his side twice as fast as she could. Other trollers tacked back and forth, keeping distance so the wires wouldn't tangle. At the top of the waves she could see the snowy crags of the Fairweather Range before the boat dropped back into the trough. She kept her eye out for the *Spanker*, but Zachary had said they were fishing the other end of the island.

In the wheelhouse she checked on Keta. He had his head between his paws, and didn't move when she nuzzled him with her nose. "You okay, monkey?"

The dog looked worried.

Through the windows she watched the rubber snubbers on the bow, connected to the lines in the water. The one on the left pulsed. The rigging made a ghostly buzzing sound.

"Hear that?" Zachary shouted from the troll pit. "You got a hog on your side, port main," he said.

Beads of water detonated in bursts off the wire as she brought in the line. Twelve percent of the deck share, that's what he had promised her, which meant she was getting a good fifteen bucks a fish.

"Pay attention, Tara. It's a big one. You want me to land it? That's gotta be thirty-five, forty pounds."

She stripped off leaders one after the other, arranging hooks on the gear-setter as she had seen him do. Through the water she could see the shape of the fish, a gray blur rising up out of the depths. When it got near the surface it shot out of the water, sun glinting off its body.

"Keep that leader tight," Zach yelled. "Hand over fist. It's hooked in the soft part of the mouth. Gentle. You got it? He wants to run to the starboard. That's a couple hundred dollars on the line there — go easy, Tara."

She gripped the leader harder, wrapping it around the palm of one hand and reaching for the gaff hook with the other, wishing he'd shut the fuck up. These fish were twice the size of the pinks at the hatchery. It was a boxing match, she decided, the fish bobbing and weaving, and she just needed to stay calm, focus on the eyes, like Gypo said. She brought the fish in closer, wondering if she was strong enough to lift this creature, with its heavy hooked snout and thick body, over the rail. With a twitch of her wrists she brought the head out of the water. As the body went slack she whacked the fish on the skull, just as she had done at the hatchery, feeling the quiver of the salmon through the monofilament.

"Yes!" Zachary shouted. "That's it. Can you get him?"

With a swipe she hooked the salmon through the gill plate, gripped the gaff with two hands, and hauled it into the bin, where it landed with a thud.

"Hot mama!" Zachary shrieked. She looked down at the fish, gills beating the air.

"That's gotta be a forty-pounder right there," he said, leaning over, his shadow dulling the rainbows playing over the scales. A second tremor coursed through its body.

"Looks like you missed the gills with the gaff. You know how to bleed it?"

She shook her head. He stretched out an index finger and swiped beneath the gill flap. "Just grab and pull."

She did, feeling the soft filaments, then the bony gill rakers. Blood spread around the fish's head.

"Let's throw it back in," he said.

She looked up at him, confused.

"I mean, the line, silly. Get the line back in. Then dress your fish. I'm assuming Jackie taught you how."

"Jackie never taught much," Tara said as she sent the line back out. "She just yelled. But I learned at the processor."

As he went forward to turn them back to where the fish had been, she cut out the accordion of gills, then reached with the knife tip to

cut the membrane around the throat. With the beveled spoon on the
other end of the knife she scooped out organs — liver, kidneys, tangle of intestines — opened the skein and scraped jellied blood. The
heart dangled in the throat, a triangle of flesh held by a white bauble
of fat. She ripped it clean and held it there, pulsing in her palm like a
frightened mouse.

She whistled over the sound of the engine. Keta came on deck,
looking at her expectantly.

"Here, monkey."

She dangled the heart over his head. He chewed, then looked to
her for more.

"Don't get that dog sick," Zachary said, watching from the galley.
"And I don't like him near the troll pit."

They worked until midnight. Stabs of pain radiated down her
spine, in the back of her neck, just as they had in the brig at the processor. She ignored it, gazing with bleary eyes over the water as they
passed another boat, the deckhand in the pit doing the same job
as her.

Zachary taught her to ice, interlocking heads to tails, filling
throats and bellies with chips. By the day's end they had eighty-eight
in the hold. "It'll put food on the table," he told her. "Let's stack 'em."

He finished winding both lines on his side, and bringing the can-
nonballs on board, before she did her first, and that annoyed her. He
noticed. "Patience," he repeated.

Zachary tidied the hold while she sautéed onions and cauliflower
and mixed them with sausage and jarred gravy. Her mother would
have been horrified. Zachary wrote "scores" from other fishermen in
black marker on the glass windows. Someone out on the Fairweather
grounds, pinnacles way offshore, had pulled over three hundred
kings. "Thinking maybe we should make a move south, especially
with this nasty bit of weather they're calling for. Wind is supposed to
switch, fifty knots from the southwest. We'll be traveling against it on
the way back if we go north. Then again, that's where the bite is."

Keta hardly opened his glazed eyes when she gave him his pills. He breathed shallowly, and hadn't touched his dinner.

"Dog's green around the gills," Zachary said.

"Don't worry, monkey. We'll get some rest on anchor." She wondered if it was the salmon heart.

She curled up with the dog, squeezed his paw. Zachary didn't change the setting on the alarm clock. Twenty seconds later he was snoring.

"Fuck," she muttered, already thinking of the snarl of the engine, Zachary's upbeat morning mood. She went down the ladder to zip into her bag.

The next day, after a morning of slow fishing, Zachary told her to pull the lines.

"That's why they call it fishing and not catching," he said.

Staring at the numbers on the glass, he said they would run north despite the prediction of strong winds. Reports were good in Icy Strait. He put the boat on autopilot and busied himself replacing a wire for the water heater. Tara tied up gear, crimping ferrules and attaching hooks to the fluorescent bugs.

As they ran, Irish, the cantankerous white-haired troller Jackie had reamed out, called for the *Revenge* over the radio. He had installed a new fathometer, he told Zachary, and it kept conking out.

"You're too hard on your gear, Irish," Zachary responded. "Give the damn alternator a spa day. You know, clip its nails, give it a sponge bath."

The old salt scoffed. "Yer a feckin' idiot, is what you are, Zach. And I'll tell ya another thing. 'Steada a home fleet built on trust, now it's ever man for hisself, one huntin' the other. No sir, that's not the world I grew up in."

Zachary stripped off wire sheathing with a flick of the wrist. "Irish, you can still get at the work pretty good, but having someone to unload on wouldn't be the worst thing for you."

He didn't seem to hear. "Fellas always gougin' each other, runnin' this guy or that into the shallows. Fellas don't even know it's starboard inside pole that's got the right a way."

"Yeah, Irish, you're coming through kinda fuzzy," Zachary said, reaching to turn down the volume. "Can you turn it onto a higher frequency, please, and repeat that?"

After about thirty seconds he turned up the volume again. Irish was still going.

"Yep, still not coming through, Irish. Try once more."

Again he twisted the knob on the volume, turning it up a few minutes later. Irish was still complaining.

Tara tried not to laugh. "You're cruel."

"It's good for him. Call it fishermen's therapy."

She watched as he replaced the wooden panel and studied the graph of tide tables on the computer. He had different gears — playful, work-serious, contemplative. He checked his watch, once more turned up the volume.

"Yeah, I hear ya on all that, old bud. I'm gonna go throw 'em in. Good morning. Clear to sixteen."

He slowed the boat. As soon as they set the gear there was a clatter — the lines whirring, the poles bending. Keta sensed the excitement, hopped off the bench, and started howling on deck.

"That's right, doggie!" Zachary shouted, pulling on his bibs. "Someone's feeling better. He knows we got fish on the line."

They each took a side, running through the lines one after the other. She did her best to haul gear without stopping the hydraulics. Zachary slapped together peanut butter and jelly sandwiches, which they ate while pulling in float bags. She tossed her crusts into the waves. It was glorious. No Fritz to check up on her, no what-the-fuck hand from Trunk, no silent, vigilant Jackie eyes burning holes in her back. She wondered if Newt would still call her slow as molasses.

Just after ten, Zachary said to stack 'em, and she arranged the leaders neatly along the gear-setter. Dinner, brush teeth, Keta's pills. The dog had started to pick at the soups and chili she gave him. "You're starting to like it on the water, aren't you?" she said, petting his head.

Moments after she climbed into her bunk and shut her eyes, it seemed, the clock was bleating. Turn of the key, press of the starter button until the low gear of the engine snarled. Rattle of the anchor, tick of the coffeemaker, lowering of the poles, and they were at it again.

That evening, setting out her side, she noticed an oil slick tailing off the stern when the bilge pumped. When she pointed it out to Zach, he frowned and mumbled something about pressure.

Wisps of white skirted across the darkening sky. A bank of clouds had developed in the west, seabirds working the leading edge of it. As she ran lines, one after the other, Zachary leaned his head out of the cabin and shouted. "That blow is headed our way. Let's pull it and get the hell out of here."

The ocean creased, and the waves took on a green tint. She heaved in her stabilizer, then returned to the cabin. Zachary rubbed his beard. "They're stacking up with the tide," he muttered as he steered the bow into a wave, the *Revenge* hobby-horsing as it rode up a face then dropped down the back side. Keta was back in his corner, licking his lips. Zachary turned on a red light to search for a wiper to clear condensation from the windows, then switched it back out. "I need you to go and throw back in those stabilizers," he said. "Hey! Pay attention out there."

The coffeepot on the Dickinson skated over the stovetop, clattering against the steel rails. Spice jars toppled onto the floor. As she stooped to pick them up, she knocked heads with Keta, who had his paws spread wide, bracing against the rocking boat.

"Leave it," Zachary said, his voice calm and steady. "Do what I said. The dog will be fine."

Outside, green water washed over the deck, flooded the scuppers. Just half an hour ago she had been fishing—now, off the port side, a wave, streaked with foam, reared back, drops skittering down the face. She was dreaming, she would wake any minute—but then the wave came down with a clap, the leading edge exploding over the gunwales. She grasped the handles of the hatch cover as the boat took a heavy roll, salt water stinging her cheeks. From inside she heard a yelp. When she stuck her head back in Keta was beneath the galley table, shaking, staring back at her.

"Tara! We need those stabies in—go!"

Holding on to the hatch cover, she dragged herself aft to the troll pit. Over the back of a roller she glimpsed land for a moment, and then it was gone. The stabilizers were balanced against the sides of the landing bins. She lifted one and threw it in the water. The orange monofilament line tightened as the steel fin dragged over the surface. She hit the lever for the hydraulics, but had it going the wrong way, and the stabilizer came back toward her, the wire skipping on the gurdey because of the weight. The metal banged against the side of the boat. "Motherfucker," she cursed. She switched directions on the hydraulics and the fins splashed. Sweat dampened her scalp. She shoved past Zachary into the house, tearing off her gear and collapsing onto the galley bench.

"Up," he said, dragging her by the wrists. "C'mon. You're not done until we're out of this." She stood, grasped the corners of the sink, hunched over, and spat. Keta whined from beneath the table.

"Listen to me. We're losing oil pressure and I need to figure this out. If our steering or engine goes, we're in serious trouble. Our hold's just about full, and we're sitting heavy. I want you to go down to the engine room and check the oil. The gauge is on the engine, toward the stern. Got it? I'll drive."

She gripped the edge of the counter as the boat heaved. She was going to throw up. "Yeah."

As she climbed down the companionway ladder she felt her bowels loosen from nausea. In the engine room wrenches swung back and forth, clattering. She could hear water sloshing against the sides of the boat, or in the bilge, she couldn't tell which. *This is not a drill,* she told herself, thinking of the class, then the curly-haired instructor, then Connor, then her father, and the quiet streets of South Philadelphia.

She dropped to her knees and threw up, vomit splattering against the exhaust manifold of the engine, dripping down into the black water of the bilge. *It doesn't get worse than this.* The thought flashed through her mind. *But if it were worse, we'd be dead.* This second idea was somehow comforting.

Wiping her lips with a rubber cuff, she scanned the block, then found the oil reservoir and tapped the sight-glass. About halfway full. The pressure gauge read just under two pounds.

Through the sweet-rot scent of vomit she smelled something dirty. To her left, on the line from the oil reservoir to the engine, a joint bled oil. She rubbed the black liquid between her fingers, feeling the silky slip.

Back in the wheelhouse, rain and ocean lashed the glass, the flapping wipers unable to keep up. Green water flooded the bow, breaking over the anchor winch. Wind howled through the rigging, the sound braiding into Keta's whining.

"You see anything?" Zachary shouted, working the wheel through the waves.

"I found the leak."

"Leak?"

"Just forward of the engine."

"A coupling?"

"Yeah. Oil was coming out of it."

"Okay, listen. I want you to keep the bow of this boat pointed into the waves. If you don't, we'll get swiped and sink. Understand?"

She nodded.

"Say yes."

"Yes."

"Use the hand wiper over here to see what you're doing. I'm gonna go down into the engine room and you're gonna guide us toward this purple X I set on the screen here, where we'll be in the lee of it. Yes? Keep one eye on the computer, another on the radar. There could be all sorts of floating junk, deadheads, even other boats. We're gonna ride this out. Hear me?"

"I need to throw up," she said.

With one hand on the wheel, he took a section of line from the binnacle board and handed it to her.

"Go. Tie this around your waist. Hurry."

Fingers shaking, she bent the line backwards, making a loop, brought the rabbit out of the hole, around the tree, and back in. A bowline.

"Go!" Zachary yelled, pushing her outside. Rain washed against her face. Wind blew the tops off dark swells. The rope grew taut. She jammed her index finger into her tonsils. Her stomach convulsed, knotted, and reknotted as she spit up into the wind.

"Get these on," he said when she came back in, pushing fleece pants and a sweatshirt into her hands. "Then your survival suit. You remember how?"

I am not going to drown tonight. My dog's not going to drown tonight. We're going to get back to the land. Maybe I won't go crabbing, but I will buy a tugboat, and then I will have a home with Keta, and then I will go back to Philadelphia, and I will discover how to love my father, and maybe I will love Connor.

"Yes."

"Look here." He opened an orange box. Instantly she recognized a yellow EPIRB, a flashlight, a strobe beacon powered by a dry cell.

"We've got hooks, foil ponchos, tarps, food, fire starter, everything here. If anything happens to the boat, you don't worry about me, you go in the water with this and swim for shore. Yes?"

"What about Keta?"

"Forget about the dog—he's got good survival instincts. The EPIRB will go off, the copter will be here in no time. Now—steer."

He disappeared down the companionway ladder. She knelt beneath the table. Keta was panting, his breath coming out in short, warm puffs.

"I will protect you. I promise. Okay?"

She stripped naked and put on the fleece, then the survival suit, keeping the hood off so she could hear Zachary. Her fingers trembled.

When she looked up again through the windows, she found herself staring at a wall of water—twice as large as what she had seen on the stern deck. Her stomach lurched as the *Revenge* skirted up the face. She reached out to the back wall for balance. The boat became weightless, and for a moment she could see the shoreline on both sides, even the dim glow of the moon as it shone through a rip in the storm clouds to the east. Then the bow dipped, and the boat shuddered as it skidded into a trough. The windows turned a sickly green. She lost her balance, hitting her elbow. Her stomach turned and she retched again onto the floor, holding her hair back, then pushed herself up again and seized the wheel.

"What's going on up there!" Zachary shouted.

The dog kept licking her cheeks. She pushed him away. "Got it!"

The boat on the computer screen inched closer to the purple X. Another wave, smaller, arched over the bow and crashed across the deck. They were blown off the line, and she began to make the turn to starboard when Zachary came from behind and took the wheel. The drumming of the wind and water diminished as they moved into the bay.

"We're in the lee of it," he explained. "We can wait it out here."

He went out and dropped the hook, signaling to her to put the boat into reverse.

"You okay?" he asked, coming back into the cabin. She had her arms around the dog and was whispering in his ear. Zachary put a hand on her back, and she stood. The man smelled of oil and fish and cigars — like her father, except Alaskan.

"Good catch on that leak down there. Saved our butts. Felt like we took a real monster — did you see it?"

She nodded, still not sure if that wall of water — it must have been thirty feet, she thought — had been real. He flipped the switch on the bilge pump, then went outside, Tara following behind in her survival suit. At the mouth of the bay she could see the wind whipping up the waves.

"Guess you can probably take that thing off now," he said.

"Okay if I sleep in it?" she asked. His face broke into laughter. And she realized that he had been scared too.

He put a spotlight into the water. A sheen of oil spread as the bilge pumped out. "If we fixed it good that should start running clear," he said, squeezing draughts from a bottle of Joy to disperse the oil. "Damn, hope old Irish made it through that blow all right. Feel bad now for giving him such a hard time."

As they watched water splash out of the bilge, Tara thought of Irish out there with his alternator, in his wooden boat, battling those waves alone.

After a few minutes, the black disappeared. "Now, that, my friend, is a sight for sore eyes."

Back inside, Keta came out from beneath the galley table. She hadn't given him his hip pills. She helped him onto the bench, pushing him from behind.

"It's over, monkey. We're good."

78

BACK IN PORT ANNA, the storm was the news on the docks. A skipper and deckhand had stripped naked to keep each other warm in the woods after their boat sank off Chatham Strait. A young troller floated in a tote for two days before being picked up by the Coast Guard helicopter. Also, Petree told her, a boat tied up on the transient float, near the *Pacific Chief,* had sunk, its tie-up lines wrenching at the dock. The harbormaster had been the one to cut the rope, releasing the *Dancing Fox* into the deep.

She gave Laney a call. "Tug's still for sale," the woman said. "How's the saving going?"

"Two weeks king crabbing, and I'll have it."

"I'm rooting for you, lady."

It rained well into September. Salmonberries turned moldy, purple knots over the river. Chalky carcasses of fish melted into the sandbanks. She and Keta stayed on the *Revenge,* waking early in the morning in the rainy gray to take daytrips for chum. "Fishing tough," Zachary called it, working through the wind and rain. They filled the hold quickly with the greenish tiger-striped salmon, saving time by pig-sticking the gills instead of dressing, plunging the fish into slush instead of icing each one individually. She had developed a routine on the boat, giving Keta his kibble, then his hip pills, plugging in the space heater and drying her socks by hanging them on the netting over the bunk each night, stowing books about various disasters at sea by her head. In the morning she strolled the docks with a mug of coffee, checking on the *Pacific Chief.*

"You still thinking of wasting your money on that slab?" Petree asked. "Jesus, there you are, learning to fish on one of the best trollers in the fleet, and you want a tugboat. You don't think before you punch, do you?" He gave her a winning smile. "C'mon. Make me an offer on the *Invictus*. Start out with something that makes you money instead of costs you."

"Yeah, but a fishing boat isn't a home."

"Why not?"

She missed Newt. Petree said the *Spanker* was up in Yakutat — "Yak-a-scratch," he called it, for how little fish you caught — far north. Meanwhile, King Bruce had radioed the harbormaster: the *Alaskan Reiver* would be tying up October sixth. They'd run to Dutch Harbor, about eight days, and she'd crab for the opener. Thelma and Zachary had agreed to look after Keta. She had started to think about a plane ticket to Philly for Christmas.

But first, the tug.

On a Monday afternoon in the middle of September she went down to the Muskeg, tying Keta outside. The silence in the room made it hard to concentrate. In just the four days of the salmon opener she had made about three grand with Zachary, plus money from chum. After taking out for food, a survival suit, new rubber raingear and bibs, food and pills for Keta, her account hovered around twenty-three thousand. When she got the tug, she thought, it would be good to have a bit left over for repairs; the upcoming crab trip would sort that out.

"Sonofabitch had it coming," someone murmured at the table beside her. She glimpsed the front page of the newspaper. LOCAL MAN KILLED IN COLLISION WITH BUOY. There was a photo of a skiff, the bow crumpled.

A low-level alarm sounded in her ears. She knew that boat. She went outside, crossed the parking lot into the newspaper office. The printing press, about the size of the *Chief*'s Fairbanks-Morse, chugged behind the front desk. She set down fifty cents and took a paper, still warm, out of a basket.

Port Anna community member Peter "Betteryear" Johns was killed yesterday evening when his skiff collided with Jameson buoy, just west of the airport. Port Anna Mountain Search and Rescue discovered the body off Hellebore Beach.

She gasped. He had been running alone at night with no lights, returning with a boat full of halibut, the article said. The running lights he had meant to fix. He hit the buoy, was thrown from the console, and shattered his skull. On the back page of the paper was a grainy photo of him as a younger man, a bearskin draped over each of his long arms.

The service for Betteryear was held several days later at the ANB building. A Native girl wept openly. An older woman stroked her hair. Tara heard about Betteryear's hunting abilities, how he loved his walkabouts through the country. Dancers in tasseled boots made of speckled seal fur stomped on stage to a slow, steady drumbeat.

How little she knew about the man, Tara realized. He had two daughters, one of whom came back from Tucson, where she ran a spiritual retreat center. She said a few words about her father's intelligence, how he wasn't always the easiest to be around, but had a good heart. That was true, Tara thought.

The second daughter stood up. A few people murmured, and then the room went quiet. The girl was heavy, with a long, thick braid. Her underbite gave her a bulldog quality. She opened her mouth, then shook her head. "I can't," she said, and returned to her seat.

For a moment Tara was about to stand, to say no matter what others might think, Betteryear was a good man. He had taught her things, had been patient, and had persisted when she was difficult, hard to know. But some weight she could feel in the room stopped her. It was the first time on the island she sensed a darkness, the dimensions of which she couldn't quite fathom. She knew then, sitting in that room, that she never would. She didn't have rights to it.

79

THE EVENING OF OCTOBER SIXTH Tara waited with her duffel on the deck of the *Chief* for King Bruce's crab boat. She had asked everyone she knew about the skipper, and she didn't like what she had heard. A crazy man, seemed to be the consensus, although people agreed he had a knack for finding crab. Just get through these weeks, she told herself, then come back, collect her dog, and this boat beneath her feet would be their new home.

Before heading out, she had called her father.

"Tara. You're safe?"

"I'm good, Pop. Are you okay?"

His voice sounded ragged. "I'm well. Listen — Connor stopped into the bakery the other day. He said you might be coming home for Christmas."

She tried to detect something in his voice, some acknowledgment of how he used the word *home*. But nothing came across. No recognition that she would be walking into a house he kicked her out of two years ago.

"There are a few things I have to do first. But yeah, maybe."

"Good, Tara. Good."

After she got off, she stopped by the post office, where she found a short letter from Connor.

September 17, 1999

Dear Tara,

Writing quickly to say I got your note. I'm back in New York, into the swing of things once more. Do you have plans for the millennium? This summer when I got back from Kansas I used money from bricklaying to buy a shell of a house at a sheriff's sale in South Philly. It'll be a project. I'm looking forward to it.

I guess I also wanted to say that I've been thinking. I feel bad for sending that first letter a couple years back now. There was a lot in there I could have kept to myself, or at least figured out a better way to say it. I think I was going through my own weirdness at NYU. I hope you accept my apology.

Sometimes I think all of this would be easier if we could see each other. Which is why I like this idea of yours to come back for Christmas. In the meantime I got a mobile phone. If you ever need to call I'll include my number.

More soon,

Connor

She put the letter in the envelope, folded the slip of paper with his number into her pocket, intrigued by this new idea that she could reach him at any time.

A black shadow of a boat moved through the gap in the breakwater. As it drew closer she made out white letters on the bow — *Alaskan Reiver*. Cages were stacked on the forward deck. Black smoke rose from the stainless exhaust over the castle as the captain gunned the engine. The boat swung around, narrowly missing the *Chief*'s prow.

She picked up her duffel, walked down the gangway and along the dock to where the boat was mooring up. Rust streaks ran down the hull. A line landed with a thud on the planks. An amplified voice said, "Tie off that hawser to the steel posts." Tara looked around, then picked up the rope, whipped a starfish stuck to the steel pier into the water, made a wrap with the line, then two neat half-hitches.

"You don't wanna go to the bull rail?" someone yelled, and she thought it might be addressed to her until a voice on the speaker responded, "I'm not gonna have my dick out in a storm."

A ladder clattered over the side, followed by a broad-shouldered deckhand with a mousy beard over his cheeks.

"You don't tie off a crab boat with half-hitches," he snapped, then strode over to the hawser line and unlooped her knot. He made a bight and cinched up a clove hitch. She was about to shoot something back when an older man, bald with a red goatee, came down the ladder. He was short, slightly hunched, with a scrape over his forehead.

"Tara Marconi?" he asked. A blurred crab was tattooed on one side of his neck, and *Trust No Bitch* was stamped in Gothic letters around its base. He wore a threaded wool workman's cap, which he removed, then performed a small bow, revealing tattoos of red and green flames above each ear.

"King Bruce, skipper of the *Alaskan Reiver*. That's Hale over there with the line." A couple more deckhands had joined him on the docks. "Boys? Manners?"

One extended a thick, oil-smeared palm. "Jethro. Skip's son."

A kid who appeared to be in his late teens, with a scraggly beard, stepped forward. "Jeremy. Folks call me Coon-Ass."

Hale tapped a foot and looked toward the harbor ramp. "And this is Rudy. Skip, we should get moving if we want one of those booths down at the Front."

"Care to join us, Ms. Marconi, for a beverage or two?" King Bruce asked.

In a quiet parade they went along the docks, up the ramp, through the parking lot, and along Pletnikoff Street. Hale stayed out in front, his long arms swinging. Jethro fell back beside her. "You crabbed before?"

She shook her head.

"Well, in case you pick up on some weird vibes, I'm just gonna tell you what you're in for. Hale's best buddy, Thibault, got crossed by a pot and had his leg crushed, so he couldn't make the trip. No one thought the old man would take on a girl."

"And now they think I won't be able to pull my weight."

He didn't say anything. He had a calm demeanor, and his slow, careful speech reminded her of Connor. "Just giving you a heads-up, that's all."

At the bar the crew slid into the booth beneath the jukebox. Hale ordered popcorn and tater tots from Cassie. King Bruce went next door for Chinese food. Hale poked Tara in the arm. "You ever see any of these troller pussies in here throw a punch? Or are they too busy keeping their balls warm in their armpits?"

Already she hated this kid. Maybe Petree would come in and kick his ass.

Coon-Ass, who also had a tangle of half-grown beard over his skinny adolescent face, and a red handkerchief loosely tied around his neck, ordered a row of Jagermeister shots. He set the tray on the table, lifted a glass, and said in a southern drawl,

> *May there be crawfish in your nets,*
> *And gumbo in the pot.*
> *May the Sac-au-lait be biting*
> *At your favorite fishing spot.*
> *May God's sun be —*

Hale cut him off. "All right, Coon. We all know you're from Louisiana. Boys?"

They tipped back the glasses, banged them hard on the table, then ordered another round. An Asian girl arrived with pot stickers, cream-cheese wontons, and egg rolls. When King Bruce gave her a twenty-dollar tip on the fifteen-dollar tab, Hale shook his head. "Basic demand-side economics—invest in areas of the economy that will show a return. That's money wasted."

King Bruce waved a hand. "Maybe I'll marry her, who the hell knows?"

One of the deckhands, the one who reminded her of Little Vic with his olive skin and broody eyes, ripped open a soy sauce packet and squeezed it down his throat.

"Rudy's from Portugal," King Bruce explained to Tara. "He's addicted to salt. Ain't that right, buddy?"

"Time to get this party going," Hale said, standing. Wiping their mouths, Coon-Ass and Rudy followed.

King Bruce clapped Jethro on the back. "What's up, son? Don't want to join in the fun? Cat got your tongue around the pretty new girl?"

She thought of Newt and looked around the bar. If he found out she had a job on a crabber, he'd start whooping.

"You writing letters in that head of yours?" King Bruce said. At first she thought he was talking to her, then saw him shake a finger at Jethro. "I know you got aggressivity in you. Soon or later it's gotta come out."

Shouts came from the pool table. King Bruce set aside his pull-tabs and his half-eaten egg roll. "Here we go."

"I didn't see you put down those quarters," Hale shouted. Then, "You calling me a fucking liar?"

Tara recognized the troller from the docks, an attractive young man who had married a Norwegian woman. They had recently had a daughter, and the man was chatting with Petree about how to deaden the noise from the boat's engine and make a baby-changing station in the fo'c'sle. He always wore the same small animal skull of some creature tied with leather twine around his neck. He had probably come down here tonight for a bit of peace and a pool game, Tara thought.

"Hey!" Hale shouted. "Don't walk away from me. The fuck you think you are?"

She could see the skull rise and fall against the man's chest. She knew enough about fighting to see he didn't want to be involved, even though he had a good six inches on Hale.

Cassie yelled from behind the bar and grabbed the bat from beneath the popcorn maker. "I'll whale the tar out of all y'all if you don't quit it!"

Coon-Ass, standing behind Cassie, knocked a glass from the bar. It shattered over the linoleum. He followed this with a low, woodsy howl. Hale hit the young troller in the temple. The man stumbled, swinging wildly. Hale charged, grabbing the man's hips, driving him into the wall and rabbit-jabbing his stomach. Frames fell to the ground, the glass shattering. Cassie held the bat over them, continuing to swear. Hale was on the man's back, with a seat-belt hold around the troller's neck.

Shaking his head, King Bruce slid out of the booth. "You shoulda been part of this," he said, shaking a finger at Jethro. He stepped in front of Cassie, keeping one hand on the barrel of the bat while he hauled Hale up by his hood.

"Let go, for godsakes. Nuff!" he growled.

The troller was bleeding from his forehead. King Bruce held out an arm and helped the man to his feet. Someone handed him a napkin.

"You all right, hoss?" King Bruce asked.

"I'm callin' the police on y'all," Cassie said, going back behind the bar and slamming the rotary phone down. "Fuckin' crazy-ass crabbing fucks."

King Bruce fanned five hundred-dollar bills on the counter. Cassie's chest heaved. "For your troubles," he told her.

She flashed another five fingers. He sighed, peeled them off, and turned to Hale and Coon-Ass.

"That'll be coming off the top of your deck shares, you can be sure about that."

Cassie took the money, opened her cash register with a ding of the bell, and poured out five tequila shots.

"You boys drink these down, and then heigh-the-fucking-ho on outta my bar."

Rudy, Coon-Ass, and Hale whooped their way back along Pletnikoff, pounding on truck doors and peeing in the street. Jethro walked with his hands shoved into his pockets, looking down at the wet pavement, while King Bruce tacked back and forth between the sidewalk on one side and the humming processors on the other, his cheek lit white by his cell phone.

"You don't want to do this," Jethro said to her. "Trust me."

It sounded like a challenge, but not one that interested her. She just wanted the check at the end of the trip.

"Is your dad a good captain?"

Jethro bowed his head, thinking. "He knows where to drop 'em, for sure. We make money."

She thought about this as they crossed the parking lot. "I got a boat I want to buy."

"Oh yeah?"

"Yeah — that one parked aft of the *Reiver*."

"The old wood thing?"

"It's a World War II tugboat."

When they reached the harbor Hale hoisted an unlocked bicycle out of the rack and rode it down the ramp, roaring as it slid out from under him. Coon-Ass convulsed into laughter as Hale tumbled onto the planks. Rudy clapped. The fall looked bad enough to break a bone, but Hale seemed to be constructed of some superhuman substance, just blasting through the world without a care. She made a note to herself to keep calm around him. People like Hale drove her nuts.

Back at the boat, the boys climbed the ladder. She followed Hale, bleeding from an elbow, into the main house. The galley bench, which made a horseshoe around the table, was torn up, with plugs of yellow foam punching out from the holes. The boys scattered to their various bunks. Jethro put coffee on.

"Here's our food for when you cook," he said, opening a cupboard. Hot sauce and boxes of Aunt Jemima and cans of corn and beef stew and powdered milk were arranged on the shelves. Bags of mini candy bars stacked on the bottom.

"You're gonna be crashing down here," he said, walking behind the galley to a bunk. "Only single rack. Pop thought it was proper, seeing as how you're the girl." He pushed open a louvered door, revealing a toilet in a corner. "Head."

She threw her duffel on the bunk. The boat trembled as the engines fired. King Bruce's slurred voice came over the speaker.

"Cut 'er da fuck loose, boys. We're gettin' the fuck outta this fuckin' fuckhole."

"He's operating this boat?" Tara asked. "He can hardly see straight."

"Aw, he's been driving boats drunk since he was twelve," Jethro said.

Tara went back out on deck, watching as the boys undid the lines. It wasn't too late, she thought—she could still leap. Hale yelled up at her from the docks. "Your hands cold?" Cursing to herself, she pulled them out of her pockets. "Catch." He tossed the bitter end toward her, but it hit the hull and flopped into the water.

"I said 'catch.'"

She hauled the wet hawser line onto deck and looped it. *Patience,* she told herself. *You will not react with anger. Just let it slide.*

With a grumble and belch of black smoke the *Reiver* pushed away from the dock. Swim, she thought, she could still swim. But then they were gathering speed. Tara pinched her mother's medallion between her fingers as the tugboat tied to the corner grew small, bobbing in their wake. *I'm doing this for you. Wait for me.*

80

TIME DRAGGED, one day after the other, as they ran north toward the crab grounds. The plan was to make it to Unalaska, work on the boat for a few days, then crab twenty-four/seven for the opener. She chopped onions and carrots and made stews with crushed tomatoes and peppers. She waited to be asked to do a night wheel watch, thrilled by the idea of guiding this 106-foot steel boat through the black. Although she knew it would mean sitting there staring at screens and staying awake. But it never happened.

When the boys weren't on watch they took food into their bunks, emerging later with egg yolk or bread crumbs caked in their beards. A stench of seawater and moisturizer leaked into the galley. Bits of burnt bacon were stuck in their teeth, the enamel stained yellow from coffee and cigarettes — she wondered if they ever brushed. She felt like a ghost on the boat. Except for Jethro, they continued their campaign of ignoring her, limiting communication to nods or one-syllable responses.

Jethro spent his days curled at the far end of the galley booth, hood up, the tips of his long, oily seal-colored hair framing his jaw, and devoured books she still hadn't read but had seen in the woods among the Alaskan Travelers: *The Alchemist, The Prophet, Ishmael, Celestine Prophecies.* When he wasn't reading he wrote letters to his "hippie chick," as Hale called her, back in college at Santa Cruz.

Hale asked Jethro to start prepping the cages. Tara watched out the porthole as he leapt from pot to pot, coiling line in twists, moving in a fury that she didn't recognize from the calm reader. She wondered what he'd be like as a lover—tender and gentle, or the madman on the pots, looping line between his elbow and hand.

At night, after wiping down the galley, she lay in her bunk, steel bulkheads sweating above her, dripping onto her sleeping bag. She recalled first arriving in Alaska, sure the island would free her, allow her to rediscover some happiness taken by her mother's death, by what happened at Avalon. This wasn't the case—she knew this now. If anything she felt cordoned off, wrapped in yellow emergency tape. Waiting. To get the tug, perhaps, which had become, in her mind, the way forward.

She reached out and wiped a drop from the bulkhead, closed her eyes. Thinking of that warm spot on Keta's brow when he woke up. His blond eyelashes.

Just get through these next few weeks. The final sprint, and then she'd be there.

After five days of travel, under a dome of cloudless blue sky, they idled past the narrow spit protecting the womb of Dutch Harbor from the Bering Sea. In the distance she saw the steam-obscured rectangles of a processor in Unalaska, and, farther on, teardrop shapes of the steeples on the Russian church, similar to the one in Port Anna.

King Bruce angled them into the harbor. The sun, at her back in the south, reflected hard off the flat water. The *Northwestern, Aleutian Sable, Cape Caution,* the fleet of crab boats tied up in the harbor made the seiners back in Port Anna look like small dogs.

"We're headed to the Elbow Room," Hale said to her, pulling his hat brim over his eyebrows. "Second-most-dangerous bar in the world, right behind some goddamn place in Rhodesia. Ten bucks Jethro's gonna mail a pile of love letters off to his hippie chick back in San Francisco, ain't that right, Romeo?"

"Santa Cruz, asshole."

They piled into a pickup, rented by King Bruce for the season, and parked in town. Tara decided to wander.

"Okay, lone wolf," Hale said. "Meet us back at the rig in an hour."

There was the tang of pre-battle excitement in town — she could taste it, that hysterical current running through the men before the opening. Scrums of deckhands outside the Elbow Room, a bar the size of a doublewide trailer, stared out from under their soiled caps as she passed. One catcalled. It was warm, almost sixty, but she pulled up the hood of her sweatshirt.

Alaska was not a place for a lone wolf — she knew this by now. Once you got kicked out of the pack, like Betteryear, or Irish, or even Keta, it was almost impossible to get back in. You grew a particular type of bitterness — she could see it in Keta, how he disliked Fritz. Or just complained how things used to be, like Irish.

Quiet, detached, maybe a little scared — in her view, this was how the boys on the *Reiver* regarded her. They were feral. She needed to become louder, cruder, more aggressive.

She crossed the bridge back toward the harbor. A greenish-purple front of clouds, underside reflecting the gray of the ocean, moved toward town. She had never been in a place with no trees — there were just these wind-scraped, bald mountains, snow blanketing the peaks.

On the boat she spooned cans of beef stew into a pot and spread frozen tater tots on a cookie sheet, salting them and sliding the tray into the oven.

"Soon enough we're gonna run outta the ready-made stuff," King Bruce said as he passed through the galley, popping a tot in his mouth and wiping ketchup from his whiskers. "Hope you know a bit more than how to open a can."

"Your boys prefer the canned stuff," she said.

"My boys?" He shook his head, took another handful of tater tots. "This is your crew, sweetheart. We're gonna be keeping each other alive out there on the big waters. Where are those boys, anyways?"

"At the Elbow Room. I walked back."

He looked at her for a moment, as if considering something, then went up the stairs. "Call me when that stew's warm," he shouted behind him.

The following morning, the stars still out, she heard Hale in the galley and smelled bacon. She pulled on fleece pants and found him by the stove, spooning grease over egg yolks.

"Wakey-wakey, Snow White. Hope you like swine."

"Jesus, dude. The sun's not even up, and you're already busting balls."

"Whose balls would those be?" he asked innocently. "Here."

With a spatula he worked a couple eggs loose, and passed a steaming plate to her. The other deckhands came out, poured coffee, and helped themselves to food. "Grab your plate," Jethro said to her. "I'll give you a crash course in crabbing."

She poured more coffee and followed him out on deck. It was just after eight, and the sky was lightening to a raw white. Jethro gripped a steel bar on a pot, a square cage webbed in nylon netting, taller than Tara. "Seven-bys," he said. "Each cage weighs about seven hundred and fifty pounds."

Inside the trap yellow line connected a set of three pot buoys: one pink rubber, the other green rubber, and the third made of Styrofoam, sprayed-painted emergency orange.

"That's our sea lion buoy, in case the little bastards puncture the other two. So how it works is our pot goes here" — he patted a pock-marked sheet of steel — "called the lift, rack, or the pot launcher. We swing the pot up into the lift, bait it with herring or codfish or whatever, and shut the door. One of us, usually Hale, hits the hydros, and splash, down she goes. Five hundred feet or so to the bottom. Throw out a shot of coiled line over the side, which connects the bridle on the pot to these two buoys, which float on the surface. Unless . . ." He looked at her, waiting.

"Unless a sea lion eats them, in which case just the sea lion buoy will remain," she finished.

"I could tell you were smart," he said.

It reminded her of being at the processor, having to learn how to make boxes with Trunk. Except this time people expected her to fuck up.

"So the pots soak for how long?" she asked.

"Day or two, then we swing back around, find the buoy, toss a grappling hook to catch the line, strung between the pink and yellow buoys, and bring her on up. This is where it gets tough, especially when it's blowing. You've got pots swinging around and we're all trying to rack 'em and get 'em in the lift. So that's done, then we tilt up the cage and open the trap and out come the crabs onto the table, and then we start sorting, which will be one of your jobs. We keep only legals, which means males over the size limit. Females go back down. Keepers get thrown into a lined chute leading to the live hold, filled with salt water. Goal is pretty simple — plug the hold. Got it?"

They returned to the galley. The tour made her feel better about things. Hale was at the table, bent over his pad. He looked up when she came in.

"Cap wants to see you."

"Me?" Jethro said.

"No. Our Italian American friend over there."

She went up the narrow stairwell leading to the bridge, her first time topside. King Bruce slouched in the mounted shock-suspension chair, socked feet up on the binnacle board. His face was lit up by the screens of his radar and fathometer and computer. A cage hung in the corner of the room, swinging gently, a blue parakeet cowering on the perch. When Tara held her hand out, the bird thrust its beak.

"Minnow don't take to girls," King Bruce said. And she saw, with a sinking feeling, that his glass eye was out, sitting on a plate beside a coffee cup. Flesh in the socket appeared pink and moist. With a pang of sorrow she thought of Newt.

"'Caught betwixt the devil and the deep blue sea.' Ever hear that saying?" King Bruce inquired.

She focused on the coffee cup, imprinted with a woman naked save for a slip of kilt covering her hips, blowing on a bagpipe. *If it's not Scottish, it's crap.*

"I've heard people say it before."

"Know what it means?"

She thought. "Like you've got a choice between two bad things."

He sipped his coffee, then folded his puffed hands. "Devil means where the water touches your boat. 'Caught betwixt the devil and the deep blue sea.' That means you're sunk. Drowned. You ever drowned?"

She shook her head.

"Well, I came near one time. Result of bad luck on the water — that's why I got Minnow here, my bird — we're old pals, we keep each other safe. Now, I'm not talking about an open-hatch-cover bad luck, leaving on a Friday, bananas on a boat, any of that stupid shit those little mom-and-pop troller operations get their panties in a twist about down in Port Anna. I'm talking about two people not getting along on a hundred-and-six-foot crab boat."

Her breath grew tight. "Listen, dude. I'm here to work, to make money, and go home. That's all."

The bird hopped to a higher perch, its small head jerking back and forth between them. King Bruce spoke slowly.

"Me, I know how to crab, been doing it since the age of seventeen, was just about born for it. I don't give two shits who I'm working with, swinging dick or not, don't affect me none. Ain't had much else in my life save for a cheatin' whore of a wife, and that quiet boy of mine who ever'time he seems about to get his wang out of his pants his Injun mother slaps the little thing right back. Rest of 'em are full of piss and vinegar, like me back in the day."

He seemed to catch himself. His glass eye made a faint sucking sound as he nestled it back into the socket. "What I'm trying to tell you, Tara" — she winced as he leaned on her name — "is that, as captain of this boat, I can't let things get out of hand, see? It would be a risk to our season, and all our deck shares. So I need you to cooperate, and be part of the team. If they give you a little shit, you take it. That's how it goes when you're green."

"I'm not gonna be some whipping post," she said.

"That's not what I'm asking. Now, just . . . don't be so keyed up. That's all. Go on. Back to work."

She took the stairs by twos, pulled on her jacket, and went into the sun, wanting to walk and consider the situation. Instead Hale shoved a plastic drill into her hands. "Take one of these bait jars, and make ten holes in it." He pushed a couple crates of the plastic containers in her direction. "There's the rest of 'em."

"Fuckin' prick," she muttered.

"If you were a guy I'd deck you," he said matter-of-factly.

She splayed her hand in front of his face, showing her bruised knuckles. Her heart thudded. "This didn't come from knitting, asshole. So go ahead, start a fight with me."

He shook his head. "You're a crazy bitch is what you are."

As the sun rose, she thought about dropping the drill in the ocean, finding the airport, and catching the next flight to Anchorage. The plane ticket would take her to under twenty-four thousand. Plus her ticket back to Philly. Still, it would get her away from this floating circus.

Hale jockeyed the pots, the crane wheezing as Jethro cleared space around the lift. "Coon-Ass, quit jerkin' your Cajun meat and gimme a hand shuffling," Hale shouted. Coon-Ass hopped from one steel support to the next, the spring-loaded safety snapping as he hooked into the eye of the bridle.

"Mud, don't fucking push that thing," Hale said as Rudy threw his weight behind a pot. "Lemme get it with the crane — you're gonna crack your back."

The rubber of her jacket grew soft and pliant in the sunlight. King Bruce looked down from the bridge of the wheelhouse, the deck like a stage beneath him. Hale circled back around to check on her. He held up a bait jar, sunlight bright through the holes.

"What about knots?"

"What about them?"

"Can you tie them, smartass?"

"Yes."

"Carrick-bend?"

She panicked. "I can tie a bowline, trucker's hitch, clove hitch, double half-hitch, anchor bend —"

"Old fart troller knots. What about splicing line? Back splice? Eye splice? Cunt splice?" He emphasized the word "cunt."

"What?"

"Did I stutter?" He smiled, then took up two ends of line and placed one over the other, the empty space between making an oval. "C-U-N-T. Spells *cunt*. See that? A cunt splice. Personal favorite."

He stood there, a cockeyed grin on his face. The tips of her fingers itched. Unlike with Jackie, she was confused as to whether she should hit this kid, how it would come off to the rest of the boat. Her confidence gone, she suddenly felt that her weather-bleached raingear and scarred brown boots were just parts of a fishing costume. Here at the far end of the Aleutian chain, this asshole was shaping her into a punch line.

Coon-Ass yelled down from atop a stack of pots. "What the fuck, Hale! You gonna get this deck cleared or what?"

Hale shook one end of the line at her. "Maybe you were hot shit down in the rainforest. But you're in Dutch now, where the big boys play. I'd say you got some work ahead of you, greenhorn."

81

A FEW DAYS BEFORE THEY WERE SUPPOSED TO head out to the Bering Sea, Hale lowered the boat's skiff with the crane and proposed taking a ride over the water into town instead of going over the bridge. The boys piled in, and Tara was left doing dishes in the galley, scrubbing the bottom of the casserole pan where a roast had burned.

"Fuck this," she said, flinging the sponge into the sink. If she was supposed to be part of the pack, then she should be in that boat. She slipped on her rain pants and coat, went out into the squall, and climbed over the rail into the skiff. Hale had already started the outboard. He took a last swig from a whiskey bottle, tossed it over the side, and looked at her. "Where the hell you think you're going?"

"The hell does it look like? Town."

"You done with the dishes? Because Skip said—"

Before she could stop herself she torqued her body, landing a right on his jaw. His hands clamped down on her ribs and they both went overboard. The cold was instant—she saw only specks of bubbles in the darkness. Her head went light as she felt her neck choked by someone yanking her by the hood back over into the skiff. Then there were hands clawing at her coat, and she was laid out over a bench, coughing, trying to find her breath.

"You okay?" Jethro said. She gasped. A cold she had never experienced seeped into her bones. Her hands and feet had vanished.

"Fucking menstrual cunt!" Hale shouted, ripping off his rain pants and rubbing his jaw. Bright white mast lights came on. "The shit's going on down there?" King Bruce yelled over the deck speakers. Tara sat up, looking around, trying to get her bearings. She saw Coon light a cigarette, shake his head, and snicker. "I guess someone had enough."

Back in her bunk she changed into dry fleece. King Bruce called her topside, his good eye bleary and red with sleep. Hale watched as she came up the stairs.

"I got Bering Sea storms, blown engines, uncharted reefs, blown hydros, ADF and G up my ass — all manner of bullshit to deal with, and now I got my crew in-fighting?"

Hale worked his lower lip between his teeth, his boxy chin shifting. "You gotta leash this bitch, man."

Tara stared at the sonar, the computer screen, the blinking satellite phones. Anywhere but at King Bruce.

"Don't bullshit a bullshitter, deck boss. I seen how you ride her. And you" — he turned to Tara — "didn't I just have you up here? And now you're out throwing punches? On a skiff, for fucksakes?"

She decided to gamble. "He was being a dick. So I hit him. Now he's gonna cry about it?"

King Bruce looked back at Hale. She had overshot. Wildly.

"Look at that, Cap. She's not safe, doesn't know her own ass end. She's gonna get herself — or worse, one of us — killed. She's a fucking liability."

"Go on, the two of you," Bruce said after a moment. "Get the fuck out of my sight. I'm too old for this candy-ass shit."

In the galley she grabbed a fistful of candy bars and pushed past the others, past rows of dual-wheeled trucks in the parking lot, their flatbeds stacked with crab pots. She chewed a 3 Musketeers in a fury as she crossed the bridge, finding the Elbow Room on the other

side. The bar smelled of beer and grime. The walls were hung with
a harpoon, green-glass Japanese buoys, a life ring, scraps of net, and
bullet-shaped Styrofoam corks. Xtratufed men in cable-knit wool
sweaters with blackened singe holes, buck knives in leather scab-
bards attached to their belts, looked up from the red Formica tables
as she crossed the floor, her boots sticky on the worn linoleum.

She ordered a can of Rainier, looked for paper to write Connor.
Any sort of outlet for this rage. How would he do here? It was funny
to think about. Initially she had thought he'd be swallowed whole by
Alaska, not a match for the state's hard-bitten, zany ways. Now she
thought differently. He was strong without having to throw punches
and cause a ruckus. He was also intelligent enough to avoid being
caught in a situation like this.

"Bar's dangerous enough without a pretty girl to rile the waters."

She turned to see an old-timer with a map of wrinkles over his
forehead. All she wanted to do was have a drink. Just one goddamn
minute of peace.

"I can see you don't wanna be bothered. But it's either me or
those boys over there getting ready to buy you a redheaded slut. I
figured I'd save ya the trouble. Tuffy," he said, putting out a hand.
"What's got you in Dutch?"

"Tara. I'm working on the *Alaskan Reiver*."

"Ah, the one-eyed Jack," he said, finishing his drink, ice knocking
against his teeth as he tipped the glass. "With the mixed-up flame
tattoos on his head. Folks say he thinks like a crab 'cause he's actually
been in the cage. Can I buy you a pickled egg? Or another a those
beers?"

"Sure, why not."

As they drank she relaxed, warming up to the man's stories of the
Japanese occupying Attu and Kiska Islands. "Folks down south don't
know the nippers actually invaded us," he said, wiping egg from his
gray beard. A few more crews arrived, each set of eyes landing on her
before taking in the rest of the room. He noticed. "Bet the boys on

the *Reiver* don't mind having a good-looking girl like you on board neither."

"There's one guy who would just as soon have me off," she said. "He might be the devil himself."

"*Aqetak*," the man said. "Old Inuit chant to drive out evil spirits. Say it five times before you sleep. Might make him leave you in peace."

She stood to zip her jacket. "I gotta go."

"Sure you don't need a ride? Happy to do it. Also score me major points with the youngsters if I was seen leaving the bar with a pretty woman like yourself."

She smiled. "Next time, Tuffy."

"*Kaya*, Tara," he said.

"What's that?"

"That's the only other Inuit word I know. And it should be the second part of the Alaska state motto."

"What's the motto?"

"North to the future."

"And what does *kaya* mean?"

He thought for a moment. "It's Inuit for 'whatever you do, don't look back.'"

82

IT WAS ONLY THE ANTICIPATION of being out on the Bering Sea that kept her from taking the next plane back to Port Anna. Finally, it was upon them. They were heading out the following day.

In preparation for the two-week opener—what Hale had described as fourteen sleepless days running from pot to pot, sorting through crabs—and because everyone seemed so "keyed up," as he put it, King Bruce gave the crew October thirteenth off.

From the top of the harbor that morning she dialed Wolf Street.

"*Figlia*, I can't find you on the map," her father said.

"I'm on the Aleutian Chain, way down at the end, a place called Unalaska."

"Ah. Let me see."

"Where are *you*?"

She heard a shuffling. "In the parlor. Wait. I still don't see."

The thought of his finger skating along the map, beneath the photo of her mother, crushed her. Also, it was thrilling. "Can you find Anchorage?" she asked.

"Yes. Anchorage. I've found that."

"Now take the tip of your finger and drag it left. Keep going, right along that line of islands until you reach Unalaska."

"Ah. I see it here."

"That's where I am."

"So far out, *figlia*. Now tell me what it's like."

"Well, no trees, but it's sunny. Mountains rise straight out from the water. Tomorrow we go on the Bering Sea."

There was a pause. "But it's dangerous, no?"

"I'm on a good boat," she lied. "What's up in South Philly?"

"Oh, well, I have these new neighbors, young people. The stairs are difficult for me. Vic wants me to move, to a condo up on Broad and Washington."

"Out of Wolf Street?"

"Perhaps. The neighborhood changes. Listen, *figlia*. I have a question for you. And I promise, I won't ask about this again."

The possibility of a move rattled her. She couldn't imagine him not being at Wolf Street.

"When this happened, that night, your birthday. This, the last thing. Did your mother know?"

She turned her head, considered the snow-covered peaks. Remembering the smell of peppermint oil and her mother kneading her skin. Then of her parents in front of the television. She answered honestly. "I don't know."

"But you never told her?" he asked. His voice was strained, desperate, even, as if he needed an answer.

"No. No, I didn't. I think she knew. Maybe she was ashamed for me, you know, about what happened."

He coughed, swallowed. "She would never be ashamed. She loved you so much. It's just—I have these days where all I do is think about her. And then I think about you." After a moment, he went on. "The other day I was thinking—I have a memory of a time when you were a child. Maybe eight. Do you recall this? You were running around, and your mother . . ." He paused. "Your mother, she grew so angry, like she sometimes did. Do you remember?"

A tremor ran through his voice. She wanted him to stop. "Pop, I don't know . . ."

"And I, well, I didn't know what to do. But I put you in the freezer, you know." His voice broke. "The walk-in at the bakery. Do you re-member this?"

Her throat seized. Silver bowls. Bricks of butter. Light of the door opening.

"Tara, I am so sorry. I'm sorry for this, and I'm sorry for that night. When I yelled at you, for saying those words. For telling you to leave."

She didn't know what to say. Never had she imagined living with-out the heaviness in her chest, the weight that sometimes caught fire and kicked her out of herself, made her fists fly before she knew what was happening.

"Please, Tara," her father said. "Please just come home."

It wasn't right. That was all she could think as she walked to the post office for stamps. Here was his daughter, thousands of miles away, about to leave civilization for two weeks to search for hard-shelled spiders on the bottom of one of the world's most dangerous oceans, and he was back in Philly waiting for her. Her father. Fat, difficult, often mean. But sorry. And she was going fishing.

There was a sign in the window, BACK IN TEN. She stood for al-most forty minutes, cursed Alaska and its mediocre employees, then returned to the phone bank by the soda machine, beneath a canopy. From the parking lot she could see the crew sitting atop the crab pots, drinking beers on the deck of the *Reiver*. The generators in the harbor made a collective hum.

I don't care, she thought. *I just want to speak to him.*

She punched in Connor's mobile number. A hurricane of noise came on the line.

"Connor?"

"Who's this?" he shouted.

"It's me!"

"Who's me?"

"Tara!"

There was static, followed by silence.

"Tara? Jesus. Where are you?"

"Dutch Harbor, Alaska."

"Wow," he said in a quiet voice. "Isn't that serious?"

She pressed on the clear plastic buttons of the soda machine. Crystal Pepsi, Mountain Dew, an obnoxious green can called Surge. She felt shy, unsure of herself. All this time, these letters, and it was still awkward on the phone. "Aren't you supposed to be in New York, in school?" she asked.

"Not on the weekends," he said.

It was what — a Saturday? The days of the week had stopped mattering.

"Can you do something for me?" she asked.

"Of course."

"Just talk."

He paused. "About what?"

"It doesn't matter. Tell me stuff about Philly. Like in that one letter you wrote."

He took a breath. "Oh, I don't know. As I said, the whole place is getting built up."

She knew he hated this, saying anything substantial over the phone. "I'm sorry. I just miss the city."

"Well," he continued, "they've got new lights on the scrolling sign on the PECO building, different colors instead of the white bulbs. Oh, and a playhouse opened downtown. I actually spoke with them, they might need help with lighting and stage direction. They're trying to clean up the Italian Market, as I said — you know, make it more tourist-friendly, even stopping John Banks. Can you believe that?"

John Banks was the man with a cross around his neck who wheeled groceries in his cart for a small fee. His refrain, which she heard so clearly now in her head, was "Bags for sale!"

A light breeze blew. She stared at the soda machine. One of the cans had a character from the new *Star Wars* movie, a young boy with straight hair. "Can You Find Your Destiny?" it read. Down on the *Reiver* she watched Hale push Rudy on the shoulder. An empty beer can made a tinny sound as he tossed it on deck.

"Your father seems good. Eva's always with him. Last time I was there I saw her coming down those back steps, from the billing office."

"We just spoke," she said. Silence again. She heard the creak of a floorboard. "I miss you."

"When are you heading back?" he asked.

"Christmas."

"To Port Anna?"

"Oh — no, I'll be back there in a couple weeks."

"Good luck on the water," he said. "Call me when you return."

"Hey, Connor?" Her face flushed.

"Yeah."

"I'm hopeful."

"Good," he said after a moment. "Me too."

After they hung up she stood, pressing her thumb into a button on the soda machine, trying to separate Connor's phone self from what he really might be feeling.

"Don't matter how hard you push," Hale said, coming up the ramp with a toothpick between his lips. "Red light means no more sody-poppy."

"Go to hell," she said.

He turned as he passed her. "Not to worry, darlin'. We'll all be there together in just a few days."

83

THE FOLLOWING MORNING they cut loose. King Bruce picked his way through the boats pivoting on anchor. A storm was creeping west over the islands, and he wanted to get out ahead of it, not to mention putting some distance between them and the other 269 crabbers with permits.

"We're gonna be first to come back plugged, first to unload, and that's just the way of it," he announced to the crew.

As they set out, the sun glowered behind the clouds. She went out on deck. As land disappeared behind them, the ocean grew into an eight-foot tide-spawned chop. Wind flattened the waves into streaks of foam. Her stomach began to sour.

Back inside the boys sat around the galley table, sections of rubber grip rolled out to keep their playing cards from sliding. Her stomach felt filled with cement. Saliva curdled on the back of her tongue. Her teeth grew hot.

"You wanna play?" Jethro asked.

She picked up a magazine, knowing full well she wouldn't be able to read, and shook her head.

Hale chewed bacon and greasy eggs, smacked his lips over buttered toast and muffins with custard melted over the tops. Sweat spread over the lining of her hat, and her hands began to shake. Hale slapped his cards onto the table, egg whites and yolk stuck to the roof of his mouth. His knife made a scratching sound as he dragged it over his toast.

The vessel shuddered as a wave knuckled the hull. She braced herself for a roll, her stomach heaving. Cells of her body felt spread around the kitchen, her head boiling somewhere in the engine room. Vomit rose in her throat.

"Easy, *chère*," Coon-Ass said, looking up from his cards. "You look like a goddamn ghost."

Out on deck she gripped the gunwales as the boat dropped down the back side of a roller. Gusts sheared off wave tops, slapping a salt spray against her cheeks. She stuck her finger down her throat, coughed, her stomach convulsing, sending breakfast into the black water. Tears arced behind her in the wind. She heaved again, a green-yellow, syrupy bile dropping from her lips.

"There's some leftovers in there if you want 'em." Hale stood beside her, wiping his lips with the back of his wrist. She managed a weak "Fuck you" and heaved again, coughing from the back of her throat. She breathed through her nose, focusing, willing her stomach to settle.

When she turned back, Hale had climbed the ladder and stood on the foredeck. The *Reiver* bucked over the crest of a wave, the wind throwing spray. Up came the sharp bow, and Hale crouched, then leaped skyward as the boat fell away and the bow knifed into a wave trough, leaving him suspended in the air. His tongue lolled out as he wheeled his arms, his booted legs scrambled, his feet searching for the deck as it came back up. He did it again, this time going higher as they skidded down the back side of a wave. And she could swear that she saw him, as he came back down, wink at her.

She retreated to her quarter berth, shut the door, and bunched her fleece into a pillow. Her stomach clenched, and she tried to breathe down the nausea. Tendrils of hair were stuck to her forehead with sweat. Her body grew alternately light and heavy as the boat pushed farther out to sea. She thought of going to Six Flags as a child — this was the worst park ride in the world, and she'd be on it for the next thirteen days.

There was a knock on the door.

"Yeah?"

Jethro shifted his tall frame into the room, nesting strands of waxy brown hair behind his ears. From a plastic bag he produced patches, pills, a jar, and two wristbands.

"Transderm, Bonine, Rugby, and Psi acupressure bracelets. A pinch of pickled ginger helps me. There's also ginger gum. And most important," he said, "don't watch Hale when he eats."

84

KING BRUCE'S VOICE BOOMED over the speakers: "We got some work ahead of us, boys."

White deck lights lit up the ocean around them. They had dumped forty baited pots in a straight line, what Hale called a string, and now Bruce was circling back to the front, ready to pick the first out of four hundred feet of water. She had figured out a cocktail of Bonine, ginger gum, and the acupressure bands to ease her seasickness, even though she could feel how the Bonine thinned her awareness.

The first pot came up with a few dozen crabs. Jethro stood beside her, flipping one over to show a flap on the underbelly. "Female," he said, flinging the creature over the side. "Those and shorts like this get tossed back. If you can't tell"—he held up a measuring stick—"when you get good males, keep a count in your head, then report back to Hale."

She counted only two males, and yelled over. "Tara, you got those jars ready?" he said back.

She had been given the job of baiting—making sure jars were filled with herring, or that whole codfish were ready to be hung in the pots. Jethro showed her how to check to see that shots of line were strong, that the two rubber floats and sea lion buoys were ready, the nylon webbing intact.

King Bruce circled back around as Rudy changed out the bait, then tossed over the pot. Coon-Ass slung out the buoys, the yellow line unraveling on the surface as the pot sank to the bottom. It wasn't like the herring fishery or even trolling — these were big, wide-open seas, with no other boats in sight.

They did a few more pots, taking about fifteen minutes for each one. She snapped to attention when Hale yelled. "Hey, Tara, you can swing your fists okay — how 'bout you try tossing a buoy. Rudy, you run the grapple hook."

Finally, the chance to prove herself. She took hold of the line, stepped into position like she had seen Rudy do. King Bruce set them on course for the next pot, the lights illuminating the streaked ocean. Rudy tossed the treble hook, missing on their first soaker.

"Git in there, Mud," Hale shouted. "C'mon, it's all in the wrist. God knows you jerk off enough." They came back, and he snagged the line. The four of them worked in silence, sorting crabs, males banging down the live chute, females tossed over the side. They waited for King Bruce's call whether to reset the pots, sending them back down to soak for another round, or switch spots, which meant a brief period of rest.

"Back down she goes," came the speaker voice.

With a sigh Coon-Ass threw the first shot over the pot. A wrench of the launcher as Hale hit the knob followed by a splash. Rudy tossed out the coil of line, and Tara followed with the three buoys. Except this time the yellow line, snickering across the deck, caught the toe of her boot. She was slammed onto her back, dragged by the weight of the pot, her head bumping against the planking.

Time slowed as the rail rushed toward her. She felt a fingernail split when she dug her hand into the wet wood. She didn't have a knife to cut herself loose, and realized she was about to be taken betwixt the devil and the Bering Sea, where no warm-blooded Anthony, saint of miracles, could save her. Just before hitting the stanchion she felt a tightening over her chest, wrists gripping her hard enough to press the wind from her lungs. She arched her foot and the boot slipped off, knocking against the top of the gunwale, hanging for a moment in the air before it disappeared into the black.

She lay on deck, panting. There was a huffing on the back of her neck and whiskers against her skin. "Goddammit, Tara!" King Bruce yelled over the speakers. "When those lines play overboard, give 'em room! What the fuck!"

Slowly, Hale loosened his grip. Coon-Ass and Rudy stood watching. "There's another set of boots in the gear closet," Hale said, releasing her. "Go grab 'em and get back out here."

She went inside and lay on the bench, sucking the blood from her finger where the nail had torn. The galley was quiet save for the sound of water dripping from her sock onto the floor. She heard the pop of the mechanical winch, the boys resuming their work, and pushed herself back to standing. In the gear closet she found a set of boots, duct-taped and too big. "Boys, on second thought, let's set 'em aboard," Bruce said. "Seems like this string might be bad luck."

When she went on deck, the crew was ganging up on pots and pushing them by hand, not waiting for the crane. No one said anything to her, so she just stood there, nursing her finger until the work was finished.

"Try not to kill us in our sleep," King Bruce said, nodding toward his seat behind the screens. The cushion was still warm with his heat. "Rudy will be up to spell you in two hours. You good? Your back all right from that spill?"

"I'm fine," Tara said.

"I got the shallow water alarm set. Watch alarm, too. When it starts blinking, just hit the button before it beeps and wakes the whole boat up. Your finger good?"

"I'm fine," she repeated.

She stuck three squares of ginger gum into her mouth and began the two hours of monkish silence, eyes making rounds between the bright green lines of the radar screen, the grainy fathometer, and the GPS. Every ten minutes she reached over to stop the red blinking light, worried about the alarm. After an hour she mixed instant coffee and hot chocolate to power her through the second half of the watch.

She reached to reset the watch alarm, heard steps, and turned, expecting to see Rudy. "You hanging in there?" It was Jethro coming up the stairs.

"Fine."

"Finger okay?"

She held up the bandage. She felt relaxed and queenly in King Bruce's cushy chair.

"What about the seasickness?"

She told him her cocktail. "Use the Rugby instead of the Bonine," he said. "Won't make you half as drowsy."

He pushed his hair behind his ears, stood over the chair. King Bruce snored in his berth behind them, on the other side of the door. Outside the water shifted in the lights. It had been two years since she had touched another person, at least in that way. She waited.

But he didn't move. After a couple minutes Rudy came to spell her.

Alone in her bunk, she thought of what she might have done. Imagined hands on her ribs, leaning up to kiss him. But soon it was Connor who came to mind, his birch oil smell, and his slow movements. She slipped her hand into her underwear, but her finger throbbed, and her body was tired. Annoyed, she sat up, patting the bunk for her book.

Dudes jerking off all around her, and she didn't even have the energy to try.

The next day the crew worked in a dry fury. Tara kept waiting to hear King Bruce on the radio, comparing notes, plugging his fishing partners for intel on their quarry. But aside from the occasional twitter from Minnow, there was only silence from up top.

Their eighth night on the water. As they ran between pots she found Jethro in the galley, standing over a frying pan of sputtering sausages. He wore a doleful expression that matched his beard, which had grown in soft and sparse.

A pot of rice steamed, covering the cabinet face with drops of moisture. Cooking shifts on the boat had disintegrated — people made food at all hours, sometimes sharing, sometimes not.

She tore apart two hamburger buns and set them on a baking sheet, cracked a yolk into a bowl of burger meat, sifted in bread crumbs, then turned the knob on the oven.

Jethro smiled. He ripped off a section of paper towel, laid it over a plate, and forked out the sausages.

"So where'd your dad get those tats?" she asked.

"Jail."

"Ah."

"You want one of these?" he asked, holding up an oily sausage.

"Sure. You want a burger?"

"Sure."

"What about the red and green flames on his head?"

"Jail too. Victorville, California. 'Cept the dumbass mixed up the colors, so now he's got green for port and red for starboard."

"And 'Trust no bitch'?"

"That came right after he caught my mom in bed with a charter fisherman."

"And that's how he ended up in jail."

"You got it."

Hale came in off the deck, water dripping from his bibs. The hydraulics on the crane had been having issues. "Yoke up, lovebirds. This stretch's supposed to be crawling with bugs — other boats have been killing it out here."

In just a few seconds the galley was a-flurry with the sound of zippers and the snap of buttons, clicks as yellow life vests were fastened. Tara scarfed down the sausage, set the burger meat in the refrigerator, and turned off the oven.

"She's blowing a gale out there. Buckle up," Hale warned. "If we don't get anything on this pull, we're fucked."

Rain appeared like tracers in the glare of the metal halide bulbs. On the horizon she could see a few lights, like stars, blinking in and out of view, as other boats pulled pots. Jethro climbed atop the stack. Balanced between the steel bars he affixed bridles, making sure each was ready to fish. Rudy took his position with the grappling hook, and Coon-Ass let out a whoop as he tossed it, snagging the line suspended between the two buoys. Tara stood by with bait as Hale fit the polyester crab line into the winch. It popped and crackled as it fed through the block.

The whole crew was silent, leaning over the cap rail to see if the pot had any color in it. If it did, it suggested that the rest of their line would be good. And if it didn't, all that work setting the pots was wasted.

The whine of the hydraulic power block, the shudder of the boat as the pot knocked against the gunwales, slamming into the rack. Inside were just a few small, confused crabs. On the next pot the bait jar was askew, the door tied shut in a sloppy knot, line tangled. A few undersized crabs mopped the air with their spiny legs.

"Well, boys, looks like we've been robbed," King Bruce said over the deck speakers.

A pall came over the crew, lifted only by Rudy's half-English, serious-sounding vows of old-world vengeance. "Tara, get food going," King Bruce said over the speaker.

She was in the cabin chopping onions, dabbing her eyes with a paper towel, when she smelled King Bruce's sweaty chestnut scent behind her. A few red hairs fell into the onions as he stroked his goatee. She didn't look up.

"Seein' now it was a mistake takin' you on." She stirred the onions. "Just not right havin' a girl on a crabber. Bad luck. I got a son who can't seem to focus on shit since you come aboard. Yer probably in love with him, too. Look at you now, you're all worked up."

She looked at him. "Bruce, I'm chopping onions."

"That'd be King Bruce to you," he said softly. He looked down at her chest and her heart quickened. "Just watch yourself."

As she stood there in front of the sink she imagined going up those stairs, into King Bruce's semen- and sweat-scented bunk, and suffocating him with a pillow. Standing aloft in the rain on the bridge beneath the sodium crab lights, proclaiming to Hale and the rest of the boat that from now on, she was captain.

Outside the boys kept working, resetting the pots. In the early morning Hale told her to get two hours of sleep. Clad in long underwear and fleece pants, a synthetic turtleneck zipped to her chin, she stared up at the steel-beamed ceiling. She could hear King Bruce snore just above her in ragged, phlegmy snuffles. She thought of Connor, his smell and his voice and his calmness, how he said he was hopeful. The words were a blanket she pulled over her head to shut out the world.

With only five days left in the opening, the boat seemed to be running less like a well-oiled machine than a spaceship about to disintegrate — the shouting and cursing, the wheeze of hydraulics and the shudder of the bulwarks as Hale slammed another pot into the launcher. The rasp of crab line against the blocking, the pot crashing down seconds later, a few crabs thrown against the webbing. King Bruce began coming down from the castle, lurching around, pointing and spitting, streaks of tobacco in his goatee. A matte of orange stubble had grown over his flames.

He ordered her to deep clean the galley. As she got on her hands and knees, breathing in the chemical scent of the cleaners, the squall of nausea returned. She went out on deck. An opaque, bluish dawn bloomed over the soft sea. A yellow crab line uncoiled as Rudy threw a buoy. The boys hardly paid attention as she heaved over the side, vomit slapping the surface.

That night before bed, their eleventh on the water, she stared back at herself in the mirror. Her eyes were sunken, and the edges of her lips downturned. The tip of the toothbrush poked between them like a thermometer. She checked her curls for gray hairs.

Back in her bunk she turned off the light and squeezed her eyes shut.

"*Aqetak. Aqetak. Aqetak. Aqetak. Aqetak.*"

85

WITH THREE DAYS LEFT, they switched fishing spots. It was a blowy day, whitecaps on the tips of the waves. The string had been soaking for twelve hours — this was their final shot.

"One string can make the difference," Jethro said. "One good haul."

Even King Bruce came down on deck as their first pot came up from the depths. Silence all around. And then a bloom between the bars, crab claws bulging against the nylon.

"Yippee ki yay, motherfucker!" Hale yelped. Crabs convulsed as the cage slammed into the launcher. The boys whooped and slapped hands and grabbed their crotches. A crunch of shells as Coon-Ass released the trapdoor and dumped a writhing pile onto the sorting table.

"We're in 'em, boys!" King Bruce yipped over the loudspeaker. "We can still plug it. Work, you motherfuckers!"

Tara did her best to keep her balance in the heaving boat as she reached into a tangle of red backs and white undersides. Pointed legs clinked and clattered against the sides of the chute, the male crabs landing with a far-off slap into the salt water below. Rudy held out an orange-gloved hand and yelled, "Bait!" She sent over a jar of chopped-up herring.

"Send her back down, then," King Bruce said over the deck speakers. "Don't wanna be running in this shit. Cod instead of herring.

You wanna be walking off this boat with ten thousand or twenty, boys? Let's find another gear."

Coon-Ass hurled a twenty-five-fathom shot of line on top of the pot, baited with codfish.

"Clear! Twenty, Cap!"

"Handful more pots like that and we'll be golden," King Bruce announced.

They brought up another pot, this one even more packed. The hold was halfway to full, Bruce announced. The euphoria of catching—large and legal crab pulled from the depths, all spiked legs and that glorious white underbelly—made the seasickness, Hale's ribbing, all of it, shrink away.

They set down their last trap on the string, and King Bruce swung back to start picking pots along the rocks. Coon-Ass and Jethro coiled shots of line and organized gear. One of the larger eight-by pots stood in her way, by the castle. She looked around for Hale, to ask him to fire up the crane, but he was busy with a pair of pliers, on top of a stack, working on the hinges of a trapdoor.

She'd seen the boys push these bigger pots, usually ganging up on them. Hale could do one by himself—like Jethro said, he had some sort of superstrength, which she had felt when he saved her from going overboard. But never Jethro or Coon-Ass. Or King Bruce, for that matter. Despite his puffed knuckles, she hadn't really seen him do shit over the trip, other than touching a couple stanchions with his grinder.

Curious, she wrapped her gloved hands on the horizontal support bar running across the pot and leaned her weight against the metal, trying to get a sense of the heft. Her pulse quickened. She waited for a shout, one of the guys laughing at the absurd idea of her pushing this box of steel across the deck. But they were all either inside or occupied.

She readjusted her position and bent forward again, letting the cold bar rest against the back of her neck, nestling her shoulders against the pot. She thought of Gypo in his corner. *Jab, Tara, stick and move.* "C'mon, motherfucker," she whispered. She felt the roll of the sea beneath her, hinged at the legs, then pumped her thighs, timed her push with the waves, threw her hips forward, straightened her back, and heaved. Blood rushed to her head.

When she opened her eyes she looked up to see three men on the foredeck, looking down at her, disbelief on their faces. She had moved the pot to the bow.

Hale spit over the side, shaking his head. "Sweet lord above. They ruined a hell of a man when they cut the balls off you."

86

ON THE SECOND-TO-LAST DAY they idled into a secluded bay, anchored up alongside a few other boats. King Bruce announced that they could sleep in until sunup while the pots soaked. They had found a honey hole, crawling with crabs, and he intended to get the most out of it.

In the early morning Tara took her coffee outside. A silver tincture lay over the bay. Rectangular buildings of the cannery were situated on the eastern shore beside a runway. A few single-prop planes were lined up at one end. On the other side of the bay, along the mud flats, she watched a bear scrounge among tidal grasses. Her muscles felt tired and quiet. It was comforting to know, as she stood in this mysterious outpost, that the pots were making money.

When she went back into the house Jethro said they were calling for a storm out of the southwest, which would blow them off Dutch Harbor. King Bruce wanted another couple thousand pounds before heading in, to top off the hold. But after almost two weeks the crew was ready for home.

"All right, we'll pick 'em up then blow this Popsicle stand," Bruce said over the speakers.

A cheer went up on deck as he pulled the hook and pointed them east.

Back in Dutch they unloaded and tied up, and Bruce went to the bank, returning with thick envelopes. In her bunk she counted her share. Sixteen thousand three hundred dollars. She knew the boys were all sticking around for opilio crab season in January. King Bruce hadn't asked her. She didn't want the invitation, anyway. She had toughed it out, and now held the check to prove it.

In the late afternoon she climbed the ramp to use the phone. First she left a simple message. "Hi, Laney, it's Tara Marconi. I have twenty-five thousand in cash. I want to buy your boat. Call me back." Then Connor's cell. No answer. Finally, she dialed Wolf Street. Just the machine. He was probably at the social club.

On her way back down to the *Reiver*, she passed the boys. Jethro slowed as the others walked on. "We're headed to the Elbow Room — come?"

She watched his expression, knowing how the night would end.

"Maybe I'll catch up with you. Hey!" she shouted. "Hey, Hale!"

Across the parking lot his stocky body turned. She lifted a hand. He seemed confused. After a moment, he lifted one back.

Then she was in her bunk, punching clothes into her duffel, wrapping her raingear in a bungee. At the harbor she used the payphone to call for a cab. A minivan in the parking lot flipped on its lights, drove over to where she stood.

"Elbow Room?" the man asked.

"Airport," she said.

"No planes till morning."

"Just drive, dude."

He went the short distance to the tip of the island, taking sips from the beer in the cup holder. "Keep the change," she said, handing him a hundred-dollar bill. "Actually, gimme two of those beers."

"No shit," he said, clicking on the vanity and holding the bill up to the light. She slid open the door and yanked her duffel free. He handed her the beers. "Thanks, honey."

She was about to snap back at him, saying she wasn't his honey, but was too tired.

At the airport she sat on a bench, sipping from a can, watching images on the soundless television of army tanks rolling around in the desert. These maps with curved red arrows describing troop movements appeared as hieroglyphs from some distant world. She felt loopy and starved.

In the restaurant she ordered the special, a big bowl of wonton soup with crabmeat. The rich broth and doughy noodles calmed her. And then, like a bad dream that steadily works itself back up around you, there was that chestnut-whiskey smell. She looked up to King Bruce's blistered hand pulling at his goatee. His good eye matched the glass one for shine.

"Making a run for it, are you?" he said. "Not even goodbye?"

She tapped the plastic spoon against the table.

"Don't know what I was thinkin', takin' on a girl like you. Hale's right. You're a liability."

Slowly, she stood, taking a hundred-dollar bill from her envelope, slipping it beneath her water glass. She wanted to say that the world would be a much better place if he had stayed in that crab pot and sunk to the bottom of the ocean, but instead found herself reaching out, feeling his body stiffen when she hugged him. "Thank you for taking me on, Bruce. Good luck in January."

She picked up her duffel, looking into his stunned, rubbery face, and then walked toward security.

87

SHE STEPPED OUT OF PORT ANNA AIRPORT into the late-fall scent of wet spruce and rotting alder leaves, and hugged Zachary, pressing her face against the waxed cotton of his oilcloth jacket, inhaling his familiar tobacco and fish smell.

"Geez," he said, patting her back. "You okay?"

"I missed it here," she said, not letting him go.

"There's someone in the cab who misses you right back. He insisted on sleeping out last night, beneath the truck."

When Tara opened the door Keta leapt, sidestepping her, curling around to show her his haunches, whining as she tried to pet him.

"Oh, monkey, come here. I'm sorry, I'm so sorry."

Finally he gave up and filled the air with a mournful howl, white whiskers shaking as his black lips puckered. A few tourists loading into a van took pictures. She sank her head into his fur, pulling him near.

"I know, it's awful, every little bit of it."

"You sure you're okay?" Zachary asked again, setting her bag in the pickup bed. "You look like death."

"I'm fine. Tired. Thelma's good? The kids?"

"Everyone's good. Thelma's answering all sorts of 911s about bears in the trash. And the kids couldn't get enough of the dog."

"I pushed an eight-by crab pot across the deck."

"Oh yeah? One of the big boys?"

She nodded. He held the door open for her. "Not bad. Load up, doggie."

Keta leapt onto her lap, arranging himself over her thighs. "You seen Newt at all in town?" she asked when Zachary got in.

"They were up north in Yak-a-scratch, hear they did pretty good. Then he went down south to pick up some girl."

The little guy was actually doing it.

"Where am I taking you?" he asked.

"To my new boat, if it's not too much trouble."

He looked at her. "You didn't."

"I did."

He shook his shaggy head. "Now I know you're not okay."

"I've never been better. Promise."

88

ON MONDAY SHE WIRED LANEY her twenty-five thousand dollars — then half jogged with Keta trotting by her side to the DMV and filled out the change of registration.

The top read:

Year: 1944
Make: Clyde W. Wood
Hull: wood
Type: tugboat
Propulsion: propeller

The woman behind the desk hovered her stamp over the paper, looking at Tara. "You know what they say about boats. Two happiest days are when you buy 'em and when you sell 'em. And this here's a big one."

"I know."

The stamp thudded down. "Well, congratulations. You're now the proud owner of a big wooden tugboat. Lord help us all."

Outside she held Keta's cheeks and kissed him on the snout. He stood still, eyes shut, allowing her to clean the brown threads from the ducts. "You ready for your new home?"

They cut through the gravel floatplane turnaround, crossed the parking lot, and went into the harbor office. When Tara announced she had bought the *Pacific Chief,* the room went quiet. "I'm giving you till Thanksgiving to get that ugly bird under power," the harbor-master said. "Then she becomes fish habitat. Laney knew it, now so do you."

She went cold. All the elation from the DMV drained away. "That's not enough time."

"You're the hot shit girl just back from the Bering Sea. I heard the stories. You know how to put in a day's work. Boat's yours now. So is the responsibility to move it."

"Laney never told me about the deadline. The engine block's cracked."

"Learn to weld."

"You can't weld to cast-iron." She had read this in one of her books.

The harbormaster fastened her weary eyes on Tara, the same blue as the faded, ugly banner around her neck. "Sweet lord, why didn't you just stay away like I told you?"

Before Tara could respond, the phone rang. The woman tipped the microphone to her lips. "I'll give you till Christmas. Now git."

89

HER FIRST NIGHT on the boat she stretched out in the rope hammock and stared up at the hemlock tongue-and-groove ceiling, making constellations of the knots. She could hear Keta snoring in the salon below. How many times had she imagined this, smelling the salt brine coming through the open portholes? Somewhere, she was sure, her mother was smiling.

In the morning she brought out a bucket of bleach and scrubbed the moss-stained lettering of *Pacific Chief*, using a toothbrush to root out mold. For lunch she rested a sandwich on the whale vertebrae, settled into the Adirondack chair, and opened her notebook.

The volcano appeared purple over the water, clouds spinning around its peak. It would rain later on, she thought. Or perhaps this was just the winter settling in. It seemed like yesterday it had been summer solstice, when it never got darker than twilight. She took a bite of her sandwich, propped up a leg, and started a letter.

> *Dearest C,*
>
> *Just wanted you to know — I bought the boat. Army TP-125, with an engine the size of a school bus. Which I've got until Christmas to get running. And after that, I'll*

"Y'all rentin' out berths on this here beast?"

She turned. At first glance she didn't recognize the thick-necked man standing on the dock with a woman beside him. But then she saw the eye patch, pushed aside her notebook, and threw her arms around Newt. His head was shaved, and his fingers were wrapped in tattered tape, gummy with dirt. The woman stood about his height, with plank shoulders and knit gloves.

"T, I'd like to introduce my one true love, Ms. Plume Rand."

The woman wore shorts over rainbow-striped tights, a wool sweater with half-dollar wooden buttons. She left off petting Keta, stepped forward, and extended a hand. A bolt of jealousy shocked Tara.

"I'm real, for better or worse," she said, smiling at Newt. Even his teeth looked whiter.

"This guy back here," Newt said, pointing to a bright-eyed toddler with a felt cap. "This is Luis."

She looked between them. Plume reminded her of herself a couple years back, her eyes working over the tug, mesmerized. Luis chewed his fingers, gurgling.

"I don't know, Newt," Tara said. "You'd have to baby-proof it."

"Ain't nothing hard liquor and a hammer won't fix, right, babe?" he said to Plume. "Plus, this guy's a tough little gummer. Rugged stock."

They both turned at the sound of footsteps. Petree and Irish stumbled along, Irish carrying a suitcase of Rainier.

Petree slurred his words. "Kangaroo, tell me the news ain't true."

"Still up for helping to get that engine going?" Tara asked.

He gulped back a beer. "C'mon, Irish. Girl's got a temper on her. You stand around too long, she's like to smack you one."

Stung, she looked out over the water.

"Go on, boys, drink somewhere else," Newt said. "We got business to discuss."

"Is that basil?" Plume asked, pointing toward one of the portholes.

Tara looked at the plant, which she had picked up at the hardware store. "It is."

She watched Petree and Irish make their way toward the dead end of the dock. After a moment she started up the gangway. "C'mon inside."

She'd finish the letter later.

90

SHE SMELLED PETREE before she saw him — the scent of ginger and hops. He had a plate of the Fairbanks-Morse on the engine room floor beside him, and was shining a light into the crankcase.

"Who let you on my boat?" she asked.

"Your friend Newt."

"Oh yeah?"

"Your buddy and me struck a deal. I get this girl running, he'll buy the *Invictus*. Plans to fish it with his family."

She continued to look at him, wary. He tore open another ginger chew.

"We'll have to grind down the cracks, seal 'em with JB Weld, see if they hold." He caught her gaze. "Look, word is you have until Christmas. You gonna help or what?"

She rolled up her sleeves. There was no time to waste.

"Teach me."

After a morning of feathering a grinder blade over the belly of the exhaust manifold, eyes throbbing from the orange sparks, she walked through town to the library and called her father.

"*Figlia.*"

"Hey, Pop."

"Where are you?"

"Back in Port Anna." There was a lightness to her voice, she could hear it. An airiness in her muscles she hadn't felt before.

"I tell the boys down at the club what you are doing and they cannot believe it. Was it good? Did you make money?"

"Enough for a ticket back to Philly." Silence. "Pop?"

"Yes. I just — I thought, I just wasn't sure."

"Weren't sure about what?"

She heard some talk, followed by Eva's laughter. He came back on the line, his voice frail. "Just, it's nothing. Vic wants to see you. Acuzio's back from Santa Fe. Little Vic, too."

"There's just one more thing I need to do. And then I'll be there."

"Is it money?" he asked after a moment. "I can send some. Just — come home."

"I'll be back soon."

"You come straight to Wolf Street."

She smiled at the order. "Okay, Pop. I will."

91

FOR THE NEXT FEW WEEKS she worked twelve, sometimes fourteen hours a day in the engine room, helping Petree rebuild the compressor, run WD-40 through the braided lines, clean and polish the oil strainers. They moved onto the Deutz three-phase generator, taking apart each of the six cylinders, Tara cleaning the heads and rings and rods with a soft cloth while Petree measured tolerances.

"We'll show her, just you watch," he said. "Hell with a hundred yards. We'll do a drive-by, drown 'em in our smoke." She began to get the sense that running the engine was Petree's final revenge not only on the harbormaster in Port Anna, but on all the harbormasters who had ever given him grief when he arrived into port with one of his hard-luck boats.

Around Thanksgiving, Miles, back home from college in Bellingham, stopped by. It didn't take long for him and Petree to bond. He took on the job of cleaning out the heat exchanger over the boiler, reaming out each of the rods, then making a new gasket on the fifth, smaller air compressor cylinder. When she handed Miles a container of Locktite to smear on the bolt threads as he tightened up the cylinder head, he smiled back at her as if it was the nicest thing anyone had ever done. "Thanks, Tara."

Fritz came by to check their progress. He followed the beam of her headlamp as she showed him where she had mixed up the two-part JB Weld epoxy, then grinded it down, using sandpaper, then emery cloth, before putting on another layer. "These old beasts need attention," he said, running a finger over the fix. "They like to be taken in hand, held close. Loved. They're like dogs. When their owners leave them, they lose their hair, get bitter."

"I don't think I've ever heard you get sentimental," she said. "It's touching."

He gave a slanted grin. "Speaking of which, you and that dog of yours holding up okay?"

"He's taking to the boat, I think. He likes peeing on the docks."

Fritz shook his head, running his fingers along the maze of pipes above. "What can I say? This boat just needed someone crazy enough to take her head-on. Hey. You mind if I snip off a couple of those basil leaves for Fran? She needs some for her Thanksgiving stuffing."

"That's why it's there."

"Tara Marconi," he said, shaking his head again. "You'll forgive me if I still can't get over it."

She picked up her tubes of JB Weld. "I forgive you. Now you'll forgive me for kicking you off so I can get back to work."

92

AT THE LAST MINUTE she decided not to go to Fritz and Fran's for Thanksgiving, and instead collapsed into the salon cushions, still in her oil-stained mechanic's suit. Newt bounced Luis on one leg, holding a bottle in one hand, a can of Rainier in the other, staring into the wood stove.

"How's Old Man River and his trusty sidekick down there? He ready to turn this beast over?"

"Soon."

"And then you go back to Philly for Christmas?"

"It depends if we run the hundred yards. But that's the plan. How would you guys feel about looking after the boat, and maybe the good monkey here?"

Hearing his nickname, Keta pulled himself up from the bed, made a show of stretching, and walked into the galley to rest his chin on Tara's thigh. "I know. But it will only be for a little, okay?"

Newt tried to fit the bottle between the baby's lips. "You are coming back, right?"

"What do you think? I'm gonna get the boat running, then abandon it, along with this love?"

"Sometimes it's hard to figure that curly head of yours, that's all."

She thought about looking out the window at the Delaware, the navy yard as the plane descended. And then Connor. It couldn't help but be awkward. They could hardly speak on the phone.

"You thinking about your feller back in Philly?"

She took the can of beer from him, tipped it back until it was gone. "Apparently I'm not that hard to figure."

"You get this far-off gaze. What's it been? Two years?"

"Two years and two months."

He crunched his can beneath a heel. "But who's counting?"

"Careful of the floor," she said.

"Feels like yesterday we were out on that breakwater, ain't it? And me thinking what in the hell has this girl gotten herself into."

She laughed. "Feels like years ago when I was thinking just about the same."

93

A RAINY DECEMBER SEVENTEENTH. Petree was back after a break, eager to make the final push on the engine. She was in the galley, studying the manual, waiting for her welds to dry. Plume had Luis on her back and was busy unscrewing the oak edges of the counter-top, cleaning them down with white vinegar and oil, leaving a sharp scent in the air. Despite her "free love" appearance and soft voice, the woman was neat and organized. Whenever a leaf on the basil plant turned yellow she nipped it off with her thumbnail. Tara lit lint and cardboard and yellow cedar scraps in the firebox of the Monarch, then set the kettle on the burner for coffee.

Plume was dribbling water into the dirt of the basil plant when she looked over at Tara, then back through the window. "There's some guy out there. He's been standing with his backpack for the past ten minutes, looking lost." She checked again. "Actually, he's kind of cute."

Tara checked her watch. The welds could use another half an hour at least. She closed her book, stood, and warmed a coffee mug with hot water. When she parted the leaves of the basil plant she saw a tall man in a leather jacket and sweatshirt with the hood pulled up against the rain. He was scruffy, with a high forehead, slow move-ments as he took something from the top pouch of his backpack. "Holy fucking shit," she said, pulling away.

"What?" Plume looked over her shoulder. "You know him?"

She opened the door and went out on deck, expecting the spot where she had just looked to be empty. But it wasn't. Connor's face broke into a smile. He flipped his palms to the sky, shrugging. She ran down the gangway and gripped him, holding the back of his head, pressing him to her. Breathless, she managed to say, "What are you doing?"

The features of his face were more defined. His freckles lighter, almost disappeared over his cheeks. Fine wrinkles at the edges of his eye.

He looked up and down the length of the tug. "So you actually did it."

She watched his lips, the dimples in his cheeks, the one on the right deeper than the left. She glanced down and flipped the brass zipper of her oily mechanic's suit with one finger.

He pulled up her chin. "Is it okay I'm here?"

She searched for the right words. After a moment of silence, all she could think of to say was, "Wanna help?"

"Yes," he said, his features relaxing. He hefted his backback. "And, how?"

94

WHILE CONNOR SHOWERED she went into the engine room, setting Petree's coffee on top of the hot water heater. Her hands shook.

"You okay?" Petree asked. "Look like you just seen the ghost of
Soapy Smith."

"I'm fine. What do we got going here?"

He splayed his fingers over one of the cylinders. "Touch," he said.
She reached out. "It's warm."

"That's right. Know what that means?"

"My welds are holding."

"Damn right they are. The boy and I reamed out the pipes on all
the heat exchangers. Opened up the sea chest to bring raw water in
to cool her. All we need now is to clean out the oil strainers in the
manifold. Take a look at this."

He flipped a light switch and a glass peephole on a metal box lit
orange, the flame reflecting off tanks strapped in by the oil reservoir.
"Rigged that up myself. We'll change out the diesel filters, bleed the
air lines. You give the oil screens a good scrub with a wire brush until
the brass shines. I'd say a couple days and we're in business."

Connor ducked beneath the bulkhead into the engine room.
He was Petree's height, but looked unmarked, fresh-faced after the
shower, so young beside the old salt.

Miles came back from the bow, where he had been working on
the compressor. "Who's this?" he asked, wiping his hands on his suit,
looking at Tara.

"My friend Connor," she said. "From Philadelphia."

Connor shook their oil-stained hands, then rapped his knuckle against an empty CO_2 tank.

If there was a way she could take all she had learned over the last two years — not only about engines and combustion, but about biases and predilections, habits and quirks — she would share this so he would say the right thing. *I wish I could help you,* she thought. *All the missteps I have made, please don't make them too.*

His mouth opened. "So where do we start?"

It was perfect.

95

WHEN SHE CAME DOWN THE LADDER the next day, Connor was sitting at the table, drinking coffee with Newt. The Monarch gave off waves of heat. The manual for the Fairbanks-Morse was open to the page on the oil manifold.

"When do we get some sunshine around here?" Connor asked, nodding toward the volcano. It was just after eight. "Doesn't the dark drive you nuts?"

Newt stood. "We're going out to the cape to try and rouse up some winter kings. Y'all have fun down there in the dungeon."

"You get used to it," she said, pouring herself a cup, watching Newt step out on deck. She looked over his work pants and sweatshirt. "Sleep well?"

"Like a baby," he said. He clapped his hands. "So what's the schedule? I've been reading about brass strainers."

She finished her coffee, grabbed an apple. "Let's get to it."

In the light of the headlamp he traced the engine manual with the pad of his finger, from a white steel tank just aft of the bilge pump through two brass filters, into the crankcase, to the Manzoni injectors, hitting three sides of the cylinders. He tapped a wood plank with the tip of his shoe. "Which means our filters should be here?"

He looked at her questioningly. Using a crowbar, she brought up the plank. Beneath, screwed into a timber, were two pint-sized cast-iron filters. "Bingo," she said, catching his eye and giving a thumbs-up. He kneeled, shifted a lever, and removed the caps. Inside olive-colored residue was caked around the screens. Without waiting he reached in, his hand going black. With a squelch the screen lifted out.

"We've got gloves, C," she said.

"Ach, it's fine." He held the screen with the tips of his fingers, residue dripping into the bilge. If Miles or Petree had been here they would have yelled. Work smarter, not harder. She saw then that he was trying to impress her. He'd have to use industrial soap, even diesel to remove the oil from his hands.

They went back through the cargo hold and climbed topside, the strainers wrapped in diapers. A gentle gray rain made a shine on the silver deck. In the galley she lit candles and set out newsprint, and they both used wire brushes and brass cleaner to scrub.

There were so many things she wanted to talk about, she didn't know where to start. He appeared content. She wondered then how she had ever thought they were going their own separate ways.

There was an "Ahoy" from outside. Petree peeked in his head. "We're not straining cocktails in that thing, buddy," he said to Connor. "Just so they're not gummed up is fine."

Connor grinned across the table at her, as if this were an inside joke of theirs. His quiet, contained movements reminded her of Betteryear.

When she stood to make sandwiches, she noticed how Connor watched her. She allowed herself to feel his gaze, and didn't mind how his eyes rested on her back, kept her close.

"Nice job," she said, picking up his strainer. It gleamed in the galley light.

"Not bad," he agreed. "Not bad at all."

Later that afternoon, Petree insisted Tara take his truck and show Connor town. He wanted to see the payphones at the library, the apartment where she first lived. "But first, show me that river you smelled when you arrived."

It was three P.M. The air was already taking on a twilight glow. Shreds of cloud skirted across the sky as they drove north. The volcano appeared enormous across the water. Keta whined whenever Connor stopped scratching his head. Fur swirled in the air, blowing through the sliding cab window, catching on Connor's leather jacket.

"So you gonna give me a good improv line, or what?"

"Oh, man. You give me a prompt. Two of them."

She squinted out the window. "Watermelon. Spanish Inquisition."

He thought. "Can I tell you how hard it is to burn a watermelon at the stake? It's, like, ninety percent water. Doesn't work."

"Are you kidding?" she said. "That's really good."

"You think?"

Just beyond the ferry terminal she pulled onto the gravel road by the river. The few leaves clinging to the alders waved in the fading light.

"I kind of can't get over it. You coming here. It's not the Connor I remember," she said.

"Yeah, well." He opened his door and looked down toward the river and the grassy estuary beyond. "People change."

She led him to the bank, holding back thorny branches of devil's club. Keta darted off through the salmonberry bushes, nose near to the ground as he worked some invisible trail.

She thought back to more than two years ago, when she stood on this same riverbank with Fritz, fish gasping in the shallows. Now she noticed the low angle of the winter light, how the sun reflected off the water and honed the lines of the trees. She knew she could walk farther into the valley, then up the side of the mountain into the muskegs and marshes, where the tufted bulrush would be turning yellow, the blueberry shrubs crimson as winter continued its dark, wet press.

Hands on her wrists snapped her out of her thoughts. He ran his fingers over her chapped and hardened skin. She looked down, pressed the toes of her boots into the gray sand, then up again, seeing what the light did to his green eyes. He brushed a curl from her face. Stretched out in those scarred wooden beds at the Bunkhouse, building the platform with Thomas, sharpening knives with a file on *Leda's Revenge* — through all this she had forgotten what it felt like to be touched.

Keta's white head appeared upriver. Panting, he watched them. Connor leaned over and kissed her, quiet and warm. She drew back when she felt the dog against her legs.

"It's okay, monkey. I know what I'm doing."

96

OVER THE NEXT COUPLE OF DAYS she noticed how Connor paid careful attention to the idiosyncrasies of the boat that she was just herself learning. How far to turn the butterfly valve after using the toilet so that it wouldn't overflow the black-water tank and make the boat list to starboard. The importance of warming mugs before pouring coffee so the liquid wouldn't go cold. How to start the wood stove with yellow cedar, then spruce, and, before bed, putting on splits of hemlock, the night wood.

To her surprise, Connor and Newt hit it off. When the fridge handle broke, Connor took a set of deer antlers he found lying around, countersank them, and made a handle. This pleased Newt immensely. "An Alaskan brain on that guy."

Connor slept in the quarter berth across from the head. They hadn't kissed since the river. He seemed to be waiting for the boat to run its hundred yards, or maybe he was waiting for something else. There was a reticence in him she recognized — but now it reassured her. She trusted it. One step at a time. Running the boat was what counted now.

The plan was to start the engine on the docks on December twentieth, steam the hundred yards the following day, then fly out on the twenty-third.

On the way back over the bridge, after buying tickets, he surprised her by reaching out, taking her necklace between his fingers, and examining her medallion.

"What?" she said, reaching up to settle the chain.

"I wanted to ask—you sure you're okay flying on the twenty-third?"

She rested her hand on his mouth. "I think my mother would love it."

"Yeah," Connor said. "I think that's right."

97

PETREE WAS LIKE A HIGH SCHOOL ORCHESTRA CONDUCTOR, pointing to this hose, that check valve, bleeding the filter at the end of the run. He sang as he went. "So we go here, and then to there, on down to you, and you . . . where do you go . . . ? Ah, here you go, da da-da . . ."

It was just past eight in the morning on December twentieth, two days before winter solstice. The sun hadn't yet risen. Connor came down with a box of doughnuts and coffee.

"A simple beast," Petree muttered, reaching for a cruller, patting the exhaust manifold, leaving powdered sugar on the paint. "If only all —"

"If only all women were so simple," Tara finished for him, impatient. "Should we turn her over?"

Newt and Plume were outside on the docks — they had agreed to keep an eye on the lines. If the engine ran, that meant the boat would move, and Petree wanted to be sure they didn't break off the dock.

"Don't rush it, Kangaroo. I need to see it all in my head before we take her for a spin around the floor."

After a couple more minutes of talking to himself, he twisted a selector dial to make sure the starter was taking power from the car battery. "Okay. Let's see if we can't build us some air."

Miles walked around and gave the starter a couple thwacks with his wrench. Tara pressed the button on the generator, which shook and rumbled, hiccupped and stuttered, then roared, trembling on its mount.

"Boy's a good wrench," Petree yelled to Connor. Miles loosened a nut on each injector, tightening it back up when diesel spurted out. He let the Deutz idle a few minutes before throttling, setting the rubber stopper to maintain RPMs. Tara slipped headphones over her ears and handed a pair to Connor, who looked confused when Petree pulled a lever. They were in the dark until there was a second clunk, and the lights flickered up again, dimmer now. Petree tapped the voltage dial — just over two hundred amperes — and flashed a thumbs-up.

The needles on the twin PSI gauges rose steadily from five, to ten, to fifteen as the compressor ran and they made air. For a moment she saw Petree Bangheart before the hard winters up north, the alcohol. Fixing engines took the years away. Or maybe it was working with Miles, who checked each of Tara's welds for droplets of water, nodding at her good work. Petree bent to lift the planking by the engine. Toes balanced on a bulwark, Miles twisted the wheel on a valve in quick, muscular motions. She knew this opened the sea chest to allow salt water into the system to cool the engine. Petree throttled down the Deutz, letting it idle for a couple of minutes before shutting off the generator.

The silence echoed. Miles and Petree walked around, checking gauges, wiping down the brass knob for pumping oil through the lines with a rag. Petree turned a yellow gate valve above the engine. It was hard to see his eyes beneath those swollen folds of skin, but she could tell he was getting nervous. "If the cylinders go and the prop turns, I need you and your guy here checking our wash outside."

"Roger," Tara said, hurt that she was given the stupid job, but so ready to have this over with.

"Miles? We still good on air?" Petree asked.

"All good."

"Here we go."

Using both hands, he twisted the black cast-iron wheel to AIR. The pipes whispered, and a bumping sound started in the crankcase, like a rollercoaster being pulled up an incline. Blue smoke leaked from the head of the fifth cylinder. When he went to FORWARD, the engine died. He checked the PSI gauge, then turned the wheel again. The pistons accelerated, the hull shifted forward, and then the engine fell silent.

She began to sweat. Doing the math in her head, factoring in her plane ticket, she figured she would have about ten thousand dollars to put into the boat for repairs — a drop in the bucket. It needed to start.

"She's just burning off old oil," Petree insisted. "When did she last run, Tara? Six years? These beasts are like horses — they need to stretch their legs, otherwise they go to seed. See how we do this."

He turned the wheel all the way to the left, then hit START. The vibrations in the bulwarks felt different now as the pistons and crankshaft changed direction. When he brought the wheel to ASTERN the engine died down, then came back up, chattering the timbers and shaking the floor planks. He exchanged a glance with Miles, who turned the wheel on the governor, opening the valves on the cylinders, feeding fuel. The clanging fell off for a moment, loped, then accelerated.

"More!" Petree shouted. The pistons settled into a rhythm. He turned to Tara and Connor. "Go!"

They ducked beneath the bulkhead, sprinted through the cargo hold and up the ladder, lifted off the hatch to the deck. The boat shook. Off the stern, Irish, in a rowboat, a bottle between his legs, spun in the wash of the five-foot propeller. He gave a gummy laugh as he twirled, caught in the stew of barnacles and sea anemones.

"The good gods favor ya, young lady!" he shouted.

The engine rumbled to a stop. The lines slackened, then grew taut again when Petree switched directions on the crankshaft. She could see this in her head, recalling the diagrams from the instruction booklet.

There was a bark. Keta paced along the docks, panting, watching her. Plume stood behind Newt with the baby, watching as mouse-gray smoke rose in rings against the lightening sky.

"The thing actually works," Newt said, picking at his fine hair. "Connor, I owe you fifty bucks."

Petree came up from the hold, smiling. "We'll run her a bit, then take her offline. Pump the bilge so she's light. Tide's high at about noon tomorrow. We'll back her out, loop around, burn off old oil, and that should be our hundred yards. Sound like a plan?"

"Is it okay if I hug you?" she asked him.

"I'll take that over a fist to the jaw," he said, reaching out his long arms and gripping her. "Listen, I set up a bilge pump down there. Just run the hose over the side and turn her off once she pumps down — should be around nine this eve."

"Got it."

"You call the harbormaster?"

"Not yet."

"I'll do it."

As she went below to plug in the pump, she heard him say into the VHF handheld, "Port Anna harbormaster, this is *Pacific Chief*. Engine is running. We'll be driving by tomorrow morning. Make sure your windows are shut — otherwise you're gettin' smoked the hell out."

98

THE MORNING OF DECEMBER TWENTY-FIRST. She lay in the hammock with Connor, her head on his chest, rising and falling with his breathing. Keta snored in front of the wood stove.

The night before, he had kissed her in the galley when she had come up from shutting off the bilge pump. Except this time it wasn't soft or quiet, but with urgency. When he asked if there was room in the hammock, she said yes. Except once they reached the top of the ladder, Keta began to whine.

"He's lonely," Tara said, looking down through the cutout in the floor.

"Well then, let's get him up here."

She watched as he went about rigging up a system, threading Keta's life vest with a blanket. The dog went limp as they pulled him up, then sprinted around the exhaust stack in the middle of the room.

Connor held her hands to his chest as they danced to some beat in his head. His quiet nature from high school still existed. But there was a sureness in his movements, a confidence. She snuggled closer. Keta rested by the fire.

Now she lay beside him, smelling the salt-rot of low tide: anemones, limpets, fucus drying in the morning breeze. Connor snored softly, a naked leg thrown over the side of the hammock. The harbor so quiet, the boat so still. She patted the carpet remnant for Connor's phone—4:12 A.M.—then pulled herself up on an elbow and peered out the aft window toward the volcano in the west. A curtain of northern lights reflected radar green over the snow-covered cone.

"Connor. Hey." She nudged his shoulder. "Wake up."

Keta heard the commotion and came over, his ears pointed.

"Oh my lord," he said, making the hammock swing as he looked out the glass.

She slid the door open, and they walked onto the aft deck into the salt air, her feet cupped on the asphalt roofing against the cold. The lights danced off Keta's coat. The dog leaned against Connor's shins, whining as the sky pulsed.

"My friend Betteryear told me Inuits think it's their ancestors laughing," she said.

He pulled her close, kissing the top of her head.

"You'll have to tell me about him one day."

All of her days, she thought. All of her days for this.

99

WHEN SHE WOKE AGAIN the sky was beginning to lighten. She heard a sound below. Usually Newt and Plume were up early, feeding the baby, the scent of coffee wafting topside. But when she rose, careful to not wake Connor, she went into the galley and there was no one.

In the month she had been living and working on the tug, she had come to enjoy the tap of the cast-iron and copper skillets, hung from nails in the ceiling beams according to size. This morning, though, the pans were silent. It was as if the boat was holding its breath before the move.

She stuffed newspaper and lint into the Monarch, dropped a match into the firebox, and listened for the whir of flames. When the water boiled she went out on deck and sat on the cedar cap rail, eating an apple, drinking her coffee, watching the blues overhead lighten by degrees.

She loved these mornings, the mountains purple and sharp against the sky, revealing their heft. This land that had so unsettled her that first day when she arrived now filled her with such contentment. In another few hours a splinter of light would work over the rim of the volcano, the sun peeling back shadows. And this boat beneath her would move.

She checked Connor's mobile, in the pocket of her flannel. 6:47. She scanned the docks for Zachary, then walked down the gangplank, at a weak angle this morning. The *Spanker* was already out, winter king fishing. Most of the trollers that had been tied to the bull rail were gone—the price for king was good, and folks were catching.

She hated to look in the water around the tug. Algae bloomed on the keel. Anemones pulsed in the current. This morning, though, it was the colonies of mussels, shells agog in the ebbing tide, that annoyed her. Normally they clustered right up to the waterline. Now they were nearly a foot below.

Fear moved up her spine. Her eyes went to the bow, searching for the stenciled white letters of *Pacific Chief.* The words were almost level with the bull rail.

She sprinted up the gangway, slid off the hatch leading to the cargo hold, and peered down. Her throat constricted. Water, black with engine oil, returned her reflection. Shreds of insulation, rags, a loose section of hose, her chest freezer with its lid open, floated in the scum. From far off she heard splashing.

She ran down the gangway and threw the breaker at the post to save the boat from being electrocuted. Using Connor's phone she dialed 911.

"Thelma—it's Tara over on the docks. The *Chief* is sinking."

"What?"

"My boat—*Pacific Chief,* she's taking water. Zachary's supposed to be by at seven. Call Fritz at the fire department. I gotta go."

She hung up, thought for a moment, then ran inside to wake Plume, who slept with Luis sprawled over her. "What's going on?" the girl asked, fumbling for her glasses.

"Just take what you need and get off the boat. Go."

Trailing a length of muslin blanket, Plume pushed past Tara and ran through the salon out the door. "Connor!" Tara shouted. "Wake up. Off the boat. Bring the dog."

"Wha?" she heard.

"The boat's taking water. Time to get off!"

Not waiting for a response, she went back out, pushed the hatch cover farther aside, then lowered herself into the black water. It flooded the cuffs of her boots and saturated her fleece pants, her legs already beginning to numb. A Jerry can, the yellow plastic container for diesel that she had been using to power the generator, nudged her arm. Gasoline swirled in rainbows on the surface.

Taking a breath, she stepped forward into the darkness. But the floor planks were gone. Ocean closed over her back, and she spit out a mouthful of salt water.

"Connor!" she hollered.

His face appeared above, sharp in the low sun. "How can I help?"

"Is the dog off?"

"He's on the dock with Plume."

"Throw me a headlamp. Hanging in the mudroom. Hurry."

What to do, what to do . . . where was Zachary? And Newt, of all days to leave early to fish. If Thelma called the fire department, Fritz would pick up on his radio.

Connor dangled the headlamp. "You want me down there with you?" he asked.

"No. Look out for Zachary. Tell him what's happening when he gets here."

Tucking her chin, Tara pushed off the bottom rung of the ladder, breast-stroking in the direction of the splash. The headlight illuminated the outline of the bulkhead. She ducked under it, kicked. A Styrofoam cooler bounced off her shoulder. Her breath came in gasps, her feet throbbing with cold.

"Stay calm, Tara," she recited.

The white beam flashed over the bronze "Fairbanks-Morse" plaque on the engine. Water lapped against the belly of the exhaust manifold. Her breath came in ragged gasps.

As she swam the tip of her boot brushed a boat rib. She stood, balancing, water almost to her chest. Rafts of yellow floor planks floated around her. She gritted her teeth against the cold. And then she saw it — a flash of white in the headlamp's beam, water gushing in around the sides of the loose through-hull.

Right then she understood what had happened. The end of the hundred-foot hose they had used to pump out the bilge had been left in the ocean. After the bilge level dropped she had unplugged the pump. Overnight the hose had back-siphoned, gulping ocean, flooding her boat as they slept. And now there was water coming in around the seal of the through-hull, which had been put beneath the waterline by the growing weight of the boat.

From back in the cargo hold she heard a noise. She curled her fingers around the lead pipes, swinging herself forward, pedaling her feet in the water. Just before ducking beneath the bulkhead, she stopped. The pump, she thought. Get the pump out of the bilge, stop the water from back-siphoning, that was a start. Even better, find the plug end and start the pump up, start emptying the boat. How quickly she had worked in the simulated engine room, clamping on a shred of rubber, tapping in a wedge with a hammer. She needed that same speed now.

Seawater lapped against her chin. She tasted again the dull, rotten flavor of used engine oil. Her fingers ran over the iron lever on the strainers for the oil manifold. There! — the cord of the 110-volt pump. She pulled and up it came, its plastic casing dripping oil. She gripped the metal handle and slipped beneath the bulkhead.

"Tara! You down there?"

Above the hatch she saw the dark outline of two men, Zachary and Connor. She found her footing on the stationary planks beneath the water, elbowed aside the open chest freezer and blocks of insulation, and pulled the pump through the water. The end of an extension cord dangled in front of her. She reached up.

"Careful. Don't get your fingers in the —"

One hundred and ten volts shot through her bloodstream. "Motherfucker!" she screamed, jumping back.

"Standing in water — not the best time to put your finger onto the hot," Zachary said.

Angry now, feeling that old urge to box whatever dark force had shocked her, she grasped for the soaked plug. A vibration moved through the water and she felt the bilge pump gulp between her feet, followed by the holy sound of water splashing into the ocean above.

"Take this," Zachary said, handing down a black marker. "Draw a line at the high-water mark so we can keep track. You got that Honda trash pump? We need to start gaining — further down she sits, the quicker she'll get heavy."

She recalled another lesson from the class on the importance of storing a backup trash pump high in case of emergency — which she'd done while organizing the workbench.

The pump was too heavy to carry with no footholds. She found a section of planking, got purchase on a bulwark with the tips of her boots, and lifted it onto the floating island of wood.

"Bridle this to the frame," Zachary said. She took the line he handed her and made a triangle, then fastened the end with a double half-hitch.

"Good!" she yelled up. She reached the ladder and pushed the pump from the base as he lifted. Connor offered a hand and she took it. A few people had gathered on the transient dock, watching with the confused expressions of drunks in the morning.

Zachary popped out the choke on the pump, then pulled the cord. Silence.

"Did you prime it?" she asked.

He gave her an incredulous look. At the thud of rubber boots, they both turned. Headlamps bounced on the planks as a group of firemen jogged toward the boat, two carrying a pump between them. Fritz was out in front, his stomach, framed by suspenders, shuffling as he ran.

"Hop-skip! We got a boat sinking." He pushed a kid with canvas pants bunched at his knees up the gangway. "Fire department charges extra when I have to run," he told Tara. "You got a hatch forward? Looks like she's way heavy in the bow. We're gonna need more pumps than just the one. Horn, set that pump up forward. Top o' the mornin', Zach. That pump shit the bed?"

"She won't turn over. Moisture or bad gas."

"Horn, head back to my truck for a can of ether out of the box. Grab that gas jug too."

Tara lowered herself back into the cargo hold. "Where we at, kiddo?" Fritz asked.

She shined her light across the area. "Leak around the through-hull on the forward starboard side," she said. "An inch in the last five minutes."

He crouched down, gripping either side of the hatch rim and peering around.

"Listen to me now. As the boat drops down the sea's gonna start pouring through planks that have lost their caulking. We've got to lighten her load. That through-hull leak is the least of your worries."

"Okay. I'm going in — if you drop down your pump from the boat I can catch it."

"Look for Horn up around the fo'c'sle hatch."

The higher water level made it easier to swim. She stopped in front of the through-hull. White water came in from all sides now — like Fritz had said, the deeper the boat sank, the faster the water. Very soon, she knew, it wouldn't be safe to be down here.

Boots pounded the deck above. As she swam she imagined water sloshing around the big oak wheel, picking up her mattress like a leaf. The cross-shaped mast sinking in a rush of foam and bubbles, the caged trouble lights flickering as the boat went under.

White light shined in her eyes. She brought a hand to her face. "Can you not point that at me?" she asked.

"Sorry," the kid said. He held up the hose end from the pump with one hand, and his pants with the other. "Fritz told me to put this in the bilge somewhere."

She muscled through the water. "Give." He had no urgency about him. She wanted to slap his face.

"Get that deep as you can!" Fritz shouted from somewhere above. She plunged the pump end with its plastic cage into the bilge.

"Get out of the way," she said when the hose caught on the kid's leg.

"Set!" she yelled up.

"Fire in the hole!"

The hose shook in her hands, and a shadow of water pulsed through.

A midship hatch to the engine room opened, and she saw an oblong shape of a head, a snorkel and mask.

"Hey there, darlin'," Newt said, shielding his good eye from her headlamp. He pulled a blue gallon bucket of roof tar into view and waved a spackle knife. "Gonna try and muck up that starboard leak from the outside. You okay?"

"I'm not okay."

"We'll plug it. Listen, there's a Coast Guard prick out here who says he needs a word."

Then he was gone, but leaving behind his lighthearted confidence. It would be all right. Grace and wonder come from heartache. Newt had said that once, and she was beginning to realize how true it was.

She pulled herself up the ladder and out on deck, where pumps worked — two on the stern, one smaller fire department pump amidship, and the larger one dumping off the bow. A steady chorus of water splashed overboard. Diapers floated around the hull, soaking up oil. Her boat was in intensive care, tubes and wires attached, everyone working to keep her alive.

Connor, in his flannel pants, was speaking with a gray-haired man in a dark blue windbreaker who matched him in height. A Coast Guard insignia was stitched over his left breast. Marine Safety Detachment.

"Can I help you?" she asked.

The man turned. "Are you Laney Mitchell?"

"No. Tara Marconi."

"Are you the owner of the boat?"

"I am."

"Ah. The records must not have gone through." He checked his clipboard, then handed over a card with his name embossed on it, alongside the crossed anchors of the Coast Guard. "I'm gonna need to ask you a few questions here. Ms. Marconi. Ms.?"

She looked toward the hold. "Yeah. It's not the best time, to be honest."

He rubbed the back of his head, scrunched up his face. "So it appears. Is that oil dripping off you?"

She observed the ring of black water gathering at her feet.

"We'll come back to that later," he said. "I'd like to start with the layout of the boat. Can you tell me how the tug is partitioned?"

"Partitioned?"

"I mean, is the lazarette separated from the cargo hold, and is the cargo hold separated from the engine room?"

"Everything's separated by a bulkhead, if that's what you're asking."

"That's *not* what I'm asking," he said, in a sharp tone. "If you knew about boats, you'd be able to give me a clear answer."

"I know enough about boats to see that mine is sinking, how about that? If you'd like more information, you're welcome to come down and help stop this leak."

She turned to go, felt his fingers close around her arm. "Ms. Marconi. I —" She sprang back, tamping down the urge to swing. Connor stepped in front of her.

"Whoa, whoa, whoa. Trust me, buddy. You don't want to be doing that." The man stared at Connor, and was starting to say something when Petree came forward. The three of them converged on him.

"I-I'm trying to do my job here, okay?" he stammered. "Sinking will mean oil spill. It will mean diesel spill. Both classified as federal emergencies and crimes. Not to mention a two-hundred-and-twenty-ton boat on the bottom of the ocean."

Tara ground her molars. The man looked back at her, waiting. She heard steps, was pushed to one side. "Macclenny, did someone forget to lock your cage this morning? Go on, man. If there's an investigation, I'll tell everyone you did your job."

It took her a moment to recognize Jackie's blond hair peeking out of the faded blue handkerchief, tied in a neat triangle over her head.

Fritz yelled across the deck. "The hell's going on over there?"

"You know this boat, Jackie?" the man said, jabbing his clipboard.

She looked older, tired. "Yeah, the skipper used to work with me. Heard there were issues."

Without waiting Tara climbed down into the cargo hold, and soon the sound of their voices drowned out. They were gaining on the water level, which had lowered back down to the black line. It was working. The boat was rising. In broad strokes she swam into the engine room and moved the forward pump as far aft as the hose would stretch.

Fucking useless Coast Guard, she thought. If the boat floated, she'd make Zach, Fritz, Newt, Petree, and now Jackie a box of cannoli. Each. She couldn't believe the woman had come to help her. She'd bring back from Philly soppressata sausages and pepper shooters stuffed with provolone and prosciutto from the Italian Market. Hell, she'd make them all godfathers of her first child, never mind that her father would insist on Little Vic. And Jackie the godmother. But please, let this boat float.

She brought the 110-volt bilge pump aft into the cargo hold, followed by the tip of the fire department's pump. Already, the waterline had dropped another inch and a half, thanks to all the pumps sucking from one spot. Their plan was working.

Water from the hoses gushed over the side. She could almost feel the boat growing light beneath her feet, and it left her with a weight-less, breathy excitement. Zachary stood by the railings. "Good thing you were up early, to get on top of this before it got too bad," he said.

She hadn't thought about that—if she and Connor had lazed around in the hammock just a few hours longer, she could have gone down with her boat. Along with Keta, Plume, Newt, and the baby. It was too awful to think about.

They both watched Newt, his back pale as a seagull's breast, fin-ish smearing black roofing cement over the through-hull. He gave a thumbs-up, then swam toward the stern of the boat where Fritz had set up a rope. As Newt climbed aboard, Zachary sighted down the cap rail.

"The hell's going on?" he said, his voice rising as he spoke. She felt a shift of weight beneath her boots. Zachary walked forward toward the windlass, then glanced back at her with an expression she recognized from the night of the storm. "Hey—hey! Fritz! She's going ass-over-teakettle!"

And she was. As soon as Tara saw it, she jumped into the hatch, not bothering with the ladder, landing in the water, twisting her ankle against a bulwark. She heard Connor calling her name, and then Petree, yelling for her to get out of there. But she was already swimming, pulling herself along the manifold, ignoring the burn in her leg, yanking at a pump cord to unplug it. Water sloshed against her chest as the boat continued to tip forward. The aft pumps had made the stern light, and the weight of water in the bow was taking the tug down. It was her fault.

She heard a noise. There were arms around her waist. Connor was dragging her through the water toward the cargo hold.

"Get off me!" She kicked and hit her foot against the engine. Her leg rang with pain. She wrenched away from Connor. "You're not helping," she shrieked. "We just need to get these pumps forward. Get off me! Newt, help," she pleaded.

Newt, shirtless on the ladder, said, "T, listen to me. In seven seconds water's going to be coming in through that hatch above us. And we will drown. Either you move aft and we go out that back hatch, or the two of us will drag you. Choose now."

"I need to stay."

"No — no, you don't."

The boat lurched forward. Her head hit the engine block. "Go!" someone shouted. She felt a wetness on her forehead, then arms pulling her beneath the bulwark, into the cargo hold, slanted now at a steep pitch. She grabbed a ladder rung and hauled herself up through the hatch with Connor pushing her from behind. Then she was on deck, trying not to slip back into the house as the boat tipped to vertical. People shouted. She glimpsed the harbormaster swinging what appeared to be a machete, trying to hack the last line that connected the *Chief*'s stern to the docks. Fritz held her back.

"Jump!" Newt said, hanging on to the rails on the starboard side.

She grabbed Connor's hand, and then they were sliding off the deck into the aquarium-green water and bubbles, the pain in her ankle numbed by the cold. Hands scooped beneath her arms and she was pulled over the bull rail onto the planks. She watched from her stomach, Connor coughing beside her, as the boat continued its pitch forward, water closing over the house, flooding through the stern door into the galley. The tug paused, dragging the corner of the dock down. Fritz stepped away as the harbormaster swung furiously at the line attached to the boat's cleat. With a pop the threads gave, the dock snapped back, and the boat moved quickly into the churn of water. The stern paused for a horrible moment before plunging into a froth of bubbles.

Then it was just empty space on the corner of the dock, and the ocean below. Steadily sealing up the wound until it was as if nothing had ever been there.

100

A RAVEN HOPS ALONG THE BULL RAIL. Snowflakes melt on its black feathers. Gripping her crutches, she leans over the water, imagining for a moment she can see the tugboat below. "Careful," Connor says, setting a hand on her shoulder.

The still water mirrors their reflections. There are gouges in the wood an inch deep where the lines pulled. She touches her bare neck. The medallion, now on the bottom of the ocean, had been a talisman, proof that what she was doing — coming to Alaska, working on fishing boats, buying this tugboat — made sense. Also the basil plant, so carefully pruned. Her mother's photo of the men from Aci Trezza. Fish swimming through the netting of the hammock.

A rumble from the west. Diamonds of light hover in front of the volcano, its rim wreathed in cloud. Fuselages come into view, cutting through the swirling snow.

They stand for another minute there at the outer corner of the docks, snow melting into the water, thunder from the arriving plane echoing off the mountainsides. If her mother were here she could tell her that she understands now, how where you come from braids itself, wildly, into the place you choose to build your life.

He matches her slow pace as they walk toward the work float. A new film of snow covers the docks. She centers her weight over her crutches, taking small steps, trying not to slip. He rests his hand against the back of her head. "You okay?" he asks.

She turns, glances back at their prints, the scuff of her crutch beside his steps. A sea lion surfaces, diving as a troller backs out of its stall. Again she touches her chest, feeling for the medallion.

"*Okay.* That's my word for the day."

He smiles. "It's a start."

Newt stands on the work float by the truck, arms folded over his chest. Green specks of fish blood dot his T-shirt. "Aren't you cold, buddy?" Connor asks. Newt slings the duffel onto the flatbed. She recognizes Fritz's rig from the bumper sticker, CUT KILL DIG DRILL.

"We good?" Newt asks. She nods, slipping into the jump seat, letting Keta, waiting in the back, arrange himself over her legs, just like he had on that first trip from the ferry terminal.

They curve along Pletnikoff Street. Snow beats on the windows, leaving slow trickles of water on the windshield. Long-line bait shacks, black seine nets, gillnet drums, are scattered around the gravel yards, dusted with white, each piece of gear with its own particular use, meant for its own season. The Bunkhouse. Ugh. She wouldn't miss that place.

"You guys set up?" she finally asks Newt. "The *Invictus* gonna work out?"

"We'll need to munchkin-proof it. Might send your dog off to Zachary's for a spell—boat's small for a wolf like that."

In the back she presses Keta's head to her cheek, feeling the wetness of his eyes. He sighs, then sits up to stare ahead through the windshield. In long swipes she smoothes his fur, flicking away loose hairs, wrapping her arms around his broad chest and hugging her to him.

"When you think you'll be back?" Newt asks.

The question hangs in the air as they accelerate over the bridge. Gulls flock in front of the processor, blending in with the snowflakes. Connor leans against the headrest, staring forward.

She knew floating two hundred and twenty tons would be no small project. Salt water was corroding the engine at this moment. If she didn't do it, someone else would. By law, the boat would be theirs.

"Soon."

Newt finds her in the rearview mirror. "Don't be worrying now. We'll keep an eye — well, three of them between us — on the dog, and the boat."

They park and unload. Keta won't rise from her legs. He just looks at her, his brown eyes unblinking. She lifts one of the dog's ears, whispers into it, "I'll be back. Promise."

The three of them stand beneath the overhang. Newt shuffles his feet, looks down at his hands. His knuckles are swollen. Snow catches in the downy hair of his arms. She's never seen him at a loss for words.

"Hey," she says. "You remember that day in the woods, when you stood up for me after Bailey said something stupid?"

"'Course."

She reaches out to hug him. "You're just the best. Do you know that?"

"Don't you go forgetting about us here."

He loads into the truck. She and Connor wave, keep on waving as the vehicle turns around the bend, no brake lights at the stop sign. Newt.

The brushed metal rollers clatter as Connor pushes the duffel onto the conveyor belt. The heavyset agent, whom she recognizes as a troller from her AMSEA class, tells her not to worry about the crutches.

"Heard about the tug. You'll get her up again."

In the airport bathroom, beneath the bright white lights, she looks in the mirror and traces an index finger beneath her eye. There's dirt under her fingernails, calluses on her palms. A saying of Newt's finds its way into her head: "A cat always blinks before you hit it with a sledgehammer." She never understood what this meant, until now.

Inside the plane she uses the backs of seats to hobble down the aisle. There's a murmur of greetings as belts click. The flight is full, and she and Connor are separated. An older man in a camouflage hat stands as she slides into the window seat. As they taxi out to the single runway, her heart begins to race.

Outside, fronds of red seaweed and pebbles are strewn across the concrete. Waves break against shale boulders skimmed with snow. She turns to see Connor peering out the window.

The jets power up, and the brakes release. She can make out the docks, the empty corner. Then they're floating, white streamers whipping off the wing tip. For the first time she sees Port Anna from above — grid of downtown, harbors, roads stretching out on either side dead-ending into mountains, all of it powdered white. Higher above, ice fields, those same blue glaciers she saw so long ago from the ferry.

The plane banks over the channel. She cranes her head to catch a glimpse of Betteryear's cabin, thinks she sees its square shape along Salmonberry Cove before it disappears off the edge of the wing. Lights wink, houses meld into trees. And then, like that, town is gone.

Puddles in the muskegs flash silver with the plane's reflection. Waves split on the outer edge of the island. The plane shudders as it slips into a cloud. They're lost in the cottony blankness, gradations of white. Again she looks back, wanting to catch Connor's eye. His forehead, resting against the window, turns golden as the cabin grows luminous with sun, a ripple of cloud-tops beneath. There's a chime, and the flight attendant speaks into the public address.

"Ladies and gentlemen, the captain has turned off the Fasten Seat Belt sign. It is now safe to move about the cabin."

She looks back out the window. The volcano crater is above the blanket of clouds, the edge of the rim sharp and bright in sunlight. The man with the camouflage hat sighs, tugs at the bill, wet from snow. He is curious, perhaps, about this woman in her scarred Xtratufs and ripped wool jacket staring so intently out the window.

They have forty minutes to Ketchikan, then two hours to Seattle, time she intends to use making up for sleep lost over the past twenty-seven months. She tilts back her seat, folds her arms over her chest, and shuts her eyes.

Her mind works over the tug, the broken frame of her mother's photograph, fishermen of Aci Trezza waking to find themselves on the bottom of the frigid North Pacific. The thought makes her smile. She thinks of the plane, arcing over the rest of the country, dropping out of the clouds, and, finally, the winking trouble lights of the oil refineries below. Dry docks of the navy yard on the muddy Delaware. Ribbons of row homes cutting through the Italian Market, burn barrels with gashes aflame.

"So where you headed this eve?" the man beside her asks.

Branches of the sugar maple scrape brick. Connor stands behind her, waiting. Like an immigrant returning to some ancestral land, she pulls open the storm door. She turns the brass knob. Her father rises slowly from the couch, his cardigan untucking as he stands. His hair is thinner, his movements stiff. She takes in his smell, lovely and so long forgotten, as he presses her head to his chest.

She opens her eyes.

"Home."

ACKNOWLEDGMENTS

Perhaps the finest part of this project is how it placed me — at times obnoxiously — in the path of others. People opened their homes, refrigerators, tents, trucks, hearts, and minds over the past ten years. To all involved — too many to mention here — thank you.

Artistic residencies made the first attempts at writing this book possible. I'd like to thank in particular the Macdowell Colony, the Ragdale Foundation, and the Island Institute for taking a chance on a lost writer with no MFA, no publications. Support was also given by the Elizabeth George Foundation, for which I am grateful.

For sharp outside reads I'd like to thank Rick Nichols, John Maxey, Nancy Szokan, Vicki Solot, David Leverenz, Daniel Sheehan, Andrew and Annette Dey, Brenda Levin, Heather Haugland, Peggy Anderson, and Meghan Rand — Meghan, who believed in this book all those years ago. It's been a long time, but Jennifer Suhowatsky for early, unqualified love and support. To Robert Bly, who answered my letter when I was nineteen, and said yes, he would read a poem a month if I left college for the woods of Alaska. You are a great mentor. And to Jenny Pritchett: I've got your back, just as I know you have mine.

For unfaltering company along this windy path, heady thanks to my coconspirator Suzanne Rindell, who has been there since '99 — or is it '98? You would know. Will Chancellor, Katch Campbell, Katey Schultz, C. B. Bernard, Andy Kahan — in all capacities, thank you.

368   Acknowledgments

Big love to the boys of the forty-ninth state — Rick Petersen, Xander Allison, Kyle Martin, Steve Gavin, and Ryan Laine, for their reads and long-winter company. Here's to not many more years of hemlocks falling on cabins, boats sinking at the mooring buoy, scoping ourselves — and many more indeed of deer heart and onions at Fred's Creek, waiting with whiskey for the bear to eat the honey-drenched goat. To Nick Jans for the good company along this path, and the clean boot prints in the snow. Pam Houston, for helpfulness from way back in the day, and her commitment to Sitka and its arts. And a toast to the lassies, Darcie Ziel and Sarah Newhouse, for the early reads and constant nudging. To Matt Goff for his generosity, both with his time and his intricate understanding of Sitka and its landscape. Thank you, also, for guidance, homes to stay in, insight, and helpful reads, to Nancy Lord, Dale Ziel, Peggy Shoemaker, Deb Vanasse, Vivian Faith Prescott, John Straley, Shannon Haugland, Michaela Larsen, Richard Nelson, and Tom Kizzia. To Scott Brylansky, for sharing his knowledge of wild foods. And to William Stortz, who first took me hunting, and shared his homebrew and dry wit, I promise to carry this debt of kindness, and to pass it on in your memory.

On the waters, badass fishermen, skippers, deckhands, and close readers Sierra Golden on the F/V *Challenger,* Spencer Severson on the *Dryas,* Eric Jordan on the *I Gotta,* Grant Miller on the *Heron,* and Karl Jordan on the *Saturday* — and to Karl and Spence for correcting my knots, both in the book and elsewhere. Tele Adsen on the *Nerka* for a great read, to Marsh Skeele on the *Loon* for telling me about blooms of jellyfish, and Charles Medlicott for Dutch Harbor crabbing knowledge.

And my 215 machos, Alex Auritt, Rob Sachs, Jeff Marrazzo, the true crew. And to Philly the city: I'll always carry your big spirit in my heart, and fists. Much love to Justin Ehrenwerth for believing in this project from the first, giving who knows how many reads, sketches by the wood stove, beers when required. *Hineni,* brother. Always.

I follow in the wide artistic wake of my godmother, Deborah Boldt, who has been helpful and encouraging throughout, and my aunt Denise Orenstein, whose generous reads of the manuscript have buoyed me up in tough times. I give thanks to Eavan Boland and Stanford University, and to Stegner years '14, '15, and '16. To Molly Antopol and Chanan Tigay, for just being fun and hilarious and so smart and cool. And, of course, to the best carpool ever — Rachel Smith and Brenden Willey, and their partners, respectively, Kevin Fitchett and Zoe Grobart. Anything I write you will all write better. Thump thump thump.

For guidance and friendship, insight and wisdom, and for the deep footsteps you leave, I give thanks to Toby Wolff, Elizabeth Tallent, Adam Johnson, Richard Ford, and Rick Powers. For insight not only into this world of writing, but also on children, love, work, boxing — all the important things.

To Kent Wolf, for taking a chance on a glorious mess of a manuscript, and to Jenna Johnson for believing in this so early, for lighting up this project with her razor-sharp intelligence, even if she would hate all those metaphors. To Pilar Garcia-Brown for the close read and guidance, and to Michelle Bonnano-Triant, whose love of writing and the world is infectious. And, of course, to Taryn Roeder. I'm so glad I stalked you that first year in college — one of the best decisions of my life.

Thanks for the unfaltering love and understanding of my uncle and aunt Fred and Mary Jo, and for having the Farm, and the pickup to borrow — you were my own geography of hope as a kid. To Donna Lee and Lou DiNardo, I feel very lucky to have scored you as in-laws. To my father, Cecil Jones, who was committed to this book from its inception, and to my sister, Laura Jones, whom I love and am so proud of. To my stepfather, Joseph Lurie, thank you for your strength, your constancy, your goodness; I will always look to you.

My daughter, Haley Marie: you are my heart. Everything. All of it.

And Rachel, tug dweller, eagle-eyed copy editor, rough-stock, gorgeous wife. Who knew we would even be allowed to dream such things? And I get to walk with you through this life . . . crazy luck of mine.

READING GROUP GUIDE

At eighteen, Tara Marconi is stumbling into adulthood unable to anchor herself in a world without her mother, losing her connection with the people she has loved, and haunted by a dark secret. She hasn't felt at home in a long while — her mother's death left her unmoored and created a seemingly insurmountable rift between her and her father. Desperate to put distance between herself and her pain, she makes her way to "the Rock," a remote island in Alaska governed by the seasons and the demands of the world of commercial fishing. In the majestic, tough boundary lands of the forty-ninth state she begins to work her way up the fishing ladder — from hatchery assistant all the way to crabber on the Bering Sea. She learned discipline from years as a young boxer in Philadelphia, but here she learns anew what it means to work hard, to do something well, to connect, and — in buying and fixing up an old tugboat — how to finally make her way toward home.

DISCUSSION QUESTIONS

1. What do you know after reading the opening scene? How did the descriptions of the landscape and of Tara's experience on the boat bring you into the story? How is Tara affected by her surroundings, and how did the environment compare with the preconceptions you had about Alaska?

2. One of the things that brings Tara to Alaska is the idea of living off the sea and being involved in the fishing world, as her moth-

er's Sicilian family has done for generations. Compare Tara's experiences in Alaska to her imagined Sicily. Do you think they are more alike or more different than Tara expects?

3. When Tara sets eyes on Laney's old tugboat, the *Pacific Chief,* it's love at first sight. There also seems to be an instant connection between her and Laney, even though they are very different people. "What is it with that old tug and you pie-in-the-sky girls?" the harbormaster asks Tara (p. 97). What do you think the two women have in common? What drew each of them to the tugboat?

4. Though they talk about being on separate paths, Connor still has a powerful hold over Tara and influences her throughout the novel in a variety of ways. For example, it is after receiving his letter and gift of pajamas that she asks Newt to get her a job at the processor. What is it about Connor's letters that seems to galvanize Tara? What does Connor come to symbolize for her during her time in Alaska?

5. Tara and Connor often compare where they live now—Alaska, New York City—to growing up in the old Italian neighborhoods of South Philadelphia. Discuss the differences in culture between their childhood home and Alaska. What kinds of things would you put on a list defining the cultural chasm between Alaska and the lower forty-eight? What traits and preoccupations are shared across such different communities and landscapes? How do these fit into your sense of a national identity?

6. Tara's cousin Acuzio tells her of Alaska, "It's a man's world, shows you what you're made of" (p. 10). But afterward, Tara's mother contradicts him. "Your cousin, he don't know nothing," she says, explaining that it's the work that makes you strong; your gender doesn't matter. Who, in the end, do you think was correct? Discuss the various ways in which this novel explores themes of gender identity and relationships between people. How does Tara defy these stereotypes, wittingly and unwittingly? Do you

think there is something about the novel's setting that changes the usual dynamic between the sexes?

7. There appear to be two defining moments that push Tara toward her decision to move to Alaska. Describe how each of these events influenced her and led her to make the decisions she did.

8. Through her relationship with Betteryear, Tara gains another perspective on the conquering of the Alaskan wilderness. What meaning for her lies in the tragedy of Native peoples like the Tlingit? Why do you think Betteryear takes such a shine to her, and what do you think they are standing in for in each other's lives?

9. Tara often thinks about her father's stubbornness and how much pain his temper has caused her over the years. Were you surprised at how things changed for them over the course of the novel?

10. What does home mean to Tara? How does her idea of home evolve over the course of the novel?

11. What does Alaska teach Tara about teamwork and community? How does her new community come together in the novel's final chapters?

12. The book's title comes from Newt, who explains, "We're all tumbling around in the Alaskan laundry out here" (p. 172). What does he mean by this metaphor? Do you find the description apt for Tara and the other characters she encounters? Why do you think the author chose *The Alaskan Laundry* as the novel's title?